CODE OF ARMS

GIDEON RYKER
BOOK 1

JACK SLATER

Copyright © 2024 by Jack Slater

All rights reserved.

No part of this book may be reproduced in any form or by any electronic or mechanical means, including information storage and retrieval systems, without written permission from the author, except for the use of brief quotations in a book review.

Cover design by Damonza

❀ Created with Vellum

PROLOGUE

"We're here," the driver announced. They were almost the first words the girl had heard come out of his mouth in two grueling days on the road. They'd stopped only for fuel and gas station sub rolls in all that time.

Julia swallowed as the warehouse's roll-up doors clattered open, revealing a vast black maw where answers should have been. The last forty-eight hours had been a surreal dream. Nobody told her where she was going or what to pack. She was given no warning before the men came to her dormitory and told her it was time to leave her friends, her family, and her entire life behind.

She followed the route through the real world she'd never known only by reading road signs and matching them up to a map she created in her mind. The car's rear doors were locked at all times. Not that she would have run.

Where could she go?

The driver—he never gave his name—gently feathered the gas and guided the car into the unlit warehouse. He waited for the metal doors to rattle their way back to the concrete before he pressed a button to his side, and the rear locks thunked open.

"What now?"

His dark, beady eyes met her gaze in the rearview mirror as they had done dozens of times during the journey. Usually, Julia looked away, the glances sending uncomfortable shivers running down her spine. Now she was so desperate for reassurance, she clung to anything she could.

"They'll come."

And they did. The overhead lights flickered on seconds before a woman and a girl not much older than she was entered the cavernous, mostly empty space flanked by two muscular men in dark suits.

"Who are they?" Julia asked plaintively. When no response came, she tried again. "Why am I here?"

Still, her driver didn't answer. He just kept watching, his eyes wide and dark and hungry.

One of the two men—guards, Julia surmised—pulled open the sedan's rear door and gestured for her to climb out. Her legs felt like jelly as she complied. The guard moved her aside and closed the car door before stepping away.

Julia grew uncomfortably aware of her appearance in the harsh, bright-white overhead glow cast by the warehouse's strip lighting. She hadn't washed in two days. Her hair was a mess. Her gray dress, the only item of clothing she could remember wearing, was dusted in cookie crumbs. She hurriedly brushed them aside as she felt the touch of the older woman's gaze on her.

The woman stepped closer. Her eyes were a piercing green and her lips were tightly pursed. Julia had never seen her before, but she immediately sensed that she was in charge. She had an air of command.

"Pleased to meet you," she said, bowing her head.

"Oh," the woman replied, tilting her head to one side as she studied Julia with a disconcerting level of intensity. "You're a pretty one, aren't you?"

Julia swallowed. "Thank you."

"How old?"

"Sixteen!" Julia answered, feeling a desperate urge to prove herself to this woman.

"You arrived just in time," the woman said without any obvious emotion in her voice as a young woman appeared at Julia's side. "Emily, clean her up."

She turned and strode back toward the metal door that seemed to lead into another section of the warehouse. The two guards trailed behind her. As they walked away, Julia noticed the distinct outline of a handgun holstered at the hip of each man.

"Arrived just in time for what?" Julia said, her voice barely audible as she turned to Emily, desperate for comfort.

The first thing she noticed upon meeting the girl's gaze was that her eyes were empty. Despite her age, her entire demeanor seemed drained and empty of life. Unlike the women back home, she was wearing makeup, and the blush on her cheeks faked a life that wasn't there.

Emily stared at her without answering for several seconds. Her pupils were tiny pinpricks in her eyes. It was almost as if she was looking past Julia, or through her, to a world that no longer existed.

"Come with me," she said at last, turning away and beginning to walk toward the door behind which the other three had disappeared.

"Where?" Julia said, her voice squeaking with desperation.

Emily flinched and stopped. She turned slowly to face Julia, and this time, her pupils were a little wider. It was as though she'd shaken herself free of some trance. "It gets easier. Just try *not to feel. Find a place in your head you can escape to and just... stay there."*

"Escape from what?" Julia whispered.

Instead of answering, Emily led her through the door. As they left the warehouse, Julia heard the sedan's engine rumble into life and the big metal door squeal as it opened once again.

She followed Emily into a dimly lit hallway. There were half a dozen doors on either side.

"These are the dormitories," Emily said, pointing at three of them. "We'll find you a bed afterward."

Julia didn't bother asking this time. The nervousness that had gripped her before was gone, replaced by cold fear. Something about this place smelled evil. It was a heady mix of bleach and perfume and bodily fluids, and it was wrong.

Emily opened a door on the left and led her into a room that was a strange combination of a bathroom and dressing room. On the right-hand side was a shower stocked with high-end soaps, shampoos, and conditioners. Thick towels hung on a warming rack on the wall.

On the left side of the room, a wooden cabinet groaning with different items of makeup sat next to a full-length standing mirror. The length of the other wall was taken up by built-in wardrobes.

Emily pointed to the right. "Get cleaned up."

Julia stripped awkwardly and left her clothes in a neatly folded pile on the side of the shower. It wasn't the nakedness that bothered her. She was used to undressing and washing among other girls her age. But usually, she was just one of many. It was different here. It was too quiet. She could hear herself think.

And she didn't like it.

She stood under a boiling stream of water and scrubbed her skin until it stung. She let the water run down her face and the dark strands of hair on her back for as long as she dared, and then she finally twisted the faucet and stood in the steamy silence with water dripping off her skin. She held her breath, barely daring to open the shower door.

Because Julia knew now why she was here. And she was terrified.

With trembling fingers, she reached out and slid the shower open. Emily was leaning against the wall. She was holding something in her left hand, but it was difficult to see what it was. Julia stepped out and swaddled herself in the towel.

"Put these on when you've dried off," Emily said, handing her a tangle of wire and lace.

She looked down with a furrowed brow. She turned her hand over and saw that she was holding a red lingerie set. The cloth was barely there. It would reveal far more than it covered.

Julia started to tremble.

"What...what's going to happen to me?" she whispered.

"I told you," Emily answered in a harsh tone that grew deeper with every word, as if she was struggling with her own emotions. "Don't ask questions. Don't think. Don't feel. Believe me, I tried the other way. It's not worth it."

Julia sank to her haunches. The shaking grew in intensity until she was practically rocking back and forth. Her stomach was clenched into a dense ball of fear. Silent tears coursed down her face.

"Shit," Emily swore. "Stop crying. You can't go in like that. They don't pay to see you scared. Most of them, anyway."

But Julia couldn't stop. She'd been taken from the only life she'd ever known and spirited halfway across the country to this hellhole. The tears kept falling. The muscles in her core grew tense and strained from the contractions.

Emily shook her shoulder, but Julia couldn't stop. She tried again, digging her fingernails into her bare skin until the pain cut through the depths of her terror and momentarily silenced her.

"All right! Stop. I'll cover for you this one time. I'll tell her you're bleeding."

"What?" Julia whispered. The skin under her eyes was raw and tender. She could taste the salt from her tears on her lips.

"You'll have to watch," Emily said, picking the lingerie set up from where it had fallen on the floor. She hurriedly undressed and climbed into it. "The first time is the worst. After that, you get used to it."

Julia swallowed. "Watch how?"

"You'll see. It's all recorded."

ONE

The mountain had called to him for weeks. Not by name, since he did not know it then, but even when his tortured body was too weak to respond, he'd turned his head to watch it through the window of his small cell-like bedroom.

When the thin mattress underneath him was soaked through with sweat and stained by droplets of blood, he promised himself that he would scale its peak. He didn't even know whether he could.

And now he stood in front of it, Montagne Sainte-Victoire in the French region of Provence. In ancient times, it had been the site of a great battle between Roman forces and the barbarians. Today, it would be his proving ground.

He gazed up at the base of the great limestone ridge as dawn broke over the sky. The face of the mountain, so beloved by the locals, looked to the west. At this hour, it was still shadowed by darkness. And though by midday the sun would be punishing, even so early in the year, it was not yet.

Even so, the man began to strip. He wore only a pair of hiking pants and a corduroy quarter-neck sweater to combat the cold. He folded the sweater and the T-shirt underneath it neatly at his feet. The hiking pants unzipped at the knee and turned into shorts. The extra material joined the other clothing on the ground.

He wore a canvas belt around his waist from which hung a small bag of chalk, borrowed from a local in the village who had advised him on routes to the top, and a dented stainless-steel water bottle that was his only possession.

His skin went up in goose pimples as a chill breeze swept over him. It was not the mistral—the icy northwesterly gale that swept through the region all winter long, but it was cold enough. The hairs on his arms and the back of his neck stood to attention.

But he felt none of it. He had the strangest sensation that he was observing himself from afar, as though he was watching from a camera suspended in the air behind him.

The feeling shouldn't have been strange, and yet it was. He had felt this way for months, ever since he woke up and saw the craggy face of the old soldier tending to his wounds. As though he was already dead, and his soul was watching what remained of his body eking out its final days on earth.

"Can you tell me your name?"

Somehow the American knew that the man was speaking French. More strangely still, he understood every word.

"Non."

"Then what should I call you?"

The answer came naturally to his tongue, though only a blankness followed when he tried to question why. "Nomad."

Though the American spoke little, he did at least respond to this granted moniker. And now, Nomad began to climb.

At the start, the face of the mountain was not technically challenging. He dipped one hand into his chalk pouch, then rubbed his palms together to spread the powder. As he watched himself, he felt as though he'd done this a thousand times.

There was an adhesion of scar tissue on the left side of his torso where the blade had cut through his abdominal wall three months earlier. The wound was—at least visibly—healed. But Nomad winced with pain as he dug his fingertips into an outcropping and brought his right leg up, nestling the tips of his bare feet into a crack in the limestone wall.

He looked up but could no longer see the summit. It was up there somewhere, thousands of feet above him. A glance down told him that he'd scaled only a couple of hundred. Though he'd established a fitness regime over the past few weeks along with some of the other invalids, many of them were in their sixties and seventies. Light jogging and calisthenics were no way to prepare for a climb this challenging.

The thought didn't concern him. Little did, these days. The old soldier had told him that he suffered from a condition called depersonalization—a sensation that he didn't really inhabit his body, but rather observed it from a distance.

"Dammit," he grunted as his hand slipped and came away from the rock, leaving him with only two points of contact. He wobbled in midair before somehow digging the toes of his left foot into a fissure. His back was marbled with a thousand tiny droplets of sweat, a few of which were coalescing into a rivulet that began to course down his spine.

His biceps, shoulders, and back ached. He pushed on. About midday, the sun broke over the peak of Montagne Sainte-Victoire, and Nomad found a ledge to perch on, a thousand feet up. He unscrewed the water bottle and drank sparingly despite his thirst.

He was tired, but he felt truly alive for the first time that he could remember. More than that, the sensation of depersonalization was less pronounced than usual. He felt almost himself.

Whoever the hell that is.

His peripheral vision caught a flash of movement and snapped instantly to focus on it. He saw a short-toed eagle floating on a thermal at almost the same altitude as him. He watched it for a long time, amazed by the way it hung almost unmoving in the air, only its neck rotating like a gimbal in search of prey.

When it dove for the ground, Nomad felt a rush of elation wash through him. He almost convinced himself to jump after the bird.

"It's not the fall that kills you," he muttered.

Once the majestic bird of prey was lost to view, he turned back to the mountain. He had a little over fifteen hundred feet left to climb. The Croix de Provence at the mountain's westernmost peak was waiting for him, as it had awaited adventurers for hundreds of years.

Five hundred feet passed quickly. He came to the base of a steep couloir—a narrow gully down the mountain, and for the first time felt a measure of fear. The sensation was so alien to him that it almost didn't compute.

The air at the bottom of the couloir was freezing cold. The trench was ten feet deep and probably saw no sun at any time of day. Ice crystals nestled in the deepest cracks in the rock. The cold air swept across Nomad's soaking flesh and sent a tremor down his spine. He had the strange sense that the person he'd been before the incident would have turned back, deciding that the mountain was best left for another man on another day.

But Nomad found that he was able to dispassionately examine his fears and anxieties as though they were locked like zoo animals in a transparent box and he was merely an observer. He pushed the uncertainty out of his mind and gauged the terrain above him with a practiced eye. The rock looked stable, and there were plenty of footholds. On the other hand, somewhere above him was a spring, not powerful, but enough to cause a constant trickle of water down the limestone. The larger, flatter sections were particularly slick.

It was dangerous. There was no doubt about it. But it could be scaled.

He pressed his cheek to the side of the mountain and stuck out his tongue. Cool, clean water sluiced away some of the dust and dirt that he'd inhaled over the previous few hours. It felt good.

And now he was ready.

He grunted as he kicked up with his right leg and found his first foothold. He moved almost like a spider, never breaking his three points of contact, as though an instructor had drilled that necessity into his head over and over again.

A hundred yards up into the couloir, Nomad encountered his first major hurdle. The gully had widened above him into a single steep, slick face of stone. There were a series of horizontal ledges in the rock that were particularly pronounced on his right side. They offered a route up, but it was bound to be a difficult climb—the face was soaking wet and covered in a thin coating of green algae.

He looked down and chewed his lip. Returning to the bottom of the couloir might be an equally dangerous challenge.

Puffing out his cheeks, he muttered, "I guess the only way is up..."

Nomad had almost made it to the top of the gully before he regretted not climbing in his hiking shoes. He tried using the rough skin on the inside of his left forefoot to provide some friction on the slippery rock just as he was reaching up with his right hand to cling onto a fresh handhold.

It didn't stick.

"Shit..."

His left foot slipped and continued to fall out from under him. His left hand was still dug into the rock, as were his right toes, but the force of the fall jerked his right shoulder painfully, and he sent his left arm windmilling backward in a frantic search for balance.

For a moment, panic completely overtook him. He looked down and saw nothing but a thousand-foot drop onto jagged rock. For once, he saw it through his own eyes and not through the lens of an imagined camera.

And Nomad finally realized that he didn't want to die.

TWO

The silence was excruciating.

Every scratch of knife against plate was like a bell ringing in the otherwise mute emptiness between them. The sound of chewing, of teeth scraping against each other, of morsels of food being swallowed was impossible to ignore.

"How was your day?" Julia said, breaking the truce that only he adhered to.

As always she was perfectly put together, her hair straightened, nails perfectly manicured. It was the blankness in her eyes that he loathed—but not quite as much as the manic devotion that sometimes replaced it.

Not for him. *Never* for him.

McKinney forced a smile. He wondered how obvious the stiffness in his posture was to her and found that he didn't care. He had no doubt that she reported every detail of their relationship back to her handler in New Eden—perhaps even to Father Gabriel himself.

Do you tell the truth, little girl?

"Busy," he said.

"Is there anything I can do to help?" Julia instantly replied.

"You know my work is classified."

"Not to me," Julia said, her posture ramrod straight, her knife and fork poised elegantly in those slim hands of hers.

"You don't have a security clearance."

"What does that matter? Our only loyalty is to Him, not to earthly constructs."

McKinney's lips tightened. "I was being polite, Julia. I don't need your help. Remember your place."

I'm explaining myself to a child, he raged internally.

Julia wasn't a child, even if it sometimes felt that way to McKinney. She was in her early twenties, though he didn't know her precise age. And she wasn't his wife, either, other than in a strictly legal sense.

Except she was in every sense that mattered. They ate together. They lay at night in the same bed. And they prayed together: she with fanatical devotion, he with belief ground down by experience and opportunity in equal measure.

The situation was intolerable. Of course it was. He was a man of power and respect in the nation's capital—a power base that he had cultivated assiduously for decades through whatever means necessary.

"I only want to help, Sheldon," she said in a wheedling tone. "You always look so tired. My duty as your wife is to share your burden, but you don't let me in. How do you think that makes me feel?"

I don't give a shit!

Of course, Sheldon McKinney didn't voice those words out loud, though he suspected she felt the force of them emanate from his every pore.

She was undeniably beautiful. Tall, elegant, her body toned from the relentless exercise she took—quite shaming his own reticence to adhere to the Mandates he'd sworn to live his life by.

But that was decades ago, he reasoned. *Times change. Men change.*

"I'm sorry," he said, forcing himself to relax.

He needed her to think that her efforts were working—that she was succeeding in grinding down his defenses. If he gave her evidence of progress, even if the signs were tiny, it would buy him time.

"You do help," he said, gesturing at the plate in front of him—which he realized he'd practically licked clean. Aside from everything else, Julia was a damn fine cook. He resented her presence in his life, but that didn't mean he couldn't enjoy the fruits of her labor. "This is how you support me. Your job is to keep the household so that I may do my work."

"I can do more than that. You know Father released me from some of the usual obligations. I can help with your work. But you need to trust me."

"I do trust you."

"It doesn't feel that way. Not always."

Not ever, he saw in her eyes.

"I was alone for a long time," he said, laying his cutlery onto the empty plate in front of them. "You have to understand that a man develops routines. It will take a long time to unlearn them. But I promise you, I'll try."

Would it be enough?

"Thank you," Julia said softly. "And what about the other thing?"

It was obvious from the way her cheeks colored what she was referring to. A baby. The one mandate that she simply would not allow him to duck.

McKinney felt his hands clench by his sides, though he forced himself not to reflect the way he was thinking in his expression. His inscrutability was well-practiced. Washington's parlor games required that he be as impossible to read as a sphinx. He'd never expected that his decades of experience going toe-to-toe with the country's fiercest political minds would be training for managing his relationship with his wife.

This too was an intolerable predicament to be placed in. He could hide a wife—half the nation's senators either maintained mistresses or acquainted themselves with the type of woman whose numbers were listed in little black books. A child was another matter entirely. She would have to live at the Middleburg place if she fell pregnant. She wouldn't like it, but what other option was there?

"Tonight," he said, reaching out and taking her hand. "We'll try tonight."

THREE

"Colonel," the young woman said, smiling broadly as she entered his office with her cameraman in tow. "Thank you so much for agreeing to this. I'm Emily, and this is Colt."

She winked. "He doesn't talk much."

"It is my pleasure, Emily," Colonel Jacques Fournier said gallantly—in English, no less, a major concession for the proud Frenchman.

It helped a little that the American girl was startlingly attractive. She had short, dark hair that fell just below her chin and perfectly framed her face. She was clearly athletic—as was her cameraman—and her makeup was so skilfully applied it appeared entirely natural.

But, he mused, that was the way of the Americans, wasn't it? All style over substance. They understood little of the tradition of the institution that he led. There was evidence of human habitation on the site of the castle in the vineyard's grounds going back all the way to the Gauls, two thousand years earlier. He was just the latest custodian in a proud line.

Fournier chided himself for thinking this way. The American production company had offered a donation of €30,000 to the foundation that funded the activities of the institution. And since the brasserie needed a new roof, he couldn't afford to look a gift horse in the mouth.

"Corporal," he said, gesturing to his assistant, a man in his fifties who was still lingering by the door. "Please bring us coffee."

"Yes, Colonel." The corporal nodded sharply, then closed the door after him.

"So you still refer to each other by your military ranks?" The woman asked, her eyes sparkling. "Fascinating!"

Fournier nodded. He was sure that she knew a little of the history of this place, especially since she was filming a documentary on it for American television, but he couldn't resist indulging in his favorite topic.

"The French government and the leadership of the Foreign Legion understood that legionnaires returning from the war in Indochina—you call it Vietnam—needed a place to recover from their wounds. Both mental and physical."

"Yes, you had your own war in Vietnam," Emily said, sitting down in one of the two chairs on the opposite side of his desk. "I read all about it."

"History repeats itself." Fournier shrugged. "The first time in tragedy…"

They paused as Fournier's assistant entered with a tray of small cups. To the obvious dismay of the two Americans, the coffee was served in the European style—with little water or milk.

Fournier shook his head. "Anyway, we've been improving on the facilities here at L'Institution des Invalides de la Legion Etrangere—the Institution of the Invalids of the Foreign Legion—since the 1950s. We have legionnaires here who fought in Indochina, Algeria, Mali, Afghanistan—every conflict that

France has been involved in during the lifetime of any French citizen. We have ninety-five residents at present. The youngest is in his early thirties, the oldest, ninety-three."

"Wow," Emily said, reaching into an inside pocket and pulling out a reporter's pad. She scratched a note. "It's a beautiful place. I can see why people come here to heal."

Fournier looked out the window, and the view over the rolling vineyards up to the *montagne* took his breath away, as it did every time. "The government was very foresighted when it chose to establish this place. It is not always so. I think also in your country." He smiled. "We produce now over two hundred thousand bottles of wine per year. It's sold to buyers all over the world. Even you Americans have a taste for the Legion's wine."

"I look forward to trying it," Emily said. "Will you be giving us the tour yourself?"

"Of course," Fournier said. "Have you any other questions before we begin?"

Emily looked up, her pen poised over her pad. "Is it only former legionnaires who are permitted to retire here?"

"Any legionnaire with a good record of service and an honorable discharge," Fournier confirmed. "We charge €500 monthly in rent. That's not enough to keep this facility running, of course. Our residents also assist in the vineyard and help produce wine and ceramics, as well as run the museum."

"But only legionnaires?" Emily pressed. "No other French soldiers, or, I don't know, American veterans?"

Fournier frowned, unsure why the reporter was asking this question. It could be answered with a simple web search. As he studied her face, he saw a keen interest in her eyes that was supposed to be hidden by the layer of artifice these American media types daubed on themselves like lipstick.

"Just legionnaires," he said, rising. "I understand your camera equipment is still in your van? Please, follow me…"

He led Emily and Colt to the stairs outside his office, then patted his pockets absentmindedly. "Please, wait here a moment."

He went back into his office and stopped at the corporal's desk. He spoke in a low, sharp voice. "Etienne, have you seen the American this morning?"

His assistant shook his head. "No, Colonel. Why?"

Fournier wasn't sure. But the colonel was nobody's fool. Perhaps because he'd never married, he'd devoted his entire life to the Foreign Legion, eventually rising to command one of its premier regiments. Now he led the Institution with the same rigor he'd devoted to his military career—a career that had taken him all over the world and forced him to sit across from hundreds, perhaps thousands of men and women who were trying to pull the wool over his eyes.

And he sensed that was exactly what this American woman was attempting to do.

"Find Jean-Luc," Fournier said in response. "And tell him to keep our guest out of sight until the camera crew is gone."

"SENATOR?"

Sheldon McKinney, chairman of the Senate Select Committee on Intelligence looked up with some reluctance as his long-time fixer Ronan Haynes entered the small private reading room in his Middleburg residence. He came here whenever he felt he needed to escape his wife's overbearing presence.

Which was often.

It was early morning, and he'd slipped away from the bed they'd shared to brood on what he could do about his marital problem.

"What?"

Ronan's expression barely flickered in response to his master's sharp tone. He looked unaffected by the early hour. "The wet team is in position."

"Do they have a confirmed sighting?" Senator McKinney asked.

The aide shook his head. "Not yet. But WISHBONE indicates they may only get one shot at taking him out. They want to know if they have a go-order."

"I haven't had them hunting the globe for three months so they can give him a fucking massage," McKinney snapped, slamming his palm down hard against the sofa cushion to his side. "They are to kill him and ensure they return with DNA samples and photographic evidence of the kill. Or they don't get paid. And I want the scene sanitized. They leave nothing behind. You understand?"

"Yes, Senator," Ronan said, nodding quickly. "Do you want to monitor the live feed?"

McKinney paused to consider the question. "I'll watch in the library."

"There's...one more thing."

"Spit it out, man," McKinney said.

"What about collateral damage? The target location is sensitive. This could cause an international incident. It will definitely make the news."

"I don't give a shit if some retired French mercenaries get popped. Just make sure they don't leave any evidence behind."

FOUR

As the afternoon dragged on, Colonel Fournier grew convinced that he was being taken for an idiot. French television stations had visited the institution on many occasions to share the work that was done here with the public.

Their camera crews were professionals and carefully tested the light before shooting, capturing footage in dozens of different locations. These reporters had interviewed more than a dozen of the retired legionnaires despite having slots of only several minutes on the evening news. Most of the footage never saw the light of day.

The woman Emily and her purported cameraman Colt did little of this. Oh, they made cursory attempts to operate their equipment, but not like the French reporters had done.

And why the focus on the Americans?

The Institution was home to two retired American legionnaires. Both had French passports, and one had renounced his US citizenship. But they still spoke with American accents—a Lone Star drawl and a New Jersey twang. One was in his sixties, the other relatively sprightly at forty-nine.

"Are you sure that's it?" Emily asked after talking with the younger of the two American residents. Colonel Fournier led her out of the brasserie—the mess hall that served the residents their meals—and toward the vineyard so that she could get a sunset shot. "You're not hiding any more of my countrymen here, are you? Our viewers really respond to a local angle."

Fournier was certain now. This girl was playing him. She was no reporter, and her cameraman was nothing of the sort. His camera bag was much too large for the relatively small digital Nikon, even with the attached microphone boom. Why such an oversized bag?

He shrugged, choosing his words carefully. "As you know, many nationalities join the Legion to leave their prior identities behind. But no, there are no others. I have shown you everything."

The two Americans exchanged a coded look. Despite the warm afternoon breeze, Fournier felt a chill run down his spine.

"Let's speed this up," Emily said, her tone cold, instantly discarding all her former charm. Colt knelt on the ground, then placed his bag on the dirt and unzipped it. Fournier couldn't see what he was doing, but he backed away nonetheless, sensing trouble.

Colt handed Emily—Fournier now doubted that those were their real names—a black pistol and kept one for himself. A Glock, if the colonel wasn't mistaken. Colt held it in a steady double-handed grip. He was clearly no stranger to firearms.

Neither was Fournier. But since he didn't have one, he was at a disadvantage.

"Jacques." Emily smiled with no warmth in her eyes. "I respect what you're doing here. PTSD is no joke. Some of those guys in there, you can see they're real messed up. The last thing they need would be for a gunfight to break out in their sanctuary."

She glanced at Colt. "You think that would set back their recovery?"

"No doubt," the previously taciturn faux cameraman growled. "But I'm going to have to correct you."

"On what?"

"It's only a gunfight if the other side gets to shoot back."

Fournier glanced up at the castle, the Institution's main building, desperately hoping to see a friendly pair of eyes looking back. The last rays of the afternoon sun painted the limestone in an enticing orange glow that contrasted with the terror he felt. He had looked up at that view countless times in his two decades here. It always represented a warm blanket of safety. If someone saw what these animals were doing, they would surely raise the alarm. But the windows were empty.

And now he felt only terror.

"Jacques." Emily whistled. "Look at me."

"This is madness," Fournier protested, shaking his head violently from side to side. It still hadn't fully hit home that this was real. "You cannot hope to get away with this. My brother is a government minister!"

"Listen, no offense," Colt said. "But this will go quicker if you realize that we really don't give a shit. You are hiding someone who is very important to us. We have orders to kill him and take his body home. You can see how our two positions are at odds with each other."

"We're not hiding—"

"Shut the fuck up, you French piece of shit," Colt snapped. "You lie to me again, I'll put a bullet through your kneecap. You really don't want to know where I'll go after that."

Fournier took a step backward. He'd served in Lebanon, Djibouti, Zaire, and Yemen during his time as an active-duty officer in the Legion. He'd never been afraid to die, even when the enemy was pounding his positions with everything they had. But that was then, and this was now, and he didn't have a gun in his hands. And they did.

"Who are you people?"

"We're the fucking Avengers," Colt snorted. "Does it matter? Where is he?"

Fournier saw movement out of the corner of his eye. The doctor—his name was Jean-Luc, and he was really only a medic—emerged from the castle, his head moving right and left. He was clearly searching for something.

Or someone.

As if he were watching a movie, Fournier saw Jean-Luc's gaze slow and settle on the scene taking place down in the vineyards. It was too far away, and the colonel's eyesight was not what it had once been, but he was certain he saw the doctor's pupils widen with shock. The old man froze there for a moment, the scene not making sense in his mind.

And then Jean-Luc cried out in warning.

"Shit," Emily muttered with all the energy of someone who'd dropped a bunch of bananas in a grocery store. "This is about to get messy."

Colt snapped to his right, lined up a shot, and squeezed the trigger of his pistol twice. Matching gunshots rang out, a horrific invasion in a place as peaceful as this. Jean-Luc spun and went down, hitting the deck out of sight beneath the vines.

"All units, check in," Emily said. For a moment, Fournier just stared at her, thinking she'd gone insane. Then he realized that the lapel mic that he'd assumed was used for the video camera's audio was in fact a radio system. She touched her left ear as she waited for an incoming transmission. "Yeah. We couldn't keep it contained. Cut the signal and line the old bastards up."

"You're insane..." Fournier mumbled. He couldn't take his eyes off where Jean-Luc had disappeared below the vines. He pictured the old man's blood staining the sandy dirt. A tear stung his right eye.

"No, we're motivated," she said in a bored voice, gesturing at him to walk back up to the castle. "Move!"

Fournier dragged his feet as the two Americans marched him back up toward the chateau, his brain working in overdrive. He hadn't thought this clearly in years. Not since the last time somebody nearby was shooting at his men. One of the legionnaires inside must have heard the gunshots. They would get a message out to the local gendarmerie.

"Hurry the fuck up," Colt said, grabbing him by the lapel and dragging him through the rows of vines. As they reached the end, he gave Fournier a push, and the retired colonel stumbled and fell onto the dirt. He looked up, expecting to see Jean-Luc's body. His blood was there, soaked into the ground. Too much of it.

But the old man was gone.

"Huh," Emily said. "Guess you need more range time, Colt."

"Yeah," the guy muttered. "Guess so."

FIVE

Nomad had a broad smile on his face when he heard the first gunshot. By the time the second one rang out, his expression was black.

The adrenaline from the climb and his brush with a nasty and unplanned fall to the bottom of a very steep cliff had him feeling better than he could remember. His heart was still pumping from the effort, and the combination of endorphins flowing through his system had him centered for the first time in weeks.

Pistol. No suppressor. 300 yards.

He didn't know how he knew any of these pieces of information. But he did, just as he knew that the sound of gunfire had come from the direction of the castle. He'd been recuperating there for almost three months, ever since getting out of a French hospital with a stab wound in his side, a fierce concussion, and evidence of torture that scarred his entire body.

In all that time, he'd heard a couple of rifle shots and the occasional blast of a shotgun to deter some local critter. But no pistol fire. He instantly knew something was very, very wrong.

If he thought he was riding an adrenaline high before, the clarity he felt now was almost overwhelming. It was as though the chemical was scouring years of corrosion from his mind.

"Gideon," he whispered. "My name is Gideon."

A very strong part of him wanted to question himself on how he knew this. For months, he'd known himself only as Nomad. The nickname had caught on among the old legionnaires, at least on the infrequent occasions when he emerged from his quarters to eat or work with them.

The only true memory he had before now was a girl whose face haunted his dreams. She always came to him in the boundary between wakefulness and sleep. But she was only a ghost, an empty shell he thought he knew. He was *certain* he knew. And then he woke again and the certainty was gone, replaced by an aching hollowness in his soul.

Not now.

Because one thing was clear. The Institution had just passed seven decades without a violent incident. Nobody had ever invaded its grounds and fired weapons. It couldn't be a coincidence that it was happening now. It was his fault—and his responsibility to do something about it.

Gideon started to act before his conscious mind told him why. He looked down at his clothing, which he'd found undisturbed at the base of the mountain after his descent. The hiking pants were a steel gray, but the corduroy sweater was pale and would be clearly visible even in the half-light of the evening sky. He scanned the ground, looking for one of the foul-smelling puddles he'd passed in the last few minutes—all that was left of the previous week's rain. He realized now that his brain had been hard at work in the background cataloging his surroundings, even when he wasn't consciously aware of it.

There.

He scooped up handfuls of filth and covered the pale

sweater with it, not stopping until the clothing was fouled and dark. The skin on his arms and face had a rustic tan from being outside with the legionnaires over the past few weeks. But he dragged his dirty hands across his skin even so, smearing dark lines of mud over every inch.

The last thing to go was the stainless steel bottle. He kept the pouch of chalk, just in case.

Gideon climbed up the small bank at the side of the small French country road. The full foliage of the trees around him had yet to return after the winter, but there were enough perennials to provide some cover.

He broke into a run, feeling no discomfort from the fresh scar tissue on his side or exhaustion from his long climb. He felt like a finely honed instrument, a weapon of war finally being unleashed.

There was a farmhouse coming up on his right, he knew. The owners were away and had asked someone from the Institution to check in on their property. They hadn't meant like this.

He smashed a window by the front door, wincing as he waited to hear if an alarm would sound. There was no box on the exterior of the property.

Clear.

He picked up a piece of firewood from a pile neatly stacked on one side of the porch and used it to clear the glass, then hopped through. The decor inside was rustic. He headed for the kitchen and found a set of gleaming steel chef's knives on a magnetic stand. He chose one that was about six inches long and razor-sharp.

It never occurred to him to pick up the phone and call for help.

Though it wouldn't have worked even if he had.

Back outside, Gideon worked his way through the farmhouse's grounds. A chain-link fence separated them from the Institution's vineyards. He couldn't ever remember feeling this alert. This alive. It was as though he was made for this.

This early in spring, darkness fell fast and early. The sky darkened further with every passing minute. By the time he made it to the fence, he was practically invisible. He paused there, sniffing the air like a dog. Allowing the sounds of the countryside to soak into him.

Somewhere to his right, a bird cawed. Startled or just hungry?

Gideon went to investigate. He crept along the hard-packed ground and barely made a sound. Somehow, even when he stepped on a twig, he was able to arrest his full weight before it snapped and betrayed his position. His certainty grew with every step he took.

Definitely startled.

He could smell a man somewhere in the darkness, not far. Perhaps twenty or thirty yards at most. He had to be on the opposite side of the fence, which posed a problem. There was no way of climbing it without the chain metal ringing out like a burglar alarm.

A snap of a twig. Not caused by him.

Then a voice. "Nothing to the north. Golf out."

The speaker had an American accent. But Gideon had known he would, even before he remembered his own name. Because these men were here to hunt him.

Gideon found his quarry unerringly, despite the darkness. His eyes were completely adjusted to the gloom. Now that he knew where to look, he saw his opponent staring down at the glowing screen of an electronic device. His lips drew back in a disgusted snarl.

Too easy...

He pressed himself into the dirt, hiding in a jungle of vegetation about three feet from the fence. He slowly cast around for something to toss and found some small stones and pebbles. He placed several in the center of his left palm and grasped one in his right.

He threw the stone toward a spot five feet to his left, parallel with the fence. It landed with a thud. Instantly, he sensed movement from his quarry. The guy had heard the sound and was coming to investigate. The glow from the electronic screen diminished, and he watched a silhouette pad through the trees with a weapon—a rifle—raised. It was attached to his chest rig. The barrel extended farther than he'd expected, and he realized the weapon had an attached suppressor.

Good, Gideon thought as he tensed every muscle in his body in turn, preparing for what was to come. *That'll come in useful.*

He tossed another stone, a little closer to him this time but still away from the foliage. He saw the man who referred to himself as Golf close on the fence line, then push the suppressor through the chain link. He came closer than Gideon had allowed himself to hope, pausing just a couple of feet away from where he was hiding. His breath stank, hot and heavy, and came out in a nervous, uneven rhythm.

His night vision was evidently impaired by the glow from the screen. It would recover. But not fast enough.

Now!

Gideon exploded out of the darkness. He grabbed the barrel of the rifle barely half a second after his fast-twitch muscle fibers began to fire, pulling the weapon violently both toward and away from him to prevent a stray gunshot from filleting him. His prey should have dropped his main and gone for his secondary weapon, the one that Gideon could see in the holster on his thigh rig.

He didn't.

Instead, he instinctively attempted to drag the rifle out of Gideon's grasp. In the process, his finger squeezed the trigger and half a dozen rounds spat out of the barrel of the Heckler & Koch G36.

The element of surprise was over. Suppressed or not, the bad guys would now know that their target was active. But Gideon knew even as he struggled for control that the suppressor's real benefit was that it prevented them from knowing exactly where the gunshots had come from.

And he wasn't going to wait for Golf to tell them. With a final burst of strength, he yanked the rifle toward him through the fence, bringing its owner with it because of the attached sling. Before the guy could bring his foot up and use it for additional leverage, Gideon sank the blade of the chef's knife into his throat, driving it as far up as he could before the chain link stopped its forward momentum.

The commando was dead the moment the twisting blade cut through his Adam's apple. It just took him a couple of seconds to realize it.

Gideon let go of the borrowed knife and, without stopping to process what he'd just done, grasped the horizontal bar at the top of the fence to pull himself up and over. He landed lightly on his feet just a few seconds after Golf's gunshots split the night's calm.

His now-dead opponent was slumped face-first against the chain link, his entire body slack in death. Gideon saw to his distaste that the knife was acting as a hook and holding the man's entire dead weight.

As if checking off items from a list that he couldn't remember being drilled into his head, he reached for the man's radio earpiece. He pulled it free and twisted it onto his right ear.

"—units, radio check."

"Bravo, copy."

"Charlie, copy."

When Delta checked in, Gideon realized that he had to assume he was facing at least five opponents, and probably more.

"Echo, copy."

"Fox, copy."

There was a long silence. Gideon contemplated trying to mimic the dead man's voice, but he hadn't heard enough to be confident of his chances of pulling the trick off. And besides, a part of him that he didn't recognize wanted his enemies to understand that one of their number was dead.

He wanted them to fear him.

"Golf, do you copy?"

Gideon started to pat down the dead man's equipment. He liberated the man's thigh rig, complete with a Glock 17 pistol and two additional magazines, and secured it around his own leg. He quickly realized that it was going to be difficult to free the guy from his rifle without lifting his body off the fence.

"Golf, how copy?"

He let another long, empty pause drag out.

He was also aware that time was ticking. The leader of the enemy unit would have had a rough idea of Golf's location. The second he realized that one of his guys was dead, a whole world of trouble would be heading this way.

"Switch radio channel," said the clipped voice that Gideon assumed belonged to the team leader. "Mark."

Before they had a chance, he squeezed the push-to-talk button hanging off the earpiece's wire and said, "Your buddy can't come to the phone right now."

"Who is this? Gideon?"

Gideon reached over the fence and pulled the knife blade

free of Golf's throat, holding him by his Kevlar vest as he did so. The knife made a sucking sound, then came free, covering his hands in slick blood in the process as the dam holding it back broke. He wiped them on the man's dark fatigues, then slowly lowered him to the ground before tossing the knife aside.

You didn't disrespect the dead.

At least, he didn't.

The H&K was attached to Golf's chest with a two-point Vickers sling. Gideon freed it, then clipped it to his own torso.

"If that's you, buddy," the team leader said sardonically, "I'm impressed. Hell, I can't believe you can still speak. I heard they did a real number on you."

Gideon knelt and continued frisking Golf. He added three rifle magazines to his haul and stashed them around his person. Sadly, no grenades.

Time to go.

Though he wanted nothing more than to continue his conversation with this man who seemed to know things about him that nobody else did, Gideon knew such a desire was a weakness. He wanted his enemy to know he was out here. He wanted them jumping at shadows in the darkness. He couldn't afford to allow them to play the same trick on him.

"I'm better than I ever was," he said. A white lie. He had no idea who he even used to be, let alone how good. "Something you're about to find out."

SIX

Colt—whose codename was Alpha, unsurprisingly—grimaced. It wasn't supposed to go this way. That rat bastard Gideon was supposed to be in a fucking coma, not running around taking his guys out.

Still, he had seven shooters remaining. And the girl, and even he had to admit that she was a fine shot. Probably also had a cooler head than some of his testosterone-juiced door-kickers. They were here for the money more than the mission.

"Who's closest to Golf's last known?" he radioed once everybody had checked in on the backup frequency.

"I guess that's me," Echo said.

"Go take a look. Don't do anything stupid. I guess our target's not as crippled as we hoped."

"Don't worry, I'll take him out," Echo bragged. "He gets one free hit. That ends now. I ain't here to play."

"Charlie, go with him. Take this prick out. The rest of you, get back to the castle. Comms, anything to worry about on emergency service frequencies?"

"That's a flat no," the guy in the van radioed. "I put a

blanket over the whole area. Some of the neighbors probably think their cell service is down. Landlines are out as well. If anybody still uses those."

Colt acknowledged this piece of good news with a double tap on his radio transmit button. At some point, he knew, somebody would let the cat out of the bag. Maybe a technician at the cell company would notice a fault and send out a service engineer. Or perhaps one of the neighbors had a satellite phone. It wasn't completely impossible out here in the sticks.

The trick was to be gone before that happened. Tomorrow morning, the local gendarmerie would find a few bloodstains and a whole lot of traumatized pensioners. But if he did his job right, they wouldn't have a fucking clue what to do next.

"I want four guys on the prisoners," he radioed. "Make sure none of them do anything stupid. If you have to pop one of them to reinforce the point, go ahead."

He strode back into the castle, his face screwed up into a snarl. He didn't like losing guys. Not because he was the one who had to write the letters to the families—he didn't bother with that, and most of his men didn't have families anyway. It was a matter of professional pride. He just didn't like his opponent getting one over him.

The prisoners—about ninety of them, mostly men and a couple of women who worked to keep the old legionnaires fed or from losing their minds—were assembled in an ancient hall on the second story. They sat on the wooden floorboards. Those who still could, anyway. A few, pained by aged hips or other joint problems, lay on their backs or sides.

"Fournier, up front," Colt snapped, letting his rifle fall against its sling. He didn't bother drawing his pistol. The old guys were covered from multiple directions, and the consequences of playing the hero had been made abundantly clear.

"What's going on?" The old colonel asked, drawing himself

up to his full height and doing his best to put on a front of indignation. "What was that gunfire?"

"Tell me about him," Colt said.

"Who are you talking about?"

Colt dragged his teeth over his bottom lip. He reached down for the pistol strapped to his thigh. "Don't take me for a fucking asshole."

He drew the pistol and swept it across the assembled group of pensioners. They all looked back up at him with scarcely concealed fury. It was impressive, he had to admit. They might be old, but they hadn't lost any of the spirit that had drawn them to join the French Foreign Legion as much younger men.

He picked one of them at random, possibly the oldest, definitely the most haggard. The guy was knock-kneed and milky-eyed and probably couldn't walk ten feet without assistance. Colt lined up his pistol, flicked the safety off, and squeezed a single round into the dude's head. He was probably doing the guy a favor. Better to go out quick.

The report of the gunshot was explosive in the echoing castle hall. The two men sitting cross-legged behind the corpse were instantly splattered with blood. It took them a couple of moments to realize that their brother-in-arms was now a former brother-in-arms.

And then the yelling started. Colt expected that. He didn't expect them to be more angry than scared.

"Putain!" *Fuck.*

"You piece of shit," one of the Americans yelled. "You better hope you don't get out of here alive. Because if you do—"

Colt shot him too, then raised his pistol directly upward and fired three more shots into the rafters. A fine mist of plaster, likely decades or even centuries old, fell around him like snow.

"Enough!" He shouted. "I really don't give a crap if I have

to cut you down one by one if that's what it takes for you to sit down and shut the fuck up."

He grabbed Fournier and stared him directly in the eyes. "You will tell me everything I want to know about your patient. Or I will keep killing until you do. Understand?"

The colonel blinked several times in rapid succession, then slowly turned his head to survey the scene behind him. He focused for a long time on the corpse of the first man that Colt had shot.

"He was Italian," Fournier said in a faraway voice. "Fought in Algeria, then spent a decade living on the streets before he found his way here. You could never meet a kinder man. You are a monster."

"Yeah, yeah, tell me something I don't already know," Colt snapped. He jabbed the muzzle of his pistol hard against Fournier's forehead. "What condition is Richter in?"

"Richter—?" Fournier muttered, his brow furrowed. "Oh. That was his name. I see."

"Is he wounded? Any injuries? What about mentally?" Colt tapped his temple with a finger of his free hand. "I heard he went completely loco. Surprised he made it this far. Guess you guys did a good job patching him up. Shame we'll have to waste him after all that effort."

Fournier glanced back at the old men arrayed behind him. It was a pitiful army, Colt thought.

Put a bullet in me before I end up like this.

The French colonel seemed to derive some comfort from whatever he saw. He straightened, turned back to Colt, and said, "This man you call Richter. He is fit. But I think you will see that yourself, very soon."

SEVEN

Gideon barely touched the ground as he ran through the grounds of Domaine Capitaine Danjou, the vast area of vineyards in which the castle was situated. The buildings were almost completely dark. All of the running lights that usually lit up the space at night had been doused.

Dammit. Should've checked for optics.

The term came so easily to the forefront of his mind it almost shocked him. An hour earlier, he had no idea what night vision was, at least not consciously. Now he felt more alive than he could ever remember. He was a predator moving through his hunting grounds. Even without a scope, he drank in every detail of the darkened castle and the semicircular dormitory building that housed the retired legionnaires. The cries of birds and scratching of rodents came individually to his ears.

And though an untold number of smells assaulted his nostrils, his brain cataloged them separately, filtering out all those that either presented no threat or were not otherwise interesting in some way.

The fact that the lights were out meant that the bad guys

were using night vision. Most likely thermal optics as well, which meant if anyone was watching the grounds, he would be lit up as bright as a Catherine Wheel.

And that meant he had to get inside. Fast. The buildings here were built in a French countryside style, with thick stone walls that would hide his thermal signature.

He sprinted for the residents' building, the semicircular structure that faced the many hundreds of acres of vineyard that fed the winery's fermentation tanks. His room was there, and he'd grown to cherish the dawn breaking over the mountain ridge each morning, along with the first tendrils of light that pierced the low shroud of fog that sometimes hung over the vines.

In just the last few weeks, fresh foliage had begun to sprout where before there had been nothing but skeletal remnants of the previous year's vegetation. Gideon had watched the fresh shoots grow, as if keeping pace with his recovery. Nobody had told him why he was here. Not even Jean-Luc.

I never asked.

The legionnaires had accepted him as one of their own. Many of them had colorful, sometimes even criminal pasts. They had forged a brotherhood and a new life together. Nobody ever asked where he came from, and he returned the favor. They had offered their friendship and given him space.

And he had brought death to their sanctuary.

The Institution of the Invalids of the Foreign Legion was supposed to be a place where broken men could find peace in their final years. Instead, it had become a place of violence and death.

Gideon froze as once more gunfire split the calm of the night. He knew instantly that it was not directed at him. The sounds were muffled and almost indistinct. Possibly coming from the castle. A single shot, followed by another. Then three more in quick succession.

And then nothing. Silence returned. Gideon held his breath and listened for the sound of sirens screaming up the dusty lanes that led to the castle. But there was nothing. He had no cell phone, and he realized he didn't even know the French emergency number.

But Jean-Luc had a phone.

Gideon pivoted from the castle. His first duty was to get a warning out. He cursed himself for not thinking to do so at the farmhouse. But as soon as he thought of the remonstration, he dismissed it. It was now an irrelevance. He had a task to fulfill, a mission, and he was going to get it done. The time for blame and guilt would come after.

He flooded his body with oxygen as he brought the Heckler & Koch up to his shoulder. It felt like a natural extension of his body. There was a short courtyard space between the edge of the vines and the residents' rooms, a two-story structure. The rooms were accessed by a sheltered balcony, both on the ground level and the first floor.

Gideon swept the automatic rifle left and right, trusting his instincts to pick out any shooter in an overwatch position. The search was hindered by the fact that the building was almost 250 yards long, providing an abundance of places where a sniper could be hiding.

He exhaled.

There was only one constant in battle: the trade-off between certainty and speed. Both were opposing sides in the battle to remain alive. To be certain took time. And time wasn't something Gideon had in abundance. Not after hearing the gunshots in the castle.

So he chose speed.

He sprinted across the courtyard, kicking up dust in the

darkness. As he ran, the wind sent clouds scuttling overhead, momentarily revealing the moon in all its glory. It wasn't fully waxed, but close.

He was away from cover for just five, maybe six seconds. Nobody shot him in that time, despite the moon's untimely appearance.

It occurred to Gideon as he crept down the long, endless balcony on the first floor with his rifle raised that he didn't need to stay and fight. He sensed that the version of the man who had occupied his body before might have simply left the invalids to their fate.

But they were the only reason he still drew breath.

And he wasn't going to leave them behind to suffer a fate that he had caused.

A quick glance to his left revealed that he was passing room 21, the numbers stenciled in black paint on a white door. Jean-Luc occupied room 66 on the floor above, right next to the room the Institution had assigned him.

"Drink this," the old man urged. "You have a fever. It will burn you up unless you're careful."

He inserted a plastic straw through Gideon's cracked lips and coaxed him into sucking. Gideon tried, but the liquid only burned his lungs. He began to cough, and the wracking agony this drew forth brought tears to his eyes.

Jean-Luc didn't ask him to go through that again. Instead, he dipped a cloth into a bucket of water beside the bed and brought it up to Gideon's lips. The old man squeezed the cloth gently, sending a slow trickle of liquid through into his dry mouth.

It tasted like an elixir.

Gideon let out a slow, shaky breath. He didn't know why the memory had come to his mind. Until now, he hadn't even realized he remembered that part of his recuperation. But Jean-

Luc had been nothing but kind to him. Gideon had no doubt that the old Frenchman had saved his life.

In a way, he'd started to view him as a father figure.

The stairwell to the second floor was ten feet to his left. Gideon crept toward it, then ducked out in an instant with his weapon raised.

Clear.

He instinctively knew that staircases were kill zones, so he moved fast, getting to the midpoint, then pivoting as quickly as he had before.

Clear.

He finally emerged onto the second-story balcony. He was now roughly in the center of the long, narrow structure, which meant enemies might appear on either side. He inched forward and checked to the right, quickly determining that the coast was clear, then the left.

He heard nothing. Smelled nothing. Sensed no one. It was time to move.

Jean-Luc's room was ten doors down. He covered the distance in a matter of seconds. The old man never locked his room, but as Gideon stopped in front of it, he realized that something was wrong.

The white door was two inches ajar. And there was a bloody handprint on it.

A wave of rage and panic almost kicked the legs out from underneath him. Jean-Luc was the only source of stability he could remember. The thought that something had happened to the man was almost overpowering. For the first time all evening, he felt true, unbridled terror.

He didn't want to push the door open. He didn't want to see what was on the other side.

But he did.

He reached out with his left hand, keeping the rifle pushed

out against the sling with his right. It wasn't a completely steady grip, but it was better than nothing. He pushed the door slowly. Like every door in the castle's grounds, it was perfectly oiled, and the hinges moved silently. The legionnaires took maintenance seriously.

The room was dark. It could have been empty.

Except for the groan of heavy, labored breaths.

"Old man? Are you in there?" he whispered.

"Nomad?" Jean-Luc gasped, his voice thin and reedy. "Is that you, boy?"

Gideon dropped his rifle against its sling and sprinted for Jean-Luc's bedside. He fell onto his knees, his natural night vision enough to show the scene in front of him in all its bloody horror. Jean-Luc was bleeding heavily from his side. He was lying on his back, some kind of cloth pressed against his rib cage. The mattress underneath him was soaked with blood.

"I thought I could make it," he wheezed, turning his tired eyes to look at Gideon. "But I'm dying. My lung's punctured."

"The hell you are," Gideon said, instantly falling into a predrilled routine.

He turned for the first aid box, a kit of Jean-Luc's devising. He knew it well since the old man had been his doctor for the last several months. He had been a medic during his time in the Legion and hadn't let his skills fade after returning to civilian life.

Gideon dragged the heavy steel box from underneath the small basin attached to the wall at Jean-Luc's bedside. He didn't care about the noise it made. He snatched the scissors from the top drawer and cut the bloodstained olive-green T-shirt from belt to neckline.

He slowly pushed Jean-Luc's hand aside, and the bloodstained rag that was stemming the blood loss fell away. Gideon felt how little strength the old man had left.

"You're right, punctured lung," he said, his tone businesslike despite the situation. He lifted Jean-Luc's body just a couple of inches and peered underneath. "No exit wound. It must be in there somewhere."

Shit.

Gideon looked away to conceal the expression on his face. Jean-Luc was right, he was in a bad way. But even though he knew it rationally, you couldn't confront a patient with the reality of their situation. Gideon had seen many times how hope could keep a person fighting for their life. Sometimes it was enough, even when all hope should have been lost.

"Do you have a chest seal in this thing?" he asked the second he turned back. He began routing through the first aid kit, searching for the familiar packaging. His fingers brushed against the notepad in which the old man had recorded the progress of his own recuperation day by day for the previous three months, and he felt a compulsion to set it to one side.

Jean-Luc slowly, regretfully shook his head. "I thought I had every base covered, as you Americans say." He smiled weakly. "But I never expected anyone to shoot at me. Not again."

Gideon felt the comment like a knife through his heart, even though he knew that Jean-Luc hadn't intended it that way. "Okay. We can make it work. Maybe… Yes!"

He pulled out a square of plastic and some adhesive tape. It wasn't a perfect solution, and it would let more air in and out of the lung cavity than he would like, but it was better than nothing. He just needed to stabilize the old man until help could arrive.

The phone.

Later.

He began tearing the packaging off the items he would need. He didn't see Jean-Luc reaching up to place his hand on his shoulder. It was only when he felt the old man's fingers clenching around his upper arm that he looked up.

"What is it?"

"Leave me. I'm bleeding internally. We both know it. There is no saving me. You have to get out of here. Go for help."

"We'll call for help. There must be a helicopter at the hospital in Marseille. They could be here in—"

Jean-Luc gestured feebly with his other hand at the cell phone lying on the bloodstained sheets to his left. "No signal. I tried already. That's why I came back here. Please, don't waste your time trying to save my life. I know there is no hope. I'm at peace with that. I will go to God, if he will have me."

"Bullshit!" Gideon said, tearing open the roll of adhesive tape. "I'm not leaving you here to die."

"You are," Jean-Luc said firmly. As the words escaped his mouth, Gideon saw that they had consumed the last of his strength. "I have a few minutes left at most. I have seen men die; I know the signs. As I say, I'm at peace. I only wish for you to get out of here alive. The only answers I have are in my journal. Take it when you go."

Gideon sank back onto his haunches and stared at the old man's pale complexion. He knew that it was the truth. He could see Jean-Luc's life force ebbing away with every passing second. The punctured lung was barely sucking now. He'd lost too much blood.

He wanted to be sick. He'd cost this man his life.

And how many others?

"What happened?" he whispered.

"It was an American camera crew," Jean-Luc panted, speaking slowly and taking great care to enunciate each word. "At least, it was supposed to be. I saw their van in the parking lot. But Colonel Fournier must have sensed that something was wrong. He sent me a message to keep you out of sight. I was looking for you when..."

He coughed, and his eyes closed.

"Jean-Luc?"

They opened again, but now they were staring into space, the light in them growing fainter by the second. "I saw them gather the others...into the castle. That's all I know."

EIGHT

Gideon didn't make an immediate move for the castle. It was another nugget of intelligence from Jean-Luc that stuck in his mind.

He moved through the darkness as two men. Compartmentalized. But not like before. Jean-Luc was the one who had given him a term to describe, perhaps explain the way he felt: depersonalization. This wasn't that. Half of him was hot rage. The other half, cold fury.

This was a groove he'd greased many times before. Though never with such intensity.

Gideon knew that he would have to deal with the grief he'd locked up at the back of his mind. It hung heavy, like a weighted rucksack on a long march. But now wasn't the time to open it.

Now was the time to avenge Jean-Luc's death.

The adrenaline coursed through him in a steady flow, just enough to keep his finely honed senses keyed up to the max. Twice he spotted members of the OPFOR—opposing force— sneaking through the grounds. Both times, he avoided them, expertly blending into the darkness so that his presence was never even sensed.

He found himself in the parking lot that Jean-Luc had mentioned before he passed. The van was right where it was supposed to be, parked on the opposite side of the fountain in the center of the driveway. It was a Mercedes Sprinter with a magnetic decal on one side. He couldn't read the words in the dark, but he guessed the sticker had the name of some production company printed on it.

Probably a shell.

Gideon squeezed himself into a rosebush hidden from the castle windows by the low-hanging branches of a young pine tree and watched. He switched his attention from the castle windows to the parking lot every minute or so. There was movement inside the main building, but as far as he could tell, no one was obviously keeping a steady watch on events out front.

He returned his attention to the Sprinter. It was dark, but not dark enough. He could see that someone was inside the cargo compartment. Almost no light leaked out, but the few glimmers that escaped were enough to tell Gideon that somebody was home.

He crept around the wall at the edge of the parking lot, barely more than a couple of feet off the ground. His back ached from the day's earlier exertions, but he blocked out the discomfort. His nostrils were bathed in the earthy scent of the dirt that he'd smeared all over his arms, and he welcomed the reminder of his camouflage as he worked himself into position.

Here.

The Sprinter was parked in such a way as to block the view of a small segment of what lay behind it to anyone in the castle, unless a spotter had been placed on the roof. That was possible, but it would be difficult for any single lookout to cover a full 360 degrees. It was a risk, but one worth taking.

Gideon positioned himself dead in the center of that blind spot. He paused for thirty full seconds, flooding his lungs with oxygen as he studied the Sprinter one last time and made his plans. Its front end was pointed toward him. There was no obvious access from the driver's cabin to the cargo compartment.

Before he moved, he studied the terrain ahead of him. The parking lot was covered with gravel, so he slowly kicked off his running shoes and left them in the flower bed. Then he crept toward the vehicle.

It was only ten yards from him. The gravel dug into the tender flesh of his soles, but he felt little discomfort. After all, he'd climbed a mountain barefoot just a few hours earlier.

He relaxed just a fraction when he was within five yards of the van. He knew enough basic trigonometry to be certain that he was now invisible to any spotter in—or on—the castle. He slowed even further as he approached the nose of the Sprinter, inching around the side to test the driver's door. He reached out slowly with his right hand, pressing the rifle against his torso with his left to make sure it didn't bump against the side of the vehicle. His fingers rested on the door handle, and he slowly—barely—applied a little upward pressure. Just enough to test whether it was open.

The handle gave. The van was unlocked.

Dumb move.

Gideon calmly released his grasp on the handle, careful not to let it ping back and reveal his presence. He paused for a second to listen after he withdrew his hand. Somebody was definitely inside. There was a low hum of electrical equipment, and every few seconds, there was a little rustle of movement. A quick glance at the roof showed some kind of satellite antenna peering up at the sky.

It was easy to understand why the legionnaires had thought this was a TV crew truck. It was impossible to tell in the dark, but Gideon guessed that somewhere inside was the jamming device that had screwed up communications in and out of the castle grounds. The shooters would be using a hardened radio network designed to operate in such environments.

He also briefly considered whether he was walking into a trap, but he instantly dismissed the idea. If someone had overwatch of the courtyard, they could easily have picked him out with thermal optics by now. If the bad guys knew he was here, he would already be dead.

Time to move.

He sprinted barefoot around the side of the van, pivoting nimbly around the back edge and drawing the Glock pistol from its thigh holster as he pulled open the cargo compartment's rear door.

A tech working on a ruggedized laptop looked up, startled by the unexpected intrusion. He was wearing a pair of canned headphones with a boom microphone. That explained why he hadn't heard Gideon's approach. His eyes flared, the light from his laptop screen reflected in them.

Gideon held one finger of his left hand to his lips. Seeing the kid glance at a handgun that lay on the pull-down table in front of him, he shook his head slowly from side to side.

He spoke in a voice that was barely above a whisper. "I wouldn't do that if I were you."

The tech nodded slowly, blinking rapidly as the shock of his newfound position crashed over him. Gideon took advantage of his surprise to pluck the pistol out of his reach, then close the cargo compartment door behind him.

The space was lit only by the glow from the laptop. A

number of weapons and ammunition crates were visible, which was a concern, especially if his companion decided to do something stupid. But none were immediately within reach. Gideon circled the kid and came around behind him, making sure he knew that there was a pistol pointed at the back of his head. He studied the headphone setup for a moment, then flicked the button on the side of the left can.

"I guess I'm supposed to be impressed," he said now that the microphone was muted. The tech was staring at a daytime satellite image of the Institution's grounds. Ten dots moved about on the screen, each clearly indicating the GPS location of one of the team's shooters. Nine of the dots were shaded blue, the last was red.

"Huh?" The tech's voice cracked. "Why?"

"Lot of you guys for little old me."

Gideon took the headphone setup off his companion's ears and listened to the left can. He heard a couple of garbled radio transmissions, mainly position checks and reports that one area or another was clear. Unless the bad guys were trying to pull one over on him, they didn't yet have any idea what was coming.

"Get me some zip cuffs. Do it slowly and make sure I can see what you're doing. I don't really need to kill you."

But I wouldn't lose any sleep if I had to was the obvious implication.

The tech did as he instructed. He rose to his feet with exaggerated caution and fumbled through a couple of black duffel bags by the far wall of the compartment, before turning with an entire handful of black plastic zip cuffs on show.

"Toss 'em over."

There was a rattle as the kid complied with his instruction.

"Now back up to me."

Twenty seconds later, the tech was secured with his wrists

manacled tightly behind his back. Gideon shoved a half dozen other cuffs into an elasticized pocket on his thigh rig. He knew he was going to need one very shortly, and the others might come in useful.

"Sit down. Don't do anything stupid."

He kept one eye on the comms technician as he searched the van for anything that might prove useful. In the process, he found an entire crate of grenades, which made up for the disappointment of not finding any earlier, as well as a spare chest rig with a dozen empty pockets and pouches that were quickly filled with the spare magazines he'd liberated earlier, along with a variety of other useful supplies.

There was also a jerry can of fuel. Gideon looked at it for a few seconds, knowing that the clock was ticking, even as a plan formulated in his mind. He pocketed a cell phone, then began to build an improvised pyrotechnic. The finished product didn't take long. It was messy, but it would work.

"LISTEN, KID," he muttered as he dumped the technician onto the gravel in the van's blind spot just ten minutes later. "If I were you, I'd crawl as far as you can as quick as you can. I don't exactly know how long it's going to take that thing to blow, but I'm pretty sure you don't want to be here when it does."

NINE

Four blue dots roamed the grounds. Gideon had committed each of their locations to memory before leaving the van behind. He knew that the intelligence was time-sensitive, so he rounded the castle in search of the closest of the enemy shooters.

His goal was simple: close with the bad guys and eliminate them.

Five of the enemy team remained in the castle itself, or at least they had been there a couple of minutes earlier. The logic of the deployments was clear. Though many of the retired legionnaires were either elderly or infirm, several weren't. The château was home to those nursing mental or moral injuries as well as physical disabilities or age.

Even the true pensioners were hard men who had put themselves through the most grueling military training France had to offer and had then spent years, sometimes decades toiling in the castle's vineyards.

Hard men make dangerous captives.

Gideon suspected that the prisoners were most likely being

held together. The bad guys, though heavily armed, were significantly outnumbered, so that course of action made the most sense. If they were together, they could only be in the large banquet hall on the second floor of the castle. Unfortunately, the GPS data didn't give him elevation, but that was his operating assumption.

The question of how to rescue them... was still hazy in his mind.

The first step in any attempt, however, was obvious. He needed to even the odds. And he wanted the shooters in the castle—and their leader—to grow fearful and jumpy. It never occurred to Gideon that he was outnumbered nine to one. For him, solitude was an advantage.

And he intended to press it to the limit.

The ground was dry underfoot, baked by the punishing Provençal sunshine. It was covered in a thin layer of pine needles. Gideon's first task after rising from his sickbed a few weeks earlier had been to sweep them away, an endless chore that had nevertheless provided his bruised mind some space and time to recover.

He bounded past a sign on his right that told him to "Respect the Environment!" and touched the tips of two fingers to his temple in a mock salute. No sooner had he made the gesture than he froze. A neuron fired somewhere in his brain, and Gideon obeyed it instantly, even before he knew what he was being warned about.

He slowly lowered himself into a kneeling position on the dusty road that ringed the small vineyard in front of the main residence building, the G36 assault rifle light in his grip. The safety was off, but his trigger finger customarily bracketed the trigger guard.

There you are.

A man in black combat clothing crept past a pine tree about

fifty yards in the distance. As he stepped out into the vineyard from underneath his canopy, he was momentarily illuminated by a shaft of moonlight. Gideon paused just long enough to sight his aim, then rested his finger on the trigger.

Inhale.
Exhale.
Hold.
Squeeze.

A burst of sustained fire erupted from the rifle's muzzle. Gideon expertly let off the pressure after five rounds had chewed through his enemy.

At least three of the rounds had impacted the man's chest armor. It was impossible to know whether those bullets had penetrated the Kevlar. It didn't matter. The fourth and fifth had bucked up slightly, one entering just beneath his collarbone, the other blowing apart most of his chin.

"Two down," Gideon hissed, his face twisted into a bloodthirsty snarl as an image of Jean-Luc's death mask filled his mind. "Three to go."

"WHAT THE HELL WAS THAT?" Colt snapped, rushing toward the window on the castle's side where the sound of gunshots had come from. The hit team's leader instantly picked out the sound of the weapon of choice for his team.

But that meant little. Gideon had stripped Golf of all his weapons after stabbing him in the throat. The useless bastard probably hadn't even injured their target. He'd died for nothing.

"Who's shooting?" he radioed. There was a long pause before, one by one, the team's roaming gunmen checked in. None of them reported opening fire.

"Shit," Colt muttered. Fox was down. Two men dead, for what? This was supposed to be an easy hit—no mess, no blowback. The boss wasn't going to like it.

One of the legionnaires started to laugh. He was a younger man, probably in his forties, with an enormous frame and a bald head. The back of it was craggy, and Colt wondered offhandedly whether he washed the cracks with soap. All kinds of shit might be growing in there.

"Something funny?" he yelled, gesturing with his pistol. "We'll see if you think the same way when your gray matter is painted all over the guy behind you."

The massive legionnaire shrugged. He was wearing a tank top that was already stained with blood. His face was creased with amusement.

"I made my peace a long time ago," he said in an Eastern European accent. "You think I give a shit about some punk like you?"

Colt resisted the urge to put a bullet through the man's forehead. Every additional death would increase the blowback. This op was likely always going to end up in the media. But a massacre of some of France's most respected veterans would turn this into an international incident and take it from a news story that would fade from the front pages in a day or two to one that would dominate the media landscape for weeks.

Still, he was this close to pulling the trigger anyway.

"Mobile units, close on that gunfire, now! I want the target eliminated."

"Roger," came a series of clipped acknowledgments. Then only silence.

GIDEON CUT a several-meter length of twine away from one of the vines, then tossed it on the ground by his feet. He pulled one of the grenades from his chest rig and zip-cuffed it halfway up the nearest vine. Next, he carefully tied one end of the twine to the grenade's pin, before gently spooling out the remainder of the distance he estimated a man would move in four seconds.

Next came the tricky part.

His heart pounded as he pulled the twine taut. He needed it tight enough to yank the pin free the second a wayward foot knocked it out of place, but not so tightly wound that he accidentally blew himself up in the process of setting his trap.

After tying the trip wire in place, he quickly surveyed his handiwork. The whole process had taken only seconds. The brown twine was almost impossible to see against the similarly colored dirt underfoot, but even so, he would need some luck to successfully pull off the ambush he had in mind.

The tiny vineyard he was operating in measured about a hundred meters by forty and was bracketed on two of its four sides by outbuildings—the Institution's shop, museum, and a number of administrative facilities. The dead shooter lay at the far end, his upper torso still on the dusty road, his lower half off.

The field itself undulated underfoot. The center rose up into a mound, which meant that the east and west ends sat in a depression. If you stood about where the dead man lay, you could see down the vines only to the middle of the vineyard. After that, the earth dropped away on the other side.

Gideon quickly set additional trip wires on several of the parallel rows of vines, daisy-chaining the IEDs—improvised explosive devices—together for added effect. His internal clock warned him that almost a full minute had passed since he'd last opened fire.

You're out of time.

He quickly tied the final knot and retreated to a spot about twenty feet short of the high ground at the center of the field. It was impossible to be certain, but the dead guy was likely the only shooter who had been freely roaming on this side of the castle's grounds. The others would be coming from the buildings to the south and the west.

Probably.

It was a gamble, but so was everything in life. And Gideon was outnumbered. He was going to have to take a few risks if he wanted to shift the odds in his favor.

Footsteps in the distance. Hurried, foolish. But they reinforced the knowledge that he was out of time. He lay flat on the earth, quickly searching around for fallen leaves or twigs with which to break up his silhouette, but he found nothing. He cursed his memory of helping to prepare the vines for this year's growing season just a few weeks earlier.

Still, he was covered in dried mud and the dust of a hard day's climbing, as well as his borrowed chest rig, which was made of dark canvas. As long as he held still, he would be almost impossible to spot.

The footsteps grew closer. Gideon slowly reached for the spare magazines he'd secreted around his person. He also set one of his last remaining grenades within easy reach.

Gideon sensed he had company. Not close, somewhere on the west side of the vineyard. Probably two of them. He reasoned that the new arrivals had probably noticed the splayed-out body of their comrade in arms and were conferring over what to do about it.

"Don't keep me waiting…"

They didn't. Two men emerged from the cover of the buildings on the west side of the field of vines. They moved in a low crouch, hugging the shadows for concealment. Gideon pressed his cheek against the side of the rifle and peered through the optic. He had a bead on one of them but knew he couldn't take the shot.

Not yet.

Because the second he did, the other would go to ground. He needed to take at least two of the OPFOR out simultaneously. That left just one free-roaming shooter. It was better odds than being triple-teamed in reverse.

Though it hurt him to do so, Gideon lifted his aim a few feet. He double-checked that the shot selector was on sustained-fire mode, then rested his finger on the trigger. He exhaled slowly, then squeezed, pivoting his rifle left and right as though he were laying down suppressing fire.

He kept the trigger depressed until the twenty-five remaining rounds in the magazine were spent and the ground to his right was coated in shiny brass casings.

Gideon immediately threw himself upright. Even as his feet scrabbled for purchase, he ejected the spent magazine and fed a fresh one in. It seated with a comforting click, which he heard despite his ringing ears. He dumped the empty and started running.

Already, incoming rounds cracked all around him, chewing the upcoming year's harvest into splinters before the first grape had been seen. Twice, Gideon heard the waspish sting of a bullet just inches from his ear. The shots were being fired randomly to keep him pinned down, but that didn't mean the enemy couldn't get lucky.

He squeezed off several short bursts as he ran, crouched low and mostly firing blind. He needed them to know he was moving. His muzzle flashes—though dampened by the suppressor fitted to the gun—would quickly betray his position.

And the other team always got a vote.

Still, he needed them to run right into his booby trap.

Which meant he needed to give them a target to chase. And he was the only bait going.

Gideon threw himself to the ground as he hit the brow of the hill. His chest was heaving, but he didn't feel out of breath. A level of elation beyond anything he'd ever experienced pushed out all physical discomfort.

He was high.

Five, four, three...

He held his breath. It should be right about now. More gunshots in the distance. Footsteps, low voices. Then...

Boom.

TEN

Senator McKinney had the frame of a football player gone to seed, which was both artfully and effectively disguised by his choice of tailor—always English, always Savile Row. His study was the library of an eighteenth-century country house near Middleburg, Virginia, where a fire crackled despite the mildness of the season.

"Lock the door behind you," he said in a low growl without looking away from a seventy-two-inch television that sat on a wheeled cart so as not to upset the aesthetics of the space when it wasn't required. "And throw another log on."

Ronan Haynes did as he was instructed, pulling closed the heavy wooden doors behind him and sliding a heavy metal bolt into place to secure them. He didn't audibly acknowledge his principal's instructions. The senator preferred it that way.

McKinney finally looked away from the screen—and the constant stream of radio chatter broadcast through the speakers—as Ronan approached. His expression was sulfurous. The air in the room was thick from heat, the scent of wood smoke, and a distinct lack of fresh air.

"It's a mess," he spat. The remnants of a cigar were stubbed out next to him. "They're dropping like flies."

"The target?"

"No sign of him."

"There will be blowback," Ronan said.

He stood at the side of the studded leather couch currently occupied by Senator McKinney. He knew his place. He was not a man of overweening ambition. He saw little sense in flying too close to the sun. No matter how tough any man was, he was still made of human flesh. His wings were easily clipped.

"Why the fuck do you think I sent for you?" McKinney exploded. He clenched his right hand into a fist several times, practically vibrating with scarcely repressed rage.

But it was more than rage, Ronan knew. It was fear. Fear the likes of which McKinney had not felt in years.

You flew too close…

The issue for men like Ronan was that they were by their very nature tied to more ambitious men. No matter how carefully they operated in their own lives, if their masters chose to roll the dice, then they tumbled with them. And so it was today.

He said nothing and looked at the television screen. He saw a map display overlaid with roughly a dozen GPS locator dots. Several were now shaded red, which he presumed from McKinney's statement meant that they had been removed from the board.

Gideon Ryker was supposed to have been a fucking potato. But apparently not. He'd gotten lucky. Perhaps he'd been forewarned, or maybe the Agency hit squad had simply been overconfident. He'd seen it happen before. Even when their lives rested on their caution and good judgment—maybe especially then—men could be supremely arrogant. It was difficult to truly believe that your opponent was better than you. Because if you really believed that, then going up against him was too terrifying to contemplate.

It was easier to tell yourself a story that your enemy was weak, naive, or incompetent. Because how could you fail to defeat such a foe? Even better if the adversary was all three. Then he was beatable. Then the mind didn't shy away from a fight.

But it was a slippery slope, one that Haynes resisted at all costs. It was the reason he had survived a lifetime in the shadows. He believed—had to believe—in his core that his enemy was both invulnerable and omniscient. Because to beat such a rival required both dedication to one's craft and mastery of it.

"What do you want me to do?"

McKinney glowered at the screen as another dot shaded red. "Is it possible that we've been compromised?"

"I check both houses for listening devices weekly," Haynes said. "And that's on top of the Bureau's countersurveillance sweeps."

"And what do you find?"

"I would tell you if I discovered anything. I never have."

"Then maybe you're not looking hard enough," McKinney snarled. "Or perhaps they're using something new. Something you can't detect."

"The detectors are sound."

"My wife?"

Haynes tightened his lips. "We know she's a...liability."

"That bitch reports every word I say back to New Eden," McKinney said scornfully. "But she knows nothing. I'm sure of it. She thinks I still sing from the same hymn sheet."

"Then it's Occam's razor. The simplest explanation is the correct one. Richter—he calls himself Ryker, now—was in better shape than we expected. Or the Agency team fucked up.

Hell, that French retirement home was full of vets. Maybe they played a part."

"It doesn't matter how," McKinney said, clenching and flexing his hand. "We've got dead Agency operatives. You can't sweep this kind of mess under the rug."

"Colt will handle his people," Haynes said confidently.

"And what about Langley? What about the Hill?"

Haynes refrained from pointing out that the Hill was Senator McKinney's business, not his. Another dot blinked out.

Despite his belief in Colt, Haynes also knew that McKinney was right. The CIA would need someone to blame for the mess in Provence. They would need their pound of flesh.

"It was a rogue operation," he said, thinking out loud. "The local station chief was corrupt. He deployed the WISHBONE asset to settle some gangland squabble. We can make it go away."

"And what if Asher has an insurance policy?"

Haynes shrugged. His expression remained the same even as he said, "He has children."

McKinney thought about it for a few seconds, then nodded curtly. "Put the wheels in motion."

"Yes, boss," Haynes said. He paused. "What about New Eden?"

The senator slapped the side of the leather sofa with an open palm. The crack that resulted echoed off the rafters high above. "Dammit, Ronan. I know. He'll get wind of something this big. I'll tell him that we saw an opportunity to execute the standing order to hunt down Ryker."

"He doesn't like failure."

It was McKinney's turn to shrug. The fabric of his rumpled suit jacket bunched up against his collar. "But he can't move against me, either. It's a stalemate. *Fuck.*"

The senator imbued his last word with such fury and loathing that even the ordinarily unflappable Haynes felt a chill run down his spine. It wasn't because he feared that his master would turn against him. He had his own insurance, though they'd never directly addressed the issue. Such things were expected between men in their respective positions.

The problem was that despite McKinney's confidence that the deadlock between Washington and New Eden was unchanged, that was manifestly not the case. With every month, the noose tightened. McKinney had been unable to resist the imposition of his wife—a mole in his own household. She was half his age—a potential political grenade just waiting for the DC press pack to pull the pin.

Haynes's master was growing more desperate by the day. Using Agency assets to tie up this loose end instead of deniable local cutouts had been an insane decision. Colt was reliable, but the inherent risk was now presenting itself—dead American operatives provoked questions that could not be ignored.

"What about Ambassador Tilley? Should I make arrangements?"

A brief flash of regret crossed the senator's face, though the emotion died quickly in a territory that was inhospitable to such sentiment. He collected himself and shook his head sharply.

"No. She'll do the right thing."

"And if she doesn't?"

McKinney slapped the sofa once again, though with less enthusiasm this time. "Dammit, Ronan. You know the answer."

ELEVEN

"What the fuck was that?" Colt yelled, getting to the windows just as the flashes from the multiple detonations faded away.

"Grenades?" Emily suggested.

"Thanks, Einstein. I figured. Who the hell's throwing them?"

"Alpha, this is Bravo, shit," a voice panted over the radio in his ear. "I think I'm the last one left out here. The other two ran right into an ambush. Fuck!"

"Are they dead?"

"Either that or they'll make a helluva pincushion."

Colt's face contorted into a silent scream as he stared out the window. The room behind him was mostly dark, but he knew it was still a risk. Gideon was good—as he was proving with every minute that passed. He didn't let the rest of his team see his frustration.

"Pull back to the castle. I'm done playing by his rules. It's time to take this to the mat."

IT TOOK Gideon two full minutes to realize that nobody else was coming. His makeshift daisy-chained IED had been far more successful than he'd expected. He'd staggered the grenades on vines that were each about six feet apart and raised them off the ground so that each explosive's fragmentation kill zone was maximized.

Still, he'd only hoped to wound one of the enemy shooters and to buy himself a moment to flip the script—emerging from behind the brow of the hill to fight toe to toe with a pair of hopefully stunned survivors.

This was...*better*.

He'd poked his head up from cover about a minute earlier to survey the aftermath. One of the bad guys was definitely dead. The fragmentation grenades had torn most of the budding foliage away from the vines, giving him a clear field of view. That tango was lying on his back and had an R-rated chest wound on show.

The other guy was wounded, likely critically. Gideon could still hear him moaning. It took him another thirty seconds to determine that this wasn't a trap before he slowly advanced down the hill toward the ambush area.

All three grenades had detonated, so he didn't have to worry about unexploded ordnance, but he knew that already. Due to the connected trip wires, they had each exploded about half a second apart.

Gideon crept silently, part of his mind marveling at the way his footsteps neither left a trace on the dirt nor made even a whisper of sound. He was standing over the surviving shooter before the man noticed his presence.

"Just get it over with," the injured man groaned, attempting to lift his head off the soil. His strength failed him, and it fell back. He let out a heavy, shaky sigh.

Before responding, Gideon reached down and unclipped the rifle from the man's chest sling and ejected both the round in the chamber and the live magazine. He tossed the useless weapon aside, then did the same for the pistol in the shooter's thigh holster.

"Fuck you…" the man said, spitting a dark, bloodied glob of saliva out of his mouth. He was unable to generate any power, and it landed on his own cheek.

Gideon said nothing. Instead, he took a moment to study the shooter's wounds. His lower legs were dark with blood, and his pants were peppered with at least a dozen cuts. He wouldn't be slipping unnoticed through an airport metal detector for some time.

If he made it at all.

"Looks like a piece of shrapnel nicked your femoral artery," he observed, squatting in a low crouch over the man.

"Tell me something I don't know," he whispered back, the strength in his voice fading with every passing second.

"You carrying a tourniquet?"

The man's lips were peeled back, his teeth bared, but his expression was pale and terrified. "What do you care?"

"You don't need to die today."

"I'm screwed. I'll never walk again."

"I've seen worse."

Have I?

The comments seemed to cut through the man's false bravado. "Top left pocket."

Gideon had it free from its packaging in seconds. It was a length of strapping about two feet long with a couple of Velcro patches and a plastic torsion rod. He tore away what remained of his patient's fatigues and found the site of the bleeding.

"Dammit!" The man said, losing what little remained of the

color in his cheeks. The whites of his eyes dominated his face. "Screw it. I'm better off dead. Just give me my fucking pistol, man. One round, that's all I need."

"You don't think that," Gideon said, looping the strap around the man's thigh about three inches above the major shrapnel wound, which was liberally leaking blood. "You want to live. Don't be afraid to admit you're scared to die. Everybody is."

The man started to scream as Gideon fastened the strap into place and began tightening the tourniquet with the supplied plastic rod. He reached for the magazine he'd discarded a couple of moments before and shoved it between the man's teeth—mostly to avoid attracting unwanted attention. He was pretty sure the last roaming shooter had left his buddies to die.

But it was difficult to maintain situational awareness when you were acting as a battlefield medic.

"I guess," the man panted as Gideon finished tightening and pushed the rod through a Velcro loop to keep the tourniquet tight and secure, "you would know all about that. I heard they really fucked you up, and yet here you are."

Gideon cocked his head to one side. The timer in his brain that had been running ever since he left the enemy team's comms van was almost at empty. He needed to move, couldn't afford to waste time indulging his own questions.

And yet...

"Who fucked me up?"

The man let out a bitter, half-delirious laugh. He was panting rapidly, only capable of drawing a series of tiny, shallow breaths. "The Brotherhood."

"Who?"

The injured man's body grew slack on the ground. Gideon

recognized the signs of shock. Unless he got serious medical attention fast, he wasn't going to make it, despite his best efforts. Still, he was able to speak. "Don't ask me. Colt's the one who would know. I thought it was all an urban legend. And yet here you are."

TWELVE

"Something's happening," Sergeant Jabari Bekka observed quietly.

He was a North African legionnaire, probably Tunisian, though he'd never shared that information with any of his comrades. He was in his late fifties and still capable of acts of great physical prowess. He had a distance runner's frame, which he paired with a lean, wiry strength. He was neither tall nor visibly muscular, but those who knew him well knew better than to doubt his abilities.

Fournier nodded. There had been no gunfire for several minutes, a break that the five armed men—now six, after the recent arrival of one of the shooters who'd been sent to sweep the grounds—and one woman had used to first confer, then organize themselves.

The prisoners, himself included, had all been pushed back against the far wall upon which a dusty tapestry hung. The windows were mostly above chest height and were too narrow for most of the retirees to climb through, even if they had been physically capable of doing so. The entrances to the long hall were situated on the other side of the room.

The new disposition meant that only a couple of the members of the armed team were required to cover his fellow legionnaires. The two guards—one man and Emily, the woman who had posed as a reporter—maintained a twenty-foot buffer between them and their captives. They both carried automatic weapons. It had been a long time since Fournier commanded an infantry regiment, but he remembered enough to know that there was likely a thirty-round magazine in each rifle.

Fournier grimaced with defeat. *If we try anything, they'll cut us apart.*

And yet it was undeniable that the two closest guards were distracted by something, as were their comrades on the other side of the hall. Both he and Bekka were seated near the wall—and hence the windows that looked down over the courtyard to the front of the building.

"Stand up," he instructed the younger man quietly. "Pretend to stretch or that you have cramp. Tell me what you see."

Bekka needed no great encouragement. He stood with obvious relief and ran himself through a series of stretches.

"The van..." he whispered as he folded himself into a forward bend, which allowed him to bring his mouth close to Fournier's ear. "It's smoking. It looks like something inside might be on fire."

"Nomad," Fournier murmured in response, raising one eyebrow with appreciation. "He's planning something."

Two of the shooters were currently facing the same window as Sergeant Bekka. They began to confer with growing animation.

"The fire is spreading," Bekka explained.

A loud whistle split the room. Colt summoned one of the

two men watching over them to him. Fournier couldn't hear his words at this distance, but his meaning was clear.

Get out there and see what's going on.

The armed man reluctantly jogged toward the hall's main door. Before he reached it, a loud crack rattled the castle's old single-pane windows. Several of them shattered from the force of the explosion.

Fournier didn't wait for Bekka to fill him in. He jumped to his feet, his problem knee strangely giving him no trouble as he did so, and looked out the window. The van that had carried the fake camera crew to the Legion's Provence retreat had gone up in flames. A pillar of black smoke surged into the sky, backlit by the inferno below.

Several large pieces of the chassis had been thrown twenty or thirty feet by the initial explosion. As the retired colonel watched, a number of smaller detonations took place.

"Grenades cooking off," Bekka murmured, motioning for Fournier to get behind cover.

Almost the entire group of legionnaires were on their feet now. Only those few who were too dead or too infirm to stand remained on the floor. Despite the continuing gravity of their shared peril, some of the survivors slapped each other's backs or let out grim chuckles.

"He's coming for you," a voice called out of the crowd, speaking accented but obvious English. "The Nomad is coming for you."

"And when he does," Fournier said gruffly, speaking to Bekka alone. "We need to be ready. Instruct the men. Anyone who is able to move is to pick a target. Don't act until I give the word. There are more of us than there are them—but they have the guns. If we go too soon, they'll massacre us."

"Sit the hell down." Emily—whatever her real name was—barked. She had her trigger finger on the trigger itself. She looked half-panicked, her face glowing from the flames outside. Fournier sensed that it was best not to test her. She might just snap.

He raised his voice. "I will calm my men," he said, showing her his palms to indicate that he was no threat. He maintained eye contact until he was certain that her twitchiness was subsiding. "But please, take your finger off the trigger. We mean you no harm."

"Listen up," he said in a low, urgent tone as he turned to face the group of men huddled around the windows. Some still stared out at the flames, their teeth bared, but most were close enough to listen without being overheard. "When you move away from the windows, you will push up closer to the guards. I want the younger, fitter men in the first rank. We strike when they are distracted. Are you with me?"

His guys were too smart, too experienced to answer verbally or even to give him a nod of the head that would betray his intention. But he saw in their determined expressions and hard eyes that they understood the task ahead of them.

And that some would die in the process.

THE INSTANT GIDEON heard the incendiary in the Sprinter van ignite, he reached for Jean-Luc's cell phone. He pulled it out of his pocket as he hit the walls of the castle, pressing himself against the old stone to minimize his profile, and scanned the screen. He already had a full block of signal, confirming that the fire had destroyed the radio jammer in the van. He dialed 112—the European emergency number—and hit the call button.

"Bonsoir," a businesslike female voice answered in a matter of seconds. *Good evening.* "What is your emergency?"

"Bonsoir," Gideon replied in excellent French, the courtesy of the greeting throwing him for a moment. "Men with guns are attacking L'Institution des Invalides de la Legion Etrangere. I just heard an explosion. I think the castle might be on fire. Please, you must hurry."

There was a brief, almost nonexistent pause as the operator processed what he'd just said. "Monsieur, can I take your name?"

"Come quickly," Gideon said instead. "I have to find somewhere to hide."

The nearest town—Puyloubier—was only a short drive away, but only a few thousand people lived there. It had a police station, but it probably wasn't manned at this time of night. Still, he expected that at least a handful of local police or gendarmerie would be able to reach the vineyard within the next twenty minutes or so, drawn from the scattering of similar communes and villages in the area. They would be armed but likely instructed only to observe what was happening and report back to their superiors.

Otherwise, the closest major counterterrorism unit was the National Police's elite RAID team in Marseille, an hour's drive, but quicker with sirens and motorcycle outriders. If helicopters were available, which was likely, then reconnaissance elements could probably be on the scene inside half an hour.

Interestingly, the Foreign Legion's main base was in Aubagne, just thirty miles away. And since the Legion was activated as part of Operation Sentinel—a military outfit fighting against terrorists who periodically staged attacks on French soil—it wasn't outside the realm of imagination that very shortly, a number of extremely angry armed legionnaires might turn up and show no mercy to those who had defiled their unit's ancestral resting place.

In short, Gideon had just set the cat among the pigeons.

The enemy shooters would have to make a decision fast. They couldn't know that Gideon had called in a warning, but they would have to assume that somebody in the area had. If they weren't moving in the next few minutes, then there was no hope of making a successful escape. At least, not without risking a running shootout with the French police, its elite counterterrorism units, and eventually the military itself.

No matter how good they were, those were impossible odds.

They'll have backup vehicles, he thought. The van they'd driven here wasn't big enough to accommodate near a dozen operatives. They likely also had a couple of SUVs. They would be parked somewhere outside the vineyard's grounds but close enough to reach on foot.

But that meant that the enemy had at least a few hundred yards to cover on foot. They would know by now that he wasn't the injured cripple they'd expected to encounter. They would understand that he knew the land.

So they would take hostages when they left. Worse, they would probably booby-trap the legionnaires they left behind so that they couldn't be rushed from the rear.

Once more, Gideon pictured Jean-Luc's pale face in the seconds after his death and remembered the kindness the old man had shown in nursing him to health over the past several months. His lips drew back in a snarl. No more of these fine men would die on his account.

He would make sure of it.

THIRTEEN

The sinews and muscles in Gideon's back strained as he began his assault on the castle's walls, rising vertically with a hand-over-hand climb using an iron drainpipe for a rope. His rifle was slung over his back, his chest webbing cinched as tightly as possible. Movement made noise, and noise got you killed.

Halfway there.

In this quiet period between battles fought and those yet to begin, he felt his adrenaline start to fade. The exhaustion of the day's initial exertion still clung to him. With it came a sense of unreality, as though he were watching himself climb the walls from a distance. He almost didn't recognize himself.

No, that wasn't right. He *definitely* didn't recognize himself.

What kind of person could do the things he'd done over the past few minutes? He'd killed as though it came as naturally to him as breathing, as though he'd been raised and trained for only one purpose. Now, without bullets cracking overhead and the imminent fear of death, doubt reared its ugly head.

Surely only a monster felt at home in the middle of the chaos of battle. Was that what he was?

As he turned these questions over in his mind, Gideon's body continued its mechanical ascent. He heard shouting from inside the castle's walls—the voices of terrified and angry men. Occasionally, there was the crack of a gunshot, but he sensed—or maybe hoped—that they were fired only in warning.

There it was: just a few feet above him, the castle's great hall. This was the dangerous part. The windows he was hanging just below were the only way inside. At least, they were the only way in that was unlikely to be under guard.

Or rigged to blow.

Gideon understood human nature, even if he didn't yet know his own. His enemy would expect an assault from the front or perhaps to be picked off as they made a break for their escape vehicles. That is what they would be prepared to defend against. The last thing they would anticipate was to be attacked from behind before they were able to make their escape.

There was no time to think. Above him, the shouting reached a crescendo. Only two or three voices. He guessed the bad guys were backing toward the great wooden doors, threatening their captives to stay back.

He lifted himself another couple of feet so that he was hanging like a spider right under the window ledge.

Nice and quick.

Gideon popped up, raising his eyeline just an inch above the bottom of the window. The pane directly in front of him was cracked from the aftereffects of the van's explosion and dirtied with age, but enough visibility remained for an instant tactical picture to form in his mind.

As he expected, most of his opponents were clustered around the door. Only two of them remained close, their rifles aimed toward a crowd of angry legionnaires.

Right as Gideon was about to drop back down and prepare for his assault, a pair of eyes inside the crowd turned to face him. Perhaps he'd made a noise, or maybe it was just chance. But the man focused on him, his gaze wide and fearful.

Gideon raised his finger to his lips. The man blinked. Nodded. He turned back.

As he popped below the window ledge and took a deep breath, he heard a voice carry through the glass. "Sit the fuck down!"

Don't think I will.

He slung the rifle back over his shoulder and flicked it to single-shot mode, then pulled himself above the window ledge for a second time. It was far more challenging this time with only one free hand—since the other was locked around the drainpipe for support.

"Here goes nothing," he muttered.

He held his breath as he used the muzzle of his rifle to deftly smash a single small pane of glass, just one in a latticework of lead. It fell away from him, into the hall, but nobody seemed to notice in the chaos.

Only the man who'd seen him, who stood stock-still.

Gideon had his left foot twisted behind the drainpipe, his right propped against a tiny crack in the wall for support, and his left arm carrying most of his load. The scar tissue on his side ached from the effort. The barrel of his rifle rested only on a thin length of lead. It wasn't exactly the perfect firing position.

But it would have to do.

He exhaled slowly, focusing his full attention on the two shooters backing toward the great wooden doors as they provided rear security. Occasionally, he caught a glimpse of activity behind, likely whoever was rigging the explosives.

A tiny, niggling worry at the back of his mind warned that it would only take one stray ricochet to detonate whatever the explosives tech had in his pack. This was an old building. It definitely wasn't built to modern-day code. The outer shell would probably last another thousand years. It was built solid. The wood-timbered floors and ceilings, the carpets, and the upholstery...not so much.

But he didn't have a choice.

It didn't bother Gideon that his first target was a woman. She was part of the crew that had brought terror to this place of peace and rest. Either by her own hand or indirectly, she'd killed men who had atoned for any crimes they had ever committed many decades earlier.

Through the rifle's sight, he could see that she had dark hair. She looked panicked, her finger on the trigger of her rifle. She was waving it wildly but turned away to check on the progress behind her. Gideon took his shot the second her muzzle aimed away from the crowd. He squeezed the trigger.

And then she looked dead.

The woman fell with a single dark dot at the center of her forehead. Before her unfortunate partner had a chance to identify where the single gunshot had come from and respond in kind, Gideon pivoted the muzzle of his rifle about an inch to the left and calmly squeezed the trigger a second time.

The man fell, but not before reflexively jerking his own trigger in his death throes. A burst of half a dozen rounds spat out of his rifle, mercifully only chewing up the wooden floorboards in front of him, sending splinters flying from trees that had been felled hundreds of years earlier.

Keep moving.

Gideon barely needed to remind himself. His body had already shifted into action before the second shooter dropped. He reversed the rifle in his hands and smashed through the remaining glass and lead with its stock.

Or at least, he tried.

In reality, it was almost impossible to force enough leverage from his unstable perch on a drainpipe that was now creaking ominously with every move he made. As he drew back the rifle for a third time, attempting to break through the surprisingly sturdy window lead, he heard a metal fastening rattle above him.

He looked up slowly.

"Shit."

A chunk of rubble came loose above him, falling directly toward his head. Gideon dodged just in time, but the additional motion only added to the strain on the rusted brackets that held the drainpipe in place above him. The topmost of these had now completely snapped. There was only one more above him, and it was visibly coming free from the wall.

"Gidi, take my hand," a voice called. Gideon returned his attention to the window to see a group of men forcing the shattered frame open. Two held it out of his way as the wiry, familiar North African legionnaire held out his arm.

Gideon grasped it gratefully, momentarily dropping his rifle against its sling as the legionnaire hauled him inside.

"You know how to pick your moments," the man said, his eyebrows raised. Gideon remembered his name was Bekka, though they had only exchanged a few words in the time he'd been here.

He frowned as a tendril of thought tickled the back of his mind. What had Bekka said? Something familiar?

No time.

He sprinted for the wooden door, seeing that his second victim had fallen back against it, pushing it closed. That was suboptimal. He hurriedly pulled the man's corpse aside, dropping his rifle and replacing it in his right hand with the pistol from his thigh holster. He held it tight against his body.

"Get back," he yelled, gesturing wildly at a half dozen legionnaires who had hurried across the hall to strip the corpses of the two dead shooters. He didn't need to say why.

Their feet crunched against chunks of plaster that had fallen from the ceiling and rolled brass round casings across the floorboards as they grabbed their weapons and hurried backward. Gideon realized that the enemy shooters had fired dozens of warning shots to keep the legionnaires penned back. His own gunfire might have been nothing more than background noise. It was possible that whoever was behind that door had no idea his comrades were dead.

Only one way to find out.

Gideon inhaled deeply, flooding his lungs and bloodstream with desperately needed oxygen. His instinct was to charge through the door without preparing himself. His training overrode that impulse, giving him a framework to overpower his impulsive urges.

"Now."

He spoke the breaching command as he pulled back the door handle, pistol unwavering in his right hand. A black shape looked up in the open doorway. Time moved in staggered flashes, as though through a camera's shutter. The shape was a man. His eyes were first curious, then wide with shock.

The enemy shooter reached for his weapon.

Gideon squeezed the pistol's trigger. *Too late.*

Except it wasn't. The hammer clicked, but the round failed to ignite. There was no time to cycle through the causes or try and clear the jam. He tossed the useless weapon aside with a scowl of disgust tearing his face. He threw himself at the other man, who had already drawn his own sidearm and was raising it through the air.

Gideon slapped the weapon aside, his hand chopping down

against the man's wrist with punishing force. In the right place, the blow might have broken bone. Whether it did or didn't, he didn't know. But the pistol dropped and clattered across the floorboards.

How many others?

He knew he should already know the answer to that question. But he didn't. And now, locked in combat, he didn't dare check.

Gideon crashed into the other man, his momentum barely slowed by the disarming blow. They both went down hard. The impact knocked all the air out of his lungs, and he thought he felt one of his ribs crack.

But he felt no pain.

"Fuck off," the man grunted as he made a fist and rained a crushing blow against Gideon's face. He definitely felt pain this time as the cartilage in his nose crunched. A white flash filled his vision, and he reared back, hands automatically going to his face where they grew slippery with his own blood.

Not good.

Gideon kicked out, more to separate himself from the man who now had the upper hand than with the expectation of hitting him, but he landed his blow regardless. A low groan of pain erupted a few feet away as he blinked and frenziedly wiped his eyes to clear his vision.

Acting on instinct now that he could see again—mostly—Gideon scrambled toward his enemy. He pounced on him and rained a violent series of blows into his rib cage. The man was wearing a ballistic vest, but it didn't matter. The fight seemed to have left him. He was moving, but only slightly. He wasn't even struggling to get loose.

Gideon stilled his fist in midair. He took no pleasure in beating a broken man. The guy's face was streaked with blood, though whose it was, he didn't know. He was panting shakily, struggling to get oxygen into his lungs. But as Gideon stared into his eyes, he didn't see defeat. Instead, staring back at him was the spark of victory.

Shit.

FOURTEEN

The cause of his opponent's triumphant lust was instantly clear. The man underneath him hadn't given up fighting because he was defeated. He was just searching for another way to win. And he'd found it, in the form of a hatchet blade that he was now driving up toward Gideon's temple.

He ducked out of the way in the nick of time, rolling to his right and seeing the matte black blade miss his skull by barely an inch.

The unexpected appearance of the medieval melee weapon should've stunned him. But Gideon did the only thing he could and rolled with the insanity of the past few hours.

As the weapon's momentum faded as it passed through the air, Gideon reached for his opponent's wrist—but missed. His fingers connected around the top of the hatchet's handle instead. Both men's fingers were slick with blood, and somehow, he managed to wrench the weapon from the other man in a desperate lunge.

Without thinking, he brought the spiked rear end down and split his opponent's skull.

He threw himself backward, not yet allowing himself to react to the horror of the man's violent death. Instead, his gaze roved left and right to confirm that no other adversaries were present. His eyes were white and frantic, the flow of adrenaline enough to overwhelm even his carefully built defenses.

Gideon let out a sigh of relief. His chest heaved from the effort of the fight, and his muscles threatened to fail completely. But he allowed himself a moment to relax, a moment in which he could contemplate what he'd just done.

For an instant all the sound in his ears faded. Gideon's fatigue faded away. He felt almost lightheaded. But it didn't last.

He couldn't let it last.

Gideon shook off the feeling and reached forward to pull the spike out of the side of the axeman's temple. He had clearly died instantly. The matte metal gleamed with blood. Only then did he look around to see that the eyes of three legionnaires were on him, including those of Bekka.

"You did what you had to, Gidi," was all the man said.

A wave of nausea rose in Gideon's stomach. He clamped his teeth down hard until it subsided, then met Bekka's gaze. The niggling thought that had earlier faded from his mind like sand through a sieve now returned. "Why are you calling me that? How the hell do you know my name?"

The old legionnaire regarded him for several long seconds before responding. The expression in his look was soulful. "We all know you, Gideon. You're one of us."

COLT HELD up a fist once he had gained a hundred yards or so of distance from the château, then reached into his webbing and freed the satellite phone he carried. The model was designed not to make any record of incoming or outgoing numbers. He punched one in from memory, starting with a US country code prefix.

"Go," the voice of Sheldon McKinney answered on the other end. As usual, he was all business.

He spoke in a hushed tone so that he could not be overheard. "Sir, this has turned into a goatfuck. The target has eliminated over half my guys. I'm not going to be able to keep this under wraps. I need instructions."

There was a short silence on the other end of the line. Colt used it to glance around. He was a few paces away from the remainder of his team, who were securing the hostages they'd taken from the château. Forcefully. He ignored the legionnaires' glowering looks.

"How many of *our* people do you have left?"

"Just one."

Colt met the man's gaze. He guessed the senator's instructions before they were spoken and unconsciously tapped his slung rifle as he steadied himself for the killing to come.

"Do what you have to do to ensure that our involvement in this mess never comes to light. Then report back to the Center."

"Understood."

"THEY TOOK HOSTAGES," Bekka said. Gideon saw for the first time that he was carrying a rifle. He held it with a practiced ease. "Three of us."

"Who?"

"Luca, Manuel, and Novak."

Gideon closed his eyes. He wanted to keep them shut,

wanted to wake up and find that all this was just a nightmare. But he knew in his heart that it was not. He didn't know any of those three men particularly well.

It doesn't matter.

"I brought these monsters here," Gideon said. "Jean-Luc is dead because of me."

Bekka attempted to conceal his dismay at the news, but Gideon read the man's features easily. "It's not your fault," he said. "You didn't start this."

"Start what?" Gideon demanded furiously. "You didn't answer me. How do you know me?"

He caught himself before going any further and held up his palm to forestall Bekka's answer. A quick glance at his watch informed him that eleven minutes had passed since he contacted emergency dispatch. Local police units would already be on the way. It was even possible that a mobile RAID armed response team was on the right side of Marseille and would get here within half an hour. If not likely.

"Don't answer that. I have to go."

"I'm coming with you. And Marcos, too," Bekka said firmly. The retired legionnaire glanced through a crack in the heavy wooden doors in search of a man Gideon knew to be his friend. But both men were past their best.

"You can't run," he pointed out. "Not with your knee the way it is. And Marcos's heart..."

"We're coming. We understand the consequences."

"I'll be quicker alone," Gideon fired back, knowing that he could not let Bekka join him in what could be a one-way mission. Too many of his friends had died. He couldn't have more lives on his conscience.

He pointed toward the hall. "I contacted the police. They will be here soon, maybe twenty or thirty minutes. I need you to keep the guys in there safe until they arrive. Those shooters might return. If they do, you'll need to fill them with lead."

Bekka looked like he wanted to snap back, but he somehow restrained himself. He'd always been on the more erudite end of the scale when it came to the legionnaires. Some—men Gideon liked well—were a little rough around the edges. But Bekka could think. He wrote poetry in his spare time. And he understood that Gideon was speaking the truth. All of the legionnaires here were handicapped in one way or another, whether through age, infirmity, or wartime injury.

And time had come even for him.

He nodded curtly. "We'll do what must be done. What about you?"

Gideon spoke through a lump in his throat. He sensed that no matter the outcome of the next few minutes, he would never speak to Bekka again. Never return to this place that had done so much to heal him. Never sit by Jean-Luc's grave or be able to apologize for the hurt that he'd wrought.

"There will be shooting. No matter what happens, don't come out of that hall. Not until the police arrive. I can't promise to save all our people. But if I have to, I will die trying."

Bekka handed over a spare magazine for Gideon's rifle. "Go with God, Gidi."

Before Gideon had a chance to turn, conscious of the seconds ticking away and still holding the hatchet that he now saw was a tomahawk—a throwing axe, Colonel Fournier exited the hall. He carried a pistol in his right hand, presently aimed at the floor.

"You're going after them?" he asked, his dark eyes quickly taking in the situation.

Gideon nodded. His feet itched with the urge to go after the hostages, but he held himself back, sensing the colonel had something to say.

"When this is over," Fournier said, "there is a man at 167 Rue de la Marché. In Marseille. His name is Leclerc. He has the answers to your questions, and he will help."

FIFTEEN

The tomahawk axe was not an effective close-quarter battle weapon, at least not compared to the alternatives available to him. It was heavier and more unwieldy than a simple fighting knife and had far less range than a pistol.

But Gideon sprinted after the hostages with it held in his bloodied grip regardless. The rifle slung to his chest thudded against his torso as he ran, and he savored the pain that resulted.

Not just because he deserved it but because each thump dumped another hit of adrenaline into his bloodstream and fended off his growing exhaustion for just a few more seconds.

It had been impossible to conceal the passage of a group of men wearing combat boots through the gravel that surrounded the château. That was especially true if the hostages they drove ahead of them deliberately marked the ground to indicate the path they had taken.

Gideon was certain that was what the three captive legionnaires had done. The trail was too easy for him to follow for there to be any other cause. Either that, or he was heading directly into a trap.

He did the math in his head as he ran. The enemy team had started with ten shooters and a comms technician. He'd killed Golf first, then another lone operator before ambushing two men in the vineyards, followed by three in the great hall. In total, seven now lay dead by his hand. Only three bad guys remained alive.

It was a butcher's bill of slaughter.

Until just a couple of hours earlier, Gideon had no idea he was capable of committing such violence. But though he was shocked by how easily inflicting pain and death came to him, he felt no guilt for the specific lives he'd taken.

Save the introspection for after it's over.

Gideon slowed a fraction, just long enough to detect a change in the trail. The enemy had mostly followed the roads through the château's grounds. They'd stopped here, at a crossroads near the exit to the public road. Two, maybe three of them had stayed close to one another.

Those would be the hostages.

As his attention was fixed on the ground, a gunshot rang out about thirty yards ahead of him, just before the stone wall that bordered the property.

Gideon's blood ran cold. They were executing the hostages before they'd been able to make their break for freedom. Had to be.

He was too late to save them.

But not to deliver judgment on their killers. They would pay for what they had done. He threw caution to the wind and sprinted for the wall. He covered the distance in record time, ignoring all his physical discomforts and aches. He could not let the remaining enemy shooters get to a vehicle. If they did, it was over.

There.

He spotted them under a tree near the wall. Five men, and a body on the ground. He was fifteen yards away, then ten, then five before anybody noticed his approach, his running shoes light on the ground and the enemy's hearing perhaps briefly deadened by the gunfire.

He hefted the axe in his hand, then stilled himself just in time. What he saw made no sense. The body on the ground was wearing dark fatigues. So were the men with raised weapons—pointed at three men he recognized very well. In Gideon's imagination, gun smoke still rose from the muzzle of the nearest pistol.

The hostages are alive!

The joy of this realization flooded through him, and his arm drew back of its own accord. He wrenched it forward, releasing the axe as though he'd done so a thousand times. It flew true, unerring, and buried itself in the center of the enemy operative's chest. It entered with a wet, dull thud as it cut through Kevlar, bone, flesh, and sinew.

The man looked down. And then it was over. No life remained behind his eyes. He fell to his knees, then slumped onto his side.

Luca spun around, searching for the source of the axe, his eyes wide and wild as they finally alighted on Gideon, who already had his rifle in his hands and was aiming at the remaining enemy shooter.

"Go, Gideon!" Luca yelled. "Leave us."

Gideon ignored him. All his attention was focused on the last shooter. He had a perfect shot. All it would take was a couple of ounces of pressure through the trigger, and the man's skull would be split open.

But his opponent also had a shot.

"Come home, Gideon," the sole survivor said, the pistol in his hand aimed unerringly at Novak's temple. The trigger was depressed a quarter inch. He had enough ounces of pressure on it to almost ensure he would reflexively fire off a shot if Gideon took one of his own. "All this can be over. Nobody else needs to die."

"I'm sick of asking how everybody except me seems to know my name," Gideon fired back. "And at this point, I'm done caring. Let these men go, and I'll let you live. It's a fair offer."

"You know me," the shooter said, and a stirring in his mind told Gideon that he was telling the truth. "My name is Colt. I made you. Or have you forgotten?"

Gideon blocked out the man's words as he appraised his tactical situation. Colt, or whoever the hell this guy was, was only ten feet from him. The difficulty was that the group of three hostages was between them. His opponent kept edging backward and to the left to keep his aim on Novak, forcing him to follow to maintain his own clear shot.

"Fine," Colt said. "I'll make you an offer. Trade places with these men. I don't give a shit about them, you know that. Drop your weapon and come with me. I'll even be a good sport about it. You have five seconds to decide."

Colt took another step back toward the stone wall that was now only a couple of feet behind him and the car-sized opening that led to the public road. He smirked. "Five..."

Luca's eyes widened, and Gideon realized that the legionnaire was trying to get his attention. The old gray-haired soldier surreptitiously shook his head from side to side.

"Four."

Luca pointed deliberately at the ground, his gesture hidden by his own body, then held up three fingers.

"Three."

He dropped one.

Gideon finally understood what the old legionnaire was proposing. He was going to drop to the dirt and presumably drag the other two legionnaires down with him.

It would only buy him a fraction of a second. Possibly not even that long. But it would have to be enough.

"Two."

Only one finger remaining.

Gideon exhaled slowly, forcing his body to still so that his aim would be perfect. It had to be.

"One."

The word hadn't even escaped Colt's lips before Luca executed his move. He dropped to the ground, sweeping out his leg as he did so to knock the other two men to the earth like bowling pins. Gideon didn't wait for them to hit the deck before squeezing the trigger of his rifle.

Even as it kicked against his shoulder, he knew his round had missed. Colt was impossibly fast. His opponent also fired, but Novak's head no longer occupied the small pocket of air that it had only a second earlier. Colt's round went wide.

Gideon pulled his rifle's trigger half a dozen times in quick succession, but always hit a spot a couple of inches behind Colt's racing silhouette. The bullets tore splinters of stone out of the old walls, the rocky shrapnel no doubt slicing through the man's fatigues as it ricocheted back in his direction.

But he was unable to land a killing blow.

The only positive was that the hostages were no longer a factor. This was an old-fashioned gunfight. Quick as he was, Colt still didn't have the time to spare executing a trio of unarmed old men.

"Kill him, Gidi!" Luca yelled over the roar of gunfire.

At least, Gideon thought that's what he heard. Perhaps he was imagining it. The entire scene was completely surreal. His rifle kicked over and over against his shoulder as brass casings sprayed out to his right, glimmering from the moonlight in his peripheral vision.

A searing lance of fire cut through his left arm, the intensity of it throwing a white shroud over his vision. He grunted and spun back a couple of feet; doing so probably saved his life. Another bullet bit into the space his torso had occupied just a fraction of a second before.

Gideon ignored the pain and rotated back into position, bringing the seemingly heavier rifle back up and firing over and over again, even before he located a target.

But Colt was gone. He'd used the momentary distraction caused by Gideon's gunshot wound to slip around the wall.

He dropped into a crouch anyway, leveling the rifle at the gap in the wall. A combination of adrenaline and stabbing pain caused his heart to thunder erratically in his chest. Throughout it all—the icy sensation of blood dripping down his arm, the fatigue, the guilt that all this destruction was his fault—his aim remained true.

It was impossible to make out Colt's escaping footsteps over the roar of the blood rushing in Gideon's ears, but the sound of a single distant gunshot was another matter entirely. He froze just as Luca walked over to him, then spun, searching every direction for this fresh source of danger.

After no further danger presented itself, Gideon guessed that Colt must have executed the comms technician, who would have had enough time to make it to the team's predetermined rally point by now.

Another loose end?

A car's engine started in the distance before ramping up as

the driver fed it gas, then disappeared. Barely a minute later, the crump of an explosion followed from the same direction.

For a moment, Gideon hoped that the blast had swallowed Colt's vehicle. But the far more likely explanation was that the operative had left a demolition charge in another of his team's vehicles to destroy all evidence of their presence.

Gideon stared numbly out into the darkness, the rifle still raised. A cool liquid dripped down his left arm, and he understood only abstractly that it was his own blood. He didn't even look down to check how badly he was wounded. Some part of him knew that he wasn't about to drop dead. But even if he was, the sense of unreality was so pervasive that he half-wondered whether all this was merely a hallucination.

Luca came over to him slowly, his palms raised in an entreating gesture. The other two legionnaires looked on, their faces drawn with shock. "Put down the gun, Gidi. It's over."

"No," Gideon said, shaking his head slowly as the rifle came down, inch by inch. "It's only just getting started."

"Your arm," Luca said, reaching out and tracing a finger down Gideon's shirt. "You're hurt. Come, we need to get you to le docteur."

"Jean-Luc is dead," Gideon replied blankly. "He's dead."

"Merde," the Italian legionnaire said in his adopted French. He sank to his haunches, the news seeming to fall as a physical blow.

"It's shit. I'm sorry."

"It's not your fault," Luca said.

"You heard him," Gideon said, his face twisting into a self-loathing expression. "He made me."

Gideon felt the tick-tick-tick of seconds passing in his mind. He knew that only minutes remained before the first police units arrived on the scene. He had to go. Despite all the questions that swirled in his mind that the legionnaires might be able to answer—at least Colonel Fournier seemed to know something more than he'd previously let on—he knew he was out of time.

"Tell everybody I'm sorry," he said, finally turning and fixing Luca with a sincere stare. "And that I'll do whatever I have to do to make it right."

SIXTEEN

Paris Station

A CAREER WAS A HEAVY THING, Zara Walker thought as she stared at the blank, dark computer monitor in front of her. Even one that had barely spread its wings.

The judgment that had landed her on desk duty was one she would make again. Disclosing the Syrian's identity had doubtless saved lives. The man was an avowed extremist with significant weapons and explosives training and access to a network of ideological fellow travelers whose tentacles spread across Europe.

In Zara's judgment, the real crime was that the Belgian authorities were so blinded by process that after the CIA had flagged the Syrian's safe house in Molenbeek—though not his name—they'd failed to even put the building under surveillance. When they finally got around to it, it was too late.

There was that word again. Judgment. In her recent experience, it was usually used in a different context. *"How can I trust your judgment?"*

Unfortunately, the Belgians had little skin in the game. Foreign jihadists took advantage of the country's lax policing and intelligence and used it as a safe harbor before further exploiting Europe's open borders to strike the real target: France. That was exactly what the Syrian had planned to do.

He'd passed through a refugee camp on the Turkish border before paying a smuggling network to transport him across Central Europe to the West. He became Zara's responsibility when the National Security Agency intercepts flagged chatter about his final destination. She'd tracked him ever since—and had grown increasingly concerned about his interactions with known members of European weapons smuggling gangs.

Zara had successfully lobbied Gregory Asher, the CIA's station chief in Paris, to get his Belgian counterpart to pass along a coded warning to the relevant authorities. But after the Syrian slipped across the French border, she was no longer able to locate him. With every day that passed, her sense that something terrible was about to happen had grown.

Asher had resisted Zara's petitions to warn the DGSI—the French internal security agency.

The problem was, saving lives was sometimes at odds with Agency policy. The Syrian's identity had been derived from a highly classified source within a jihadist network in Syria itself. His "product" was tightly held and definitely not cleared for distribution to foreign intelligence agencies.

Since they had no actionable intelligence—neither a location nor an indication about the Syrian's plans—Asher argued there was nothing to report. And so Zara had taken it upon herself to inform the French authorities, a manhunt had duly ensued, and the Syrian was captured—along with a cache of ammonium nitrate large enough to make the Oklahoma City bombing look like a firecracker.

The US ambassador took credit for another example of successful cooperation with America's oldest ally, Gregory Asher added another notch to his win column, and Zara Walker's career went up in smoke.

That was the way it worked.

And so far, despite Zara's daily pleading for Asher to give her an opportunity to prove herself—*redeem* herself—she was stuck on desk duty, waiting for her tour in France to end, waiting for Asher to give her a scathing performance review, and, consequently, waiting for her next posting to be significantly less glamorous than Haiti.

The Democratic Republic of Congo, maybe?

For now, she was stuck on night duty in Paris Station, waiting for the phone to ring. Basically, a receptionist with a top-secret security clearance. And tonight, like every night, nothing was happening.

Noticing movement in her peripheral vision, Zara expected nothing more interesting than the night janitor—an American, naturally. To her surprise, she saw Asher himself.

She rose quickly from behind her computer so that he wouldn't be surprised by her presence. "Sir, anything I can do for you?"

Asher gave her a tight shake of the head. His expression was strained. He had a cell phone in his left hand, his fingers gripping it tightly. "Just stay on top of your duties."

He disappeared into one of the soundproofed telephone pods—not too different from similar boxes found in many offices across the world, except for the fact that they were swept for bugs on a daily basis.

Zara kept glancing at the station chief out of the corner of her eye. She could see his lips moving but couldn't hear even the faintest vibration of speech. He was having an animated conversation with someone. She frowned as she saw him wince as if he was on the receiving end of a verbal broadside.

"What does it matter?" she muttered under her breath.

The truth was that she had to own her decision. Maybe she wasn't cut out to be an intelligence officer after all. Asher certainly didn't seem to think so.

Sometimes innocent people die, he'd said in a cutting tone. *If you can't handle that, maybe you're in the wrong line of work.*

"Maybe I am."

It didn't really matter that she never wanted to be anything other than a CIA officer. Her career was out of her hands now. And Asher certainly didn't seem to be in any hurry to cut her a break.

Zara drummed her fingers against the surface of her desk, beating a rhythm that grew so entrancing that she fell into something of a daydream.

"Walker?"

At first, she thought she'd imagined Asher's voice. He hadn't willingly sought out her assistance in weeks, not since before the incident became public.

"Walker?" he snapped again. "Are you listening?"

"Sir?" Zara said, looking up sharply. She noticed to her surprise that Asher's face was pale as snow. She'd never seen him that way before. "Yes—no. Sorry."

"You wanted an opportunity to make things right."

It sounded like a statement, so she didn't respond for a few seconds. When it became clear that he was awaiting an answer, she nodded quickly and tried to ignore her growing sense that this was extremely out of the ordinary.

"Yes, sir. Anything."

"I wouldn't be so sure about that," he said. But it was as though he was speaking to someone else entirely.

Maybe to himself.

"I don't have a choice, sir. This job is all I've ever wanted. I'll do whatever it takes."

Asher nodded, but the movement was slow, his eyes somehow distant. When he spoke, the words came out in a hushed tone, as if subconsciously signaling that this was for her ears only—despite the fact that the building was otherwise unoccupied.

"Do you know who Senator Sheldon McKinney is?"

"Of course," Zara replied haltingly, wondering whether it was a trick question. "Chairman of the Select Committee."

She didn't need to state which one. In their world, only one mattered. Sheldon McKinney might as well speak with the voice of God.

"Keep your phone on you. If it rings, answer it. The individual on the other end speaks on behalf of the senator. Whatever he wants you to do, do it."

Zara fought to prevent her eyes from widening with shock. This situation wasn't just unusual; it was downright nuts. She had the horrible feeling that one day, this conversation would end up in the Congressional record.

Walker-gate?

"Sir—is this all above board?"

He stared directly back at her. "That's the wrong question."

She swallowed. "What's the right one?"

"Are you really willing to do whatever it takes?"

ZARA'S HAND shot out from underneath the covers. Before she opened her eyes, she knew that it was already broad daylight. She hit the accept call button on the third ring.

At least, she thought it was the third.

She'd waited for hours for the phone to ring, all through the remainder of her shift, and then until her eyelids became physically inseparable from each other. As she pulled the cell phone to her ear, she guessed she'd probably had no more than an hour's sleep. She felt like she'd been hit by a truck.

"Hello?"

"Ms. Walker?"

Zara automatically analyzed the man's voice in her mind. It was a trick she was particularly skilled at. Except on this occasion, it revealed little. She was pretty sure he wasn't young. There was a deepness to it, and a roughness that was usually only etched onto a person's vocal cords by age.

Other than that, she learned little. The accent was generically American. If someone put a gun to her head, she would probably guess that he had Midwestern roots, but also that she was no more than ten percent sure she was correct.

"I'm waiting," he growled.

She shook off the sleep that was still slowing her thoughts. Her response was barely audible. "Yes. I'm here."

"I have a task for you."

"Who is this?"

"You already know. No names on the phone."

Zara pulled the pillow from underneath her head and made a fist in its fabric, her fingers tightening until her wrist began to ache. Her heart raced in her chest.

"You used mine," she pointed out.

"Correct."

She exhaled slowly. "What do you want from me?"

"Don't worry," he said. "Nothing that will expose you. Once the job is done, I won't ask you for anything again. Your problems at work will disappear. It will be like they never happened."

It's not the crime that gets you—it's the cover-up.

Zara caught her breath as the thought echoed through her head. The proverb was as old as time, but it was true. Right now, she was at risk only of losing her career. Technically she'd broken the law by disclosing what she knew to the French authorities, but due to the way things had turned out, nobody higher up would want to risk the story coming out in an inspector general's report.

It was no good for the ambassador to take credit for successful intelligence cooperation, only for the truth that the CIA was perfectly happy for innocent French citizens to die to get out. So Zara would be given no further sanction. She would leave the CIA under a cloud of disgrace that only a very few would know about, and that would be it.

But then—what else would she do with her life? Go work for some geopolitical risk consultancy? Show up at 9 a.m. each morning and leave at 5 having written a paragraph in a risk update for a tech firm's executive leadership that nobody would ever read?

Zara's stomach knotted at the thought. When other kids wanted to be firefighters or nurses, she'd only ever wanted this. She couldn't bear the idea that it was over before it had really begun.

It can't hurt to at least find out what he wants, can it?

She inhaled shakily. "Go on."

SEVENTEEN

Gideon melted into the darkness as the first sirens grew audible in the distance. He judged that they were at least five minutes out and also that the first units on the scene would do little more than set up a perimeter. If the scene commander was particularly enterprising, they might attempt to establish contact with whoever was inside.

By then, he planned to be long gone.

Where he would go *to* was another question entirely. He had no home that he knew of, no family, no friends. The only connection to humanity that he could remember was half a mile behind him and growing more distant with every step.

As for his escape, high up on the agenda had to be the acquisition of a set of wheels. But first, he needed to put enough distance between himself and the Institution to be certain of escaping the police perimeter. Despite Gideon's exhaustion, the bullet wound to his upper arm, and the minor blood loss that had resulted, he was still in good physical shape. He made good time over broken ground, and it was only when he stopped to drink from a stream two miles from the Institution that he realized which direction he'd picked.

Of the four points of the compass, only three provided workable escape options. To the east lay the A8, which led all the way to Nice, a city a man on the run could easily lose himself in—a fact known to criminals all across France. Only a few miles farther down the road lay the Italian border.

To the west was Montpellier and a whole series of ports along the French and then Spanish Balearic coasts. He would easily find a ship there that could carry him to Algeria, Greece, or Turkey.

Marseille lay to the south. The city held no particular attraction for Gideon, other than Fournier's cryptic instruction to visit Monsieur Leclerc on Rue de la Marché 167. Unfortunately, it was also the largest and closest major conurbation to the Institution and would be the staging post of what would undoubtedly be an enormous police and military response to the slaughter at the castle.

Despite the immense risk of heading in that direction, Gideon knew he had no other choice, if he wanted to find the answers he was looking for. Besides, the legionnaires would not give him up. Despite the destruction he had brought to their home and the guilt that dogged his every step, Gideon felt that in his bones.

Equally clear was the fact that he could not head to Marseille directly. Untold numbers of first responders would already be surging north up the A51 and D7, roads that he would need to take. It was even possible that there would be roadblocks and identity checks—which would be a problem since he didn't even know who he was, never mind have any documents to prove it.

Trains were also out. He was covered in blood and had no change of clothes. Besides, it was too late to catch one.

The only other direction of the compass was north. It was unlikely he would meet police resistance if he went that way, but only because of the imposing presence of the Montagne Sainte-Victoire, whose limestone cliffs lay between him and the nearest roads.

The climbing routes were taxing even in the light. Attempting to tackle them in the middle of the night was almost suicidal, and the cops would know that.

Which meant it was his only choice.

"Screw it," he muttered.

With the decision made, Gideon focused on his bullet wound for the first time. He let his rifle fall against its sling, knowing that he would have to ditch it soon in any event, lest he be seen by a camper or another climber once day broke.

He carefully pulled up the sleeve of his T-shirt. The blood flow had stopped and had even begun to clot, but pulling away the cloth also tore away at whatever scab had begun to develop. Fresh trails of warm liquid began to flow down his lower arm.

"Shit," he swore, inhaling sharply as he pulled the sleeve up over his shoulder.

The moonlight provided a little illumination. He saw that the bullet had clipped his upper arm and scored a gouge into his flesh that was about half an inch deep and three inches in length. It wasn't a particularly serious wound—or it wouldn't be with proper medical attention.

Unfortunately, that wasn't on offer.

All he had was what he carried on him. He searched through the pockets and pouches on his borrowed chest rig, knowing that Golf must have had a first aid kit in his loadout. He found it in the second to last pouch and pulled out a sachet of clotting powder that he dumped into the wound, clamping down his jaw to stop himself from grunting in pain.

The powder was mixed with an antiseptic that would go

some way to preventing infection, but Gideon saw to his dismay that the wound was already dirty. He would need to properly wash it out and dress it as soon as he had the opportunity.

He wrapped a bandage around the wound, still biting down on his jaw, then finished the job with a long length of adhesive tape to keep the makeshift dressing in place. He surveyed it quickly. It was messy, but it would prevent any further infectious agents from getting into the bullet wound.

The moonlight glinted off the Montagne Sainte-Victoire, which now loomed over him in the darkness. He thought he could make out the Cross of Provence, which he had climbed up to earlier that day—an experience that seemed to belong to an entirely different timeline.

He knew the area well—or at least, he did in the daylight. Ever since recovering from the worst of his injuries in the preceding weeks, he'd felt the urge to explore the park's trails and climbing routes. Tackling them one by one had rebuilt his fitness and given him a deep knowledge of his new territory.

A number of the trails leading up the great limestone ridge weren't nearly as taxing as the climb he'd embarked on earlier that day. He found his feet following one of those paths now, first turning to the west and tracing the base of the ridge for a couple of miles before winding up and into the rocky foothills.

Gideon dragged his tongue across dry, dusty lips. More than anything, he wanted—needed—a drink of water. His mouth was rougher than sandpaper, and he felt the effects of dehydration concentrating those of his fatigue. There would be small springs and streams all around him, funneling the rainwater that occasionally fell at this time of year; he just didn't know where.

"One foot in front of the other," he whispered.

Somehow Gideon knew that no matter how tired he felt, no

matter how dehydrated or how much pain he was in, as long as he kept following that mantra, he would make it out of there. He sensed that he had overcome even greater challenges in the past. Not knowing when or where didn't affect a deep certainty that he would succeed here as well.

Within half an hour, he heard the chatter of helicopters in the air and saw searchlights beaming out of their noses and illuminating the Institution, which now lay several miles behind him. Despite the risk, he stopped for several minutes on a rock that jutted out halfway up the ridge and simply watched.

What would the police find? Who were the men who had come after him?

How does Colt know me?

That last question was the one that sent a shiver running down Gideon's spine. Colt's familiarity was disturbing. Did it mean that he had been part of the man's team? He instinctively wanted to rule out the prospect but knew he couldn't. Not after he'd killed so many men tonight with such careless abandon.

He didn't regret any of their deaths, even now. They had been in his way. Impeding the completion of his mission was their choice, and with choices came consequences. And sometimes, those consequences were final.

But what kind of person wasn't sickened by the act of killing? Shouldn't he be almost insensible with guilt? Did the fact that he *wasn't* make him some kind of sociopath?

Gideon's thoughts drifted once again to Jean-Luc's death mask. The guilt returned now, like a steel blade shoved through his ribs. He grunted out loud, had to physically resist the desire to give in to his grief. His fists tightened, and he held his posture stiffly until the worst of the pain faded into a dull ache.

Not a sociopath, then. He had emotions. Just not for the men he killed.

"Who the hell were they?"

His question was plaintive and spoken into a darkness that couldn't and didn't answer. He kept watching the growing activity at the Institution for a little longer, wondering how many of the legionnaires he came to know had died that night. How many lives would he have to bear on his conscience?

A third and then a fourth helicopter arrived on the scene, touching down on the château's grounds. They would be the RAID units, France's elite counterterrorism troops.

He heard no gunshots, though he didn't expect to. The enemy was already dead.

Gideon resumed his journey, feeling little but emptiness as he trudged up the face, following a path that thousands, perhaps tens of thousands had traced before him. He barely needed to concentrate; it was as if his body were carrying out the task by rote.

One foot after the other.

On a couple of occasions, a helicopter buzzed the limestone ridge several miles to his right. Gideon knew that the aircraft would be equipped with infrared cameras and that he would burn like a firework in their displays. Each time, he ducked and hid behind a boulder or another form of cover. But the helicopters never returned, never hovered directly overhead, and fixed him in the beams of their spotlights.

He knew that the pilots and system operators inside didn't believe that anyone would risk climbing the ridge in darkness. It was clear from this height that the search efforts were focused on the roads.

He doubted that they would turn up anything. Colt would be long gone by now.

But who the hell was he? Why had he murdered his teammates? Gideon had looked into his eyes and seen no soul in them. He was a true sociopath and the reason Jean-Luc was dead. He'd brought an evil into a place of sanctuary.

And that evil needed to be quenched.

Jean-Luc's death needed to be avenged.

And Gideon knew that he was the weapon that would inflict that vengeance. Someone somewhere had honed him into a supremely capable operator. For what purpose, he didn't know. It didn't matter. That life was left in the past.

He had a new mission.

Vengeance.

EIGHTEEN

The road to vengeance lay through the tiny village of Repentance on the other side of Montagne Sainte-Victoire. It was really more of a hamlet, Gideon thought as he looked down on the small collection of farmhouses and cottages that made up the town. He noticed a number of signs advertising holiday properties and wondered whether this early in the season, some might lie empty.

He stared longingly at the nearest of these homes, attempting to peer through the darkened windows and drawn curtains as if he could determine which had owners soundly tucked up under covers, and which were merely unoccupied.

Gideon let out a tired sigh. He knew that staying was only a fantasy, no matter how badly he could use a rest.

And a shower.

It was too dangerous. He needed a car, and then he needed to be out of here. At some point, the national police and the gendarmes would turn nothing up on the southern side of the ridge and would—however doubtfully—proceed north. They would perform the sweeps out of a sense of duty, not enthusiasm, assuming that no one would be stupid enough to stay behind. It was his job not to disabuse them of that notion.

He turned his attention instead to a 1980s Renault Fuego, a sporty hatchback whose once-red chassis had seen better days. Still, the tires seemed inflated, and though it was impossible to be sure from this distance, in decent condition. It was stored under a carport, and though a variety of tools, garden furniture, and other equipment appeared to be kept behind it, nothing blocked its path out. There were even what looked like relatively recent oil stains on the ground.

So it probably still runs.

The carport sat next to a small cottage, probably containing only one or two bedrooms. Judging by the exterior decor, Gideon guessed that its owner was elderly. This deep into the sticks, he doubted whether there was any public transport on offer that would suffice in place of an automobile.

Unfortunately, it was the only vehicle in the village that he could hotwire with little trouble, unlike the more modern cars the other residents drove.

The Fuego it was.

Gideon crept toward it, one corner of his eye on the horizon where the first tendrils of dawn were beginning to appear. Old people tended to sleep less and less with every passing year, so it was plausible that the vehicle's owner was already awake. The carport was only six feet away from a window that was obscured by shutters. It was entirely possible that behind them lay the bedroom.

The cottage's stone walls were thick, but there was no way he could turn the engine over without attracting attention. Not if the owner was that close.

Gideon slightly rephrased the mantra that had carried him this far. *One step at a time.*

He silently rummaged through the tools stored behind the

car, wincing as a metal screw dropped onto the concrete underneath his feet. He froze for several long seconds, cocking one ear to the side as he listened for movement.

Half a minute later, he decided that he was being overcautious and returned to his work.

Gideon found what he was looking for: a thin strip of metal that had probably once been used to seal a window ledge. It was a little wider than he would've liked, but it would have to do.

He inserted the metal strip between the Fuego's window glass and the weather stripping that kept the rain from dripping inside the door and corroding the internal mechanisms. The rubber seals were in desperate need of replacing—having dried out and decayed long ago. Moss had begun to grow in the gaps that resulted, but the owner had clearly made attempts to combat it.

It took his tired fingers almost a minute to manipulate the unwieldy strip of metal into position over the locking rod, and another minute to determine how the rod interfaced with the lock itself. Once the exploration was complete, Gideon simply pushed down hard and felt the mechanism open.

But that was the easy bit.

Before opening the driver's side door, he cast a quick, hopeful glance around for a fuel can. He had no idea how much gas might be in the vehicle's tank, and he could hardly stop for more in his present condition.

Not to mention the fact that he didn't currently have a dollar—or, more usefully, a euro—to his name.

Gideon trusted that it would only take him thirty seconds or so to hotwire the ancient vehicle, so he didn't bother removing the steering column cover after he gently pulled the door open. He eased himself quietly into the driver's seat, leaving the door open, then depressed the clutch and put the vehicle into neutral.

"Here goes nothing," he whispered as he climbed back out.

He started to nudge the old car forward, closing his eyes and praying that the car's internals were better maintained than its chassis. At first, his fatigued muscles barely shifted it six inches before it came to a halt. Then a foot. Then two. Then it rolled steadily down the incline toward the small country lane about twenty feet distant.

When the car reached the road, he let out the breath he'd been holding. He didn't feel any buckshot peppering his ass and back, nor could he hear any disturbance from within the small cottage. There was no obvious sign that his theft had been detected.

He kept pushing another hundred feet, straining as the gradient shifted against him, then added another fifty to be certain that the sound of the engine starting wouldn't be overheard. He only needed an hour. In that time, he could make it most of the way to Avignon, a town of ninety thousand where he could find shelter, fresh clothing, and somewhere to rest.

Gideon climbed back inside the car and yanked the plastic steering column cover away. Next, he located the ignition wires and cut them. He quickly stripped the ends of the battery and ignition wires, then held his breath in prayer as he twisted them together. A light flickered on behind the dashboard.

So far so good...

He touched the final remaining wire—the one that led to the starter motor—to his jerry-rigged electrical circuit. Instantly, he felt the motor turn over, taking the engine with it. Despite the Fuego's advanced age and the nearly two hundred thousand kilometers he now saw that it had traveled, the engine ran smoothly and the tank was three-quarters full. Easily enough gas to carry him to his destination.

It seemed that someone up there was looking out for him.

He made it to the outskirts of Avignon in good time and cruised around a number of industrial estates on the banks of the Durance river, an offshoot of the Rhône, looking for somewhere to dump the car. He found a likely spot in a wooded area near a railway line that ran along the river and far enough from town that it was unlikely the car would be spotted by police for some time.

Before leaving the car behind, he unclipped the chest rig that—insanely, given the risk of being stopped—he was still wearing. He rifled through the pouches and placed items that might prove useful, such as his single remaining grenade, an extra bandage, and some antiseptic wipes, into a plastic Carrefour grocery bag he'd found in the rear footwell, along with the pistol and Jean-Luc's journal.

It was 7 a.m.

Gideon winced as he left the Fuego behind. He hoped the police would find it and return the vehicle to its owner, instead of some teen joyrider. He'd made a note of the address he'd stolen it from and resolved to send the owner some compensation.

"If I live that long."

He jogged down to the edge of the river and found a section of the bank that had been reinforced with rock-studded concrete to combat erosion. It provided a neat ramp down to the water's edge. Before emerging from the tree line, he carefully checked to see whether he was being watched. Only when he was sure he was alone did he toss the rifle into the murky river water. After he'd filled a couple of its pouches with small stones, the webbing quickly followed.

He kept the pistol and its spare magazines. He had two of those, which were easy enough to conceal on his person. The possibility of being stopped and searched by the police was a concern, but he decided the trade-off between anonymity and security was worth it.

Gideon quickly washed himself in the river. He stripped off his blood-soaked T-shirt and hooked it on a stick to allow it to be rinsed in the fast-flowing water. It took a couple of minutes of intense concentration before he found that the skin on his hands, arms, and torso wasn't permanently stained with dried blood and filth.

His pants were only mildly spotted with blood, and the stain-resistant activewear fabric was thankfully almost wipe-clean, so the foul mud he'd daubed over himself the previous evening came off easily.

If not the smell.

Without access to a mirror, he couldn't be certain that he looked like a new man. He certainly didn't feel like one. However, Gideon was reasonably sure that his current look would at least not attract any undue attention.

Still, as he wrung out as much water from the torn and soaking T-shirt as possible before shrugging it back on, he knew that he needed to acquire a fresh change of clothes as soon as possible.

The problem was, he didn't have a cent to his name.

NINETEEN

Gideon followed ancient footpaths through the fields on the banks of the Durance until he reached a modern bridge suspended between two vast concrete pillars. A green road sign informed him that Avignon Centre was only a couple of kilometers away. It was a warm morning, and the body heat he generated by walking helped dry his clothes within a half hour or so.

He stopped for a moment at the center of the bridge to rest. He stared down the course of the river, looking at but not really taking in the reeds swaying in the morning breeze and half a dozen ducks that bobbed on the water's surface. It was a bucolic sight.

The prospect of continuing his journey was unappealing. Now that he had stopped, his body's exhaustion started to plead its case. Gideon knew that he could ignore his physical needs for only so long before his body would begin to give out. Whoever had sent the hit team to the château to find him was unlikely to simply give up on their pursuit.

Especially after he'd come close to killing enough of them to count on two hands.

To merely continue his flight, let alone think about fighting back, he needed food, water, and rest. Shortly after that in his hierarchy of needs followed access to money, identity documents, and ideally a car that wasn't stolen. Perhaps the mysterious Monsieur Leclerc would be able to help him acquire the latter three, but the former he would have to manage himself.

On the outskirts of town, Gideon found a Europrix discount supermarket. He entered cautiously after checking the parking lot for police vehicles, then checked each aisle for evidence of security guards—or loss-prevention officers, as they now styled themselves back home.

A uniformed security guard sat at a desk near the store entrance. He was in his mid to late fifties and was entirely occupied by watching a loud Arabic soap on his cell phone, completely ignoring the bank of camera feeds he was supposed to be monitoring.

Gideon grabbed a baguette sandwich—ham and cheese—from a ready-to-eat counter along with a bottle of sparkling water and a pack of paprika-flavored chips. He followed the signs to the store's restrooms, entered the accessible bathroom stall, and locked the door behind him. He crunched the entire bag of chips into dust before emptying them into the baguette, then proceeded to devour his concoction in about five bites. He didn't notice how dry his mouth was until he swallowed the final mouthful, at which point he twisted the plastic cap off the bottle of water and upended its contents directly down his throat.

Then burped. Loudly.

"Excusez-moi, ça va?" A concerned-sounding female voice asked through the door. *Excuse me, are you okay?*

"Oui," Gideon replied in perfect French. "I'm okay. I had a problem with my stomach, but it's fine now."

He stayed silent for a few moments, listening to determine whether the busybody was still on the other side of the door. When he heard departing footsteps, he stuffed the now-empty packaging into the bathroom's trash can and turned to leave.

As he did so, he caught sight of himself in the mirror. There was a speck of blood on his left cheek that had somehow survived his wash in the river. His hair, well past ear-length after several months without a cut, looked like it had been dragged through a hedge.

Backward.

Gideon pumped two squirts of hand soap into his palm, then ran it under a stream of warm water from the tap. He made a lather and used it to thoroughly clean his face and hair before rinsing it as best he could in the small below-waist-height sink. He dried himself with a handful of paper towels, then smoothed his hair until its style had some semblance of respectability.

A different man exited the restroom, thankfully unobserved. Already, the fast-acting carbohydrates that had made up the vast majority of his meal were working their way into his bloodstream. The worst effects of his fatigue—the heavy eyelids and, more importantly, slowed mental synapses—were at least temporarily improved.

With his most pressing concern sorted, Gideon felt able to think again. He grabbed a baseball cap from a rack in the clothing section, checked that it had no security tag, then pulled it over his head. The more expensive clothing was all tagged, but a five-euro black hoodie was marked down seventy-five percent and apparently didn't merit protection. It went into his Carrefour grocery bag.

At last, he walked the aisles searching for a target, for the first time frustrated that the store was so empty this early in the morning. He immediately discounted the young mother struggling with a two-seater stroller while browsing the canned vegetables section of the store. He had no idea what her financial situation was, but despite his own straitened position, dealing with a pair of twins who looked to be under six months old seemed like enough of a struggle for one person. He had no desire to add to her burden.

Gideon's eyes narrowed as the sound of raised voices carried from the front of the store near the checkout counters. He shot the young mother a slight smile as he passed her, heading for the disturbance.

"Open another lane!" a tubby middle-aged man yelled at a manager who had also been drawn toward the disturbance. He stabbed a stubby finger in the cashier's direction, causing the middle-aged woman to flush. "She's fucking useless. I've been here ten minutes already."

"Sir, please calm down," the manager beseeched. He was a short man who carried little muscle on his frame. In fact, he looked almost gaunt. "We're short on staff this morning. If you just wait, you'll be out of here in a moment."

Gideon studied the troublemaker carefully. He was wearing expensive-looking sneakers—leather, with the name of some Italian designer embossed onto the back of each heel. His jeans were nondescript, but his jacket was also a designer brand. The only contents of his shopping cart were two bottles of white wine.

The man turned on the manager, his face wrinkling into a sneer. "Are you going to pay for my time?"

"I don't understand."

"I make good money. Every second of my time that bitch wastes costs me more than she makes in an hour."

The cashier was ringing up the items on the belt even more

slowly now, fumbling with cans of tomatoes and boxes of cookies as she crumbled under the pressure of this unwanted scrutiny.

"Hey, *connard*," Gideon called out, taking a step toward the troublemaker. "Why don't you shut the hell up. Nobody wants to listen to your moaning."

The man was a couple of inches shorter than Gideon, but he had at least fifty pounds on him. The fact that it was mostly concentrated around his gut, which had the plump rigidity of a seasoned drinker's stomach, tempered the weight advantage somewhat, but not completely. Gideon had tangled with enough men to know that all hand-to-hand combat was risky. An opponent like the one opposite him could do real damage if he could bring his mass to bear.

The guy's face reddened with anger at the insult. As Gideon drew within a couple of steps of him, he couldn't miss the popped blood vessels on the surface of his nose, his distinctly rustic bodily odor, or the bulge in his left pocket that signaled the presence of a thick wallet.

"Are you looking for a fight?"

Gideon took another step closer and considered the question. Out of the corner of his left eye, he saw that tears were glimmering in the cashier's own. Nobody should have to deal with a barrage of insults in the workplace. Especially not this early in the morning.

A quick glance around the store updated his mental map of the locations of the security cameras. They were overhead, which meant his baseball cap should obscure their view of his face—as long as he was careful.

He next visualized how he would take the man down. It was a matter of course: he ran the same exercise with almost everybody he met. A quick heel strike to the man's right knee—his dominant side—would send him crashing to the ground.

Gideon knew his reflexes were quick enough to add an uppercut to the chin before he made it.

He sighed out loud instead.

"You're not the only one who's late for work," he grumbled, shaking his head as he roughly brushed past the man, bumping his left shoulder against his opposite number's right as the index and middle fingers of his right hand slipped deftly into the pocket containing the wallet and closed around the thick leather binder.

The alcoholic grunted from the impact of the shoulder blow and completely missed the flick of the wrist that caused his wallet to change owners. Gideon quickly pocketed it, knowing that he'd executed the well-practiced technique perfectly.

Practiced when?

There was no time to investigate that thought further.

"Hey! I'm talking to you," the drunk growled, reaching out and grabbing Gideon's shoulder from behind.

"You shouldn't have done that," Gideon said softly.

Before his opponent had a chance to process the warning, Gideon swept the man's legs out from underneath him. It wasn't an elegant move, but it didn't need to be. His adversary was untrained, and he toppled over, hands scrambling in the air in a desperate attempt to regain his footing.

By the time gravity dragged him to the floor, Gideon was ten feet past him. There was a moment of stunned silence before a roar of embarrassed anger. Five seconds later, Gideon passed through the store's automatic doors. He gambled that both the manager and the store's security guard would be too preoccupied with the scene inside to realize that he had absconded without paying for the goods in his shopping bag.

He didn't stop for five minutes. Only then did he examine the contents of the wallet. He was now almost €300 better off than he had been just a few moments earlier. He examined the man's identity card but discarded it into a gutter drain along with the wallet itself after realizing that there was no way he could pass himself off as François Monet.

Gideon glanced over his shoulder, but the grocery store was no longer in view. He grinned at the memory of the big man tumbling to the ground as he slipped the black hoodie on, completing his meager attempt at a disguise.

"Jackass," he muttered.

He wondered briefly whether the humiliation of the morning's events would cause François to see the error of his ways. He doubted it. You could lead a horse to water, but you couldn't make it drink. Although that was a department that the man certainly didn't have a problem with.

Finally, he studied his surroundings in greater detail. The edges of town were grimly industrial, and he couldn't see a sign for the train station. But he figured that this was France, so he would probably find one if he headed for the center of Avignon.

Which is exactly what he did.

TWENTY

Rue de la Marché, it transpired, was a stone's throw from Marseille's docks. Like most of the bits of the city Gideon had seen so far, the neighborhood was filthy. Every few minutes, a container-laden truck rolled over the overpass that ran the length of the road and blocked much of the light. The pavement at ground level was potholed and uneven, and the walls and shutters of nearby storefronts were covered in graffiti tags and half-hearted attempts at street art.

Gideon's nose wrinkled at the assault of the scent of stale urine that seemed to thicken the farther he walked down the street. Not for the first time, he wondered who exactly Monsieur Leclerc was supposed to be. His conscious recollection of the French Foreign Legion was limited to his recuperation at the château, where former legionnaires filed off what remained of their youthful edges by toiling together in the bucolic fields and sleeping in artfully designed stone dormitories.

His present location didn't exactly jive with those experiences. At least, not the ones he remembered.

After exiting the Bougainville Metro station, he pulled the hood of the illicitly obtained sweatshirt over his baseball cap, further obscuring his face. He walked with a measured pace, his hands stuffed into his pockets, half-pining for the pistol and grenade he'd hidden just before boarding the train in Avignon after seeing armed police and soldiers roaming the station. He'd decided the risk of being randomly searched outweighed their pros.

A cigarette would have helped complete his disguise, but it wasn't entirely necessary. He dragged his soles against the ground, a trick that would likely cause anybody watching number 167 to discount him as a person of interest. The shuffle made him look like a drunk or aged him beyond his years.

"Can you help me out?" A hopeful beggar called out as he passed. The man was swaddled in a sleeping bag that was laid out on a sparse mattress of flattened cardboard. "I'm hungry!"

Gideon didn't respond. He just kept shuffling; all the while, his eyes roved and analyzed his surroundings in exacting detail. The beggar grumbled but didn't come after him to remonstrate, disappointment being a key feature of his profession's stock in trade. Besides, Gideon suspected his current appearance was downtrodden enough that he didn't look worth the effort of hassling.

He counted down the numbers of the buildings on his side of the street. 193 was advertised as an automotive parts store, though it had long since been shuttered for good. It appeared that some of the units were residential, perhaps housing some of the many immigrants and refugees that appeared to make up a significant proportion of the area's population.

He stiffened as he passed 173—though he knew that the action would be imperceptible to anybody watching.

But Gideon reacted precisely because someone was.

A battered Peugeot sedan was parked on the opposite side of the street. It was only one in a row of parked vehicles, all of which hearkened from a roughly similar model year—and not a recent one. It wasn't even the only car with a passenger inside, but something about the occupants screamed a warning to Gideon.

Both front seats were occupied. Gideon studied the car out of the corner of his eye but didn't alter his speed or direction. The two men were both swarthy of skin tone and clothed in casual streetwear that could have been found on any of the neighborhood's residents. They were young, most likely in their late twenties, and probably of mixed ethnic descent. They were definitely dressed for the part.

But it was their posture that felt out of place to Gideon. They sat upright, both heads slightly angled in his direction—or, more accurately, toward the front door of number 167.

Were they gendarmerie? Or perhaps even agents of the French internal security service—the famed General Directorate for Internal Security, or DGSI?

Gideon kept walking. He briefly felt the watchers' gaze pass over him but gave them no cause for further interest. He continued shuffling until he rounded the next corner. Twenty yards down the street, he found a shisha café. It was a grand name for a cramped space that hadn't been updated in at least two decades. Clouds of flavored tobacco smoke filled the cramped room, courtesy of its sole occupant, who it appeared also wore the owner's hat.

He sat down and ordered a coffee as his mind raced. Why had Fournier told him to look up Leclerc? Had he known that the man was being watched?

The elderly owner hobbled toward a pot of filter coffee that sat on a burner behind the bar. He just nodded when Gideon placed his order. He looked Tunisian or perhaps Moroccan. He took his time preparing the coffee, shuffling to and fro to pick up a bag of coffee beans, then a fresh cup. The whole process took several minutes, during which Gideon lost himself in the almost meditative experience of watching the old man practicing his craft.

"You're good," a voice said softly. *In English.*

Gideon looked up sharply, surprised that, well, he'd been surprised. He hadn't noticed another man enter the café. And yet, here he was, standing in front of him, his head cocked to one side with interest.

"Although I knew that already, didn't I?" The man continued rhetorically. He was only about five foot five, probably in his late fifties or early sixties, his face as deeply tanned as it was lined. He carried a cane.

"Do I know you?" Gideon asked.

"So it's true," the man observed.

"What's true?"

The guy grinned broadly. "You lost your fucking mind."

The elderly café owner laboriously tottered back over, a stained cup of coffee in his left hand. He thumped it down in front of Gideon, then stared questioningly at his unnamed guest.

"I'm fine," he said, this time in native French.

The proprietor returned to his spot on the couch on the other side of the bar and picked up his tobacco pipe once more. Gideon shuddered at the thought of the state of his lungs. Still, he was probably in his seventies, and he wasn't dead yet.

That seemed a better deal than Gideon himself was likely to get.

"Mind if I join you?" the man said.

Gideon shrugged. His musculature was coiled, prepared to fly into action once again despite his exhaustion and injuries.

But he sensed no immediate danger from this individual. It was almost as though he recognized him, even if the knowledge wasn't conscious.

"You're Leclerc?" he asked.

"The one and only. It's good to see you again," Leclerc said, groaning as he lowered himself into the seat opposite Gideon. He grasped his cane with both hands and used the leverage to counterbalance his weight for the final few inches. "That's better."

"So we know each other?"

Leclerc raised an eyebrow. "It's really no act?"

Gideon shook his head slowly. He should have felt excited or on edge, he supposed, now that he'd made his first connection with his past self. But he didn't. He just felt…

Comfortable.

Somehow, his mind recognized that he was safe with Leclerc. Which he presumed meant that he knew the man.

"Are you going to tell me how you spotted me?" Gideon asked.

"The colonel sent me a message before dawn to inform me to expect you. I have a…robust surveillance system. I was monitoring it all morning. You're late."

"You're being watched," Gideon observed. "Anything to do with me?"

Leclerc grimaced. "No, no. An arms deal that went wrong. Never sell guns to the fucking Yemenis, that's my advice. At least not in this political climate. I had the blessing of the state until I didn't. Anyway, I thought it prudent to keep you from knocking on my front door. Your presence might raise questions."

"Am I a wanted man?"

"No," Leclerc said. "Not yet, anyway. The attack on the château is being treated with great sensitivity. I understand that

DGSI has already identified half a dozen dead Americans, at least two of whom are known to have deep links with the CIA. The matter has naturally been escalated to the Ministry of Foreign Affairs and by now, no doubt, the President in the Elysee Palace, but nobody wants to pull the curtain back too far for fear of what they might find."

Gideon raised an eyebrow. "Oh?"

Leclerc shrugged. "The American ambassador has been summoned, and he will deny everything, of course. That is to be expected. But he knows that the CIA was playing dirty tricks, and so does my government. A Frenchman is dead, after all, along with many veterans of the Legion. But this is business. The DGSE and the CIA will converse through back channels, a deal will be struck, and eventually, the whole matter will be swept under the rug."

Gideon winced as a memory of Jean-Luc's face filled his mind. The old man was never more than a thought away at present. The guilt dogged his every step.

"That's impossible," he countered, not yet fully processing what Leclerc had told him. *CIA?* "You can't just cover up the deaths of over a dozen men. What the hell were they doing there?"

Leclerc raised his eyebrow. "They were there for you."

Gideon slammed his palm down on the coffee table in front of them. His cup jumped a quarter inch, and as it bounced back, droplets of coffee flew in every direction. The proprietor stood up sharply and jabbed his finger at him.

"Sorry," Gideon muttered, slightly red-faced. He gestured apologetically at the owner, who sat down slowly, his eyes fixed on his two customers.

"Don't be."

"I wasn't talking to you," Gideon said, his tone lower but no less firm. "You clearly know who I am. So why don't you start by telling me?"

"Okay," Leclerc said, settling back into the couch. "Your name is Gideon Ryker. At least, that is the name that you chose when you left your past behind. I don't know who you were before that. I never asked."

"Did we meet in the legion?" Gideon asked. He felt a sense of unreality at the conversation, as though he were an archaeologist attempting to learn about the politics of an ancient civilization by dusting off small shards of faded pottery one at a time.

"*Non!*" Leclerc snorted. "I did my time when you were just a twinkle in your father's eye. I am something of a broker."

"Guns?"

"Among other things," he nodded. "But that's just a small part of my business. Mostly, I offer protection."

"To who?"

Leclerc shrugged. "Anybody who pays. After I left the legion, I realized that it produces a conveyor belt of men trained in the arts of war—many of whom have no homes to return to. There is plenty of demand for such individuals."

"So you sell us as mercenaries?"

With a measure of amusement on his face, Leclerc nodded. "You weren't so outraged when you came to me looking for a job."

"I worked for you?" Gideon asked, cocking his head sharply. He felt like he'd uncovered another section of an ancient mosaic.

"For a couple of years. Always on your own terms."

"What did I do?" Gideon asked, not sure he really wanted the answer to that question.

"Protection details, mostly." Leclerc gestured at him. "You're young, attractive. Your market was wealthy women paranoid about protecting their assets. Don't worry, I never asked you to pull off a coup in the Ivory Coast."

"Did I ever kill anybody?"

Leclerc rose swiftly, reaching into his pocket and pulling out a €10 note. He gestured at the café owner to keep the change. "This is a conversation we should continue in private."

TWENTY-ONE

Instead of leading him back to Rue de la Marché, as Gideon expected, Leclerc turned right out of the café. He crossed the street and entered a store that sold both electric scooters and nicotine vapor fluid. The Vietnamese woman behind the counter didn't look up as he strode past her into the rear of the store.

"Where we going?" Gideon asked.

"DGSI appears to be under the impression that there is only one way in and out of my home. I usually oblige them by using my front door. Sometimes it's better to take a more discreet route."

There was a narrow alleyway behind the store. On either side, the buildings rose several stories into the air. The ground underfoot was sticky with black liquid. Glancing down, Gideon realized that it was the residue of cooking oil vented out of nearby restaurants and kebab shops before falling like rain to coat the pavement.

Leclerc walked quickly down the alleyway, appearing to know his route by heart. He pulled a keychain out of his pants pocket and stopped in front of a doorway into a nondescript commercial unit. He inserted the key into the lock and twisted it firmly while pulling the door handle inward and slightly up.

"It's a bit sticky," he explained. "The whole row was bought by a developer several years ago, but some of the residents went to the courts. They haven't succeeded in kicking us out yet."

A moment later, they were inside a vacant commercial unit. It looked like somebody—perhaps a family—had lived here for a time, though not recently. Gideon observed faded plastic children's toys and empty packs of diapers. He wrinkled his nose at the smell of damp and mold.

Leclerc led him up a stairway, then through a doorway on the second floor that seemed to lead into the next unit across—a residential apartment, equally abandoned—before returning to a hallway on the first floor. He stopped in front of a battered but evidently sturdy steel door with several locks. It took about 30 seconds to open them all up, but when they did, the door swung inward on well-oiled hinges.

"Welcome to my humble abode," Leclerc said, gesturing for Gideon to enter.

He did so. The lighting in the unit—another commercial one—flickered on automatically to reveal a space that looked like a converted restaurant. Not a fancy one. The floor was laid with chipped white tile, and a commercial kitchen filled with old but clean steel appliances lay at the back of the open-plan room. The walls had open gouges where previous fittings had been removed.

The front of the building was covered in metal shutters that must have led onto Rue de la Marché. While they were closed, there was no natural light. The center of the room was filled with stacks of military-green ammunition and weapons crates. Gideon wondered whether they were just mementos, or if they actually contained live munitions. On the left-hand wall was a desk with multiple computer monitors, and on the right, a single mattress rested on a row of green crates. Squinting, Gideon made out markings that indicated they had once—*presently?*—contained Turkish grenades.

"You live here?" Gideon asked.

"Of course not," Leclerc said, looking affronted. "But I sleep here from time to time, when business requires me to."

"And when DGSI agents are sitting on your front door," Gideon noted.

"There is that," Leclerc agreed amiably. "They don't want to get a warrant to search this place because that would be a formal process, and they know they might find items they would rather not know about—and certainly don't want recorded in court documents. I have been a useful asset for my government from time to time. My suppliers don't trace back to French arms manufacturers. And many of the Legion's men hail from Central Europe or Africa."

"So they are deniable," Gideon said.

"Precisely!" Leclerc said, his face lighting up. "I knew right from the start that you weren't just a trigger puller, Gideon. You understand that this world we operate in is messy. Sometimes the government wants a consignment of rifles sent to Yemen, and sometimes they don't. Sometimes the left hand doesn't know what the right has asked of me."

"Is that what I was for you?" Gideon asked. "Deniable?"

"Sometimes," Leclerc shrugged. "I pay well, and I don't ask questions. My contractors say that I'm a very amenable employer."

"I thought you were a broker."

"Semantics."

Gideon ground his teeth together. "Enough beating around the bush. Why did the colonel send me to you?"

Leclerc gestured at a pair of deck chairs that sat against one wall. His knuckles were white around the handle of his cane, and the effort of remaining upright was clearly costing him.

"I'm done sitting," Gideon replied. "Just answer the damn question."

"A woman came to me asking for a protection detail. She came well recommended, and she offered to pay cash. She wanted five men. She was strict about her requirements—they all had to speak native English, had to be between twenty-eight and thirty-two years old, and were required to be a certain height."

"My height."

Leclerc nodded. He walked to the kitchen at the back of the room and pulled open a metal door that led into a walk-in refrigerator. It was almost empty, save a couple of crates of beer and a single limp lettuce leaf that lay on the floor. He picked up two bottles and twisted their caps open before walking back and handing one to Gideon.

"I'm going to sit, if you don't mind," he said.

Gideon inclined his head, not churlish enough to fire back a fresh demand for answers but frustrated enough to want to force Leclerc to stand until he revealed everything he knew.

"I only have a dozen native English speakers on my books. When I narrowed it down by height and weight and age, you were one of only three men that I could offer for this woman's detail. I told her as much, and she accepted the offer."

"And I accepted the job?"

"You did. This was about…I don't know, three months ago. The client didn't request armed security, so I figured she just wanted a show of force. Many of my customers really just want bodyguards to use as accessories. For them, it's like showing off a new fur coat or string of pearls. Attractive six-foot men in suits…"

Leclerc trailed off, but Gideon understood the message.

"You gave her our names?"

Leclerc shook his head. "I only ever share assumed identities with my clients."

"What happened next?"

"I don't know," Leclerc said honestly, his jaw tightening as he looked up at Gideon. "You understand that I'm only a broker. I match customers with assets that meet their requirements—whether that's human capital or munitions. Once my matchmaking is complete, I have no further part in the transaction."

"You must know where I was to go with this woman?"

"Cannes, on the coast."

"I know it," Gideon said, feeling a strange chill of recognition.

"Still, I usually expect some contact from my contractors, if only to work out the details of payment. But after the job started, I heard nothing for over a week. As far as I could tell, you dropped off the face of the earth."

"Is that unusual?"

Leclerc's face wrinkled as he considered the question. "It's uncommon but not abnormal. Many of my clients have unusual lifestyles. Sometimes they fly off to their home country for a month and take their detail with them. My contracts are ironclad. If they leave the country, that incurs additional costs."

"So where did I go?"

"I have no idea." Leclerc gritted his teeth, and suddenly his expression was grim. "I heard nothing until you turned up at the hospital in Cannes, covered in blood and carrying your two colleagues in either arm. They were half dead. So were you. I've seen the video..."

He trailed off, and a tremor visibly ran the length of his spine. His eyes widened with frank astonishment. "I still can't believe anyone could survive what you went through. If it wasn't for you, all three of you would be dead."

Gideon said nothing for a while as he processed what Leclerc had told him. Some of the pieces of the puzzle were beginning to be filled in, but he still had only an outline of the whole story. He still had no idea who he was.

"You arranged for me to be treated at the château," he said finally.

Leclerc nodded. "It was too hot for you to remain at the hospital. The moment I learned where you were, I worked my connections to get all three of you to safety. I waited for the authorities to investigate and yet.... It seems my client was too well connected. The law doesn't apply to all of us the same. The other two—"

"What?" Gideon snapped, frustrated by the broker's momentary hesitation.

"You're bleeding," Leclerc said, gesturing at his left arm. "Badly."

Gideon glanced to his side and realized that the man was right. His shirtsleeve was sodden with blood, and the unctuous liquid was beginning to flow more freely down his skin. The wound had clearly opened up. But now wasn't the time.

"It's fine," he said. "I've survived worse."

"I know you have," Leclerc observed softly. "But it isn't fine. It looks serious. Have you taken any antibiotics?"

Gideon shook his head sullenly, knowing in his heart that Leclerc was right but hating the interruption even so. He suddenly felt weak from the lack of sleep, the previous day's climb, the exertion of fighting so many men who wanted him dead. All of it.

"You're going white," Leclerc said, rising from his low deck chair more rapidly than Gideon would've believed possible. He grabbed his good arm and pulled him toward the other chair. "Sit."

No longer able to resist the offer, Gideon sank into the chair. He started to shake.

"Have you eaten today?" Leclerc asked, grimacing as he bent over to retrieve his cane.

"Just a sandwich."

"You need calories. You're in shock."

Leclerc hobbled over to the commercial kitchen and began rattling through cupboards and drawers. He made a face as he seemingly realized he had little to offer before pulling out a half-devoured multipack of snack-sized Mars bars from the last drawer he searched.

His cane rattled against the concrete floor as he hurried back over to the deck chairs. He tossed the Mars bars toward Gideon before turning back toward the door he'd used to enter his makeshift headquarters. "Here, eat these. And drink that beer. It'll do you good."

Gideon looked down at the beer in his right hand as though he was noticing it for the first time. He lifted the neck of the bottle to his lips and gulped the foamy liquid down obediently. Only then did he realize that Leclerc was leaving.

"Where are you going?"

"You need medical supplies, and I don't have them here. Food, too. I won't be more than an hour."

"Dammit, Leclerc," Gideon muttered, even that speech taxing him in his diminished state. "I need to know what you do."

The broker paused by the door. His face briefly knotted with indecision before he seemed to pick a side. "There's a folder on my desk. Read it. It contains everything I know."

TWENTY-TWO

"You smoke?"

Zara Walker knew instantly from the scent of marijuana that clung to the man's clothing like a monkey to vines that he was in the retail business, not looking to bum a cigarette.

She shook her head, adding a brusque "Fuck off" for good measure.

The dealer shuffled off, not seeming to take any offense. Having spent almost three years in-country, Zara's experience was that the French expected rudeness. It was different in the countryside, but in the big cities, it was par for the course. Paris most of all, but Marseille wasn't far behind. And especially in this armpit docklands neighborhood.

Her response was perhaps accentuated by her general feelings of unease about her present predicament. Agency case officers weren't usually contacted by representatives of the Senate Select Committee on Intelligence, let alone dispatched on personal errands for the chairman. What she was engaged in was most likely illegal. It was definitely against the rules.

After some digging, she'd discovered that the man who'd

called her was named Ronan Haynes. He was a longtime associate of the senator, and yet it seemed that nobody knew a damn thing about him. Or at least, nothing they were willing to divulge. The mystery worried Zara.

But what choice do I have?

"There you are," she murmured under her breath as she caught sight of her target.

She'd committed everything the Agency had on Jacques Leclerc to memory. It didn't take long. He was an arms dealer and mercenary fixer with links to the French government. The French state had many such cutouts. They weren't exactly shrinking violets when it came to intervening in conflicts in the territories that had once formed part of their far-flung empire.

Why exactly Leclerc had come to the personal attention of Senator Sheldon McKinney wasn't exactly clear. But Zara had an unpleasant sense that it was connected to a number of American deaths in Provence the previous night.

"Merde," she added for good measure. *Shit.*

The problem was multifaceted. Most immediately, Leclerc was clearly a practiced member of the criminal underworld. She'd instantly clocked the pair of DGSI agents sitting on the street outside his known operating location. That was probably the point. They weren't really there to remain inconspicuous—they were supposed to send a message.

They would be easy to dodge, but their presence was a complication nevertheless. The United States wasn't really supposed to spy on the territory of its nominal allies. Not even the French, who treated the idea of being beholden to Washington, DC, with considerable disdain.

It happened, of course. The NSA listened in to the French president's telephone calls, and Agency operatives trailed Russian spies on the streets of Paris. The French external security service, the DGSE, no doubt returned the favor back home.

Sometimes, the respective nations' counterintelligence services fingered an operative in the wrong place at the wrong time.

And usually, it merited little more than a rap on the knuckles.

But usually, more than half a dozen Americans with Agency connections weren't lying dead in a damned retirement home for French veterans. That precise detail hadn't yet made the news broadcasts, but Zara had instantly connected the dots to her station chief's panic the previous night once the news broke in her circles.

"Merde!" she repeated for good measure.

No, she decided after a moment's reflection. The most pressing problem wasn't just that Leclerc was no doubt practiced in the art of detecting a tail. It was that she was being asked to tail him solo.

There was in fact a handbook for running effective surveillance operations. Probably many of them. And whether the textbook of choice was written by the FBI, Britain's MI5, the Chinese Ministry of State Security, or the Agency itself, rule number one was always the same: never tail a suspect alone.

The reason wasn't just to ensure the safety of the surveilling intelligence officer—in this case, Zara herself. It was because surveillance operations were by their nature unpredictable. Suspects—especially those trained in countersurveillance—behaved like atomic particles, their movement inherently random. They switched modes of transportation, entered buildings only to exit them swiftly from a different door, or ducked into an alcove to watch for anyone entering a room after them. Maintaining an effective line of sight on such a creature required numerous well-trained surveillance operatives.

Never just one.

Worse still, Zara was operating without the logistical support that might have compensated for her deficiencies in boots on the ground. There was no drone or chopper overhead to provide overwatch, nor was anyone monitoring the neighborhood's cameras. She had to follow Leclerc—a known arms dealer and mercenary broker—on foot, knowing he was probably armed, and somehow remain unnoticed.

It was a tall order.

An impossible order, she seethed.

And yet what choice did she have? Senator McKinney had the power to make or break her career. All she knew of him was gossip and scuttlebutt. None of it was good. He was a vindictive bastard who went out of his way to crush those who opposed him, whether they did so in the political or intelligence spheres.

There were even rumors that he had confined his first wife to an involuntary guardianship, abusing his wealth, power, and influence with the judiciary to keep her under his control despite flimsy—if any—evidence that she was actually psychologically unstable. She wasn't sure she believed that particular nugget of information, but the fact that she was even considering its veracity spoke volumes.

Zara exhaled, keeping her eyes on Leclerc as he hobbled down the tired street, pushing off his cane for extra speed as if he was in a hurry. When he was twenty yards ahead, she stepped out from underneath the awning of a rundown tabac—a particularly French innovation that was a café, bar, and newsagent all rolled into one.

"Okay, eyes on the prize," she whispered.

She'd learned at the Farm that the key at times like this was to let all the noise in her head fall away. Success required her intense, undivided attention for as long as it took. Good operatives weren't those who never felt stress—they were just better at blocking it out.

Leclerc walked for about ten minutes without obviously looking back. He passed under the flyover that bisected Rue de la Marché. Zara trailed at a suitable distance the entire way. The most challenging moment came as Leclerc walked through a long stretch of roadworks. The local gas utility was installing fresh pipes.

Long coils of plastic piping sat on wooden pallets waiting to be laid, and the entirety of the road—along with both sidewalks—was roped off. Only a narrow pedestrian walkway remained open for foot traffic, squashed between heavy concrete blocks that were presumably in place to prevent walkers coming from into contact with the heavy machinery that was in constant and noisy operation.

Shit.

Zara sensed Leclerc's posture shift just before he entered the one-way pedestrian walkway. She quickly came to a stop and hung back behind an illegally parked Amazon delivery van. She held her breath and counted out five full seconds, then another five for good measure.

Only then did she inch out from cover. Leclerc was once again walking, but it was clear from the fact that he was only yards into the pathway that he'd paused to scan for a tail.

The noise in the back of her mind ratcheted up a few decibels. Zara irritably forced it out. She waited until Leclerc was almost out of sight before resuming her pursuit. After the roadworks, the street widened out once again. The other side was full of noise, traffic, and pedestrians, which gave her an opportunity to lose herself in the maelstrom. She fell in behind a large woman heading in the same direction, expertly using her size as a shield.

Leclerc took a right at the end of the road. Zara took off her jacket and quickly tied her hair up in a simple knot before rounding the corner herself. It was a meager disguise but all she could manage under the circumstances.

Anxiety gripped her stomach as she turned right and found that Leclerc was nowhere to be seen. What the hell would the senator say when she reported back that she'd failed her assignment?

Don't worry about that. Worry about what he'll do...

Zara froze despite all her training. Leclerc hadn't skipped her after all. He was standing outside a building, using the handle of his cane to rap the metal shutters.

Keep moving...

She crossed to the opposite side of the street and concentrated on keeping her movement easy and relaxed. She reached into her pocket and pulled out her phone, pretending to stare down at it even as she tracked her target out of the corner of her eye. Everybody was a shuffling zombie these days, infected by their social media feeds. Contrary to Hollywood's propaganda, it was human nature not to suspect that such a creature might actually be a predator in disguise.

As she watched, a slit in the metal shutters opened. A pair of eyes flashed from behind, and the slit closed again. After a couple of seconds, the shutters began to hesitantly roll upward —emitting a rusty shriek of protest in the process.

What the hell are you doing, Leclerc?

Zara ducked into a rancid kebab joint on her side of the street. The shop's windows were wrapped up to about neck height in a decal that prominently featured distinctly unappetizing pictures of the restaurant's fare, along with prices and special offers. The advantage this offered was that only the top of her head remained visible, and since the interior lighting was gloomy at best, she doubted that Leclerc would be able to see her at all.

She reached into her pocket and fished out a couple of small euro notes as she ordered a portion of fries. The restaurant's sole worker took payment then trudged toward the fryer, which wasn't yet turned on.

Zara turned back to the window, keeping her posture angled toward the sales counter even as her attention focused back on Leclerc. The shutters were finally fully rolled up, revealing a tired-looking pharmacy. The paint on the front was peeling, and the windows were covered in brown paper.

As she watched, a man opened the door. He peered out, glancing left and right down the street, then hurriedly ushered Leclerc inside.

A smell of rank grease filled the air—and no doubt clung to her hair and clothing—as the oil in the fryer came up to temperature. Zara reached once again for her phone. She brought up a secure messaging app, noted the pharmacy's name and address, and sent a query to a contact in the gendarmerie she had recruited the year before.

She retreated to the back of the store as she waited for Leclerc to emerge. He did so just as the shopworker handed over her fries and pointed at the bottles of condiments on the counter behind her. She ignored him as she tried to make out the items the arms dealer was clutching.

Gauze?

Zara's phone buzzed. She took her eyes off Leclerc just long enough to read the short response from her typically efficient contact.

The pharmacy was investigated by ANSM 2 yrs ago for diversion of opioids and other controlled medicines. Investigation terminated due to lack of evidence.

She frowned as she performed a quick Google search for the acronym. ANSM, it turned out, stood for the National Agency for the Safety of Medicines and Healthcare Products—

something akin to the DEA, though she suspected its agents didn't carry guns. This was Europe, after all.

As Zara kept her eyes on Leclerc, who was already halfway down the street and clearly rushing to retrace his steps, a suspicion formed in her mind. This had to be connected with the deaths of Agency contractors the previous night.

Now a shady broker connected to the Legion was hurrying away from a pharmacy carrying bandages and likely also restricted medication. Was it possible that the target of last night's operation had escaped—and that he was here in Marseille?

Zara rushed for the door, leaving her fries and change untouched on the counter. The phone call she needed to make had to be done in private.

"You're not hungry?" The surprised worker called out after her.

She tapped the number she'd memorized for Ronan Haynes's burner phone as she stepped out onto the street. Leclerc was already out of sight, but Zara was no longer worried about losing him. She had the intel she was looking for.

"They're all yours."

TWENTY-THREE

Gideon barely remembered downing the bottle of beer, let alone stumbling over to the walk-in refrigerator to retrieve another. Between the calories from the snacks that Leclerc had provided and the warm flush of alcohol now washing through his system, he was significantly more relaxed than he had been a few minutes earlier.

The worst of the shock had faded, and his brain seemed to be running at something close to its usual speed once again. He pulled himself out of the deck chair that he'd slumped into for the previous half an hour. As he stood, he felt as though a cloak of exhaustion slipped off his shoulders. He knew the sensation was fake, that the alcohol was only pulling energy from his future, but he didn't care.

Right now he needed it.

The folder on Leclerc's desk was thin, perhaps fifty or sixty sheets of printer paper in total. The file itself was made of brown paper and was unmarked. Gideon lifted the front cover, noticing how easily it slipped open. It had clearly been pored through on multiple occasions.

Inside, he found about half a dozen separate documents, each stapled in the top left corner. He quickly leafed through the folder, initially scanning only the top sheet on each. The first was a background report for a woman named Mariella Tilley. Like the rest of the folder's contents, it bore no classification markings and was likely typed up on a simple word processor.

"So you're the client," Gideon murmured.

Other documents included a number of bank advisory slips detailing confirmed money transfers, images of and property records for a luxurious seafront home with visibly Mediterranean styling—terra-cotta roof tiling and white wooden shutters, printouts of email communications between Leclerc and the client, and thin personnel sheets for the mercenaries that the broker had supplied—John Stamp and Victor Glenn, who were both ex-legionnaires of about his age.

Gideon read through the primary background report first. It was thin. Mariella Tilley was an American citizen. She was fifty-seven and had French residency dating back over a decade. She paid taxes in France, and her place of residence was listed as Cannes—the same address as the seafront villa. She was a native of Texas, born in 1967 in San Angelo. She had no criminal record, no children, no record of marriage.

"And you're a ghost," he added.

Whoever had compiled the background report had been thorough. Mariella had a French checking account with Societe Generale that contained €37,000. Most of her purchases were located in the city of Cannes. She didn't spend much—mostly at grocery and homeware stores as well as midrange clothing outlets.

Of more interest was the source of her finances: a firm listed as Germanus Capital Partners. The next sheet in the background report outlined that it was a Cayman Islands corporation with no public accounts—in other words, a dead-end. GCP paid Mariella roughly €15,000 a month and had done so for almost a decade—though the sum looked like it had risen in line with inflation over time.

Gideon turned to the next page. It was a printout of GCP's website. The copy was bland and might have been churned out of an AI generator. GCP was a "world-leading venture capital firm" with "global expertise" and "a particular focus on the Middle East and North Africa."

It was what wasn't written that was more interesting. There was no list of investments, no contact details, no office address, and definitely no lookbook of the firm's executives. Whoever the capital partners were, they clearly wanted to remain in the shadows.

If they exist at all.

The background report analyst had clearly shared Gideon's sentiments. They had written: "Germanus Capital Partners bears all the hallmarks of a shell corporation." There was, however, no recommendation for Leclerc not to do business with Mariella Tilley.

But perhaps that was no surprise. Men in Leclerc's line of work didn't have the luxury of being picky. Almost by definition, anybody who requested the services he could offer was likely to be comfortable swimming in legally murky waters. He suspected that almost all of Leclerc's clients used shell corporations to hide the source of their wealth and provide an air gap against any potential blowback—legal or otherwise. Anonymity was a precondition in certain lines of work.

Gideon sighed and put the background report down. He rolled his neck and briefly caught a glimpse of the time on his host's computer screen. Leclerc had been gone about forty minutes. He would be back soon.

He picked up the next set of sheets—printouts of

surveillance photographs. They were all taken from the street, along with one from a boat, and featured the seafront villa listed as Mariella Tilley's home address. It was beautiful. And, according to a printout from a commercial valuation website, it was valued at almost €11 million.

Gideon let out a low whistle. "Not bad. So who the hell are you, lady? And who's paying you to live the life of luxury?"

Was she old money? The daughter of some Texas oilman, perhaps? Maybe she was some kind of trust fund beneficiary who had left America behind to live out her days in the Mediterranean.

Don't speculate.

The truth was that Mariella Tilley could be anyone. Gideon was certain now that he was looking at a cover, or a legend, as it was known in the intelligence trade. That didn't mean she was working for an intelligence agency. Plenty of people had cause to disappear. But it was definitely suspicious. Most people didn't have access to an eight-figure mansion and a couple hundred thousand euros a year in walking around money. They certainly didn't have access to a professionally designed cover story.

But then, most people didn't hire mercenaries from Jacques Leclerc, either.

"You're going around in circles."

The next two documents were personnel records of the men Gideon had clearly been partnered with. They consisted of little more than a file photograph and a short biography. Both men were American, had joined the Legion in their early twenties, and had served with distinction.

Gideon stared at each man's likeness for a long while, yearning to sense a tingle of recognition. Finally, he tossed the records aside, gritting his teeth with frustration.

Nothing.

How was it possible that he remembered *nothing*? He'd supposedly spent days with these men, working side-by-side at this villa on the sea to guard a ghost. Not just that, but he'd apparently saved their lives and dragged them to a hospital covered in blood.

And yet they might as well have been strangers to him.

Well, it wasn't quite *nothing*, was it? There was the girl whose face visited his dreams. She was maybe thirteen or fourteen years old. In his dreams her features were so distinct he thought he'd be able to wake up and draw her; only to rise from bed and find the details disappearing like sand through his fingers.

A distant scrape of movement caught his attention, and he looked up from the folder on the Leclerc's desk. He saw that one of the sheets of paper was smudged with fresh blood, and he grimaced as he noticed a trickle of dark, sticky liquid on his left forearm. He stood up quietly and walked over to the crate of Turkish grenades. He lifted the lid and grabbed a pair, placing one in each pocket.

Just in case.

Gideon glanced around the confined space with a wry smile. If he stuck around after pulling the pin, it wasn't just an intruder who would be turned into a pincushion.

He stiffened as the door into the room opened but relaxed when he saw that it was only Leclerc, who observed: "You look better" as he shuffled into the room.

The broker rifled through his pockets and unloaded antiseptic spray, gauze, bandages, medical scissors and tweezers, Steri-Strips, and boxes of antibiotics and painkillers. In addition, he pulled a squashed burger in paper wrapping out of his jacket pocket and handed it to Gideon.

"Eat," he said.

Gideon instantly realized that he was still too hungry to

turn up his nose at the condition of the flattened sandwich. The meat was more of a hockey puck than a patty, and the slice of tomato beneath the top bun was decidedly skinny. But it tasted incredible.

"Good," Leclerc said after he was done. He gestured at the half-drunk bottle of beer on his desk as he opened the packet of antibiotics and popped two of the blister packs. "Now get these down your throat."

"I thought you weren't supposed to drink while on those things?"

His host just snorted.

Gideon popped the two pills into his mouth without bothering to read the packaging. If Leclerc wanted him dead, he could have killed him a dozen times already. He washed the pills down with the now-warm beer, then complied as Leclerc gestured for him to take off his shirt, wincing as his arms rose above his head. The action caused the fresh scab that had formed under his makeshift dressing to pull and his grimace to deepen.

"There's pain medication, too," Leclerc said as he ripped open the antiseptic spray.

"I'm good," Gideon said with a firm shake of his head. "That shit messes with my head."

He paused for a second, then erupted with a short, sharp laugh. "Not that I would know."

"It'll return," Leclerc said. He set the antiseptic spray, tweezers, and scissors on his desk, then jerked his chin toward Gideon's beer. "I have something stronger if you want?"

"Just get it over with."

Leclerc picked up the scissors and began cutting the dressing off Gideon's upper left arm, forcing him to contort his face and grit his teeth from the pain.

"How much did you read?" The broker asked, clearly to distract him. Gideon played along anyway.

"Enough to know you didn't do your research on your client," he growled, his throat raw. "How often do you send guys out on info that flimsy?"

"More than you'd think," Leclerc shrugged, apologizing as he cut too quickly into the dressing and ripped open the scab that had formed underneath. "This isn't the CIA."

Gideon glanced around his host's makeshift headquarters and rolled his eyes. "I hadn't noticed."

On reflection, though, perhaps it was a good thing. After all, as far as he knew, Leclerc hadn't attempted to murder him the previous night. He couldn't say the same for the Agency.

"Did you get to the interviews in the back?" Leclerc asked as he tossed the dressing aside. He didn't wait for permission before liberally soaking the wound in antiseptic spray. The cool liquid dripped down Gideon's arm and spotted the floor with a pinkish tinge.

"Not yet," Gideon said, grunting through the pain. "Asshole."

"It has to be done."

Next, Leclerc got to work with the tweezers, picking fibers and other debris from the wound itself, which caused bursts of intense pain to flash behind Gideon's shut eyelids. He was given a break from the probing with the tweezers only when the broker intermittently flushed the wound with additional antiseptic spray.

"Stamp, do you remember him?"

"John Stamp," Gideon said through gritted teeth. "As far as I remember, I've never seen him in my life. But I saw the name in his file. He was one of the mercs I was working with in Cannes?"

"Correct," Leclerc said, his expression slightly sour. "But I prefer to refer to you as contractors."

"Oh," Gideon said, his expression widening theatrically. "I'll bear that in mind next time one of your jobs ends up with me lobotomized and two other men nearly dead. I hope I got paid well for this contract."

"As a matter of fact, yes. I've been looking after the entire sum for you."

"How much?"

"Your share is €190,000. I can give it to you however you want. Cash, transfer, even gold. You name it."

Gideon coughed, wrong-footed for the first time. "Jesus. That's more money than I've ever had in my life."

"No, it's not," Leclerc laughed. "I told you, I pay well. If you can't remember your bank passwords, that's not on me."

This silenced Gideon for a moment. How much had he forgotten? Was he rich? A spendthrift, or did he prefer to live his life fast and loose? Did he own a house? Somehow, it was even more disconcerting not to remember even the most mundane details about his life than it was to have blocked out the trauma that had led him here.

"Besides, Stamp and Glenn made it clear to me that you were to receive their shares also. The total comes to €570,000. On this occasion, I am willing to waive my usual commission."

"Generous of you," Gideon said, wondering if he had accidentally taken those painkillers after all.

"So you didn't read the transcripts?"

"Not yet."

"Neither Stamp nor Glenn saw much. You arrived at the Cannes property on Friday 16 February. You checked in to inform me that you had arrived. The client, Mariella Tilley, showed you to your rooms. You were informed that you were required to protect her only during her trips into town. Do you remember any of this?"

Gideon shook his head.

Leclerc dried the wound with a clean cloth, causing fresh sparks of pain to flash behind Gideon's vision. He kept patting until the skin was completely dry. Finally, he applied the Steri-Strips to seal the wound and wrapped Gideon's upper arm in a fresh bandage to keep the area clean.

"That should hold for a while," he said. "Make sure you clean the dressing as often as possible. And remember to take your pills."

"Thanks, doc," Gideon replied, an initial smile faltering at yet another reminder of Jean-Luc. "I think I can handle it."

Not looking convinced, Leclerc raised an eyebrow and said, "Another couple of days and septicemia would have set in."

"Well, thank God I found you," Gideon said, rolling his shoulder to test the fresh dressing. "Nice work. So what happened after we arrived?"

When he looked up, he saw that Leclerc was intently studying the bank of security camera feeds that covered every angle of the street out front, as well as the alleyway that ran behind the building and half a dozen other nooks and crannies in between.

Frowning, he asked, "What's up?"

"Trouble."

TWENTY-FOUR

Zara Walker barely noticed the high-pitched engine whine of the first underpowered moped that came speeding down Rue de la Marché. The noisy, smelly two-wheelers were a fixture of urban France.

Despite McKinney's fixer's instructions that her task was complete, she was still tucked into the doorway of a shuttered, long-closed ethnic grocery store. Something about this whole situation stank enough that she felt compelled to stick around. She wasn't exactly regretting her decision to involve herself in it, and yet...

The wind had swept trash and fallen leaves into the space, and the detritus now rose as high as her ankles. She decided not to look down for fear of what else she might see.

It was the second buzzing gnat that caught her attention. The moped squealed down the street, whipping in and out of traffic, several times barely missing the bumper of the car it cut off. Enraged horns added to the cacophony.

At first, Zara looked up with only mild interest. Like most European cities, Marseille was infested with moped-borne food delivery drivers, many of whom moonlighted as drug delivery couriers who conducted little packets of white powder or green herb across the city. They paid no heed to the rules of the road and were far too numerous for the police to be able to do much to combat them.

Something about these specific bikes, however, attracted her close attention.

Both mopeds carried a driver and a passenger riding pillion. Each of the latter had a rucksack slung over one shoulder and wore rigid bike helmets that concealed their faces. Their clothing was a messy assortment of streetwear brands. The bags they carried hung low, the material taut, indicating they contained something heavy. The bikes squealed to a stop at exactly the same spot.

Right outside Jacques Leclerc's front door.

"Shit," Zara whispered, knowing instantly that this development had to be connected to her phone call to Ronan Haynes. His master's fingerprints were all over the previous night's operation. Whoever he'd tried to kill had clearly escaped. And though she couldn't be certain, it looked a lot like he was sending people to finish the job.

It was equally clear that the men now jumping off their mopeds were, if not amateurs, then certainly far from professionals. She knew their kind. They were probably drawn from the Middle East and North African communities that made up much of Marseille's immigrant population. The two primary gangs—DZ Mafia and Yoda, not that the names mattered—had graduated out of petty street crime and narcotics trafficking and had escalated in recent years into a vicious gang war over control of the lucrative import routes into the port of Marseille, and then onward into the rest of Europe.

Though dozens of mostly young kids had died in the

previous year, the French police were no closer to dousing the fire of tit-for-tat killings that had spread across the city.

Many of the hits looked just like this: a motorcycle rolled up and disgorged a couple of young shooters often amped up on their own product. The kids opened fire, spraying bullets wildly. Sometimes they hit their target, and, just as often, innocent men, women, and children got in their way.

Zara's suspicion was confirmed a moment later. The two passengers swung their rucksacks over their shoulders in unison. They reached inside and withdrew handguns, one of which they kept, the other they handed to their partner.

"*Shit*," Zara swore a second time, on this occasion imbuing the curse with much greater force. What the hell was the senator playing at?

She'd specifically warned his little dog that the French security services were sitting on Leclerc's operating location. It was bad enough that CIA operatives had died on French soil the previous night. If a pair of French intelligence officers were to get caught in the crossfire of an operation hastily greenlighted by the chairman of the Senate Intelligence Committee…

What are you missing?

As Zara racked her brain for an answer to that question, a white BMW with tinted windows braked sharply to a halt, significantly more quietly than the two mopeds. The engine stayed running as all four doors opened and four more thugs poured out. Their faces were obscured, either by a balaclava or hoodie drawn tightly with a blue medical mask layered over their mouth and nose.

Two of them were armed with handguns, the third a Kalashnikov automatic rifle. She wasn't certain which model. It didn't matter. The last of the four jogged around to the trunk of the BMW sedan, popped it open, and pulled out a sledgehammer.

Zara edged a step out of the grimy doorway to open up her field of view so that she could see the parked car on the opposite side of the street that harbored the two French counterintelligence agents. She was almost certain they hailed from the DGSI. They appeared to be engaged in a heated discussion.

It ended as she watched. One lifted a radio handset to his lips and barked a swift, unheard transmission, then both driver and passenger doors swung open and the two men jumped out, bringing up their handguns.

"Police!" they yelled. "Drop your weapons!"

What followed was almost like a stage comedy. The eight armed gangsters wheeled about, looking around wildly for the source of the shouted orders. The four men in top-heavy motorcycle helmets—two of whom were so skinny and short Zara half-expected them to topple over—stared at each other like overgrown bugs.

"Be smart," one of the agents yelled as he swept his pistol across the row of startled gunmen. "Nobody has to get hurt today."

It was true. But it was never going to go down that way.

The local criminals looked at each other twitchily. Zara could almost hear them doing the math in their heads. But they didn't exactly have to be data scientists to figure out the odds.

A pistol muzzle cracked, the recoil sending the weapon up and wide. The crack echoed up and down the street. The shooter looked almost surprised that he'd fired. The shock didn't last.

"Oh fuck," Zara hissed, flattening herself into the doorway but unable to tear her horrified gaze away from an unfolding disaster that she was wholly unable to prevent.

The first gunman's shots uniformly went high, peppering

what was hopefully an empty building on the other side of the street and chewing chunks of concrete out of the facade. Dust rained down like snow.

The initial gunshot acted as a starting pistol. Within a second, the other gangsters began unloading their weapons. They were barely more accurate than the first shooter, mostly firing one-handed with poor posture. Two of them twisted their pistol sideways and jerked haphazardly at the triggers. Even so, the DGSI sedan was quickly pockmarked by bullet holes, as were cars several yards to either side.

Two of the helmet-wearing moped riders dropped to return fire from the visibly better-trained interior security agents. But even as one of the gangsters from the BMW fell, his chest already bloodied by a clearly fatal wound, the thug with the Kalashnikov finally brought his weapon to bear.

He was either better trained or more practiced than the others. He held the weapon tight against his shoulder and fired steadily, squeezing the trigger and riding the recoil calmly. The heavier-caliber rounds first chewed up the chassis of the sedan, puncturing the windshield and deflating the tires.

Finally, inexorably, and before the rifle's magazine ran dry, the chain of lead whipped into the two French agents. One of them spun, arterial blood spraying the driver's side window. The other simply collapsed out of sight.

In a matter of seconds, five men lay dead or horribly maimed. And as another car screeched to a halt and more armed men poured out, Zara saw that the carnage was only just getting started.

What have I done?

TWENTY-FIVE

"I need a gun," Gideon said curtly, grabbing the open box of antibiotics and stuffing it into his pocket, where it joined the Turkish grenade. "Leclerc, stay with me."

The older man snapped out of his reverie and pulled his attention away from the bank of security camera feeds. The situation had developed with ferocious speed.

Two French internal security agents now lay dead on the pavement, their blood spilling out onto the street. They would have notified their control room of the developing situation before engaging the targets. That meant it would only be a matter of minutes before armed French police descended on the scene.

And perhaps even less time than that.

"Okay, okay," he said shakily. He gripped the handle of his cane and hobbled toward a stack of weapons crates by the far wall. "I have some samples here. What do you want?"

"I don't give a shit. Anything that goes bang," Gideon replied.

He glanced back at the bank of screens and saw that three

men had now jumped out of the second car. That meant the enemy was now eight-strong, accounting for the three gangsters that had bled out on the street.

They were rounding on the front door, which, he guessed, was probably steel and reinforced from the inside like the other entryways into Leclerc's headquarters. That would delay them, but not for long. One of the men held a sledgehammer and looked like he was carved out of English oak, standing at least six and a half feet tall.

Leclerc popped open a crate and pulled out an H&K G36 automatic battle rifle. Also nestled in the foam insert was a pair of thirty-round magazines. He inserted one into the rifle and chambered a round before handing the weapon to Gideon along with the spare mag.

"What about a sidearm?"

"Probably wise," Gideon agreed, testing the weight of the rifle and finding it strangely familiar in his arms. He stuffed the magazine into his left pocket where it clinked against the other grenade he'd borrowed. The weight from the explosives and the spare mag conspired with gravity to pull his pants toward the ground. "And a holster, if you have one."

"Coming right up," Leclerc said, his tone businesslike and direct. He seemed to have shaken off his earlier anxiety. Perhaps that was no surprise. After all, he was a legionnaire with many years of service.

"Grab one for yourself," Gideon added.

"I know my own business, you young pup," Leclerc fired back, bristling with indignation.

Gideon couldn't help but smile, despite the gravity of their situation. "I don't doubt it."

As the words left his mouth, a series of resonant thuds reverberated throughout the building. He watched on the camera as the hulk with the sledgehammer drew it up over his head like a Viking with an axe before bringing it down over and over again.

"That won't hold," he noted.

"It doesn't have to. Just so long as it delays them," Leclerc said, his voice muffled as he turned away to root through a second weapons crate. He pulled out a pair of pistols and several loaded magazines, which he handed to Gideon. "Make yourself useful."

As Leclerc shuffled to yet another stack of crates, cane in hand, Gideon grinned. Despite the pounding echoing throughout the cramped and dark converted restaurant that signaled their impending demise, he felt entirely relaxed. He slid magazines into both pistols and racked a round before placing them both onto Leclerc's desk.

The broker emerged a moment later with a black canvas drop leg holster, which he tossed at Gideon's chest. The younger man grabbed it and fastened it to his right thigh before sliding the pistol into the holster. Leclerc grabbed his own handgun and checked Gideon's handiwork to make sure there was a round in the chamber.

"You don't trust me?"

"I don't trust anyone."

"Charming," Gideon muttered. "And here I was hoping you had my back."

"I didn't say you couldn't trust me," Leclerc replied.

Gideon gestured at the man's desk. "Grab those papers."

The broker complied. As he gathered up the scattered documents, Gideon returned his attention to the security screen. He saw that three of the gangsters remained with the sledgehammer-wielding brute at the front door. The other four were no longer in sight.

"They're looking for another way in," he observed.

"Then we should get out of here before they find one," Leclerc replied. "Follow me."

Gideon did as he was instructed. Leclerc led him out the same door they had entered through, the one that led into the alleyway at the rear of the building. He closed the thick steel door behind him. The heavy-duty lock clicked into place. It would slow down anyone who attempted to follow, though not for long.

Before Leclerc exited into the alley, Gideon grabbed his shoulder and pulled him back. He gestured at the man to stay quiet and reached for the handle of the rear door. He twisted it quietly, opening the doorway a crack. He lodged his foot against it to hold it in place, then secured his grasp on the assault rifle.

"Stay close," he whispered.

Leclerc nodded.

Already, Gideon was back in the zone. Though his freshly dressed bullet wound was doubtless vibrating with pain from the fresh demands he was placing on his body, he barely felt it. He stepped briskly out into the alleyway, bringing the rifle up to cover the left, then spinning quickly to his right.

"Clear."

"That way," Leclerc hissed, gesturing in the direction Gideon was still facing. "There's a blue door five units down. It's bolted from the outside."

"Got it," Gideon acknowledged curtly.

He moved quickly in the narrow alleyway, understanding in his bones that speed was of the essence. It wasn't just the gangsters who had been sent here after him. The French police and security services would be on the scene any moment now. With two of their own lying dead out front, they would leave no stone unturned in their pursuit of justice. Though he wasn't directly responsible for the deaths of their comrades, Gideon understood that it would be better if he wasn't present to face their wrath.

Each unit was about ten yards apart. The two men were forced to negotiate bags of trash, overflowing garbage cans, discarded kitchen equipment, and bulky HVAC units as they made their bid for safety.

They almost made it undetected.

Gideon was pulling the slide back on the bolt that held the blue door shut when another door into the alleyway swung open. A kid wearing a motorcycle helmet burst through but turned the other way as he brought his pistol up.

So close.

Before Gideon had a chance to spin and bring his rifle up, Leclerc did the job for him. He calmly squeezed the trigger of his pistol three times. One of the bullets went wide, but the other two found their target, one of them shattering the back of the gangster's motorcycle helmet. He dropped, dead before he hit the ground.

"Hurry!" Leclerc hissed.

Gideon grunted his acknowledgment, struggling with the rusty bolt before finally managing to pull it open. It screeched, and dark-red fragments coursed off. He twisted the door handle and pulled the door back, instantly bringing up his rifle to cover the dark space behind.

"Just go!" Leclerc shouted, pushing into his back and forcing him inside.

The hallway that led to the alleyway was dank and cramped. It smelled of damp mold. Leclerc grabbed the door handle and pulled it shut behind him.

"It doesn't lock from the inside," he explained as he directed Gideon to keep moving. Behind them, a commotion in the alleyway indicated that the dead gangster's friends were close on their tail.

"Where are we going?" Gideon said urgently. The chorus—it was almost an orchestra—of sirens was now clearly audible, barely even muffled by the well-built stone-fronted commercial buildings. The cops were close.

"Up," Leclerc said, pointing to the ceiling for good measure. "To the roof."

Gideon wished he had a flashlight to hand, but he knew that wishing wouldn't make it so. He stumbled in the darkness, then burst through a cobweb, inhaling chunks of plaster and probably asbestos fibers that had been caught in its silken strings. He spluttered and coughed but didn't stop.

About five feet ahead was a stairwell that led up. He entered it and took the stairs two, sometimes three at a time, before slowing when he realized that Leclerc couldn't maintain the pace he was setting.

When they reached the second floor, he stopped and pushed Leclerc in front of him. "You take point. I'll cover the rear."

Leclerc nodded gratefully, his expression strained from the effort. His chest rose and fell heavily, but he forced himself on nonetheless. A short walk along the hallway led to the next set of stairs. Gideon retreated with his back to the older broker, his weapon raised and ear cocked for any sound of their pursuers.

He heard it an instant later. A loud crack—probably the door slamming against the wall—was followed by excited yelling in heavily accented French. The precise words were inaudible. Their meaning wasn't. The gangsters were close behind.

Footsteps echoed in the hallway below them. Gideon grimaced as he realized the sound of Leclerc's cane was also clearly audible on the steps above him, as were the man's labored footsteps.

"Two more floors," Leclerc said, short of breath.

"Don't rush," Gideon said, surprising himself with the calm in his voice. "We have the high ground. They have to come to us."

"That's what I'm worried about," Leclerc wheezed.

A flurry of gunshots blasted up through the floorboards in the hallway they had just departed, sending splinters flying in every direction.

"Looks like they're on to us," Gideon noted.

"What gave it away?" Leclerc asked.

More than two sets of footsteps began to sprint up the first set of stairs. Gideon realized that after Leclerc had killed the first gangster, the crew attempting to batter down the steel door must have taken the alternate route into the block their comrades had found.

"Don't these bastards give a shit that the cops are about to fill us all with lead?" he grunted.

"I think someone has offered a very high price for your head, Gideon," Leclerc huffed. "Enough that these young miscreants think the risk is worth the reward. Prison means little to them. Death perhaps even less than that. Why not roll the dice?"

Leclerc rounded onto the hallway on the third floor. One flight remained.

But the enemy was too quick. As Gideon reached the topmost stair, he saw a pair of wild dark eyes gleaming out from behind a balaclava. Their owner clutched pistols in either hand. He was slightly slower to react than Gideon, who gently squeezed his rifle's trigger and sent a spray of bullets down the stairwell. He didn't stop to confirm the outcome.

It wasn't in doubt.

"Leave me," Leclerc yelled over the ringing in Gideon's ears. "I'm slowing you down. They don't care about me anyway."

"They'll kill you to get to me," Gideon said, grabbing Leclerc by the shoulder and dragging him down the hallway to the final flight of stairs. The death of another of their number didn't seem to have slowed the gang's pursuit. He could hear footsteps just a couple of seconds behind them.

"I thought you were doing this out of the kindness of your heart," Leclerc panted.

The clatter of an automatic rifle opened up, seemingly only a few feet away. An instant later, a row of bullet holes stitched the flimsy plaster wall just ahead of the two fleeing ex-legionnaires. Gideon wrapped his arms around Leclerc just in time and threw him to the ground. The action probably saved the man's life.

"Call it self-interested altruism," Gideon said, scrambling to his feet before hauling Leclerc to his own. He twisted and aimed his G36 in the rough direction of the stairwell to the floor below, before lowering the barrel of the weapon an instant before squeezing the trigger. "Dammit!"

"What?"

"My head's still scrambled," Gideon replied, pushing Leclerc toward the next flight of stairs as he reached into his right pocket for the first of the two grenades. He pulled the pin as he drew it from his pocket, clasped the lever tight against the casing, then tossed it down the lower stairwell.

Three.

Two.

"One," Gideon breathed out loud as he pushed Leclerc into the next stairwell, diving after him with his palms pressed to his ears in anticipation of the explosion that followed.

The detonation sent a pressure wave coursing through the hallway. Screams of shock and pain echoed from the stairwell below, followed shortly by the scent of flame and smoke.

"That should slow them down," Leclerc said, lifting a hand to his chest and groaning slightly. "I think I cracked a rib."

"Sorry."

The older man shrugged. "Better than getting cut apart by a fragmentation grenade."

Before the two men had the chance to catch their breath, a punishing wave of gunfire slammed into the bottom step, just a few inches from Gideon's right foot.

"I guess it didn't," Leclerc said dryly, raising an eyebrow as he staggered back to his feet.

"Didn't what?" Gideon asked as he somewhat more hurriedly did the same to avoid his toes being cut apart. He reached into his left pocket and pulled out the second grenade.

"Slow them down."

TWENTY-SIX

"Disgraced CIA officer Zara Walker languishes tonight in a French police cell," Zara mouthed as she stared out at the massacre on Rue de la Marché, her stomach turning as she realized that the metallic scent in the air wasn't gunpowder, but blood.

She knew that her only priority now was to disappear. She couldn't be caught here, not with two French agents dead. Especially not after what had happened the previous night at the Foreign Legion's château. Her apprehension here would throw fuel on the fire, turning what was likely already one of the most serious diplomatic rifts between the United States and her oldest ally into a damned geopolitical cataclysm.

Except…she couldn't just leave.

Senator McKinney was off the reservation. The United States could and did assassinate citizens of other countries on foreign soil, despite a long-standing executive order that prohibited the practice. There were ways of massaging the legal niceties. Assassinations rarely occurred in allied nations, but they happened. But those kinds of hits had to be coordinated at the very highest levels.

What was unfolding in front of her clearly hadn't gone through the interagency process. It hadn't gone through any process at all. McKinney had contracted with a half-cooked narcotics gang to finish the job that his handpicked team of Agency operatives had presumably failed to accomplish the previous night. It was insanity.

The question was: What the hell was she supposed to do about it?

It's not the crime that gets you. It's the cover-up.

"In this case, it's gonna be both."

Policy dictated that she should write a memo to the Agency's inspector general. The problem was, the IG was a well-known ally of the senator. He'd been only recently installed at the chairman's behest to "brush the cobwebs out at Langley," in McKinney's own words.

Zara suspected that anything she wrote would first hit the IG's burn bag, then end up with her name added to the kill list.

And besides, what proof did she have of the man's malfeasance?

You fucking idiot.

Zara dug her trimmed but surprisingly sharp fingernails into the fleshy part of her palm as she berated herself for stumbling into this clusterfuck. Would early retirement from the CIA *really* have been so bad? Now that she came to think of it, a cushy corporate salary and a house in the suburbs sounded a whole lot more pleasant than spending the rest of her life behind bars.

What about going to the Bureau?

She had a few contacts at the DC field office. There was no way she was getting out of this without an indictment for something, but maybe she could avoid getting hit by the wrong end of the sentencing guidelines if she came clean now.

The "now" problem was that both her station chief and Ronan Haynes had given their instructions verbally. Which meant there was no proof. It would be her word against that of the chairman of the Senate Select Committee on Intelligence. She would be lucky to avoid a life sentence.

Zara knew she'd made a mistake by involving herself in this affair. Two innocent men were dead because of a phone call she'd placed. She would have to live with their lives on her conscience for the remainder of her own.

But her mistake was born of desperation, not self-interest. All she'd ever wanted to do was serve her country. McKinney and Haynes had used that desire against her. They bore the ultimate guilt. It wasn't an argument that a court of law would ever hear. But she knew it in her bones.

"So what's behind door number two?" she asked out loud, her eyes fixed on a puddle of blood just thirty or forty feet in front of her. Already sirens howled in the distance. It sounded like the entire city's police force was converging on her location. No doubt the RAID counterterrorism teams would be here within minutes as well.

Rue de la Marché was about to become the hottest place on the planet. It was the kind of spot an Agency case officer simply could not afford to be caught dead in.

But it was obviously, chillingly clear to Zara now that she was a loose end. And loose ends had a habit of getting tied up.

Violently.

The truth was, she had two options. Either she disappeared right now, not just from Marseille but from the Agency itself, and for good…

Or she tried to find out what the hell was going on.

Her mind filled with visions of the media campaign that Senator McKinney would deploy against her if he learned that she'd turned on him. Newsreaders across the country would reveal her name and set fire to her cover. Her picture would be on the homepage of every news website in the nation.

Because the reality was, it wasn't good enough to simply get to the bottom of what was happening here. She had to do that *and* turn against perhaps the most powerful man in American intelligence. It was a hopeless task.

Zara realized that her feet were already moving. Her gaze was still fixed on the pool of blood around one of the two dead DGSI men. But his body was getting closer and closer. Without intending to, she'd reached her decision.

In truth, by callously using her for his own purposes, Senator McKinney had made the decision for her. The choice was stark. Either she spent the rest of her life looking over her shoulder for hired hitmen as she tried to ignore her conscience, or she risked everything on this roll of the dice.

And Zara Walker had always been something of a gambler.

She grabbed the dead man's pistol from where it had fallen on the sidewalk a few feet away from his bloodstained hand. A moment later, she crouched down at his side, averting her gaze and whispering an apology as she frisked his body for extra ammunition.

The act sent a wave of nausea rushing up from her stomach. This was the closest she'd ever been to a dead body, if you didn't count visiting her grandparents' graves. The corpse was still warm, but the flesh was strangely forgiving, like meat from the butcher's counter.

As she sprung back to her feet, as lithe in her movement as a dancer, she heard the crackling of the radio handset in the cabin of the bullet-ridden sedan. She peered into the open door and plucked it from where it had fallen into the footwell.

"Unit two, report," a tense female voice said. "Unit two, what is your status? Backup is ninety seconds out. Unit two, report. Are you injured?"

Ninety seconds, Zara thought. *That's cutting it pretty tight.*

TWENTY-SEVEN

"How many of these psychos are left?" Gideon muttered as he half-ran, half-carried Leclerc up the remaining few stairs.

As the Frenchman crested the final stair, Gideon let him go and pulled the pin on the second of his borrowed grenades. He let the lever pop out, counted out a second, and then tossed the grenade to the bottom of the stairwell.

He dove out onto the top floor at the exact moment of detonation. The shock wave rang his skull a little and gave his body a good massage but otherwise left him unscathed. He turned onto his back and fired a couple of bursts down the bottom of the stairwell for good measure.

"That way," Leclerc said, pointing to a window at the far end of the hallway. The glass was filthy and allowed in very little light, but a ladder was just barely visible on the other side.

"Cover us," Gideon said, sprinting ahead of the older man and reversing the rifle in his hands in the same movement. He used the weapon's stock to smash the glass in three places, before swiping it along each side of the frame to remove any shards.

He reached out and grabbed one of the rungs to test its strength. It was rusted, the weather-protective paint long ago peeled away, but it held. They had their route to the roof.

Gideon turned back to give Leclerc the good news. As he did so, he caught a flash of movement out of the corner of his eye. The shooter with the assault rifle emerged out of the stairwell, his face nicked in half a dozen places, rivulets of blood streaming down his flesh.

Leclerc fired. His bullet caught the gunman in the neck.

But he squeezed the trigger a second too late.

A jet of flame spat out of the Kalashnikov's muzzle. Had the gangster jerked his trigger even an instant later, the shot would have gone wide as his body went limp and he convulsed on the filthy hallway floor, spurts of arterial spray jetting out from his punctured neck.

But he didn't, and neither did the bullet.

Gideon roared with frustration. Once again, his rifle spun in his hands, as neatly as any soldier on parade, even as he sprang toward the stairwell. He brought the weapon to his shoulder right as he reached the top step. He depressed the trigger, and the weapon kicked his shoulder with mulish force again and again and again.

Only two of the pursuing gangsters were left. And then there were none, and the air was filled with the scent of blood and burnt propellant and death. Gideon stared down at the carnage for so long, he almost lost himself in it. An age passed before conscious thought returned to his mind.

The muzzle of the rifle lowered, slowly at first, then it plunged toward the floor, the weapon caught only by the sling around his neck. He felt limp, sickened by all the killing, and then by worry.

He turned and saw what he had most feared. Leclerc's

stomach was red with blood. The broker had slid down the wall, leaving it streaked red from the exit wound.

"Gunshot to the stomach," he said, his voice tight and labored. "Not a pleasant way to go."

For a moment, Gideon was unable to speak. Leclerc was practically a stranger to him—and yet also one of the only surviving connections to a life he could not remember.

And he was dying.

"The hell with that," he spat furiously, slinging the rifle over his right shoulder and trusting to fate that none of the enemy were left alive.

"Leave me, Gideon," Leclerc whispered. He gestured feebly at the broken window and implicitly at the shriek of sirens that now coursed entirely unbroken through the shattered glass like one endless moan. "Get out of here while you still can. You can't carry me out of here on your back."

"The hell I can't," Gideon said, pulling Leclerc's bloodied shirt up and away from the wound.

It was a through-and-through, as far as he could tell. The bullet had probably done significant damage to the man's internal organs, but at least it hadn't nicked an artery. He kept pulling the clothing up and over Leclerc's shoulders, ignoring the man's frantic moans of pain as he did so. He tossed the jacket aside and crumpled the T-shirt in his hand before using it to stanch the bleeding.

"You have to," Leclerc said, his voice growing fainter and displaying more of his native accent as exhaustion overtook him. "You know we can't both get out of here without being caught. Not in my condition. Besides, things are looking up."

"I don't see how."

"It was DZ Mafia's local punks who shot me," Leclerc said, gesturing with great difficulty in the direction of the stairwell as his chest rose and fell in labored, shallow breaths. "Not a CIA assassin or something harder to explain. DGSI will have to treat me before they lock me up. And I have a better alibi than I did ten minutes ago."

Gideon knew that Leclerc was speaking the cold, rational truth. Even if he could carry the old broker out of here over his shoulder, get him up the ladder to the roof, and then lower him to safety on the other side of the street, then what? How would he get him to a doctor? He would die without immediate medical treatment.

"Dammit," he said, the phrase somehow devoid of emotion.

"How's your memory?" Leclerc asked in a rasping whisper, his eyes lidding as he spoke.

For a moment, Gideon thought the broker was joking. "Not so bad. At least as long as you don't ask me about my childhood."

"You have a numbered account at the Bank of Panama. You must speak to Miguel Sanchez; he is an executive in their private banking arm. Give him this account number—761829—and use the passphrase *nomad*. That's all he will require to release your funds."

"Why nomad?" Gideon asked as the screeching sirens grew ever closer, hoping that Leclerc would be able to shed some light on the mysterious word. It clearly meant something to him. He just didn't know what.

Leclerc shrugged limply. "You chose it. I never asked why."

Gideon stared down at the broken man on the floor of the filthy hallway. He was bare-chested, the T-shirt on his stomach already soaked with blood. He couldn't see how Leclerc could possibly survive. Shame flickered in his chest at the thought of abandoning him.

He tenderly lifted Leclerc's hands, first right, then left, and placed them on top of each other on the bloodied T-shirt.

"Keep applying pressure. I'll come visit in the hospital when this is all over."

"Do that," Leclerc muttered, seeming to drift in and out of consciousness. "If I make it, you can contact me by leaving a message with Miguel. He knows how to pass it along to me. Now go."

ONCE THE DECISION WAS MADE, Gideon knew better than to waste energy looking back. Survival wasn't ensured, but there was a simple way of improving your odds. You just had to make decisions faster than your opponent. Procrastination was what got you killed. It didn't really matter if the choices you made were good or bad, only that you moved fast enough to outrun the consequences of the failures.

He dumped the rifle, knowing it was too heavy and unwieldy to carry with him, but he kept the holstered pistol and spare rounds of 9mm ammunition. He placed his concerns about Leclerc and his shame at abandoning him into a box, locked it tight, and didn't even think of it after that.

The access ladder to the roof was rusted, but it held. Enough shards of corroded iron cut into Gideon's palms to make him hope that he was up to date on his tetanus shots. After surviving the past twenty-four hours, that would be a hell of a way to go.

The roof was tiled and sloped shallowly toward the edge to allow rainwater to flow into the guttering. It was an uneven surface, but the block was almost two hundred yards long, and the slopes of the building roofs provided him a route the entire way.

As was the case with many American city blocks, the structures hadn't been built at the same time. They were different heights, meaning the roofs rose to slightly different elevations. Gideon leaped from one to the other, ignoring the jarring ache in his left arm as he sprang up to a higher rooftop and used his upper body strength to haul himself upward.

His brain gauged his chances of escape as he ran. Despite everything that happened since, the first shots had only broken out five or six minutes earlier. He trusted that his internal clock was that precise. The first police units were likely already arriving on the scene, but it would take them five or ten minutes longer to cordon off the entire area. If he could make it to ground level in the next sixty seconds or so, he might just have a slim chance of making it out of there. Dozens of other civilians would be fleeing the gunfire. He just had to lose himself in the crowd.

The block was shaped a little like a skyscraper arrowing to a needlepoint, and Gideon was headed for the narrowest end. As he reached the lip of the final building, he skidded to a halt.

"Oh, hell..."

The building in front of him had recently been leveled. The site was in the process of being cleared but was thankfully empty of construction workers. The problem was more immediate and lay right below him in the form of a huge heap of rubble, out of which lengths of sharp rusted rebar jutted like cocktail sticks on a plate of canapés.

The irony of it was that the pile of rubble was almost tall enough for him to jump down onto. But if he impaled himself on one of those spears of rusted steel, his tetanus shots would be the least of his concerns.

Gideon looked directly down. Before the next building had been demolished, it had been connected to the one he was standing on. The demolition job had been neat, but the wall underneath him was a rough canvas—jutted with outcroppings of brick, tied-off sections of rebar, pipework, and other features that could potentially be used as hand- or footholds.

Just so long as he didn't lose his footing. Because the porcupine underneath him was looking less and less inviting with every second glance.

He cocked his head to one side as a noise attracted his attention.

Chopper.

It took a couple more seconds of sweeping the skies to locate the tiny gray speck in the distance. The aircraft was probably three or four miles away, but it was moving fast and would be overhead in a matter of seconds. He couldn't afford to be here when it arrived.

So there was only one thing for it.

"Don't slip…"

TWENTY-EIGHT

A neon orange reflective work jacket found hanging off the back of a parked earth mover went over Gideon's shoulders almost as soon as his feet touched solid ground.

It would attract exactly the right kind of reaction—instant disinterest, unlike his current ripped, dusty, and bloodstained clothing. He deposited the pistol in one of the jacket's voluminous pockets along with the spare ammunition and dumped the holster onto the rubble pile.

Next, he climbed up over the fence that surrounded the worksite. A crowd of onlookers—mostly men, given that the street faced onto an enormous freight-forwarding depot—had gathered to watch half a dozen police cars scream down the road, sirens blaring and lights flashing. Thankfully, they were facing the other way, and he dropped lightly to the ground behind them without attracting any attention.

What now?

Gideon knew that he was running out of time before the local police started zipping up their cordon around the entire area. His disguise was only skin-deep. He had no papers, and he needed both fresh clothing and a long, hot shower if he was going to avoid attracting attention for any length of time. But for any of that to matter, he needed to get the hell out of here. Now.

He sidled behind the crowd of rubberneckers, glancing both ways up the street before making the only decision left open to him. The cops would close the roads first. He would be surprised if he made it to the end of the street before a police car parked in front of him and its occupants started spooling out crime scene tape.

He couldn't go back over the worksite because the yard's other side faced onto Rue de la Marché, which was doubtless now swarming with heavily armed police officers and counterterrorism personnel.

So he kept on going, hopping up onto a wall on the opposite side of the street, then leaping over the last couple of feet of a tall green-painted steel fence that surrounded the freight depot. He hit the ground on the other side with a grunt, rolling like a fresh graduate of airborne school to reduce the force of impact.

An instant later, he was back on his feet and moving down the alleyway between the fence and the warehouse. A quick glance upward revealed that the building's walls were studded with security cameras, with one positioned about every thirty feet. He doubted anybody was watching too closely. The presence of numerous cigarette butts by fire exit doors indicated the passageway was in frequent use, probably by men dressed just like him.

He followed the alley all the way to the end, took a left, and walked casually past a row of parked cars and work vans to the front of the massive warehouse, which faced another one of equal size. The unit at the end was occupied by the local postal service, La Poste, whose logo was painted on the side of fifty or sixty small mail delivery vehicles in yellow livery, many of which appeared to be in the process of being loaded.

Gideon crossed the street, his hands in his pockets and all his senses on high alert. He soon realized he didn't need to worry. Between the noise of all the commercial vehicles and a railway line that ran parallel with a spaghetti network of overpass roads that ran the length of the coastline, the sirens he'd left behind were now barely audible.

The police would get here at some point. But he had at least a few minutes.

"Perfect," he whispered as his gaze roved over the sea of parked yellow postal vehicles. He watched as a postman closed the rear doors of a small two-seater van, then walked around his vehicle to climb into the driver's seat.

Gideon broke into a trot and made a beeline for the van. It was electric and made no sound as it started up, which surprised his exhausted mind when it began moving without an engine turning over.

Think fast, act quicker.

Instead of gently tapping on the van's windows to attract the postman's attention, as he'd planned, Gideon was forced to improvise. He stepped in front of the vehicle, waving his arms wildly to attract the attention of the driver.

The man stepped on the brakes, and Gideon deliberately walked around to the passenger side before rapping loudly on the window and pointing down and out of sight at the vehicle's right-front tire, which was of course perfectly fine. "Monsieur?"

The driver lowered the passenger window, his face creased with surprise. "What is it? Something wrong with my van?"

Gideon winced, wishing he didn't have to do this. The emotion didn't stop him from carrying out his plan, however. That part of him was compartmentalized. Had to be. He reached smoothly into his jacket's inside pocket and pulled out the pistol, which he quickly thrust a couple of inches past the window so that it was out of view of any onlookers. With his other hand, he opened the van door from the inside.

"I apologize for this," he said softly, maneuvering the pistol into his left hand to free up the right so that he could climb into the passenger side of the vehicle. "You should know that you are going to be okay. I will not hurt you if you do exactly as I ask."

"What?" The postman asked, sounding far more surprised than alarmed. His brain clearly hadn't processed the implications of the firearm now pointed at his skull. Things like that simply did not happen to people like him.

After closing the door behind him, Gideon buckled his seat belt, if only to silence the annoying chime that sounded inside the van's cabin. He thumbed the pistol's safety, knowing the click that followed would get his unwitting hostage's attention.

It worked. The man swallowed hard, not knowing there was now zero chance of getting shot.

"Drive slowly, within the speed limit," Gideon said calmly in perfect, accentless French. He scanned the man's face. His driver was in his mid-fifties, with a beer gut and a kindly warmth in his eyes. "Do you have a wife? Kids?"

The postman nodded quickly, starting to quiver from fear.

"Are the kids at home?"

"Please, don't hurt them!"

"Answer the question."

"They're at school."

"Good. By the time they get home later, all this will be a bad dream. You're going to drive me for about ten minutes. Then I'll leave you, and you'll never see me again. Understood?"

"Yes. I think so."

"What's your name?"

"Gilles."

"Okay, Gilles. We have an understanding, all right? You're going to do exactly as I say, and then you're going to drive back home to your wife and forget this unpleasantness ever happened."

"Yes, yes..."

Gideon gestured at the van's windshield with the muzzle of the pistol. "Then drive."

ZARA GRIPPED her borrowed pistol tightly as she followed the path the gangsters had taken into the building. Her heart seemed to have lodged itself somewhere above her esophagus, and she wondered whether it would give out before she managed to get herself shot to death.

Too late to back out now.

She followed the trail of open doorways to a commercial unit with bare walls that was filled with ammunition crates. The presence of a desk and some files in one of the corners indicated that it was probably Leclerc's makeshift office. It was empty, so she kept on going.

Swallowing hard, she stepped over a dead body in the alleyway. And then more and more bodies as she passed through a trail of devastation the higher she climbed. She'd never seen the aftereffects of a grenade's detonation before, but that was clearly what had happened. The foot of one stairwell was almost completely destroyed, the plaster scarred black and punctured by thousands of tiny pieces of fragmented metal. The charred body she found there was almost unrecognizable as a human being.

Zara found Leclerc on the top floor. She recognized him from the background pack that Senator McKinney's fixer had sent her. He was slumped back against the wall, his torso bare and his hands limp against a bloody pile of cloth that covered his stomach. At first, she thought he was dead. It was only when she drew closer that she realized that his chest still stirred.

Faintly.

She frisked him for weapons or information but found nothing. He didn't move as her fingers danced across his body. He was almost at death's door.

"Shit," Zara whispered. She needed more than this. Her only vague plan had been to convince Leclerc—or whoever he was working with—to trust her. Now his mysterious accomplice was gone, and Leclerc was in no shape to speak.

She looked around, searching for the escape route they had been following. As she did so, her eyes came across Leclerc's jacket—and a thin manila folder poking out of it. She grabbed the stack of documents without looking at them, folded them, and stuffed them into a free pocket. She was on the point of leaving Leclerc when her conscience got the better of her.

Zara unclipped the radio handset she'd taken from the DGSI vehicle from her belt. She tensed her body and prepared to sprint for the roof the second the transmission was complete.

"There is a man on the fourth floor," she said, desperately hoping that the radio communications weren't being recorded. "He needs urgent medical attention. All the criminals are dead. Somebody get up here. Now!"

TWENTY-NINE

Gideon lay back on the thin mattress of a single bed that took up most of the space in a tired room of a bed-and-breakfast that appeared to cater mostly to the city's undocumented immigrant community.

He reached that conclusion when the proprietor failed to ask for his passport. Which was good since it saved Gideon from having to offer a bribe to convince the woman to overlook the indiscretion and thus protected his dwindling supply of euros.

The only other piece of furniture in the cramped bedroom was a small washbasin, which he used to rinse the most obvious rivulets of dried blood from his skin. Then he fixed his lips to the faucet and drank deeply before popping one of the antibiotic pills down his throat.

He'd left the postman in the back of his own van, undressed and gagged. It wouldn't take him long to free himself, but the unpleasant act had given him a couple of hours in which to freely roam around in the man's postal uniform. During that time, Gideon had purchased fresh clothes before following a convoluted route on public transport that had taken him to his current location in the northern quarter of Marseille.

The hostel's shared bathroom was thankfully empty when he arrived, which allowed him to wash the remainder of Leclerc's blood off his skin. He dumped his bloodstained clothing in a grocery bag and took it back to his bedroom.

Now he stared up at the ceiling wondering what the hell he should do next.

Rest was high on the agenda. He couldn't go on like this, not for much longer. His body needed time to recover, or it would fail him in a crucial moment. But try as he might, he simply could not fully sleep. He was too wired from the hours of combat he'd participated in over the previous two days.

The other factor keeping him awake was the mystery of who he was, and why everybody he encountered seemed so committed to ending his life.

"Fuck," he mouthed, his mind's eye filled with an image of Leclerc's bloodstained jacket.

It was bad enough that he'd been forced to abandon one of the only people alive who appeared to know who he was; he'd also left behind the information in Leclerc's folder. There were at least two documents—the testimonies of his partners on the ill-fated operation that had cost him his memory—that he hadn't had the opportunity to read before the gangsters arrived to further spoil his day.

He slapped his palm against his right thigh in frustration. He knew their names, but nothing else. A cursory internet search on the postman's phone hadn't turned up any way of finding either John Stamp or Victor Glenn, though it wasn't exactly a surprise given their line of work.

Worse, Leclerc's folder was probably now in the possession of the French authorities. And if that was the case, then his only other lead—Mariella Tilley—was likely out of reach.

What else do you know?

Gideon's face contorted with frustration. He had little more than a trail of breadcrumbs to navigate by. Worse, half of them were missing.

"You joined the Legion," he said out loud as he stared at the ceiling, which was yellowed from the effects of decades of cigarette smoke. "Why? To get a new identity?"

He turned over the idea in his mind. Perhaps Gideon Ryker wasn't his real name after all. The thought was somehow compelling. Why, after all, did men join the French Foreign Legion? It wasn't exactly the refuge of rapists, murderers, and violent criminals that it had been in previous decades and centuries, but the organization still had a certain mystique. Its recruits left their previous lives behind, gaining a new name and a new passport in the bargain.

For many, that was the attraction. The modern Legion carried out due diligence to make sure their recruits weren't actually murderers, but less serious crimes were tolerated. Many legionnaires were petty criminals or had picked up a criminal record in their native country that they wanted to leave behind.

So what did you do?

As hard as he tried, Gideon was unable to uncover any further details from the gray soup of his memory. Trying to remember who he was was like wading into quicksand. He caught glimpses of faces that faded away the moment he tried to focus on them, saw buildings and endless stretches of unbroken, dry countryside.

But all of it faded into dust.

"What else do you know?"

Gideon ran through his list of accomplishments with a sense of ironic detachment. He'd saved the lives of two fellow legionnaires after they'd been trapped in an upscale villa on the

French Mediterranean coast. The CIA wanted him dead. He had access to a numbered Panamanian bank account with an unknown balance. And for some reason, the word "Nomad" meant something to him.

"Nomad," he said aloud, repeating the word several times for good measure. It felt familiar, like returning home after a long trip, but it conjured no more detail from his mind than anything else had.

What was a nomad, anyway? A wanderer. A person who never stayed too long in any one place.

He snorted. That much was accurate, anyway. Or at least it seemed to be right now.

Gideon sagged against the mattress, his ordinarily muscular torso flattening against the surface like poured pancake batter. A sense of ennui crept over him.

Was he condemned to live this life forever? To wander the world, always glancing over his shoulder, one step ahead of his enemies until the day he wasn't?

But what was the alternative? Hand himself over to the French police and throw himself on their mercy? If he wasn't so dog-tired he could barely think, he would have laughed out loud.

What would he say if he did walk into a police station? That he just happened to be in the wrong place at the wrong time? And not just once but twice in under twenty-four hours? It stretched credulity. Nobody was that unlucky.

No one except the Nomad.

He couldn't turn himself in. That was a given. Though not at his hand, two French agents lay dead. At least half a dozen local gangsters were also now deceased, and their deaths could definitely be laid at his door.

Not to mention the corpses of nearly a dozen Agency operatives in Provence.

Gideon was certain that if he surrendered to the police, he would simply disappear. That was the way the intelligence world worked. Someone, somewhere in a darkened room would go to work on him to try to find out what he knew.

And what would he say—that he couldn't remember?

He allowed himself a quiet laugh at the picture this generated in his mind.

I swear, it's true. I conveniently forgot everything you want to know. Why would I lie? You hear this all the time? But I swear I'm the one who's telling the truth!

So surrender was out of the question. And the prospect of spending his entire life on the run wasn't too appealing, either. He had no idea how much was in the bank account that Leclerc had told him about or even how to get in contact with the mythical Miguel Sanchez at the Banco de Panama. Even if he was rich enough to spend the rest of his life sipping French 75s on some Caribbean beach, he would have to do so in the certain knowledge that one day, an assassin would stride up out of the sea and put two bullets through his forehead.

Or, more likely if less romantically, attach an explosive device to his car.

"At least I'd die quickly," he whispered, half-asleep.

This simple process of almost sub-conscious deduction had revealed that there was really only one solution to his problem. He needed to go on the attack. His first step had to be returning to the villa in Cannes to check whether it was being watched. If not, then he was going to have a very intimate conversation with Mademoiselle Tilley.

She was the missing link.

As Gideon rolled onto his side, ready to drift away for good, something dug into his thigh. He slapped lazily at it, half-imagining that a mosquito or some other biting insect was harrying him. When the pinching sensation didn't go away, he thrust his hand into his pocket—and his fingers closed around Jean-Luc's journal.

Somehow, he'd carried it with him all this way and never once even opened it. A wave of wakefulness hit him like a baseball bat, and Gideon knew that there was no chance he was getting any shuteye before he saw what was inside.

He fished the slim softcover notepad, barely larger than his open palm, from his pants pocket and scanned the front critically. It was thin, no more than sixty or seventy pages of lined notepaper, and was unlabeled except for the initials *JL* in the top-right corner.

Gideon no longer allowed himself to feel regret over the old man's death. Guilt, maybe, but he'd made his decision and now all other emotion had to be set aside. Revenge would quench his grief, and if it didn't, well—he'd cross that bridge later.

He opened the notepad.

The front page was dated roughly eleven weeks earlier. He realized that it was the day he'd been brought to the château. Rather than a classic diary, the pad was something of a treatment log for Jean-Luc's patient.

Him.

The handwriting was uniform but somehow also untidy, as if written through exhaustion. Halfway down the page was a tiny smudge of blood in the outline of a fingerprint.

Gideon fought hard to maintain his composure at the sight of it. He began to read.

The patient needs a hospital. He has suffered lacerations across sixty percent of his body. The cuts look deliberate, though neither deep nor severe enough to have caused his current comatose state. He has not spoken since he arrived this morning, nor opened his eyes. He is feverish, his skin dry and flushed. Heart rate steady at 150 bpm. Too high. Pupils dilated upon examination. Appears to be hallucinating.

Under Jean-Luc's personal observations was a bulleted list of treatment steps that had been taken. Gideon's wounds were washed and cleaned with antiseptic. The most severe lacerations were bandaged. He was administered cefazolin 1 mg via IV every eight hours, along with metronidazole 500 mg IV on the same schedule.

Antibiotics, Gideon recognized, subconsciously rubbing one of the deeper cuts on his thigh that had by now thickened into a section of pale scar tissue.

Pain medication was limited to 500 milligrams of liquid solution of Tylenol mixed in with his water.

The following day, Jean-Luc dispensed a dose of diazepam to treat a series of severe and sustained convulsions.

He may not wake up, Jean-Luc wrote on the third day.

Gideon felt a shiver run down his spine as he read those words. Even though he knew the time had proved them hasty, he somehow felt that dying in his sleep would have been a shameful way to go out. He was a warrior. He deserved to die fighting.

"A warrior?"

That was a strange way of putting it. It certainly seemed that he was trained to fight and that he was good at putting that theory into practice. But training made one a soldier, did it not? Warriors were creatures of the past.

Or were they?

Day five. *The patient remains unconscious. He talks in his sleep, though so quietly I am unable to make out the words. Only one: a woman's name. He repeats it over and over again. Julia.*

Gideon stiffened. Julia? Who the hell was Julia?

A stabbing pain in his chest caused him to crunch upright on the thin mattress and the cheap wooden bed to creak underneath him. It was as though his body had rebelled against his mind.

"Julia," he whispered, savoring the name in his mouth. Like "Nomad," it felt familiar, like his tongue was used to making those shapes.

"Dammit," he snapped, tossing the notepad aside and thumping the wall with all his strength. The blow made his closed fist sting and prompted an answering shower of thuds from some of the bed-and-breakfast's other tenants.

Slowly Gideon forced himself to relax. The answers were inside him somewhere. They had to be. The familiarity of the few pieces of the puzzle that he managed to uncover was proof that the truth was hidden, not lost.

He just had to keep digging.

Gideon returned to the journal. *I spoke today with a doctor in Paris. He suggests the patient's symptoms match anticholinergic syndrome. Still waiting for blood analysis. I am maintaining IV hydration. There are other treatments, but his condition is improving. Slowly.*

There was no further reference to his sleep talking, but day by day, his symptoms improved. His fever came down, and his pupils returned to their normal state.

The bloodwork is finally back. The patient's blood contained extremely high levels of atropine, scopolamine, and hyoscyamine, consistent with ingestion of datura stramonium. They didn't just torture him, they poisoned him!

By the start of the third week, Gideon was walking around the château's grounds. Jean-Luc noted that he spoke little. The hallucinations lasted a little longer but eventually faded.

The journal contained little more insight—he remembered the rest of his recuperation. But Gideon didn't need it to. He had a goal now: to get to the villa. And more than that, he had a lead on what had happened to his memory. Whatever datura stramonium was, it was clearly related to his condition.

He needed to find out how.

THIRTY

"How much for the kayak?" Gideon asked, gesturing at an ancient, scratched but hopefully seaworthy watercraft that was pulled up above the line of dying seaweed on the beach that indicated where the tide had reached early that morning.

It had taken him most of the previous afternoon to reach the sandy beach about three miles up the coast from Cannes. A mile to the west lay his target, one of only a handful of villas on this section of the coast that was on the seaward side of the coastal road. He'd caught only a brief glimpse of the luxurious property on his bus ride into town behind the walls and trees that shaded it. There was no obvious sign that the residence was under surveillance, but that counted for even less.

The proprietor of the small beach bar was reticent to rent Gideon the kayak without seeing either a credit or ID card, so he was forced to part with the last couple hundred euros of his cash as security. His hotel, he complained in a loud American accent, was too far to walk back to. He made no mention of the fact that he'd slept the previous night in an open doorway.

The sum was probably more than the battered vessel was

worth, but it was also a fair exchange, given Gideon had no intention of returning it when he was done.

"You can keep the cash if you throw in one of those dry bags," Gideon said, gesturing at a row of yellow roll-up dry bags hanging from a series of pegs behind the bar. "Deal?"

"It's your money," the long-haired Frenchman replied with a typically insouciant shrug.

Gideon turned to drag the kayak down to the water but was pulled up short at the sound of a loud whistle. The bar owner waved crossly at him, then pointed at a clipboard he pulled out from the side of the cash register. "You must sign ze safety waiver. You understand that you go out 'zere entirely at your own risk."

"No problem," Gideon replied laconically. "But don't worry. I'm a strong swimmer."

He paddled idly down the coast on the back of the current. He slowed as he passed within sixty or seventy feet of the villa and eyed it closely. The shutters on the front of the building were wide open, but there was no sign that anyone was home.

He spent the next two hours slowly paddling up and down the coast, creating a mental map of the seafront onto which he layered detail with every pass. The landing was rocky and rose up sharply about fifteen feet. The cliff wasn't vertical, but it wasn't far off, either. Worse still for a waterborne approach, traffic farther out to sea caused distant bow waves to batter the outcropping with unusual force for the typically calm Mediterranean Sea.

There was no place to safely stow the kayak, which meant he would have to ditch it somewhere out to sea and swim the final approach. If he tried it in daylight, he would be easily spotted. The operation would have to take place at night.

The alternative was to take the safer route and gain entrance via the busy coast road. It would likely be quiet at night, but the plan ran the risk of being noticed by anybody conducting surveillance. There were just too many places for a stakeout crew to hide.

No, Gideon decided as his shoulders began to throb from the exhaustion of holding the kayak steady against the current that wanted to tug him out toward the horizon. *This has to be done the hard way.*

CANNES, along with most of the surrounding villages, was the kind of overtly wealthy French coastal town that was populated almost year-round by the super-rich. It was still early in the season, so the marina wasn't yet choked with glittering Sunseeker pleasure boats, nor was a collection of superyachts anchored offshore.

But there was still enough of a trade for the seafront cafés to be populated with rake-thin Russian women who ordered expensive truffle-laden salads and bottles of champagne with their lunch. They lavished their attention on the liquid portion of their meal and typically ignored the food.

Gideon swooped in after one such party left and polished off a chicken Caesar salad that must have cost sixty or seventy euros, only to be left entirely untouched. He poured himself a glass of champagne from a glittering silver bucket. The bottle was almost entirely full. He took a deep swig from the flute and coughed vigorously after the bubbles went down the wrong way.

I guess I'm more of a beer guy.

A waiter swiftly moved him on, a look of utter disdain on his face as he shouted that he was going to call the police. But Gideon felt no shame. A man had to do what a man had to do.

He lounged on a nearby spit of sand for a few more hours

as he waited for the sun to disappear below the horizon. The evening air was noticeably cooler as a breeze whipped up off the surface of the sea. Gideon clasped his arms around his knees and concentrated on breathing deeply, in and out, in and out.

Before he knew it, it was time.

THE FEW PLEASURE boats that Gideon had encountered on his earlier reconnaissance paddle had returned to the marina by early evening. As he pushed the kayak off the narrow sandbar, the darkness fell fully and a string of pearls began to glitter along the coastal road.

He stripped to his underwear before climbing into the seat of the kayak, holding the paddle horizontally to help steady his rocking craft. He filled the dry bag with everything he owned then kicked it toward the tip of the kayak's interior as he made himself comfortable. The waves were a little calmer now that the tide had retreated.

The flip side, he knew, was that the first section of exposed rock he would have to climb on his way up to his target would be covered in seaweed and algae—and much more slippery than it would have been otherwise.

He rolled his shoulders before dipping the power face of the kayak's left blade into the water to start his journey into the blackness. The moon had not yet completed its journey up into the sky overhead. Still, it was a fixed point to paddle toward as he yet again made the mile-long journey back down the coast.

Gideon paddled for a full half hour before he was in position, allowing his eyes to fully acclimate to the low light conditions. He felt as sharp as he'd ever been, restored to something like his full strength after the previous night's sleep and the few hours he'd managed that day on the beach. The shoulder wound was painful but not a physical impediment.

He stopped about a hundred yards away from shore. At least, that was his best guess. It was impossible to be certain without a GPS locator. The sea has no landmarks, no permanent features. Contours appear one minute and are washed away the next.

The only change to the villa was that it was now bathed in a warm glow. He couldn't see a single lightbulb on the exterior of the building, and after a moment of puzzling, he realized that the expensive residence was uplit. Its owner had clearly spared no expense.

As he'd noted earlier, the plot was separated from its neighbors on either side by tall privacy fences that ran all the way to the cliff's edge. He'd seen no other security measures down by the water and noticed nothing now. No blinking lights, no evidence of raised cameras.

That didn't mean that the property was unprotected, of course. It was easy to hide a camera, infrared sensor, or pressure plate. But it was a risk that Gideon was going to have to take.

He circled in place for a long time, his eyes glued to the villa throughout. An hour, perhaps more. It was impossible to be certain. He saw no movement, no sign that the property was occupied.

The operational part of his brain rejoiced at that observation. It would be significantly easier to break into an empty property than an occupied one.

The human part of him despaired. He needed answers. What the hell had happened to him in that place?

It's time.

Almost without consciously realizing it, Gideon dipped the tip of his blade back into the water and powered toward the shore. He closed to a distance of barely thirty yards off the rocky outcropping before clipping the paddle to the side of the kayak. He then reached into it to withdraw the dry bag, which he tied around his waist.

And then he dove into the sea.

Gideon stifled a gasp as the bracing water reinvigorated his senses. He guessed that it was about sixty degrees, not yet ready for the hundreds of thousands of tourists who would descend on this part of the French coast in just a couple months' time to enjoy the weather. Cold enough that he picked up his stroke count to force himself to warm up.

He counted thirty strokes, sipping air on every third, then bobbing back up above the surface and treading water for a few moments to check his position. He'd covered about half the distance, the backwash from the waves stealing one stroke in every two. This time he counted out fifteen strokes before he stopped, knowing that the bottom would rise quickly up out of the water. When he became vertical once more, his toes brushed against something hard below the waterline.

The route out of the Mediterranean was more of a scramble than a climb. Gideon lost half a fingernail and was forced to stifle a cry of pain as a wave splashed salty water over the unprotected tip of his finger. He hissed with agony but forced himself to keep moving up and out of the sea.

The dry bag dragged behind him as he lifted his right foot up to gain a foothold on the cliff, which was quickly steepening as he reached the halfway point. His shoulders, exhausted from his climb up to the Cross of Provence two days earlier and further strained by the day's paddling, cried out with exhaustion.

But he couldn't stop. *Didn't* stop. Not even when his left hand slipped, and he found himself dangling off the rock with only two points of contact between him and a fall onto the jagged stone below.

A rush of adrenaline from the brush with disaster coursed through Gideon and gave him the energy to finish the job. He breathed a sigh of relief as his head reached the top of the cliff, then groaned from the effort of pulling himself up and over the edge.

He rolled onto his back and panted heavily, more drained from the climb than he anticipated. He knew he couldn't afford to lose momentum, but even so, he was completely unable to move for at least thirty seconds as his chest rose and fell like a forge's billows.

Finally, he pushed himself back up, pausing in a low crouch to survey the villa. It was right in front of him now. There was no movement inside. No evidence that his approach had been detected. Now that he was this close, he could see half a dozen cameras along the villa's roofline that had been invisible from the sea.

Was anybody inside watching him?

Gideon untied the dry bag, reached inside, and withdrew the pistol. His dry clothing came out next. He dried himself as best he could before pulling those back on. Then he looked back up at the villa, still wondering that same question.

There's only one way to find out.

THIRTY-ONE

Gideon held the pistol in a tight double-hand grip, keeping the weapon close to his body as he crept through the villa's grounds. A light breeze whistled through a row of pine trees planted alongside the path that led up from the cliff edge.

He dropped to his haunches, craning his head as a strange whooshing sound occurred only a couple of feet above him. Was it a drone? He aimed the weapon overhead, knowing that he had no chance of hitting a tiny quadcopter with a 9mm round—especially in the darkness.

"Cool it," he mouthed silently as he tracked the flight of half a dozen bats close overhead. He only ever glimpsed them as momentary dark shapes before the naturally stealthy creatures disappeared once again.

As he continued up the path, he realized why they were out. He breathed in a cloud of tiny insects and almost choked as one of them got stuck to the back of his throat. He forced himself to swallow, gritting his teeth together and tensing his upper body to prevent himself from coughing loudly and giving away his presence.

You couldn't plan for everything. But insects...dammit.

The villa's outer walls were only fifteen feet away now. Gideon paused in the last pool of darkness before he had to step onto the lighted terrace around the building to study his final approach. He moved his head in a strange, programmed figure-eight pattern, completing the full motion twenty or thirty times in utter silence. His eyes went to the right, his chin followed upward then dropped down, and his gaze went up and left.

Over and over again.

After about two minutes, he was as sure as he could be that there was no one else here—at least, not outside the residence. He studied the square granite flagstones that surrounded the villa too, looking for anything out of place that might indicate they harbored pressure sensors. He saw nothing, but that meant just as much.

There were no lights on inside the building. It was possible that the inhabitants were asleep, but it felt colder and emptier than that.

Okay. Better go find out.

Gideon trained his weapon on each of the dark windows in front and above him in turn, breathing slowly, trusting in his instincts to warn him of danger. He sensed none.

Stepping into the pool of light that bathed the terrace sent a shock of adrenaline through his body as intense as if he'd set foot on molten lava. Leaving the shadows felt unnatural. But there was no reaction. No gunshots rang out. No alarm sounded, nor did the thunder of footsteps fill the air.

Quickly.

Still, Gideon sprinted to the villa's outer wall and pressed his back against it, minimizing his silhouette. His heart raced in his chest, but his breathing remained remarkably steady. Another scan of the area.

Still no sign of danger.

He sidled toward the door. The top panel, from about waist height up to a couple of inches from the top of the door, was a single pane of glass. He studied it closely, searching for any hidden wires or magnetic sensors. Zilch.

He reversed his pistol in his hand so that he held the barrel like the shaft of a hammer and drew it back, ready to strike. His pulse increased as anxiety about the ensuing noise grew within him. Then he caught himself at the last moment and reached out with his left to try the door handle.

The mechanism turned smoothly. It was well oiled and unlocked. The door opened silently.

Gideon felt his body sag with relief. Still no alarm sounded. The house was quiet. Somewhere in the distance a mechanical clock paid homage to every passing second. He stepped through the threshold until he was once again protected by darkness.

The interior of the villa was modern, but the furniture and paintings were decidedly not. Gideon found himself in an entrance lobby that felt almost like it belonged in an old English manor house. A plushly upholstered sofa lay against one wall with a coffee table in front of it. A wooden coatrack stood empty on the opposite side of the door.

He paced through the lower floor of the villa, scarcely allowing himself to breathe. His footsteps barely made a sound, but he cringed every time his heel clipped the marble-tiled floor. The door to the right led into a large open-plan kitchen that would have had sea views during the day. Right now, all he saw was an inky canvas that stretched out to infinity, decorated with a few blinking ship's lights.

Like the rest of the residence, the kitchen was a study in contrast. The island unit was modern and gleamed with top-of-the-range appliances—there were at least three ovens, each of which told a different time. The furniture on the other side of the vast entertaining and dining space was antique and wooden and sat on top of a thick Persian rug.

There was food in the fridge. An unopened pack of salad leaves looked limp and forlorn. He closed the door.

Gideon held his breath with every step he took deeper into the villa. An instinct jangled at the back of his brain, as if warning him he was walking into a trap. Something felt wrong, that was for sure, but what? He sensed no other presence. No footsteps. No alarms.

He passed a large home office. It was empty, though the computer's hard drive whirred periodically in the gloom. The desk drawer was open an inch, as were a number of drawers in the unit that ran along the opposite wall. Gideon filed away the observation for further examination when he was finished clearing the villa.

The rest of the first floor was equally empty and less interesting. It felt austere and un-lived in, though somebody clearly did reside there. Just a sea of well-appointed reception rooms kept perfectly clean as if awaiting guests.

The stairs were tiled and didn't creak as he climbed to the second floor. A central hallway ran left and right, and half a dozen doorways faced him on either side. All were open except one. Gideon saved that for last.

His nose wrinkled as a pungent scent assaulted it. It smelled like a dead rat, though far more intense. He knew immediately what he would find up here. He understood now why the house felt so cold and empty.

And his nerves jangled even louder.

He cleared each of the open doorways one by one. Behind three of them were bedrooms, one of which also had a walk-in closet, presumably indicating it was the master bedroom. The only clothes on the shelves and rails were male, sized to fit someone of average height and weight. The bed was neatly made, but there was no evidence of personal possessions or trinkets on the bedside table.

Who the hell lives here?

Gideon inhaled a deep breath through his mouth as he returned to the hallway. The final two doorways contained bathrooms that were evidently empty. He rotated back to the closed door. He didn't want to open it.

But he had no choice.

He twisted the handle and quietly pushed it open, instantly bringing his pistol up and sweeping the dark space behind with its muzzle as he sidestepped down the hallway to the left. He panted as a jolt of adrenaline hit his system, and a foul stench assaulted his nostrils.

"Clear," he muttered.

The house was empty. At least of living people. Because he'd found the only occupant, and she was lying dead on the bed in front of him surrounded by a halo of darkened blood and brain matter. A revolver had fallen out of her right hand in death and lay on the pillow.

It was a suicide. Or at least, that was how it was meant to look, Gideon corrected himself. He couldn't afford to make assumptions.

He tipped his head back and screamed silently at the ceiling, a wave of frustration sweeping through him. He'd come here looking for answers, and instead he'd found only another branching question. Another body.

"So who the fuck are you, Mariella?" he asked as he lowered his gun to his side and his briefly elevated blood pressure subsided. He scanned the room carefully. The curtains were drawn across the windows, blocking out the moonlight. He felt the sudden urge to open them to throw some light onto this sordid scene.

And a window.

Still breathing only through his mouth, Gideon walked over to the windows, pulled the curtains apart, and cracked open both panes as wide as their fixtures allowed. A cool breeze tickled his skin as he turned back, thankfully helping to flush the room with much-needed fresh air. It was a risk since the bedroom overlooked the coast road—and thus anyone watching the villa—but Gideon couldn't face the thought of being confined in this cramped space with a dead body that had to be at least thirty-six hours old.

The dead woman on the bed was most definitely Mariella Tilley. She was a little older than the file photo he recalled from Leclerc's folder, but the resemblance was unmistakable. What remained of her face was more lined in death but also now strangely free of worry.

The top drawer of her bedside table was open. Inside he found a metal gun case with a key still in the lock.

There was no sign of foul play anywhere in the house. Though Gideon was unable to check the fingerprints on the metal case, he suspected he would find only Mariella's. It appeared that she had walked upstairs, retrieved the revolver, laid back on her pillow, and shot herself in the temple.

The only argument in Gideon's mind against the suicide hypothesis was that women didn't usually go the firearms route. But it happened.

The question was: Why?

He studied her prone corpse for several minutes longer, his mind swirling with theories, all short on evidence. Finally, he searched her clothing for clues, finding nothing. The same held for the remainder of her bedroom. He found an American passport in the bedside table, various pill bottles that treated conditions he didn't recognize, and—like the master bedroom next door—zero personal effects. It was as though she lived here in theory, not in practice.

Gideon retraced his steps downstairs and returned to the villa's home office. The windows overlooked the sea and were unlikely to be visible from any neighbors. Assessing the risk that anybody else was watching from the water, he rolled down the interior blinds and flicked on the main light.

It took his night vision a moment to adjust to a glaring white electric glow that seared his retinas and caused his pupils to narrow to pinpricks.

"Uh-uh," he muttered, noticing a table lamp that he turned on before turning the main switch back off and setting his pistol down on the red leather desk surface. The material was supple and clearly well maintained, like everything else in this cold, lifeless home. "Okay, much better."

The thought was rhetorical. At least, it was supposed to be.

"You're not a fan of the big light either, huh?"

THIRTY-TWO

Colt rolled down the window of the blacked-out Escalade and extended his arm out into the warm Texas springtime air. He surfed the onrushing wind with his palm. It did little to help his building anxiety, but it was at least better than continuing to listen to his fingertips drum against the plastic door handle for hours on end.

He'd entered the country on a false passport. He had considered skipping town, but not for long. The reach of the Brotherhood was long. He had lived an honorable life as a warrior, perhaps not by the greater public's code of arms, but by that of his people. His tribe.

He was returning prepared to die.

If others were willing to spend the remainder of their lives looking over their shoulders, not knowing if this day would be their last, that was their choice to make. But it was not a fate that he was made for.

The first of the fences that bordered the vast ranch—the largest privately owned piece of land in the entire United States—was a six-foot-high chain-link fence topped with barbed wire. Cameras mounted on poles were spaced at regular intervals and watched over the entire length. Theories abounded in the communities that neighbored the ranch as to what happened behind its borders.

Some of the wilder hypotheses were spread by members of the Brotherhood themselves. In nearby bars it wasn't uncommon for drinkers to speculate in hushed tones on whether the land was owned by the Department of Defense or used as a training site for the intelligence community.

The truth was, nobody really knew.

There was a two-hundred-yard buffer zone between the outer and inner fences. The land was liberally spread with concealed security devices—laser trip wires, infrared cameras, and other devices that, like the cameras, fed back to the ranch's security control center, which was manned twenty-four hours a day.

Rarely, however, was the security team troubled by intruders. Texans knew better than to trespass on private property. And perhaps the rumors of government involvement kept the curious at bay.

The Escalade paused at the outer fence as a technician in the distant control center checked that the license plate was on the approved list. Seconds later, the automatic steel fence began sliding open.

By the time the heavy SUV arrived at the archway over the second gate, it was already open. Colt trained his gaze on the words etched into the heavy wooden structure. New Eden Ranch. Until he was eighteen years old, it was the only world he'd ever known. Even now at closer to forty, it still felt like home.

You're not the same man you were then, he reminded himself, glancing over his shoulder and watching the inner gate slide closed, shutting him inside.

No, Colt mused, he wasn't the same man. By the time he'd joined the Agency, he was already more proficient with weapons and better able to withstand hardship than any recruit in his class.

But the Agency had given him freedom. Time away from New Eden to think. To put his life into context. Though the mandated pilgrimages back to Texas were relatively frequent, his people seemed less familiar every time he came back.

Colt shook his head. They were still his tribe. Even if his faith wasn't as strong as it had once been, at least they understood why he was who he was. He couldn't say that for the rest of the world, whose inhabitants appeared more and more feeble and pathetic to him with every passing year—enthralled not to faith or country but commerce and personal gain.

Not so New Eden's citizens. In truth, this little patch of the world was traveling in the opposite direction. Their faith was stronger and more hard-edged than he could ever remember.

The drive to New Eden's main town was only about ten minutes from the border of the ranch. The Escalade traveled down well-maintained roads that Colt knew well. In the distance he saw parties of men in gray exercise clothing jogging in tight formation.

When the SUV reached the crossroads on the outskirts of town, Colt expected the driver to turn right, to take him toward the VIP quarters where Senator McKinney stayed when he was called back to the ranch. Instead, the man turned the wheel to the left.

He leaned forward to inform him that he was going the wrong way.

"No, sir. My instructions are to take you to the parade ground," the driver replied.

Colt opened his mouth to ask why but closed it instead as a cold chill ran down the back of his neck. Despite the warm springtime breeze that wafted in through the SUV's open window, the hairs on his forearms stood to attention.

The drive took another twenty minutes and passed through a checkpoint manned by armed men. Colt recognized some of them as men he'd helped train, or at least grade, on his frequent pilgrimages. They looked back at him stone-faced.

They're just being professional.

But Colt no longer felt the self-confidence that had carried him through his adolescent Trials and then helped him to succeed at the Agency, one of the harshest meritocracies on the planet. The senator had assured him that this return to New Eden should hold no fear for him.

He'd suspected it was at best an unenforceable promise the moment it was spoken. He was certain of it now.

"Fear is natural," he whispered under his breath as the Escalade slowed its approach toward the archway entrance to the massive barracks complex. The ornate brick building was rectangular and surrounded a parade ground. The styling was vaguely European. It contained dormitory-style accommodation for close to a thousand men, though it typically housed just a few hundred.

The Chosen.

The heavy vehicle crept through the archway through a passageway that was about three car-lengths deep before merging into the sandy courtyard in the center.

Where it stopped.

Colt exhaled shakily and wiped his damp palms against his jeans. His driver hopped out, walked around to the side of the Escalade, and courteously opened the passenger door. Colt scrutinized his face as he climbed out, his legs leaden. The man's expression was blank.

A dozen men stood at the very center of the parade ground in two ranks of six, their backs facing him. Colt guessed that he was supposed to join them. He took a deep breath, inflated his lungs, and drew his chest upright as he strode over.

As he drew level with the two ranks of men, he saw familiar faces out of the corner of his eye. They stared steadily ahead and didn't acknowledge his presence. He saw why a moment later. Three men faced them—Senator McKinney and a bodyguard who stood a few paces behind, eyes constantly roving. The third was a man he'd never spoken to, but who he knew better than his own parents. Who everyone knew better.

Colt instantly bowed his head and dropped to one knee. "Sir."

"Join us," Father Gabriel said, his voice surprisingly high in person, yet somehow no less commanding for it. He wore plain olive fatigues, black boots and a rich purple sash embroidered in gold over his shoulders that resembled a Catholic priest's stole.

Colt kept his gaze lowered as he approached the man whose judgment would decide his fate. He knew better than to beg. Fear was natural, but weakness was a choice. Weakness had to be pitilessly eradicated from humanity. To display even a hint of it was to mark yourself for death.

"You failed, Commander," Father Gabriel stated in a voice designed to carry. "Do you deny it?"

"No, Father."

"Your task was simple, was it not? Find a crippled man and bring him to me for judgment. And yet you did not succeed."

"Yes, Father."

"You understand what must be done?"

Colt closed his eyes, feeling the strength sap from his body. For one exhilarating moment of madness, he considered trying to fight his way to freedom.

"I do, Father. I only ask that you permit me to go with honor."

A long silence followed. Colt wished he dared meet Father Gabriel's gaze, but the proscription against it was so deeply embedded in his psyche that even now on the verge of death he dared not break it.

"You have served me for many years, Commander, and always with dignity," Father Gabriel said, his words playing with Colt's emotions with all the skill of an orchestral conductor. "But you fucked up. I will have to make an example, or the sickness will spread."

Colt's head dipped as the sentence of death was laid upon him.

Father Gabriel stepped back, and as if the signal had been prearranged, the two ranks of commandos behind him jogged into a circle around Colt. Finally he looked up, stood up, and rotated in a full circle, meeting each of their eyes in turn. None of them were armed. They were dressed in black fatigue pants and olive-green T-shirts. Their arms hung loosely by their sides.

He saw no pity staring back at him.

As he completed the full turn, his gaze finally fell on Senator McKinney. He'd always considered his immediate superior in Washington to be a man of unbending iron will. McKinney had sent him to kill so many without ever displaying even a flicker of emotion, let alone conscience.

Now he was pale-faced and shrunken.

Father Gabriel raised his voice. "You all know what has to be done. Expunge the weakness that has infected us."

In a lower voice, but one that still carried to Colt's ear, he said to McKinney, "Don't turn away."

The circle of men surrounding Colt stepped toward him in unison. He saw fists begin to close, heard the scrape of boots on sand behind him. He gritted his teeth and made fists of his own.

The mark of a man's strength was to never give in, even

when facing impossible odds. A strange easiness came over him now that his fate was sealed. He had nothing to fear now.

It was over.

Colt stepped toward the line of men closing in front of him and drove an uppercut into the chin of a man he'd known most of his life, someone he had run with as a child. It was the only blow he succeeded in inflicting.

His gut exploded in pain as the man slightly to his left landed a powerful punch. It drove the wind from his lungs and caused the muscles in his chest to cramp and spasm. He doubled over and was barely down before a fist cracked against his right temple.

Then a kick to the back sent him crashing to the ground. As he struggled to breathe, a line of saliva dribbled from his lips.

And the blows and kicks continued raining down. Colt barely felt the pain now. His body was too far gone. Some part of his consciousness had remained reserved and accepted that he was on the verge of death. A bone in his leg snapped, then a steel-toed boot took out his lower row of teeth.

With one eye closed, Colt found himself staring at Senator McKinney's face. Father Gabriel had already turned away and was walking from the parade ground in an easy, casual step.

But McKinney's terrified eyes were fixed on his body, soon to be a corpse.

They were the last thing Colt saw before the blackness took him.

THIRTY-THREE

Gideon spun around, reaching for the pistol on the desk even as he dove for cover. It took several long seconds before the pistol's grip was seated in his palm, the barrel raised and ready to fire.

"Chill," a woman said.

Speaking English. How did she know? She was armed, but her pistol was holstered. She looked multi-ethnic; likely half-Black.

She held up her palms in a gesture of peace. "I didn't come all this way just to get slotted at the final hurdle."

"Who are you?" Gideon demanded.

He kept his pistol raised but shifted his aim a foot to the left. It was little more than a gesture of respect. He could re-center the shot and squeeze the trigger in a quarter of a second, and she likely knew it as well as he did.

"How about you put the weapon down, stand up, and shake my hand? I think you'll find we've got a lot to talk about."

Gideon blinked rapidly several times. It was difficult to process what the hell was going on. Adrenaline was flowing through his system like the springtime melt over the Niagara. His palms were sticky, the hairs on the back of his neck standing upright. How the hell had this woman got the jump on him?

He forced himself to relax, if only a little. He breathed in deeply, feeling the much-needed oxygen flood through his lungs. It was instantly calming, and he repeated the trick several times, breathing in slowly and holding the air in his lungs for a couple of seconds before exhaling.

Once his mind was clear, he considered the situation. Whoever this woman was, she could have put a bullet in the back of his head without giving him the courtesy of a heads-up that he was about to die.

But he wasn't dead. So it stood to reason that she wasn't a threat. At least, not an immediate one.

Finally, he lowered the pistol, though he kept it in his hand. Gideon was willing to take the first tentative steps, but he wasn't ready to commit himself to a trust fall. At least, not yet.

"That's better," the woman said. She took a step into the room, causing Gideon's heart rate to spike, but she did nothing more threatening than hold out her hand. "I'm Zara."

"Nice to meet you," Gideon said, feeling faintly light-headed at the normality of the exchange. "Gideon."

"That's better," Zara said, seeming pleased. She smiled. "Don't you think so?"

"Than what?"

"The whole Wild West routine." She shrugged. "You draw, then I draw, then we shoot each other in the stomach and both of us bleed to death. I prefer a good old-fashioned conversation."

Gideon winced at the reminder of Leclerc's injury. He'd tried to follow the news of the shootout in Marseille but had seen no coverage of anyone taken to the hospital. He feared that the man was dead. Another life to add to the tally that weighed on his conscience.

"I know your name," he said evenly. "But I asked who you were."

"That's fair," she nodded. "I guess I'm really not supposed to tell you. But over the last twenty-four hours, I've found myself doing a lot of things I'm really not supposed to do. So hell, what's one more?"

Gideon stared back at her, unsure whether he was supposed to respond. As he did so, he noticed for the first time that his uninvited guest was startlingly pretty. It wasn't in an overt way: she was dressed practically in dark running sneakers, black jeans, and a thin bomber jacket, but despite a lack of visible makeup, her skin almost glowed.

"I'm a CIA case officer," she sighed. "At least, I was up until yesterday afternoon. Now I'm not really sure what I'm supposed to be. I'm hoping you can help me answer that."

Gideon tightened his grip on the pistol. "You're CIA?"

Zara fixed him with an intense stare. Her eyes were dark but expressive. He sensed no threat from her, and yet...

"I had nothing to do with the shootout at the retirement home," she said. "I wasn't involved in the operation, hell, I wasn't even brought up to speed until after the senator called me."

"What senator? Who are you talking about?"

Zara narrowed her gaze, sharpening her focus on him yet further. He felt as though she was probing him for honesty, as if determining whether he was playing her.

I guess I'm doing the exact same thing.

"Senator Sheldon McKinney," she said at last.

Gideon turned the name over in his head before responding. "I don't know who the hell that is."

"No, I see you don't," Zara replied. She cocked her head to one side. "Well, he seems to know you. I don't know for sure, but I'm guessing he sent that hit squad after you at the château. And he *definitely* put a bounty out on your head with the Marseille gangs. They're still looking for you, you know that?"

Gideon filed away the senator's name, adding it to his threadbare cupboard of clues. If what this woman was saying was correct, then this McKinney character was responsible for Jean-Luc's death and potentially Leclerc's too.

There would have to be consequences.

"Who is he?"

"Oh, no one," Zara said, idly picking at her fingernails as though they were discussing nothing more important than the weather. "Just the chairman of the Senate Select Committee on Intelligence. One of the most powerful men in the American IC."

"IC?"

"Intelligence community," Zara decrypted, looking increasingly puzzled by his responses. "Okay. I showed you my cards. Now show me yours."

Gideon bit his lip, suddenly uncertain how to answer. What was he supposed to tell this woman, that he knew little more about himself than his name? Who would believe a story like that?

"I don't have much to show," he said.

"Oh no, buddy," she said, shaking her head. "That's not how this works. Something crazy hinky is going down here, and you're right in the middle of it. My career's on the line. Hell, so's the senator's—that's the only reason I can think of for him risking everything like this. So why don't you go ahead and tell me what you know?"

He closed his eyes, suddenly feeling exhausted. Upon

opening them, he set the pistol back down on Mariella Tilley's desk and shrugged. "Sure. Why the hell not?"

"That's better."

"The woman who owns this place is lying upstairs in bed with a gunshot to the temple. Looks like the body's been here a couple of days." He paused and narrowed his gaze. "Her name's Mariella Tilley."

"She's dead?" Zara muttered. "Dammit."

"You know her?"

Zara reached into a back pocket and pulled out a sheet of paper. She held it up in front of him. He squinted for a moment until he placed it as coming from Leclerc's background check.

"Where the hell did you get that?"

"You know where," she replied calmly, though not without a glance at the pistol on the desk. "And don't worry, your friend's alive. Not that you asked. I'm the one who called in his location to the French cops."

"You were in Marseille?" Gideon asked, too shocked to process the news of Leclerc's survival.

Zara nodded, glancing down at the floor before she answered. "I was. I entered the block after all the shooting started. After the explosions, too. I found these documents in your friend's jacket."

Gideon blinked. He replayed Zara's strange glance at the floor in his mind, studied her posture, which was no longer as upright and confident as it had been just a couple of minutes earlier. Almost like she was hiding something.

"This McKinney, he sent you there?"

She nodded, her lips pursed.

"You called in my location, didn't you?" Gideon asked as the pieces fell into place. "You're the reason Leclerc ended up in a hospital bed."

Zara seemed to shrink in on herself. "I was doing my job,"

she said feebly. "I didn't know McKinney was going to lose his mind like that. I had nothing to do with the gang hit. That was all him, I swear."

"Tell me the truth." Gideon said, his voice hard and untrusting. He sensed there was more to this story than she was making out.

Her voice hushed and her posture hunched forward, Zara said, "I knew what I was doing was illegal, okay? I convinced myself it was how the sausage was made."

"You sold me out to get a promotion?"

"I made that call—sold you out—because my career was already over. Doing McKinney's bidding was my only hope of saving it. And I convinced myself you deserved it. It might not have been legal but I figured I was doing the right thing."

Gideon narrowed his gaze. "Why?"

"Because you killed nearly an entire Agency contract team. In my experience men capable of feats like that don't tend to be nice guys."

"Then what the hell are you doing here now? You change your mind?"

"I'm looking for answers, just like you," Zara replied, her voice strengthening. "I wasn't lying when I said my career is on the line. Probably my life, too. I'm a loose end."

Gideon probed her face for any sign of dishonesty. He had no idea whether he would find it even if she was lying through her teeth. She was an Agency case officer, after all. He detected nothing, but...

"I know the feeling," he said dryly.

"There's more to it," Zara continued. "I'm guessing you made those two DGSI operatives outside Leclerc's place?"

He nodded.

She swallowed. "They are dead because I made a phone

call. That's on me. Maybe when this is all over I'll hand myself into the authorities for what I did."

"Why not do it now?"

"Because if I do that I will end up dead and this whole mess will get swept under the rug."

Gideon chewed his lip. He had to admit that Zara's story was persuasive. So was her demeanor. "So let's say I trust you. And I'm undecided on that. But if I did, what would you want from me?"

Zara laughed, briefly turning her eyes up to the ceiling before returning her gaze to him. "I don't know. How about you start by telling me why so many people seem to want you dead?"

Gideon smiled despite himself. Zara's humor was catching. "You're not going to believe this..."

"Try me."

"I don't have a fucking clue. A few months ago, I came here, to this villa, to do a protection job along with two other guys. Leclerc brokered the deal. I don't know what happened after that. All I know is that I was drugged, tortured, and almost lost my life."

"You're saying that you have amnesia?"

Gideon nodded.

Zara closed her eyes and started to laugh.

"I'm glad one of us finds it funny."

"I'm sorry," she said, doubling over and starting to hiccup as her body was convulsed by guffawing laughter. It took her a good minute to wrestle control of herself.

Even then, her voice was halting and her eyes glinted with tears. "But you have to admit, it's kind of amusing.... I came all this way to find you only to discover that you don't have a fucking clue."

When she was done talking, she walked over to the desk and jiggled the computer's mouse. The box whirred into life.

"What are you doing?"

"What does it look like, Einstein?" she asked. "I came here for answers, and it turns out you're not exactly the Oracle of Delphi. So it looks like we're going to have to find them the old-fashioned way. You going to just stand there, or do you want to help?"

THIRTY-FOUR

"Dammit, it's locked," Gideon said after Zara swiped the mouse and the computer screen flickered into life only to demand a password.

"No problem," Zara said, reaching into her pocket and removing an unbranded gray plastic USB drive. It looked cheap, like something ordered off of Amazon.

She tossed it to him, and he caught it automatically.

"What am I supposed to do with this?"

"Plug it in and you'll see," Zara said mysteriously as she turned her attention to the set of mahogany drawers by the far wall. The brass fixings on the front rattled as she pulled the topmost drawer open. She reached inside and brought out a ring-bound folder, which she flipped open and began reading through.

After raising a curious eyebrow at the USB drive, Gideon did as he was instructed. He plugged it into a port on the front of the tower PC and waited expectantly.

Nothing happened.

"What now?" he asked.

"Patience, young padawan," she replied, carelessly tossing the folder back into the drawer before slamming it roughly closed. She pulled open the next drawer, her body language indicating that she had little hope of finding anything more interesting. But instead of sighing with frustration as she had multiple times before, she let out a low whistle.

"Now we're getting somewhere," she said.

"What have you got?" Gideon asked after giving up on Zara's mysterious—and apparently nonfunctional—drive. He looked up from the computer to see that she was holding a tiny black cylinder between the thumb and forefinger of her right hand.

"Concealed camera," she explained. "There's all kinds of gear here. It's high-end stuff, too. It's not really my area of expertise, but I didn't think you could buy some of this equipment on the open market. If you can, somebody should probably put a stop to it PDQ."

"PDQ?"

"Pretty damn quick," Zara said, distractedly rooting through the drawer. "There's everything here. Microphones, pen cameras, GPS trackers, you name it. Who the hell was this Mariella bitch? And what was she using all this for?"

Hearing the PC's fans spool up, Gideon returned his attention to the computer's monitor. He raised his eyebrows in surprise when he saw that somehow Zara's gadget had bypassed the password lock screen. "Neat trick."

She grinned broadly. "That's what you pay your taxes for. Actually, I guess you don't. You should think about it, you know? You can still go to jail for not paying your taxes on illegally obtained income. The IRS has a checkbox on the tax return and everything."

"I'll bear that in mind next time I speak to my accountant,"

Gideon said, taking a seat in front of the monitor as he started randomly opening files and folders. "Whoever he is."

"How did you lose your memory, anyway?"

"I was hoping you'd tell me," he said dryly.

"Don't give me that. You must have some idea."

"Jigsaw pieces, that's all. It happened here. I was tortured, I guess. Drugged, too. With something called datura stramonium. Still haven't got around to figuring out what the hell that is yet." He unconsciously rubbed the scar tissue on his left thigh.

"You remember *anything*? Like, even which room it happened in?"

Gideon shook his head. "Nothing."

"Search McKinney's name," Zara said, sidling up next to him after apparently giving up on finding anything else of interest in the office. "He's the only lead we got."

His fingers danced obediently over the keyboard, but after a couple of rotations of the progress icon that lasted just long enough to tempt hope, the search came up empty.

"Damn," she whispered. "Guess that would have been too easy. You mind if I have a go?"

"Sure," Gideon shrugged. "Maybe you'll have better luck than me. Far as I can tell there's nothing on this thing. I guess maybe she just used it for the Internet."

It turned out it had nothing to do with luck. Zara brought up the command window and typed in a series of commands that Gideon inferred were to be read by a program on the USB drive she'd given him, then tapped the return key.

After a few moments, a list of file names populated the black window in white text. It was hundreds of lines long and kept growing as the seconds ticked by.

"What are they?"

"I'm not sure," Zara answered slowly. "Looks like...names. According to the file types, they're videos."

A light seemed to click on in both their minds at the same moment. Zara even twisted around to glance at the still-open drawer behind them.

"Guess that explains the hidden cameras," Gideon said. He squinted at the list of file names on the screen. "I don't recognize most of these people, though."

"I do," she replied, frowning thoughtfully. "It's weird, though. They're mostly media people. Movie directors, Hollywood producers, that kind of thing."

She tapped the screen. "He's the French environment minister, though. Weird."

Zara reached for the mouse and returned it to the search bar at the bottom left of the screen. She typed in the minister's name and hit the return key. This time the search completed almost immediately.

A single video popped up. They looked at each other, then Zara shrugged. "Guess we better watch it."

She double-clicked on the file. A window opened up on the screen with the paused video inside. The still image on the screen was graphic enough to make Gideon's eyes pop with surprise. The camera must have been positioned on a piece of furniture to the right of a double bed he remembered seeing upstairs. It was close enough that it captured the sea of naked flesh and entwined limbs without any hint of modesty.

"How French," Zara remarked. She hit play.

The film was just as graphic as the still frame. A dark-haired man with a cyclist's frame, hairy buttocks, and a large oval birthmark on his right shoulder copulated fiercely with two women at the same time. The camera was positioned so that his face was in view the majority of the time.

"That's definitely him," Zara confirmed.

"He's really getting into it," Gideon observed.

"Hookers, I'm guessing," Zara said. "But that's just a hunch. Monsieur minister is definitely not a looker, though, so I'm guessing it was transactional. This feels like a honeypot."

Gideon knew that term, even if he wasn't sure why. And given the list of other names—and presumably the similar videos that came with them—he was inclined to agree. "What's the purpose of all this, though?"

Zara clicked through half a dozen additional videos at random. Some of the same girls popped up, but the star of the show was always different. In ninety-nine percent of cases, they were men.

She shook her head. "Hell if I know. But someone—Mariella, I guess—went to a lot of effort to get all these videos. It's just a guess, but I don't think she did it out of the kindness of her heart."

"Blackmail?"

"Seems plausible. The thing I don't get is how the senator's involved in all this."

"You think he was on one of these videos? Wanted to cover it all up?"

Zara frowned as she considered the suggestion. "It's possible, but it doesn't explain how you fit into the equation. If he was compromised, then why not come after this place? He's proved he has the connections."

"Then maybe he's involved in whatever's going down here."

"I like that theory better. It fits."

She opened the desk drawer and rummaged through its contents.

"I already checked that one."

"Well, you missed this, for a start," she said, pulling out a portable hard drive complete with data transfer cable. She plugged it into the computer and waited a second for the drive to mount. "Empty."

Zara brought up the command window once again and executed an instruction that appeared to copy the entire list of video files onto the borrowed drive. "Just in case."

———

"SIR, YOU NEED TO SEE THIS," Ronan Haynes said, flicking on the senator's bedroom light as he entered without knocking, a first for both men. He carried a tablet in his hands.

"God dammit," McKinney said, his voice gravelly as his eyes snapped open. There was an empty scotch glass on his bedside table and his eyes were dark and baggy. "I told you I wasn't to be disturbed."

"The security system just triggered in the villa in Cannes," Haynes said, offering the tablet to his master.

"Tilley's place?" McKinney asked, immediately more alert. He groped for his bedside lamp and turned it on before snatching the tablet from Haynes's fingers. "Who is it, the cops?"

Haynes shook his head. "It's him. And he's got company."

McKinney pulled himself upright so that his back was level with the headboard. He squinted at the screen in his palms. "That bitch," he snarled.

"It looks like they're working together. Makes sense."

"I take it the villa hasn't been cleaned?"

Haynes shook his head, endeavoring to keep his features bland. "There wasn't time."

"Fuck. Do we have sound on this thing?"

"No."

McKinney looked away from the screen for the first time,

his eyes wide. A potent combination of fury and fear burned in his now-wakeful eyes. "Can they see this in New Eden?"

Haynes nodded, glad he was standing a couple of feet back from the bed.

The senator hurled the tablet computer toward the nearest wall. The glass screen shattered on impact and the metal chassis punched a hole in the wall. Plaster dust coursed toward the floor.

Haynes struggled to keep his tone even. He wanted to grab his boss by the lapels and yell at him that both their lives were on the line. But he swallowed that thought, like so many over the years. "What do you want me to do?"

"Get ahead of things for once!" McKinney snarled. He took a few seconds to compose himself then growled without a hint of contrition, "Put a bounty out on the woman. It'll raise fewer questions. Do it quietly but make sure the right people know. She'll need documents and transportation if she wants to run. If we get her, it looks like Gideon comes as part of the package."

"How much?"

"Whatever it takes."

THIRTY-FIVE

"The whole fucking house is bugged," Zara marveled in a hushed tone as they walked back outside.

Now that they knew what signs to look for, they saw the devices everywhere. The tiny black camera dots were even present in the kitchen, just in case a particularly horny French movie producer felt the need to get it on while fixing a post-coital sandwich.

What was equally clear was that the bugging operation wasn't a one-time thing. It seemed that the villa's very purpose was to be used to entrap targets of opportunity in order to create blackmail material—what the Russians called *kompromat*.

"You reckon that's who's behind this?" Gideon asked after Zara floated the thought.

"I have no idea," she admitted as she walked the entire property, snapping photographs on her cell phone. "If you squint, you can just about make out their fingerprints, but we don't exactly have any evidence of it. Mariella Tilley had an American passport. That doesn't rule out her being a Russian asset, but it's sure not proof she is. Most foreign intelligence agencies run honeypot traps. I've never heard of anything this... industrial. But that doesn't mean they don't exist."

"If not them, then who?"

"That's the million-dollar question. I don't see how McKinney's involvement fits with the Russia hypothesis. He's a prick, but as far as I know, he's our prick." She paused, then finished in a more thoughtful tone. "I guess everybody has their price."

Zara took particular care to photograph Mariella Tilley's bedroom from a dozen angles. She snapped individual photos of the pistol, the brass casing that had ejected and rolled across the bedroom carpet, the blood splatter, and the pale, now-bloated face of Tilley's corpse.

"Why bother?" Gideon asked, his voice a little flat as he trailed Zara through the villa. Her next stop was the first of the guest bedrooms, where she captured images of the hidden cameras.

Now that the operation was drawing to a close, the adrenaline that had carried Gideon through the previous couple of days was beginning to fade from his system. With it was his sense of self. The sensation he'd experienced ever since waking up at the legionnaire's château all those weeks earlier—that he was somehow separate from his body, watching it from a distance—was beginning to return.

Even the excitement of discovering the blackmail tapes wasn't enough to hold back the tide. He needed rest. Hell, he needed a doctor, somebody who could explain to him what had happened to his mind. Was there a medicine he could try? If it would help him uncover his memories, even just give detail to the outline of the teenage girl who sometimes intruded into his dreams, he would take it.

"Because," Zara said, turning to meet his gaze. Unlike his

own, hers glinted with energetic fury. "This is proof. Somebody's responsible for the carnage of the past few days. And they are going to pay for what they've done. I don't care how long it takes."

Gideon stiffened sharply as Zara's righteous vigor somehow began coursing through his own veins. He felt shame that he needed to leech off her life force and fear that she would leave and take it with her. They'd only just met, and yet he felt he needed this woman in his life more than he'd ever needed anyone before. She was a kite string tethering him to the earth while a feverish storm raged overhead.

Tethering him to...something more.

For a moment, his legs grew unsteady beneath him. He blinked as a sense of déjà vu overcame him. It was like he was seeing the bedroom's walls for the second time. Like he'd been here before.

"We should go," she said when he didn't—couldn't—respond. "For all we know somebody else has access to those camera feeds. I don't want to be here if they show up."

"Not yet," Gideon said, the words coming out in a husky croak.

"Why not?"

He didn't answer for the simple reason that he didn't really have one. Not a good one. All he knew was that he needed to be outside. Beyond that, he just wasn't sure.

Gideon almost stumbled over his feet, falling forward as he followed a vague urge to be in the open air that grew with every forward step. He exited the villa via the door he'd entered it by, then walked around to the side of the building.

"Where the hell are you going?" Zara hissed from behind him in a tone that sounded like she thought he'd gone insane.

He stopped halfway down the wall, certain he'd reached his destination and equally sure that there was nothing here to see. He took another step forward, and instead of unforgiving stone, the soles of his sneakers scraped against wood.

Slowly, Gideon's eyes lowered to the ground beneath him. He was standing on a pair of wooden doors set into the ground, a bit like the entrance to a tornado shelter.

"Here, I think," he said, his stomach gripped by a vice of horror at what he might find beneath him.

Unlike the villa itself, the doors were bolted and secured from the outside with a padlock. Gideon searched around for something to smash it with and found a large chunk of stone among several rocks that bordered a flower bed. He hefted it in his right palm before bringing it down hard on the shiny steel lock.

It took several attempts before the padlock came free. In the end, it was the metal hasp and staple that broke off, not the lock itself. Gideon kicked the smashed pieces of metal aside and dropped the rock just off the edge of the wooden door.

If Zara said anything, he didn't hear it. His hearing was drowned out by the ringing of a bell, his mind swallowed by a hazy fog. His stomach was no longer knotted, but instead, waves of nausea threatened to overcome him. He pushed them back with difficulty and steadied himself.

Gideon heaved the two doors aside. He stood over the space that opened up, staring down into an inky black hole. Behind him he heard a click, then a sudden flash of illumination as Zara brought out a flashlight. She brought it to bear on the basement he'd discovered.

"Is this where...?" she began, before breaking off, unable to finish the question.

He didn't answer. He took the flashlight from her unresisting fingers and crouched down, playing the beam out into the reaches of the basement. A ladder led down about seven feet to a brick floor. There were clearly objects inside, but they were difficult to make out from his present angle.

Gideon climbed down the ladder instead. The second he reached the bottom a foul—*familiar*—smell assaulted his nostrils.

Zara joined him a moment later. Out of the corner of his eye, he caught a flicker of distaste, almost disgust on her face. She might be an Agency case officer, but nothing could prepare a human for encountering a scene like this for the first time.

He held the flashlight horizontally and rotated in a full circle, slowly playing the beam out over the entire basement. The space extended about twenty feet in each direction, the majority of it below the villa itself. The air was dry but tasted metallic, like spilled blood.

The cause of that was immediately obvious. In the corner to Gideon's right lay four large metal cages, almost like dog kennels—but larger. They were big enough to hold a person. To the side of one of them was a black trash bag that looked about half full.

Gideon walked slowly, silently over to the cages. He came to a stop about two feet in front of them and momentarily closed his eyes. He tried to picture himself inside one of them, as if doing so would force open the dam that was blocking up his memories.

It didn't work.

He was certain that this was the place. Despite the basement's cool, stable atmosphere he was sweating, his senses hyper-alert to every sound and smell as adrenaline and cortisol flooded his system. His body clearly recognized that he'd been held here. But his brain still refused to admit it.

The cages stank of blood, urine, and feces. Dark stains marred the metal bars.

"My God," Zara whispered as she joined his side. She drew

her phone from her pocket, opened the camera app, and almost apologetically began recording the scene.

"Yeah," he said, his voice low and venomous.

He turned and left her to her work. The space behind him was open and empty. Except for the cages, there was little else in the basement. A few plastic boxes stored against the far wall were about it. But Gideon's gaze fixated on a metal ring sunk into the floor.

He walked over, then crouched down to examine it. It was rusty, but in places the corrosion had flaked off—recently enough that it still remained on the floor around the ring itself. He ran his finger over the sections where the metal ring had been worn smooth.

"You can make this stop," a voice said in his ear.

Gideon threw himself back.

Zara whipped around, startled. "You okay?"

He didn't answer.

Saliva drooled from his lips and yet his mouth had never felt so dry. His heart raced faster than he could ever remember. Strange shapes passed across his vision whether his eyes were open or shut. The chains around his wrists and ankles clinked as he strained against the ring on the floor.

"Just do what we want and your friends don't have to die," the voice said. "Life won't be so bad. In fact you'll live in the lap of luxury. Thousands of people will adore you, pray for you. Love you. You'll see your sister again. You can come home."

Gideon's eyes popped wide open. He saw Zara staring down at him, visibly horrified by what she saw. She reached for his hand and gripped it tight. "What happened? You look like you were having some kind of seizure."

Gideon struggled for breath, his heart still racing faster than he could remember. When he was finally able to speak, he said only three words. "I remembered something."

THIRTY-SIX

Zara, it transpired, had simply driven to the villa and parked on the public road outside. Though he was still dazed from the shock, Gideon had to admit that his kayak-borne stealth insertion now felt a little overengineered in the cold light of day.

Or at least, the first glimmering of dawn now caressing the horizon.

They drove for half an hour, mostly in silence. Zara didn't press him for information. Several times he caught her glancing worriedly in his direction out of the corner of his vision.

Gideon's head swiveled as though it was on a gimbal, constantly leaning forward to check the side mirror or peering over his shoulder to ensure that they weren't being followed. His breath came in sharp, shallow waves. No matter how hard he tried to breathe in, it was as though his lungs rejected the order, spasming and denying him air for several seconds each time.

"I'm okay," he said, the words unconvincing even to himself. His pulse was still elevated, mouth dry as a bone. It was as though his body was trapped in some kind of posttraumatic stress loop, constantly forced to relive the trauma he'd experienced in that basement.

What trauma?

Worst of all was the fact that already the memory was fading. Just half an hour earlier, he had remembered every detail of his interrogator's voice, his smell, and subtle shifts in the man's posture and intonation.

Now he only recalled what he'd experienced in the broadest of strokes. The man had said he had a sister. That he could go home.

"*Just do what we want...*"

But where the hell was home?

Zara piloted her rented sedan into the front drive of an isolated holiday trailer about thirty miles from the coast. "It was all I could afford," she explained. "And the owner accepted cash."

"It's good" was all Gideon could generate the energy to say. He felt his eyelids drooping with exhaustion.

As soon as Zara parked and unlocked the side door, he stumbled into the cramped space. At the far end of the steel trailer was a double bed that folded down from the rear wall. It called to him.

"It's okay," Zara said, her expression upbeat but her gaze deeply concerned. "Sleep. I'll keep watch."

Gideon didn't argue. He lay down on the bed without kicking off his shoes. He didn't even crawl all the way to the pillows by the rear wall before his eyes closed and he fell into a deep, dreamless sleep.

By the time he awoke, the sun streaming into the trailer's windows had already passed its zenith and was fast falling behind the trees that bordered the plot the trailer rested on. He sat bolt upright in bed and sucked in what felt like his first full lungful of air in days. The infusion of oxygen into his bloodstream made him momentarily lightheaded. He stared at Zara through bleary eyes. She was lying on a window seat at the front end of the trailer, her legs folded beneath her and her back leaning against the cabin's curved wall. She was working on a tiny laptop.

"Feeling better, sleepyhead?"

"Like someone took a baseball bat to my head," Gideon admitted.

"There's coffee in the pot," Zara said, gesturing at a filter machine next to the tiny stove. "I've been mainlining it all afternoon."

"You didn't sleep?"

She shook her head. "You needed the rest more than me. Anyway, I was too wired to close my eyes."

"What have you been up to?" Gideon asked as he swung his legs off the foot of the bed. He finally kicked off his shoes, a little shamefaced at the marks of dirt he'd left on the bedspread.

"Watching dirty movies, mostly."

"Find anything interesting?"

Gideon stood up and walked over to the metal kitchen sink. He twisted the faucet and waited for the water to run cold, then lowered his face and splashed handfuls of icy liquid onto it. The chill was bracing and rapidly woke him up. He kept going until all the sleep was washed from his eyes, then he ran his wet hands through his hair and smoothed it back into something approaching his usual style.

Zara waited for him to finish, a ghost of a smile on her lips. "All done?"

He nodded and grabbed a cup of coffee.

"I've watched about half the tapes so far."

Gideon raised an eyebrow. "Good going."

She wrinkled her nose. "You wouldn't say that if you'd seen

the things I have over the past few hours. Hair where hair has no right to be. And oh God, the beer bellies..."

He shot her a mock salute. "Somebody had to do it."

"I guess," she shrugged. Her expression turned serious. "Most of the videos were, shall we say, light on conversation. Especially the older ones. The ladies clearly had instructions to get as kinky as possible. Having video of a sixty-five-year-old man with a leather gag over his lips must make for better blackmail material."

She shuddered involuntarily before continuing. "But about a dozen of them were filmed in the last six months. I was only able to verify the identities of a handful of the subjects. They were mostly French military officers and civilian employees of their Armed Forces ministry."

"And?" Gideon prompted.

"This time the ladies had a script. They were asking questions about you."

"Me?" Gideon asked, his mind still running at half speed despite the attempt he'd made to wash the fatigue away.

Zara leapt lightly to her feet. She carried the laptop to the tiny seating area just a couple of feet away and sat on a bench. "Come."

He did as she suggested and took a seat by her side. She swiveled the laptop so they could both see the screen, then tapped the spacebar. A grainy video began to play. It had been shot in a darkened room at an angle that pointed down on one of the guest beds in the Cannes villa and left little to the imagination. The sheets were rumpled and the pillow hung half off the end of the bed.

Two figures lay back against the headboard. The man had a shock of dark pubic hair and a thick seventies-style thatch on his chest. He was smoking a cigarette. A blonde woman—at least, light-haired—lay by his side, idly playing with his chest hair.

"Did you ever go to war?" she cooed, her French accented with a twang that almost sounded American. "It must be so scary."

"A few times," the man replied, his tone gruff and proud. "You get used to it."

"Humble brag," Zara snorted under her breath. "*You get used to it.* What an ass."

Gideon couldn't help but grin at her reaction despite his burning desire to know why the hell he was of such interest to these people. Why had the man in his repressed memory seemed to think he was so important? He'd said people would *pray* for him. Why did the CIA—and the chairman of the Senate Intelligence Committee personally—want him dead?

His smile fading, he returned his attention to the screen.

"I met a guy in the Legion once," the girl said. "I was in Avignon visiting a friend."

"Let me guess," the soldier said dryly as he turned his head to one side and blew out an arrow of smoke. "He took you to bed and gave you the night of your life."

The girl slapped his chest playfully. "It wasn't like that. I think his name was...Gideon, something. He sounded American."

The man shrugged, visibly losing interest in the conversation. "We have some Americans in the Legion, that is true. But there are thousands of legionnaires. I don't know them all by name. There was no officer by that name, I'm sure of that."

He stubbed his cigarette out on an ashtray on the bedside table, then rolled over onto his chest and began toying with the girl's breast. Gideon recoiled at the image, noticing for the first time the obvious disparity in their ages. The legionnaire on the video had to be in his late thirties or early forties. His conquest barely looked out of her teens.

"Anyway, enough of this Gideon. Another man would get jealous."

"Well, he owes me money," the girl laughed, at first seeming to try to wriggle from his grasp before stiffening and then giving in. "Maybe you can look him up for me."

"Maybe…"

Zara killed the video before it went any further, her lips pursed with distaste. "There are three or four of them just like that. Looks like a fishing expedition, not an attempt to create kompromat. Someone was looking for you."

She didn't say it, but the obvious question was written on her face. *Why?*

Gideon stared blankly at the computer screen for a few more seconds, replaying the memory from the basement in his mind, even as he felt less and less connected to it. He felt like somebody had taken his brain and given it a shake so that all the pieces were thrown up in the air like glitter in a snow globe. Everything was in there somewhere, but it was arranged in all the wrong order.

But the fogginess was deeply at odds with the growing urge to find out who he was and what had caused all this pain. His desire to uncover his past was like a candle flame in the wind: buffeted and tested—but stronger for it. The more he learned, the more he knew he needed to keep going. Like Zara with the two dead French agents, he owed justice to Jean-Luc, and all the others who had suffered because of him.

He couldn't stop now, just because it was hard.

"Do you have the Internet on this thing?"

She nodded, concealing her disappointment well, but not well enough. "It's running through a bunch of private network nodes, but, you know…"

She shrugged.

"This won't link back to me," Gideon promised. He reached for the laptop and opened a browser window. He typed just two words into the search bar. *Datura stramonium.*

"Scopolamine is derived from the nightshade, or datura stramonium, plant," Zara read aloud from the first article he clicked.

"Used in microscopic amounts to treat motion sickness, the chemical is also the subject of exciting research as a potential treatment for Alzheimer's. A 2014 VICE documentary investigated claims that high dosages of the drug could be used to strip someone of their free will or brainwash them into believing a chosen set of facts. Whatever the truth, dozens of cases of datura stramonium poisoning occur each year in the United States alone, frequently leading to severe amnesia, prolonged hallucinations, and even causing irreversible brain damage in victims."

"Great," Gideon muttered. "Now I'm brain-damaged."

Further investigation revealed little more than what they'd already read. Articles in medical journals confirmed that severe neurological and psychiatric symptoms were common aftereffects of nightshade consumption. But he already knew that.

Zara reached out and tentatively squeezed his forearm. "Are you ready to talk about what you remembered?"

THIRTY-SEVEN

Gideon recounted everything the man had said—the idea that he was somehow important, that there was a group of people who believed in, what, his divinity?—and the fact that he had family.

Or at least a sister somewhere. He also described the dreams he'd had back at the château during his recuperation of a teenage girl's face and the sense that she meant something to him. It was only one drop in the ocean of his lost memories, but at least it was something.

He fell silent as a wave of almost unbearable longing swept over him. He was a man adrift, unmoored not just from his emotions but also from his past. He was anchored to nothing more than the moment he presently occupied. It was no life to live.

Zara chewed her lip thoughtfully, then reached for his cup of coffee and took a swig from it. She shot him a mischievous smile as she set it back down. "Sorry. Helps me think."

"Forget it. My heart's racing enough as it is."

"Do you have any idea why you joined the Legion?"

Gideon shook his head. A note of frustration slipped into his tone. "I already told you—"

"I know," she said, holding up a finger to forestall his coming tirade. "Just checking. I'm detail oriented. Okay, here's my theory: What kind of people join the French Foreign Legion?"

He shrugged, wondering how any of this mattered. "People looking for a fresh start, I guess."

"And a fresh identity. A new passport."

"I figured that much out myself," he answered snippily.

"Meow," Zara fired back, undeterred. "But it indicates that you were running from these people at least seven years ago. Maybe longer. You were a young man then, right?"

"I guess so."

"So you probably didn't have the resources to get hold of fresh documents any other way. The Legion would have been your best shot. The hard bit isn't crossing a border without papers; it's getting a job once you reach the other side. But you found a way."

Zara frowned. "I don't really get the rest of it. I don't see why Senator McKinney would risk so much to take you off the board. It indicates that you must know or represent something powerful enough to threaten his existence, but what that is..."

She spread her palms wide.

"I guess we'll have to ask him," Gideon said. "He's our only lead. Which means we have to get Stateside somehow without being caught."

"What are you planning on doing, kidnapping the chairman of the Senate intelligence committee?"

Gideon shrugged. "Do you have any better ideas?"

She grimaced. "No."

"And I'm not saying we go to those extremes," Gideon said. "But right now it seems like all roads lead back home. I just don't know how we get there."

"Yeah," Zara murmured, growing visibly more anxious. "I reached the same conclusion while you were asleep. You don't have any documents, and we couldn't use your existing ones as it is. Even if mine weren't locked in a safe in my desk at the embassy, they would be equally useless."

"I think I have money," Gideon offered, explaining about the numbered Panamanian account. "I don't know how much exactly, but you don't open an offshore bank account for a few hundred bucks."

"Let's hope not," Zara smiled. "That'll definitely help. But I don't know how to get hold of quality travel documents. They never covered that eventuality at the Farm. Usually somebody just hands me a packet with a perfect fake passport in it. Even if we could get some, we'd have to travel through immigration. By now my hunch is that both our images will be flagged on Border Patrol's facial recognition system. We'd never make it past the immigration counter."

"Then what—a container ship? That'll take weeks," Gideon said.

"I think it's time you rang your buddy in Panama," Zara said. "Because there are ways we could get around our little problem. But they all require cold, hard cash—and lots of it."

Late afternoon in France meant that it wasn't yet lunch in Panama. Despite that, Miguel Sanchez wasn't at his desk. Gideon listened to entirely forgettable hold music for about ten minutes over the laptop's speakers, slightly garbled by the encryption program Zara was using to route the internet-routed call and maintain their anonymity.

Once he was found, Miguel informed his valued customer that there was a little over $900,000 in the account and thanked him for his custom. Gideon explained that he would shortly email the man an account number and an amount of money to transfer.

It was that easy.

Zara explained that there was a hidden back door into the United States—and most countries around the world—that few knew about. "You just have to fly private."

"It's that easy, huh?"

She shrugged. "Kinda. It's a big security hole, and a hard one to patch."

Because they required much smaller runways, private planes were able to land at hundreds, if not thousands of additional airports across the US. Many of these weren't manned full-time by immigration officers.

Passengers were still required to be processed through the usual customs and immigration checks. "But," Zara said, "Who's to say how often that happens?"

"It's a risk, though. Maybe we get lucky, maybe we don't."

Zara grinned. "That's why my plan has a second feature. Private jets are expensive. A plane with enough range to take us from France back home would probably set us back a cool quarter of a million bucks. Maybe more. And we'd still need to give the charter company our documents for the passenger manifest."

"So how does your plan help?"

"Every single day, you have empty leg flights—planes repositioning for their next job carrying nobody but their pilots. And sometimes those pilots are willing to look the other way in exchange for a hefty contribution to their retirement fund."

"And you have a contact?"

Zara nodded, visibly pleased with herself. "And I have a contact."

Gideon raised his eyebrows. "So what, are we a team now?"

"We both want the same thing, right?" Zara said. "McKinney has to face consequences for what he's done. I owe those two French agents that much. And I figure we're stronger together than apart."

THIRTY-EIGHT

"You're sure about your guy?" Gideon asked quietly.

"I guess we're about to find out," Zara replied, her expression strained. Her contact at the Agency had located a Bombardier Global 6000 business jet due to fly an empty leg from Turin, Italy, to Montreal, Canada, early the following morning. The pilots, apparently, were willing to pretend they didn't notice they had passengers for the princely sum of €50,000.

Each.

Not bad for about nine hours' work.

The drive from the French Mediterranean coast into Italy only took five hours. They drove without stopping, save a five-minute break at a motorway gas station, just long enough to fill up the tank and empty their bladders.

Thankfully, despite the bullet-ridden chaos that France had been plunged into over the previous couple of days, there were still no hard borders within the European Union. The shift from France into Italy was barely noticeable—the only giveaway was the fact that the speed limits changed and the road signs were written in a different Romance language.

They arrived at Turin-Caselle Airport, ten miles northwest of downtown Turin, two hours ahead of schedule. Zara was presently behind the wheel as Gideon sat in the passenger seat, his eyes roving in every direction, searching for any sign that they were walking—driving—into a trap.

"Security seems normal," he said as they passed several armed carabinieri—Italian police who were easy to pick out due to the red stripe that ran down their dark pants. He watched discreetly as several off-duty carabiniere officers cheerily bid their on-duty colleagues goodbye before piling into a large police van.

"I concur," Zara agreed. She applied pressure to the car's indicator lever and followed signs to the small airport's long-term parking lot. "If they knew we were coming, they'd be working double shifts."

"Doesn't mean someone else isn't waiting for us out there," Gideon mused.

"Anybody ever tell you you're an optimist?" Zara quipped. "Because if they did, they lied."

They performed a second pass on foot after parking the car, threading through excited vacationers and scanning for any sign that security was tighter than normal or that watchers had been planted in the crowd.

Zara finally convinced Gideon that the airport was safe. They returned to the vehicle and wiped it clean but left their firearms and ammunition locked in the trunk. It was unlikely that a police dog would be trained to recognize gunshot residue —but not impossible. Besides, to get airside they would have to pass through metal detectors.

At some point the car would be towed, but it would probably languish in a municipal impound lot for several weeks or months before an official got around to opening it up. And since the serial number on the pistol Gideon had borrowed from Leclerc's selection had been filed off, it would be a dead-end. Zara's weapon would probably attract more attention, but even then, it would likely only be linked back to French gang crime before the trail went cold. Ballistics analysis was a highly inexact "science," so it was unlikely the weapons would be traced back to the gunfight in Marseille.

"Ready?" Gideon asked after tossing the car keys into a trash can.

Zara nodded, displaying more confidence than he felt. "Ready."

The meeting point they'd been given was in front of a car rental desk in the arrivals terminal of the main airport. Gideon wore a baseball cap and hoodie as he walked inside, despite Zara's protestations that this would instantly mark him as an American.

"I don't like it," he said for her ears only as they stepped through the airport's sliding glass doors. The back of his neck itched, though he swiftly realized it was only due to the sweatshirt's label.

Still...

"I'm twitchy, too," she said. "But we don't have any other choice."

A man in a pilot's uniform was waiting for them at the designated place at the designated time. He carried a cheap Nike backpack in his right hand and was wearing his flight cap. Ryker noticed that he was artfully positioned to prevent his face from being captured by any of the domed black security cameras that studded the walls and wondered how many times he'd done this.

Or he's undercover, and about to arrest us both.

"You will call me Jesse," the pilot said, waving off introductions. Given the man's tanned complexion and Castilian Spanish accent, Gideon was pretty sure that wasn't his real name. He handed Zara the backpack.

"You got the money?" Gideon asked.

The pilot pursed his lips, clearly irritated by the question. His English was good but not flawless. "We wouldn't be standing here if you don't pay."

Good point...

"Do you have a way of knowing the time?" the man asked.

Zara tweaked her left sleeve to reveal a digital wristwatch—just a cheap Casio model. Nothing with a Bluetooth connection or a GPS chip that could be traced.

"I have 11:21," Jesse said after consulting the screen of his phone. "Are we agreed?"

After checking her watch, Zara nodded.

"Inside the bag you will find two vests and two access cards that will allow you airside. You are here for trial shifts for a position at Timecafe on the other side of security, you understand?"

They both nodded.

"First you will visit the restroom and put your vests on. After that, in...now eight minutes, you will go to the access hallway opposite the sushi restaurant. You will tap your cards against the reader. I will meet you on the other side of the metal detectors. Understood?"

Again, they both nodded.

"11:30," he said, turning on his heel and striding away. "I will not wait for you if you are late. And make sure you're not carrying any contraband."

Gideon breathed a measured sigh of relief as he watched Jesse disappear out of sight without a SWAT team storming in to apprehend them. If the man was compromised by local authorities, he doubted that things would have been allowed to get this far. The moment they confirmed they were the couple Jesse was waiting for, the trap would have snapped shut.

In the end, the passage through the dedicated line for airport employee security was easy. Since they were both wearing reflective neon vests that visibly marked them as people on official business and had access badges clipped to their belt buckles like the other airport employees—Zara had noticed that particular tell—they were waved through by the bored outsourced airport security officer without further question. Zara's laptop went through the scanner without attracting attention.

Jesse greeted them on the other side of the metal detectors as promised. He instructed them to follow close behind before leading them through a set of glass doors that led toward the runway apron, where they boarded a transfer bus along with a dozen or so other airport employees, most of whom rocked white AirPods in their ears and kept themselves to themselves.

Still, neither Zara nor Gideon relaxed until they were safely inside the gleaming white Bombardier business jet without incident.

They caught only brief glimpses of Jesse's copilot, despite the fact that he was effectively a paid employee.

"He could've at least introduced himself," Zara whispered.

"The ground rules are simple," Jesse said, his posture clearly more relaxed once the jet's outer door closed behind him. "You may use the bathroom and make yourself comfortable in the cabin. Soft drinks and food in the fridge are OK. The alcohol is not. Are we agreed?"

"I never drink on flights," Gideon said, not sure whether that was accurate or not.

Jesse ignored his lame attempt at humor. It was probably for the best. "If you wish to communicate with us, you will knock once on the cockpit door, which will be locked in flight. Once only, that is very important."

"Sure," Gideon agreed. "But why?"

"Nobody will check the flight recorder. Once we land, you will disappear, and it will be like this never happened." Jesse shrugged laconically. "But if there was an incident in flight, even a minor incident, it would be investigated. And if it transpired there were passengers on board that didn't match the manifest..."

"I get it. One knock only. Don't worry, we'll be quiet as church mice."

Jesse shot him a curious look but apparently decided the unfamiliar turn of phrase wasn't worth following up. "Please wear your seat belts throughout the flight. The journey over the Atlantic can get bumpy. And while I appreciate your custom, I hope not to see either of you again.."

"Same here, buddy," Gideon groused as the pilot disappeared into the cockpit. "Same here."

Within a few minutes, the business jet's engines began spooling up. Shortly after that, the aircraft taxied toward the runway, where it sat for almost half an hour as the tower gave priority to much larger commercial jets. As an added precaution, Zara and Gideon stayed away from the windows to avoid attracting attention to their supposedly empty aircraft. Finally their takeoff slot was allocated and they were in the air.

As soon as they reached cruising altitude—which, presumably to avoid being recorded on the jet's black box, Jesse didn't announce—Zara kicked off her shoes and walked into the small galley at the back of the cabin. She emerged with two champagne flutes filled with orange juice and handed one to Gideon with a broad smile on her face.

"For you, sir. I think this calls for a celebration."

Gideon looked up at her from his exceedingly comfortable

seat. He grinned back, almost lightheaded at how bizarre the comfort felt after the adrenaline ride of the past few days. "Good job."

They clinked glasses at thirty thousand feet as Italy's green fields gave way to the still snowcapped French Alps beneath them. By the time they reached Paris, the weather had grown cloudy and they skimmed a few thousand feet over a bed of powdery clouds, which provided the only scenery until they were well over the Atlantic Ocean.

"And there's Wi-Fi," Zara said, grinning with satisfaction. "What more could a girl want?"

Gideon fiddled with the controls on his plush seat until it reclined into a flat bed. He knotted his fingers beneath his head and closed his eyes. His subconscious immediately returned to the memory it had been toying with for hours. *"Thousands of people will adore you, pray for you..."*

He drifted into a state that was somewhere between wakefulness and a dream, helped by the constant background hum of the jet's engines. The girl's face played across his mind's eye. He called out to her, she turned, and for a second her features were so clear and distinct, but as soon as he tried to commit them to memory, they were gone.

More fragments of memory tormented him, each as impossible to grasp as the last. Faces, scraps of conversation, a vision of an endless plain.

A harsh voice, like a drill instructor's. *"You're not special, Nomad. Suck it up."*

"Gideon? Are you awake?"

"I am now," he grumbled as his eyes blearily opened. The map on a screen on the wall indicated they were most of the way across the Atlantic. They didn't have too long to go. The last memory echoed in his ears. *"You're not special, Nomad. Suck it up."*

"Oh, give me a break," Zara said, entirely undaunted by his grouchy response. "I've been hard at work."

"Doing what?"

"I'm glad you asked. How bad do you want to recover your memory?"

He furrowed his brow. "Is that a trick question?"

"There's one slight problem," Zara replied, wincing. "It might be kill or cure. Is that a risk you're willing to take?"

THIRTY-NINE

"Mushrooms?" Gideon asked skeptically.

"Mushrooms," Zara agreed with a firm nod and considerably more enthusiasm than he felt. "Specifically, psilocybin, the psychoactive component in magic mushrooms. It's what gives you the funky visuals and the sense of dissociation from your body when you trip."

"You sound like you're speaking from experience."

"Don't tell the Agency," she replied sheepishly. "I'm pretty sure I certified to the federal government that I've never touched scheduled narcotics."

"Yeah," Gideon said, gesturing at their shared predicament. "Because your career's on such an upward track right now. Wouldn't want to risk it."

"Touché." She turned her laptop around so that he could see the screen. It was open to Google Scholar. "These are all the journal articles that I could find about using psilocybin to treat and potentially reverse amnesia. It looks like there are dozens of trials going on right now all across the globe. I found a doctor in Boston who has developed a protocol that can be used to recover lost memories."

"So what's the catch?"

"This is all experimental stuff," she admitted. "In about seventy percent of cases, the Spohn protocol appears to succeed. In twenty-five percent, the suppressed memories appear to be permanently overwritten by the protocol itself. I guess the hallucinatory effects somehow replace the preexisting memories."

"And the remaining five?"

"Well, that's that catch you were looking for," Zara said. "You've heard of a bad trip, right?"

"Sure."

Zara spun the laptop again and opened a page of notes. "It's a colloquial term for a psychedelic crisis. Hallucinogenics can amplify preexisting emotional states. That's why mushroom and LSD users focus on creating the right set and setting before tripping. If a trip goes bad, the user can experience intense fear, anxiety, and paranoia. People have been known to throw themselves out of windows thinking they could fly, that kind of thing."

"You're really selling it to me," Gideon quipped.

"Don't worry about that. I shouldn't have even mentioned it. The protocol ensures that someone's watching the patient at all times."

"So no window-diving. Got it."

"That's not the risk. The problem is when you use this hallucinogenic protocol to recover suppressed memory, it appears that in a very small number of cases as negative memories return, the negative symptoms of the trip are massively amplified in a kind of psychotropic storm. Doctor Spohn refers to episodes of impending doom, highly realistic visual and auditory hallucinations, time distortion, and aftereffects that have left some of her trial subjects with crippling depression, flashbacks, and anxiety. Potentially for life."

She closed her laptop. "It's not like you have to decide now."

"I'll do it," Gideon said firmly, surprised by how entirely comfortable the decision felt. "I can't live the rest of my life wondering who I am."

"Okay then," Zara said, seeming torn as to whether she'd made the right decision in telling him. "There's one other thing."

"Let me guess, you want me to shoot up fentanyl to help my gunshot wound heal."

"Heroin, actually." She smiled wanly.

"Just kidding. I also did a bit of a deep dive into Senator McKinney. Honestly, I didn't find much. He's got his shit pretty buttoned down. He's supposedly married, but there's not even a photo of his wife anywhere on the Internet. But I did find this guy—a retired investigative journalist, I guess—called David Packer. He used to work for the *Houston Chronicle*. After he retired, he wrote a couple of blogs about McKinney hinting that there was something explosive about him, something that could destroy his political career. Then the posts just end."

"You think the senator had this guy killed?"

"Nothing like that. But maybe McKinney threatened him somehow to shut down the story. As far as I can tell, he's still alive. Well, there's no record of his death anyway. Maybe it's worth paying him a visit."

"Sure," Gideon shrugged. "We just have to sneak across the Canadian border, pop into Doctor Spohn's office in Boston on our way south so she can take a chisel to my gray matter, then make it to Texas. All while avoiding the death squads that will no doubt be on our tail."

"Exactly," Zara said, a twinkle in her eye. "I knew you'd be on board."

The jet hit a patch of turbulence, almost causing Zara's laptop to slide off the edge of the table in front of her seat. She grabbed it hurriedly and closed the lid, then checked that her seat belt was buckled securely. Gideon followed suit. They were chasing the day west, so the sun was still high in the sky overhead. He couldn't see any obviously inclement weather but reasoned that you probably couldn't see turbulence anyway.

For about twenty seconds the jet flew straight and level. Then the wings began rocking sharply from side to side, causing Gideon's stomach to lurch in time with the motion. The plane's gyrations grew steadily more intense as the seconds passed by, the jet first climbing several hundred feet rapidly, then just as quickly dropping back toward the sea.

Gideon glanced nervously up at the screen on the wall that depicted their present location. The icon that represented the jet was almost touching the Canadian coast, about a hundred miles north of the US border.

"You think we're going down?" Zara asked lightly.

He shrugged. "Maybe it's time to stick our heads between our legs and kiss our respective asses goodbye."

Even as he said it, the noise of the engines audibly diminished. Gideon's ears popped as the plane rapidly lowered several thousand feet in altitude before leveling out in another G-force-inducing maneuver.

"Shame," Zara said softly. "I was really looking forward to seeing the expression on McKinney's face when we knocked on his front door."

The seat belt sign flickered on overhead, immediately attracting both Gideon and Zara's attention. It was the only piece of communication they'd had from the cockpit throughout the entire flight.

Until the intercom crackled a moment later.

"Montreal Tower, this is Bombardier November-Alpha-782 declaring an emergency, over," Jesse said, his voice strained but professional.

Gideon and Zara immediately traded worried looks.

"What the hell?" he said softly.

In a more distant tone, as if the voice was coming from the other end of a pipe, a woman said in a distinctly Canadian accent, "November-Alpha-782, go ahead with your emergency, over."

"I guess Jesse's figured out a workaround for the problem of how to communicate with us without being picked up on the black box," Zara suggested.

"We have a failure on engine one and need immediate clearance for emergency landing, requesting vector to nearest runway, over."

"Understood, 782, you are clear direct to runway 24-right," the air traffic controller said calmly. "All traffic held and emergency services on standby. Advise your current fuel and passenger status, over?"

"Copy, Montreal," Jesse transmitted. "We have ninety minutes of fuel and zero passengers on board. Repeat, no passengers on board, over."

"I guess it's going to be a surprise when the fire trucks turn up, huh?" Zara said, drumming her fingertips against the table in front of her. Her expression was tense.

"Yeah," Gideon agreed. "We'll just have to try and lose them in the chaos. What are the fucking chances?"

Strangely, despite the imminent prospect of dying in a fiery ball of igniting jet fuel as the Bombardier business jet completed a rapid, unscheduled disassembly a few hundred feet short of the runway, he felt completely calm.

Unlike the more immediately dangerous events of the last

few days—surviving the hit squad at the Legion's château, then the gang hit in Marseille—there was really nothing he could do about a technical failure on board a tin can at twenty thousand feet. He had no rabbits left or hats to pull them out of. Neither could he shoot his way out of this problem.

He stared at the screen and watched as the icon ate up most of the Canadian province of New Brunswick. The aircraft felt somehow sluggish, as though it was barely struggling to stay aloft, but the turbulence was mostly a thing of the past. The plane started descending through the cloud layer, and for almost a full minute only white was visible on the other side of the jet's body. Water vapor formed on the exterior windows.

As they dropped beneath the clouds, the intercom activated once again. For several long seconds, only heavy panting was audible before Jesse finally radioed, "Montreal Center, NA782, Mayday, Mayday, Mayday, experiencing severe hydraulic failure, losing altitude, request diversion to nearest suitable airfield, over."

Gideon stiffened in his chair. *What are the fucking chances?*

"782, Mayday acknowledged. Divert to Northern Aroostook Regional Airport, Frenchville, Maine. Squawk 7700, over."

"Diverting Northern Aroostook Regional, copy, squawking 7700. NA782."

"Boston Center is informed of your situation. Switch to frequency 121.6 for coordination with Northern Aroostook Regional, over."

"Copy, Montreal Center, switching frequency. NA782 out." The intercom clicked back off, and the Bombardier banked gently to the left.

Gideon let out a low, quiet whistle to attract Zara's attention since her eyes were still glued to the screen. "Is the Wi-Fi still working?"

"What for? Hell of a time to check your emails."

"Pass me the laptop."

Zara did as she was asked, her dark eyes staring curiously back at him.

He fired up the device and opened a commercial flight-tracking website. The Internet on board the Bombardier jet was surprisingly fast, and the overhead map quickly populated with tiny yellow icons that each represented one of the tens of thousands of aircraft currently aloft over the entire globe.

"What are you doing?" Zara asked.

Gideon didn't answer. At least not immediately. He kept zooming in on the airspace around Montreal.

"Don't react," he said in a low voice that no microphone would be capable of picking up—at least not over the background aircraft noise. "But everything we just heard was an act."

Zara's eyes narrowed. "How do you know?"

He flipped her laptop screen back around and showed her the zoomed-in view over Montreal. "Because if that was really Montreal Center Jesse was talking to, every single one of these planes would have been put into a holding pattern miles from the runway. Watch."

He moved the mouse pointer and clicked on one of the icons that was heading directly for the runway. It was British Airways flight BA95, and they watched as it dropped below a thousand feet in altitude.

"The voice on the intercom said that they were holding all traffic. Doesn't look like it to me."

Gideon turned the laptop back around and brought up an image of Northern Aroostook Regional Airport on Google Maps. It was a tiny airfield in the middle of nowhere, miles from the nearest settlement and hours from the nearest SWAT team but with a runway long enough to accommodate the Bombardier business jet. Only a handful of buildings were scattered around the runway. There was barely even a hangar. It couldn't be staffed by more than a dozen people on a busy day.

"So what are you saying?" Zara asked, now tightly gripping her seat's armrests. All the color had drained from her cheeks.

Gideon's eyes were glued to the laptop screen as he inhaled every detail of the airfield's surroundings. "If I was going to plan an ambush, this is exactly where I'd put it."

FORTY

"We need to find something to use as a weapon," Gideon said tersely as he rushed toward the galley at the back of the plane. He started pulling open metal cabinets and drawers, caring less for subtlety now that the bombardier was coming in to land. The thicker air at this altitude was generating significantly more sound—as was the lowering of the landing gear.

Hydraulic problems, my ass.

"I hate to break it to you," Zara said as she followed suit and joined him. "But we're on a plane. Best I can rustle up is a blunt butter knife."

"Correction," Gideon said as he opened a cabinet and found an assortment of clearly expensive cutlery. "We're on a private jet. And it looks like they don't play by the same rules."

He pulled out a pair of steak knives. The blades were short and would have a hard time hacking through a decent T-bone, but with enough force they would be capable of penetrating human flesh.

He doubted it would go that far. Despite the fact that Jesse and his copilot had betrayed them, Gideon didn't really expect they had done so willingly. It was far more likely that somebody —probably Senator McKinney or someone working for him— had gotten to them.

"Okay," Zara said, accepting the blade he offered her and pressing it flat and tight against her chest. "What's your plan?"

"Working on it," he replied.

She rushed over to the nearest cabin window. "Well, it looks like you've got about thirty seconds to come up with something that'll save both our lives. We're about to touch down."

"You know what they say when you bring a knife to a gunfight?" Gideon asked, buckling himself back into his seat and gesturing for Zara to do the same, just in case the pilots attempted a last-minute maneuver to incapacitate their cargo.

Zara shook her head.

"You should've brought a gun." Gideon grinned. His expression immediately turned serious. "If this goes wrong and someone out there gets the drop on you—don't be a hero, okay? This isn't the movies. They won't let you get close enough with a blade to do any damage."

"What do you mean *if?*" Zara replied through gritted teeth.

Treetops whipped past outside the aircraft's windows. The jet was briefly level with a low red brick terminal building before that, too, disappeared out of sight. An instant later, the landing gear absorbed the impact, the flaps engaged, and the Bombardier began slowing.

"I intend to even the odds," Gideon explained. "I just don't know if I'll succeed."

"Even them how?"

He surreptitiously shook his head. The small private jet was able to brake much faster than a commercial airliner, and within thirty seconds of touching down it was already rolling to a near stop. The pilots appeared to have powered down the engines—so the only sound in the cabin was the air-conditioning system.

Moments later, the jet came to a complete halt. Gideon unbuckled his belt and leaned forward in his seat, knowing he would have to time this perfectly. He concealed the steak knife between his forearm and armrest.

The cockpit door was essentially impenetrable—at least to anything he could fashion on board. He needed to wait for the pilots to exit on their own. And they wouldn't do that if they could see him waiting for them with a knife on the cockpit door camera.

Zara waved to attract his attention, then silently pointed out the window. He glanced out to see a fire truck and a black SUV speeding toward them from the direction of the airport terminal. He nodded to indicate he understood, then turned his attention back front as the cockpit door rattled from the inside. It opened a crack, then swung fully wide to reveal both pilots hurriedly pulling off their headphones and standing up.

"Quickly!" Jesse said, wearing only a white shirt. The armpits of his shirt were damp from exertion and stained yellow. The copilot, who they'd barely seen until now, was pale with nerves. "We have to get the hell off this thing before the fuel lines ignite."

"I don't think so," Gideon said firmly, leaping to his feet and closing the couple of yards' distance in a blink of an eye.

He held the steak knife in his left hand and drew his right back in a fist, lashing a powerful blow at the copilot, whose head snapped back before his entire body went limp and dropped to the floor of the plane.

Gideon quickly switched the blade into his dominant right hand.

"What the hell are you doing?" Jesse said, gesturing limply

at the jet's exit door. "This is a fucking emergency. We need to evacuate before it's too late!"

"Stop bullshitting me," Gideon said coldly. He grabbed Jesse by the shoulder and swung him around so that his left arm was pressed into a bar over the pilot's throat. "Back into the cockpit."

He gave the man a push, and both men stepped over the body of the unconscious copilot. Jesse stank of body odor; he was completely unlike the composed, suave pilot they'd met just twelve hours earlier in Turin. The scent was almost acidic. It smelled of fear.

Gideon saw Zara covering the cockpit door behind him, her eyes on the sleeping copilot. She briefly crouched and checked his pulse, then rose once more and peered out of the nearest window. "Fire truck's about twenty seconds away."

He nodded curtly, then forced Jesse into one of the two pilot seats. He stood behind him, making sure the man knew how close the steel blade was to his carotid artery. "How long does it take to start this thing up?"

"For what?" Jesse replied, his voice weak. He was noticeably no longer protesting his innocence. "We don't have the fuel to lift off. At least, not if you want to land afterward."

"I don't care about taking off," Gideon said inscrutably.

"You just want to get the engines going?" Jesse asked. "Why?"

Gideon pressed the blade against the side of the man's neck. "Just fucking tell me."

"Three minutes, maybe. There are pre-start checks, wait periods for engine pressure to stabilize…"

"I don't care about any of that. I want the engines up and running inside thirty seconds. When I tell you, do exactly as I say—or I'll cut your throat."

"They'll kill my children!" Jesse protested, his voice coming out in a pitiful wail. "Please, you have to understand—they threatened me."

"They're coming," Zara called out from behind him. "Your three o'clock."

Gideon peered out of the cockpit window. "I see them."

The black SUV was an unlikely choice for a rural airport's emergency vehicle, he thought. What Zara had believed to be a fire truck was actually a red ambulance. Both vehicles started braking and came to a stop about thirty feet in front of the Bombardier.

"Now *I'm* threatening you," Gideon said icily as he returned his attention to the pilot. "Punch the engines up. Now!"

"My kids," he stammered. "I can't..."

"Let me tell you a secret, Jesse," Gideon growled. "They don't care about your children. Killing kids attracts way too much attention. But you—you were never getting out of this alive. I don't want to kill you. I'm not like them. But I will if I have to. It's your choice."

His hands shaking over the vast sea of switches, display readouts, and other controls, Jesse did as he was told.

"Powering up the APU," he said. "It takes a sec... there."

He flicked a switch. "Engine one start," he said, his voice growing clinical and detached, as if slipping into the usual preflight routine was almost meditative.

Another switch. "Engine two start. Both engines are online."

"Good," Gideon said, watching the rear doors on the airport's ambulance swing open and two uniformed medics jump out. One of them grabbed a bag from inside the ambulance while the other made a crossed-arms gesture toward the cockpit.

"They want us to shut them down," Jesse said.

"Well, that ain't gonna happen," Gideon replied firmly. He stabbed his finger at the black SUV. "You see that?"

"Yeah..."

"I want you to drive into it. Push the throttle forward and give this thing as much power as she's got."

"Um, Gideon?" Zara piped up from behind him. "Everything okay up there? Because I thought I just heard you planning a plane crash."

"It's more of a fender bender," Gideon said, growing tired of Jesse's procrastination and reaching for the throttle himself. He started pushing it forward, mainly to prompt Jesse to actually take control. "At least, it will be for us."

The jet's engines ramped up more quickly than he could ever remember hearing on a commercial flight. It didn't sound healthy, but he had bigger problems to worry about than an airplane mechanic's future workload right now. Soon the whistle grew high-pitched and the jet started to shake.

He watched the two "medics" intently, doubting they had a clear view of what was happening behind the cockpit window from down there. They barely seemed to react even as the business jet began slowly rolling toward them, as though what they were watching simply didn't compute. The one clutching the bag only threw it to one side and began sprinting for the grass at the edge of the runway when the airplane had already closed half the distance to the two stopped vehicles. The other drew a pistol and opened fire—finally and completely revealing the ambush for exactly what it was. His rounds went high before he too dove for cover.

The driver of the black SUV also chose that moment to belatedly realize that something was wrong. The vehicle shook, then began to inch backward—but not as fast as the Bombardier was now accelerating.

"Oh God..." Jesse whispered under his breath as the business jet's nose disappeared over the SUV's windshield.

The impact was less impressive than Gideon had expected—at least until a ferocious metallic screech briefly overpowered even the whine of the plane's engines. He quickly realized that the SUV must have become trapped against the aircraft's landing gear.

As the ground speed indicator hit sixty miles an hour, two things happened. First, the landing gear snapped and the jet's nose suddenly dropped a dozen feet. Second, the underside of the jet landed on the roof of the SUV, sending a jolt through the cabin and almost causing Gideon to accidentally slice into Jesse's throat.

"Pull the throttle back," Gideon instructed the pilot as he recovered his footing, worried that the sparks now streaking out from either side of the aircraft—presumably a result of metal scraping against asphalt—would ignite either the fuel in the car or, even worse, the jet itself. "But don't stop until we reach that fence."

"You're fucking crazy..." Jesse moaned.

"Don't forget it."

When they hit the end of the runway and traded green grass for gray asphalt, the SUV somehow freed itself from the aircraft's death grasp, which caused the plane's nose to drop all the way to the ground. Jesse finally pulled back on the throttle even as the aircraft bucked wildly beneath them, his control growing more haphazard by the second.

"I don't think anybody's making it out of that thing alive," Zara said somberly from behind him, apparently catching a glimpse of the destroyed vehicle in the plane's side window.

"I won't lose any sleep over it," Gideon said matter-of-factly.

"We need to evacuate!" Jesse screamed, panic clear in his

voice as he pulled the throttle control all the way back. "We have a fuel leak. Fuck!

He leapt out of the pilot's seat, not bothering to kill the engines, even leaping over the corpse of his colleague in his mad rush for the exits.

Gideon turned calmly to Zara, dropping the knife as he did so. It would be useless outside. Fear was visible in her eyes.

He grinned. "I guess he's telling the truth this time."

FORTY-ONE

The stench of spilled kerosene stung the back of Gideon's nostrils and caused Zara to audibly gag as she clambered down the stairs that folded out of the jet's side door.

When it hit the grass at the end of the runway, the jet's left wing had pitched into the earth, causing the entire aircraft to lean in a drunken angle. She toppled out and plunged shoulder-first into the grass, then reached frantically for her spilled laptop.

Gideon grabbed the unconscious copilot by the torso and dragged him toward the open doorway. The man's face was an artwork of dark, already congealed blood that had trickled down his chin and fresher streams that were still trickling out. His nose would require splinting at the minimum and maybe significant surgical work before he would be able to breathe freely once again.

"Hurry!" Zara yelled. Unhelpful, given Gideon was well aware of the ticking clock he was working against.

He could hear the crackling of flames and taste soot on the back of his tongue. It wouldn't take long for the fire to catch in earnest. When that happened, he had approximately half a second before the entire jet exploded.

Bracing a foot on either side of the doorway, Gideon pushed his hands underneath the copilot's armpits and gripped the top of his shoulders, hooking himself in tight. Grunting from the effort, he slowly lowered the man toward the grass.

"Drop him," Zara called out. "He's close enough, and we're out of time."

Gideon followed her command and released his grip, exhaling at the relief he immediately felt in his aching shoulders and back. He slipped out after the man, landing with feline grace on the balls of his feet. He hoisted the copilot over his shoulder in a fireman's carry and sprinted away from the plane as fast as he could.

He planted his foot in a thick tuft of grass about fifty feet away and tripped, the unfamiliar weight on his shoulder causing him to spin as he fell and landed heavily on his lower back.

"Crap," he muttered.

If he said anything else, the words were lost in the explosion that followed. The remaining fuel in the Bombardier's tanks went up like a Roman candle. The first flash of white light was so searing it passed through Gideon's closed eyelids. The shock wave that followed a couple of seconds after punched the oxygen from his lungs and swept all breathable air ahead of it.

Gideon rolled onto his back and gasped for breath, hands clutching at his throat as an instinctive panic briefly hit him. A strong wind followed the shock wave, bringing much-needed air in its wake. He greedily sucked down several deep breaths, just enough to get him going again, and forced himself back upright.

Zara was on her hands and knees a couple of feet ahead of him. She was shaking.

"You okay?" he said, still struggling to speak. His ears rang from the effect of the explosion like a broken class bell.

"I'll live," she panted in response. She gripped his forearm and pulled herself upright. "It was kind of touch and go there for a minute."

"Come on, we need to keep moving," he said. "They'll be here any second."

Every fiber of Gideon's core screamed at him to stand and fight. Every neuron in his brain told him that the only choice that remained to them was to run. They were unarmed, likely suffering from low-grade traumatic brain injuries, and had just entered the United States illegally in the most spectacular fashion.

Even if they miraculously stumbled across weapons, they couldn't afford to waste the time an engagement would cost them. Someone—Homeland Security, the state police, if they had them in Maine—would have a chopper up in minutes. They had to be gone before it arrived.

"What about him?" Zara said, gesturing at the unconscious copilot.

Gideon glanced around for the man's colleague, but Jesse was nowhere to be seen. He shrugged grimly. "We've done all we can."

THE AMBULANCE CAREERED out of the pyre of smoke that coursed up into the sky from the crippled jet aircraft just as Gideon and Zara entered the tree line that bordered the airport. Neither looked back to see whether their escape had been noticed.

They just ran, branches whipping at the skin on their arms and thorns tearing into their shins. When one stumbled, the other grabbed them by the shoulder and hauled them back up.

Gideon crashed out of the woods and pumped the brakes after finding himself on the grass verge by an asphalt road. It was potholed and covered in leaves. He reached out and caught Zara, preventing her from running out into the open.

"Sorry," he whispered as he pushed her down toward the ground.

Another tree line bracketed the opposite side of the road, though that section of woods was clearly much more thinned out. If he looked closely, Gideon could catch glimpses of fields stretching into the distance on the far side.

"Open ground," he mouthed. "No bueno."

The alternative, however, was returning to the woods and the thick undergrowth that had left dead, brown pine needles in their hair and thorns and splinters of wood puncturing their clothes. Every step back there cost twice as much energy as one on flat ground. Worse, progress through the underbrush was half as quick.

They simply couldn't afford to take it slow. Speed was everything at a time like this. The longer they delayed, the less chance they had of escaping alive.

"We'll follow the road," Gideon said decisively, entirely at ease with his choice the moment he made it. "Be ready to hide the second I tell you to."

Zara nodded her agreement. They seemed to have made some sort of pact. Despite her survival and fieldcraft training at the Farm, he was clearly the expert in this domain. Despite only knowing each other for forty-eight hours, they acted as a well-oiled team. She deferred to him as absolutely in this as he did to her superior skills of analysis and investigation.

That wasn't to say that she was an amateur. In fact, she

moved with surprising precision, her footwork light and nimble over the uneven ground at the border of the overgrown verge and tree line. They were making at least five miles an hour despite the unfavorable conditions.

It was a good pace, but he knew that it wouldn't last. Both of them were running on empty. He in particular had been pushed way past his limits for days now, barely sleeping or eating. They would have to slow down or risk injury—a twisted ankle or broken leg would be far more damaging to their prospects of survival than the alternative.

"Down," Gideon hissed, trusting his tingling instincts before he was even consciously aware of what he was reacting to.

He dropped low and melted into the woods to his right. Zara reacted nearly as fast and crouched at his side, her eyes scanning left and right in search of whatever it was that had alerted him.

Gideon rotated his neck, trusting more in his hearing than his eyesight. The road curved slightly around to the right, meaning they only had visibility over about half a mile of it. He closed his eyes, exhaled...

His eyes snapped open. Pointing to their left, he tapped his ear. Zara's eyes narrowed, then she seemed to understand his meaning and cocked her head to one side to listen.

Engine noise. Something heavy.

He got his answer less than thirty seconds later. A black GMC SUV just like the one they'd run down in the jet emerged into view, driving no faster than ten miles an hour. Gideon saw that all four windows were rolled down. He made himself go entirely still, barely even breathing with the knowledge that the human eye is attracted to one thing above all else: movement.

So they have backup, he noted.

It made sense. He had already survived at least two attempts on his life—one of which had involved some of his country's most dangerous operatives. Whoever these psychopaths were, they clearly wanted him dead extremely badly and had access to the resources to make it happen. This time they wouldn't have left anything to chance.

What was equally clear was that this changed the calculation entirely. Running had been possible when all they were facing was a couple of men in a slow, unwieldy ambulance. That small party would have been completely unable to cover all of their potential avenues of escape.

But what were the chances that this was the only enemy vehicle in the area? It certainly wasn't driving in any particular hurry. Quite the opposite, in fact—the driver was acting as though he had all the time in the world.

They both held their breath as the SUV inched past. Gideon closed his eyes until they were little more than slits of vision obscured by a thick forest of eyelashes, knowing that the brain was trained to detect patterns—and nothing triggered it more than another set of eyes staring back.

Whether Zara followed suit or not, he didn't know. Either way, the vehicle passed without incident. He saw two sets of eyes staring out of the passenger windows, sweeping into the gloom. Resting on the bottom of the rear window was a rifle muzzle.

Definitely not friendly.

Neither of them moved a fraction of an inch until the SUV had completely disappeared from sight. Zara turned slowly and flashed four fingers at him.

He nodded. "I counted the same."

"Who the fuck are these people?" she said with a frustrated grimace. "How can they pull together so many shooters on such short notice? Even McKinney can't keep losing Agency assets forever without attracting attention. There's something we're missing."

"We can figure it out when we get out of here," he replied assertively, scanning the road left and right before stepping back out of the tree line.

They kept moving, but not for long. The section of woodland that ran along the road ended abruptly in a field that had been plowed for the summer crop. Green shoots were already springing out of the long rows of dark, tilled earth, but the stalks didn't yet reach knee height. It was sparse cover. The only positive was that the black SUV was no longer in sight.

"We don't have a choice," Gideon said, accurately reading the expression on Zara's face. "We can't stay here."

"Then what?"

Gideon chewed his lip, weighing the two options. If they went across the field, they risked injury, but at least they had somewhere to hide, even if he didn't rate their chances of remaining invisible too highly. The road was even more exposed.

But it would be quicker.

"We run," he decided. "Straight down the road, heading for that next patch of forest. It's what, half a mile?"

"About that," Zara agreed.

"You run, right?" he said, eyeing her up. She had the tone, lithe frame of someone who kept herself in decent shape. More than that, she had more grit than anyone he'd ever met. At least, he was pretty sure that was the case.

"Yeah," she snorted in response. "Down the banks of the Seine with Taylor pumping into my ears."

"I don't know who that is," Gideon said.

Zara laughed sincerely despite their peril. "That must make you the only person on the planet."

"Ready?"

She nodded confidently. "Let's do it."

Despite their shared exhaustion, they set a rapid pace. The road angled slightly downhill, which helped, but Zara was just as fit as she looked. Gideon's natural athleticism propelled him forward, driving her to her limits.

They almost made it.

FORTY-TWO

"Faster!" Gideon yelled as they hit the tree line, bullets cracking into trunks and branches all around them and causing leaves and twigs to fall like rain.

A black SUV had spotted them seconds before they reached safety. It accelerated toward them before screeching to a halt at the edge of the forest.

"Are you hurt?" he said, panting from exertion as they reached a streambed that had carved its way through the undergrowth. The ground tumbled down sharply toward it, the sudden change in terrain almost causing him to lose balance before he steadied himself.

A few feet to his right a massive, ancient tree had toppled in a storm and bridged the stream. The trunk was shattered and covered in green moss, but enough of the magnificent structure remained that he was certain it would hold their weight. It would be a quicker way across than clambering down into the water and then up the other side of the bank.

"I'm good," Zara replied, reaching up to dab the blood streaming from a scratch on her face only when they were safely across the toppled tree trunk. "I think I got caught by a branch."

Fresh volleys of gunfire rang out from behind them, but it was clear the enemy didn't know which direction they'd taken. It was some comfort, but Gideon knew the respite wouldn't last long. They were outnumbered. At least six bad guys remained—four from the SUV, and two from the ambulance. He guessed it was probably more than that and worked that estimation into his calculations.

"We can't keep running," he said, slowing so that they could maintain a conversation. "There are too many of them. They'll run us down."

"Then—," Zara started, before glancing up at the forest canopy, her brow furrowed.

Gideon followed her lead. He spoke in a hushed tone. "What is it?"

"I'm not sure. Maybe nothing. I thought I heard something."

"Could be a chopper," Gideon said with a grimace.

"Yeah, maybe..."

"We can't keep reacting," Gideon said, returning to his previous theme. "They've got us dancing like puppets on their strings. They'll tire us out then run us down. We need to change the rules."

"That sounds all well and good," Zara said, still raking the treetops with her gaze, "but I was hoping you had an actual plan."

Gideon cocked his head to one side, listening to yet another rattle of bullets. They sounded closer now, indicating that their opponents had exited the SUV and entered the forest on foot.

"We need wheels and we need guns, and I only know one place where we can find them."

Zara looked momentarily puzzled, then went very, very pale. "Oh, no. You can't be serious."

"I'm not asking you to fight," Gideon said, not bothering to conceal the pained expression on his face.

"No. You want to use me as bait," she said, on the verge of hyperventilating before she visibly controlled herself. She closed her eyes and breathed steadily for a few seconds before they snapped back open and she said, "I'll do it."

"We can find another way."

Zara shook her head. "I have to do this. Call it penance."

THE PLAN WAS SIMPLE. They crept back toward the spot at which they'd entered the forest together, both alert for any sign of ambush. The gunfire had subsided, and the woods were now deathly still—all birdlife having leapt into the skies at the first sign of danger.

Zara's task was to attract the attention of the dismounted shooters—ideally from as great a distance as possible to minimize the risk she was taking. With the majority of the enemy distracted, Gideon had to somehow capture the SUV they'd abandoned.

It was a shitty plan, and it definitely wouldn't be that easy. The vehicle was unlikely to be unguarded, and Zara's only defense against rifle bullets was to make sure she wasn't in their way.

Even if Gideon succeeded in capturing the SUV, Zara would still be in grave danger. He would have to find some way of attracting the attention of the men pursuing her. The plan seemed almost destined to fail.

But both knew it was their only shot.

"Good luck," she said. Her expression was determined, but

a muscle twitched on her left temple. Gideon guessed he probably looked the same way.

"Right back at ya," he said, squeezing her shoulder.

And then it was time.

They separated not far from the tree line. Zara turned left—following the sounds of men moving through the underbrush—and Gideon right. They hadn't discussed how he would know when to strike, though they both knew the answer.

You'll know.

He crept toward the tree line in a low crouch, moving foot by foot, carefully scanning the ground ahead of him to make sure he didn't step on a branch or get his foot stuck in a rabbit warren. When he closed within ten feet, he dropped to his belly and crawled, despite the thorns and sharp twigs that jabbed his exposed flesh.

The sun was dropping in the sky as the clouds turned pink and teased the arrival of evening. Already, there was a chill in the air, accented by Gideon's failure to grab his jacket in the hair-raising escape from the burning jet.

He blocked it all out.

Pushing his chest upright, Gideon raised himself fractions of an inch at a time above the brush at the edge of the forest. And then he saw the SUV. It had been driven across the field and parked almost at the edge of the woods. Another was pulled up close behind it. He'd been right about the bad guys coming in force.

His brow furrowed.

What the hell?

Three men remained by the first SUV. One of them was dressed exactly as Gideon had expected—in dark battle fatigues and armed with an automatic rifle. It was how the other two were attired that caused the gears in his mind to momentarily seize up.

They each had a device with a long antenna in their hands. It looked like some kind of radio. The VR headsets on their faces were the real giveaway, however. Gideon closed his eyes and cursed the fact that he hadn't paid more attention when Zara looked up at the forest canopy.

"Drones..."

ZARA CROUCHED BEHIND A TREE TRUNK. She'd worked her way around the party of men searching the forest for her and Gideon, finding an unexpected thrill in the task. Strangely, she was more excited than scared.

The search party didn't seem to have any idea where she was. They'd turned back on themselves several times and had even given up firing into the trees, apparently realizing that the tactic of attempting to scare her out wasn't working. She'd positioned herself at least fifty yards ahead of them. It might've been more like sixty or seventy, but it was difficult to be precise in the thick woodland.

The question was—what now?

Do I whistle?

She smiled at the thought, as though she was starring in some high school movie and trying to head off a group of bullies —not a party of armed men who wanted her dead.

The smile faded.

Still, she was far enough ahead of the gunmen to be relatively certain that she would be able to stay ahead of them. At least for a time.

Then it was up to Gideon.

"You better come good," she muttered.

She turned one last time to scout the escape route she'd chosen. She'd picked out what looked like an animal trail—deer, maybe—through an extremely thick section of forest. It would be slow going, but even slower for the likely much broader men behind her. Her other advantage was that the rows of compact trees blocked out the last of the daylight from overhead and made it difficult to see more than ten or twenty feet in any direction.

Zara scanned her immediate vicinity, recognizing the diversion she was looking for the moment she laid eyes upon it. A tree about three or four times her height had been uprooted at some point and fallen against its nearest neighbor. Their branches were deeply entangled, the timber no longer green and supple but visibly brittle.

"You'll do."

There was no time to calculate angles, and besides, Zara was no lumberjack. She simply leaned against the fallen tree, pushing with all the force she could generate until...

CRACK.

A branch high above her, possibly the last major structure keeping the tree in place, snapped. The tree wobbled for a second, and Zara looked down to see that the earth beneath her feet was wobbling.

"Shit..."

She threw herself backward just in time to escape as the remaining roots beneath the soil whipped upward right where her feet had been planted. The tree came down with a thundering crash, breaking into several pieces as it hit the ground. High above, branches kept cracking as other, smaller trees began to sway.

Despite the near miss, Zara cupped her palms around her mouth and screamed until her throat was raw, as if she'd sustained a horrific injury.

Then she ran.

She ducked and dove and dodged whipping tree branches

as if she was a character in an arcade game. In less than a minute, her clothes were torn from the full-tilt flight through the hemmed-in forest.

Male voices echoed from behind her, punctuated every few seconds by the crackle of gunfire. As far as she could tell none of the bullets came near her.

But it was only a matter of time.

Zara tripped on a root that protruded from the soil and fell hard, eating a mouthful of leaves and dirt as the air was punched from her lungs. Gasping for breath, knowing she didn't have the luxury of nursing her wounds, she forced herself back upright.

And froze.

There was something out there, she was sure of it. Something alien. The sound was unnatural and wrong.

Like a... *buzzing*.

Zara looked up, attracted by a flitting movement in her peripheral vision. She saw something overhead, flying above the level of the forest's smaller trees and bushes, where the foliage wasn't so compact.

"What the hell?"

It took her a moment to place what she was seeing, so unlikely was it. It wasn't the drone that confused her—it was what it appeared to be carrying. For a moment, she thought she saw an RPG round, not propelled on a cloud of fire and smoke but simply floating overhead. But that was impossible. She had to be seeing things.

Except it wasn't. And she wasn't.

The pieces of the puzzle clicked into place. She'd read reports about these things—even seen videos of their deployment in the war in Ukraine. Cheap RPG rounds could be attached to high-powered quadcopter drones to create what was effectively a precision-guided missile at a hundredth of the cost.

Zara stared up at the device, momentarily too stunned even to move. Maybe that was for the best. Its operator—for the drones were equipped with cameras—couldn't have seen her yet. Her lack of movement delayed her discovery a few seconds longer.

She searched her memory for everything she knew about the things. They had a single camera, usually, which pointed in the same direction in which it flew. So the operators could only see what lay in front of the weapon they piloted.

Can I outrun it?

She was certain the answer was no. The drones could fly much faster than she could possibly run. She wasn't sure how long their range was, but she was pretty confident it was measured in miles, not feet. The forest might affect that some, but it was impossible to say by how much.

And they were fast. Damn fast; she could already see that from the effortless way it skimmed the canopy, rotating slowly as it searched for a target.

Zara dropped to the ground and squashed her body behind a tree trunk, too terrified even to draw breath. Cold sweat trickled down her temple.

"Come on, Gideon," she whispered, her stomach convulsing with nerves.

She was trapped in a bind now. If she ran, the drone would surely detect her presence and complete its one-way trip. The explosive on board was easily enough to blow her to bits. But if she stayed where she was then the men with guns who she'd so confidently beckoned toward her would soon catch up.

Her only hope was to pray for a miracle.

None came.

The drone flew in a pattern of long, lazy figure eights overhead. It was hard to be sure with the way the sound bounced off the trees and was deadened by the leaves, but she thought there was another one doing the same a quarter mile or so to her right.

Zara kept her eyes on the deadly bird, circling an enormous tree trunk so that she always stayed behind it even as she heard the sound of men's footsteps crashing through the undergrowth just twenty or thirty yards behind. Her situation couldn't hold.

The drone spun fast, whether by chance or design, too fast for her to react in time. She stared up at the detonator at the very tip of the explosive round, eyes wide with fear.

And then she ran.

FORTY-THREE

The explosion echoed through the forest, shaking loose the last few birds that hadn't already flown the coop. They raced up into the sky, cawing their displeasure with every flap of their wings.

Gideon's stomach was suddenly gripped by a wave of nausea so intense he almost doubled over and retched. Even before the blast stopped echoing through the treetops, he cursed himself for being so damn stupid.

If he'd known the drones were armed...

"You get 'em?" one of the drone operators called out excitedly. He was barely out of his teens but was old enough to know that this wasn't just a video game. He was excited about killing. That was why he was here.

"Not sure," the other operator shrugged, rolling his neck before lifting up the VR headset he was wearing. "Foliage was pretty thick. Hey, Kane—come take a look. Tell me what you think."

"Tell me about it," the first said, his fingers racing across the buttons and knobs on the controller in his hands as he rotated his own armed drone. He was entirely lost in his own world.

The third bad guy—Kane, it seemed he was called—was the sentry. He was the adult with the gun who watched over the two kids with their videogame headsets to make sure that nobody did what Gideon was planning. Despite the fearsome firepower they could call down, as long as they were plugged in, the drone operators were almost defenseless to threats in their vicinity.

Kane's job was to watch over them. And right now, as he trudged over toward the operator of the drone that had just detonated—who was now picking up an iPad to replay the video like it was some kind of spectator sport—he was doing a pretty crappy job. He had almost no awareness of what was around him, barely even bothering to scan the tree line. He clearly assumed that his quarry was on the run.

Gideon's resolve hardened. He had no idea whether Zara was alive or dead. But he had to work on the assumption that she was still breathing. And that at any moment either Kane's friends in the woods or the kid with the second functioning drone might hunt her down.

The first of the two SUV's was parked almost nose-tight to the tree line. Gideon used it as cover, creeping behind it to work his way around the group of men positioned on the other side. The plugged-in drone operator was sitting on a green ammunition crate, and Kane and the other operator stood focused on the iPad.

"I got nothing," the kid called out. "You must've whacked them."

As Gideon passed, he silently pulled open the near-side passenger door of the SUV. He grimaced as he realized that there was nothing useful within reach—just a graveyard of drinks cans and candy wrappers. It looked like any additional weapons were stowed in the trunk. And there was no way he could pop that without attracting attention.

You're going to have to do this the old-fashioned way...

Gideon planted his left shoulder against the side of the SUV and sucked in one last deep breath of oxygen. He fixed the position of the three men in his mental map and ranked them in order of the risk they posed. All three were armed, but Kane was clearly the most dangerous. He doubted the other two were overly proficient with the sidearms strapped to their thighs.

"Only one way to find out," he said under his breath.

He charged toward Kane, quickly building to his top speed. The man was only ten yards away, but the distance felt like an Olympic sprint. The world seemed to slow for Gideon as Kane and the drone operators' heads spun around at the sound of his footsteps.

"Who—?"

Too late. Gideon dropped his shoulder, tightened his core, and speared into Kane's side. The fatigue-clad shooter was kitted out in body armor, which helped disperse some of the force of the blow. But not all. Gideon thought he heard ribs crack as the sentry hit the ground.

He was certain he heard the man's arm break. It sounded like a damn gunshot.

For an instant, nothing happened. The drone operator with the iPad just stared down, open-mouthed. Kane hadn't yet realized that a shard of bone was sticking out of the flesh of his forearm. He slowly lifted his wounded arm until it was at eye level.

And screamed.

Gideon reached for the man's rifle, which had fallen to the ground in the struggle. He flicked the safety even as he spun back around to face the operator, who was now scrambling to free his pistol from its holster.

"Please…" he whimpered as he realized that he was going to be too late.

"Not today," Gideon said grimly. The rifle's stock kicked back against his shoulder, and the kid with the red-rimmed pressure marks on his face dropped like a stone. Gideon turned back and fired three rounds into Kane's body, feeling nothing as the man went limp.

The other operator dropped his controller and ran, his VR goggles still strapped to his face. Just as he managed to push them up and off, he ran headfirst into a tree and stopped with a sickening crunch.

The impact didn't knock him out, but he fell back, his hands clutching his face. Gideon was pretty sure he must have broken several bones. He winced.

But his sympathy didn't last long.

He sprinted over to the writhing teenager—there was no way this kid was older than twenty. His nose was a fountain of blood, and the red marks left by the VR headset were now just a fraction of his problems.

"Up," he growled, grabbing the kid by his dark uniform jacket and pulling him upright.

"What are you doing?" the boy sniffed, more outraged than scared. At least initially.

Gideon marched the operator back to his headset. "Put those on."

"You serious?" the kid said, not seeming to understand the gravity of the predicament he was now in. His voice was squashed and mangled. He pointed at his lopsided nose. "I can't. It hurts."

"I don't give a shit," Gideon said, picking up the headset and ramming it against the kid's chest. He took a step back and aimed the rifle directly between his nipples. "You put it on, or you join your friends over there."

Despite the blood now smearing his face, the drone operator visibly blanched. He nodded jerkily, then hurriedly slipped the headset back on. "I need my handset."

"Don't move," Gideon snapped. He jogged over to the RC controller, picked it up, and gave it to the operator.

"Is it still flying?"

"Yeah," the kid said, his nose blocked up from the now congealing blood. "When they don't receive any input, they just hover in place. Until they run out of battery, anyway."

"Okay," Gideon said, carefully watching what the operator did with his fingers. "Don't think about turning that thing on me. If I see that drone come out of the trees, I promise my bullet will punch through your chest before it hits me."

The drone operator shook his head. He still seemed dazed from his run-in with the forest. "Wait..."

"You're going to do exactly as I tell you," Gideon said firmly. "Find your buddies and ram that thing into the dirt as close to them as you can. I don't give a shit if you like them. It's what you're going to do."

"You're him, aren't you?" the operator said in a hushed voice. "I was only a kid when you left..."

Gunfire rattled in the trees. Gideon's fingers stiffened on the weapon, his muscles growing so tense the barrel shook. Did that mean Zara was still alive?

Or are they just finishing her off?

"I swear, I never believed what they said about you. I remember seeing you once, right in the center of the parade ground. It was before the succession so I was only a kid, but I wanted to be you, man. With the whole world at your feet. Everything changed after that."

Gideon stared in incomprehension at the kid. What was he talking about?

"You have three seconds," he said coldly. "Get that drone moving."

"I'll do it. You're back, aren't you? That's why they want you dead. The whole thing's fucking corrupt, man. I know it wasn't always like this."

The kid's fingers raced across his controller. Gideon glanced nervously at the trees, wondering whether he was being played. He didn't have time to analyze whatever the hell the drone operator had just told him.

"Okay," the kid said, his tone growing more businesslike as he settled back into the routine drilled into him by his training. "I see movement. Too much to be just one chick."

Gideon's jaw ground together at the casual tone, but he said nothing.

The kid kept narrating what he saw. "They see me. They think I'm trying to direct them to the target."

"Take them out," Gideon said harshly.

The kid's thumbs hovered over a button, but he hesitated. His voice grew plaintive. "You'll remember me, right? When you come back, I mean. You'll remember what I did for you?"

What the hell?

"What's your name?" Gideon said instead of indulging the confusion he felt.

"Caleb."

Gideon was glad that the headset meant Caleb couldn't see his face. He was losing his battle to conceal his stupefaction at what was happening. "Okay, Caleb. I'll remember you. Now do it."

FORTY-FOUR

Gideon left Caleb with his wrists and ankles trussed with zip-cuffs he found on Kane's corpse. He puzzled over their presence for a moment—why bring them on a kill mission? It didn't make sense.

But perhaps the hit team had subdued the staff at the airport instead of killing them. No matter how important their mission and how powerful the people behind it were, the cold-blooded murder of half a dozen innocent people couldn't be covered up for long in a free society.

The events on the runway could be explained away—a drug shipment gone wrong, perhaps. The media would cover a battle between two cartel factions, perhaps wondering why it had taken place a couple of dozen miles from the Canadian border rather than several thousand miles farther south.

And then the story would be forgotten.

He ran recklessly through the thick forest, his rifle clutched tight to his torso to prevent it from becoming entangled in branches and tendrils of shrubbery. He cared little about the racket his flight through the brush generated. All that mattered was getting to Zara. Finding out whether...

All thoughts of the wider context faded away as he sprinted toward her. It didn't matter. None of it did. Neither finding out who he was nor what forces had conspired to shape this weapon and aim it at him. He'd only known Zara a couple of days, but they'd shared more hardship and overcome more obstacles in that time than many did in an entire lifetime.

As he ran, he saw evidence of Zara's pursuers all around him. They made no attempt to conceal their boot prints in the soft earth underfoot or the broken branches and squashed foliage that marked their path. All around he saw evidence of the gunfire he'd heard a few minutes earlier—pale white wounds on tree trunks and fallen branches chopped down by flying lead.

"Zara?" he yelled, despite the fact that all he could hear was his own breath and the rushing of blood in his eardrums. "You there?"

Nothing.

Still following the trail, he stumbled through the tiny clearing. He almost paid it no mind, until he glimpsed the covering of wood chips that coated the ground. He dug in his heels and spun around.

The cause was obvious. This had to be the impact point of one of the suicide drones—possibly the first he'd heard detonate. The fragmentation warhead had shredded every trunk and branch in a charred circle that measured at least five yards in every direction.

"Shit," he muttered, raising his rifle to his shoulder and spinning around and around, desperately searching for a sign.

Any sign.

Get a hold of yourself.

Gideon bit down hard on his lower lip, hard enough that

the pain overwhelmed his rising anxiety and brought with it an instant of dispassionate calm.

What don't you see?

There was neither a body nor any evidence of blood. If the RPG round had hit Zara or even detonated within a few feet of her, there would have been some evidence of her remains. But all he saw was a small crater in the ground. No clothing swept off in the blast, no blood spatter, no charred corpse.

A faint hope fluttered in his chest, sharper and more intense than it might otherwise have been on account of the despair that preceded it.

Gideon stood in the center of the circle and rotated slowly in place, this time scanning the site with intense focus.

There.

About ten feet ahead of him, just at the edge of the grenade's kill zone, was a mark on the ground where the top layer of soil and decaying leaves had been pushed aside. He jogged over and crouched to examine it more closely. It was thicker at the top and tapered to a sharp point.

It took him a moment to figure out what he was looking at. Somebody—Zara—had tripped as the grenade round detonated. She'd planted her foot, most likely her right, given the orientation of the scrape, but overbalanced and fell forward. Some of her weight pushed through her right leg, and then her forefoot and toe scraped along the ground.

There were other signs that she'd fallen. Indentations that were probably left by her palms or knees as she scrambled along the leaf-strewn, mossy undergrowth. Then a deeper groove where she'd pulled herself back upright and started running.

Gideon pumped his fist and broke back into a run, following the trail that Zara had left behind her. He found her barely fifty yards deeper into the forest, covered in blood, kneeling over the bodies of three mangled corpses.

She looked up as he skidded to a halt in front of her. Her eyes appeared glazed; her expression strangely empty. "I tried to save them…"

He took in the full scene, making a face as the taste of the carnage hit the back of his tongue and throat. There was blood everywhere. A black leather boot had been thrown almost ten feet and stopped only when it hit a tree trunk that was itself scarred by fragments of steel picked up by the explosion. He didn't dare look to see what was inside.

One of the three shooters had clearly died instantly. He must've been within a couple of feet of the suicide drone's impact point because his skin was blistered by heat, his torso shredded by chunks of metal. There was barely any blood—likely because his heart had stopped almost at the moment of impact.

The other two had lived longer. Long enough for someone—he assumed Zara—to reach them and open their first-aid pouches. She'd expertly applied a tourniquet to the blond corpse's left leg, and blood-soaked bandages and gauze were strewn all over the body of the other. Both had died despite her aid. Looking at their injuries, he doubted they could have been saved even if an evac helicopter had been on standby to race them to a fully equipped trauma center.

He sank into a crouch and reached out to touch her. "Are you okay?"

"I tried…"

Gideon reached out and wrapped his arms tenderly around her. She didn't resist as he checked her over for injuries of her own. She was physically fine, save for a few scrapes and bruises that would probably leave her feeling like she'd faced six rounds against Tyson Fury the next morning.

"I know," he said softly, pulling her to her feet. "I know."

FORTY-FIVE

"Eat this," Gideon said, grabbing a bar of chocolate from the center console and pressing it into Zara's hands the second she was safely buckled into the front passenger seat of the black SUV. It already had a bite taken out of it, but right now she needed the calories.

She was deep in shock.

Worse, the sound of rotor blades confirmed that his earlier suspicions had been correct. A law enforcement chopper was in the air, and it wasn't far away.

He tossed the rifle onto the back seat, buckled himself in, and immediately stepped on the gas. The SUV's previous driver had kindly left the keys in the vehicle, probably not expecting things to unfold as they did. The last thing he'd done before climbing into the vehicle was cut Caleb's cuffs open.

The kid was another loose end, just like so many other pieces of human detritus left behind by the storm of the events of the previous few days.

Still, the decision wasn't *entirely* altruistic.

Gideon wasn't a vindictive man. He harbored no particular

animosity toward Caleb and had no desire to find out that he'd committed suicide by shooting himself in the back of the head with his hands tied behind his back—or else slitting his wrists while on suicide watch in the county jail.

But that only meant he would give Caleb a fighting chance. And if the kid attracted the attention of law enforcement as he fled and bought them a few minutes, then he would take it.

"—plates," Zara mumbled from the passenger seat as Gideon gunned the engine and drove the SUV hard over the uneven ground of the field. The rear wheels occasionally spun as he hit a particularly deep patch of earth and kicked out sprays of dirt and stones behind them that rattled the undercarriage.

They both grunted as the front tires hit the curb at the edge of the road while traveling diagonally at nearly forty miles an hour, throwing them back against their chairs.

"What was that?"

"This SUV has government plates," Zara repeated.

Gideon glanced in the rearview mirror to check that they weren't being tailed. He couldn't do anything about the chopper overhead, but neither was it likely that anyone up there would risk shooting at him. He couldn't say that for the guys they'd just met on the ground.

He caught a glimpse of Zara's face in the mirror before returning his attention to the road ahead of them. Her right cheek was covered in someone else's blood, her teeth stained dark from the chocolate. But she already appeared a little stronger than she had a couple of minutes earlier in the forest.

Finally, her words clicked in his mind.

"Well, I promise you one thing," he said, gesturing backward with his right thumb extended. "That kid was no Fed. None of those guys were."

"They weren't from the intelligence community, either. At

least, not any agency that I know of," Zara agreed. "I don't know how I know; they just don't fit the profile."

"Who the hell are these people?" Gideon muttered, relentlessly scanning every window and mirror in his—justified—paranoia of another attack.

Zara didn't reply. Instead, she leaned forward and peered at a button on the dashboard. "Huh."

"What is it?"

Instead of explaining, Zara punched the button. An icon illuminated on the screen behind the steering wheel—a blue circle. Gideon was still no closer to understanding what she was up to when she flicked a switch to the right of the button and an emergency siren began wailing close behind.

Gideon's neck snapped around as he tried to figure out where it was coming from. It took him longer than he cared to admit to realize that the SUV itself was equipped with lights and sirens.

"Neat trick," he grumbled, shaking his head as he tried to bite down on the anxiety that had briefly washed over him.

"You're right, you know," Zara said.

"About what?"

"Whoever we're up against is more powerful than I would ever have believed possible. Whether it's Senator McKinney who's the head of the snake or not, they've got access to CIA resources, money to fund paid hits, and the capability to set up an ambush like the one we just survived on less than twelve hours' notice."

"And they got to your contact, too," Gideon pointed out.

"Dammit," Zara said, slapping the dashboard in front of her. "How the hell can we beat them?"

Gideon chewed his lower lip, wincing as he realized that he'd drawn blood when he'd bitten it earlier. It was slightly swollen, and he knew he would probably catch it with his teeth when chewing for days to come. His gunshot wound was throbbing again, and he realized he couldn't remember when he'd last taken a dose of antibiotics, so he reached into his pocket for a pill, which he swallowed dry.

"That kid back there, Caleb, he said something."

Zara turned to face him. He saw in the rearview mirror that her eyes once again sparkled with intelligence. She was still in shock, but it was fading fast. "What was it?"

"This is going to sound fucking crazy," he said, knuckles whitening around the steering wheel.

"This whole thing is fucking crazy," Zara shrugged. "Try me."

Gideon shook his head, still unwilling to believe the proof of his own hearing. "He spoke to me like I was, shit, some kind of Messiah or something. Like he thought I was the second coming of Jesus himself."

He fell silent, but Zara said nothing. When he reached his decision, it felt like it had already been made. "I'm going to have to try it, aren't I? The protocol. We don't have any other choice."

FORTY-SIX

They ditched the borrowed SUV an hour later in the small town of Caribou, Maine, but not before scouring it for every last piece of useful intelligence and equipment. The most valuable find, at least in the short term, was a little under $23,000 in cash that Zara found in the glove compartment.

"Driving-around money," she said, slapping the stack of bills against the dashboard. "They came prepared."

They both washed as best they could from a five-gallon drum of drinking water they found in the trunk. Gideon pulled on a black field jacket that had been hooked over one of the rear headrests.

But what they didn't find was just as interesting as what they did. None of the corpses Gideon had searched after the battle at the airport had carried ID. Most of them were white, which aligned with US demographics, but one of the dead had features that hinted at Latin descent.

"Which probably rules out some white supremacist gang being responsible for all this," Zara had noted as they tossed around theories before ditching the SUV.

Weapons, explosives, and ammunition were available in abundance, as was a stack of unused burner phones. But there was nothing that pointed to the identities of whoever was running this operation. No computer hardware, no documents, no paperwork. Whatever the shooters could have told them had died with them. Everything useful went into a pair of large black duffel bags. Gideon slung one over either shoulder before Zara snorted, told him off, and took one herself.

Outside a rundown ranch-style house on the outskirts of Caribou, Zara spotted a 1995 Jeep Wrangler that had long forgotten its better days. Rust spots dotted its sides, and there was a deep dent in the right-rear door.

"With a little TLC, though, she'd be a beauty..." she mused. "Tires are inflated. I'm guessing she runs just fine."

Gideon glanced up and down the street. Only a few cars had passed them as they walked into town, and he calculated in his head about how long it would take him to get the 4 x 4 started.

"What's that look?"

Noticing that a TV screen was flickering in the front room, Gideon gestured at the house and said, "You think you can distract whoever's inside?"

"I've got a better idea," Zara said. She set the duffel bag she was holding down out of view of the house and gestured for him to do the same. "Why don't we just go introduce ourselves."

She grabbed his arm and pulled him toward the house, pressing against him as though they were a couple.

"What are you doing?" he hissed as they approached the door. "Look at us!"

In a hushed tone, as her eyes took in the peeled paintwork and moss-covered front step, Zara replied, "I don't think our appearance is going to trouble whoever lives here too badly."

She knocked firmly on the door.

An old man opened it almost a full minute later. He was panting heavily despite the oxygen cannula in his nose connected by a thin plastic tube to the tank he dragged behind him. "Can I help you?"

"Oh, I hope so," Zara said, turning on the charm and adopting a tone that sounded straight out of a 1950s movie. "My husband—Keith didn't want me to do this. But I've always been a Wrangler girl, you know? My dad bought me the '87 when I was still in high school. I drove it until the doors practically fell right off."

"Uh-huh," the old man said skeptically, his voice gravel. "Honey, this ain't a car show."

"The thing is," Zara said hurriedly. "I think I can restore her. It'll take more than a coat of paint, but I can get her looking like she used to. And probably running even better. How much do you want for her?"

"She ain't for sale."

"But if you had to name a price," Zara pushed. "Go crazy. Just pick a number."

"Ten grand," the old man said, already reaching to push the front door closed in their faces.

"Done," Zara said, offering her hand to seal the bargain. "You're a good negotiator. I'll give you that."

Five minutes later, they left a very confused retiree in the rearview mirror of a Wrangler that rattled every time it hit even the smallest pothole and poured black smoke out of the exhaust. But it ran, and that was all that mattered.

Except for fuel, they didn't stop until they reached the outskirts of Boston, the first city that felt large enough to lose themselves in, where they paid for a hotel room in cash and slept in the same bed, curled up together as if they'd been married for decades.

GIDEON WOKE FEELING TRULY RESTED for the first time in weeks. Eyes still closed, he reached out to his side for Zara. His hand passed through empty air. When it landed on the mattress, he found that it was cold.

His eyes snapped open, and he went from a state of total relaxation to sitting bolt-upright in bed with cortisol flooding through his veins.

He pulled his bedside drawer open and retrieved the pistol he'd placed there the previous night on top of the Gideon Bible before jumping lightly to his feet. The coincidence had seemed funny then. It was only now he realized he was wearing nothing more than a pair of boxer shorts.

It took a couple of seconds to confirm what he already suspected: the room was empty, as was the bathroom. Zara was gone.

How the hell didn't you wake up?

Gideon heard a click from the room door and reacted on instinct. He spun and dropped to a crouch, holding the pistol with a double-handed grip as he aimed it at the entranceway.

Zara entered a moment later, reacting with a start as she noticed exactly how he was planning on greeting her.

"Relax, John Wick," she laughed, holding up a paper bag in her left hand. "I found us breakfast. And some goodies."

"You shouldn't have gone alone," Gideon snapped. "You—"

"I'm a big girl now," Zara said dryly. She hiked up her jacket and twisted her torso slightly to reveal a pistol tucked between her waistband and her lower back. "Besides, I took protection."

"—should have at least told me where you were going," Gideon said, altering what he had initially been planning to say. Zara was right; she was a trained CIA officer, not some chump off the street. He had no reason to feel so...

Panicked?

"Fair enough," she replied, extracting a cream cheese bagel from the paper bag before handing it to him. "It's a shame we didn't make it to New York, but these will have to do."

Gideon's stomach chose that moment to do his best impression of a lawnmower cranking into life. The sound was so ridiculous he couldn't maintain his composure. Both of them broke into fits of laughter.

"Still," Zara said, leaping back onto the bed and sliding up so that her back lay against the plush headrest, "it's not every day I get greeted by a man in his underwear."

"It's not every day I get breakfast in bed," Gideon agreed.

Both of them fell silent for a few minutes as they worked their way through the bagels. In Gideon's case, it didn't last more than about thirty seconds. He hopped back off the bed, pulled his T-shirt—now well overdue for a wash—back over his shoulders, and fired up the espresso machine that sat on the minibar. A moment later he carried a cup of coffee in either hand back to the bed.

"My hero," Zara said with a groan.

"What's the plan?" Gideon said when they were both suitably caffeinated. "Doctor Spohn is Boston-based, right? Maybe we go pay her a visit."

"I thought about that." Zara nodded. "But it's too risky. Everywhere we go, people end up dead. We can't risk bringing that kind of heat to an innocent woman's door."

"Do you have a better idea?"

"As a matter of fact, yes," Zara nodded. She reached into her jeans pocket and pulled out a square of aluminum foil.

Gideon stared at it, nonplussed. "Are you going to explain what I'm looking at?"

She tossed it over to him. He plucked it up off the sheets and examined it to find that it was actually a pouch made of aluminum foil. Whatever was inside was extremely light and had a bit of give. He began experimentally peeling back the foil.

A moment later he looked back up at her, a flash of frustration on his face. He was holding a couple dozen dried mushrooms. "Are you serious? You were out buying drugs?"

"I was out buying magic mushrooms, yes. And breakfast, don't forget that."

"What if you'd been, I don't know...busted by the police."

Zara rolled her eyes. "I wasn't picking a kilogram of fentanyl up from the Sinaloa Cartel. Relax. I used one of the computers in the business center downstairs and found a guy on Facebook marketplace. He was very nice."

"What if it had been a sting?"

She looked at him sideways. "When was the last time you heard of anyone going to jail for buying a hundred bucks' worth of shrooms?"

Gideon threw his hands up. "That's not the point. We're supposed to be a team. If you had told me where you were going, I could have been there just in case anything went wrong."

Zara smiled. "Next time, I promise."

She got up off the bed and walked over to the coffee machine.

"We're out of pods," Gideon said, trying and failing to stay mad. "I guess we only get one each."

"I just need hot water," Zara said, quickly washing out her coffee cup in the bathroom sink before returning to the machine and making a cup of steaming water. She picked up the foil packet of magic mushrooms from the bed and dropped them into the cup.

"I read the protocol," she explained. "It didn't seem too complicated."

"Walk me through it."

"Doctor Spohn extracts psilocybin from a specific species of mushroom, titrated so that she has precise dosages."

Gideon narrowed his gaze, his eyes flickering toward the stew of mushrooms steeping in the cup of boiling water, then back to Zara.

She grimaced. "Okay, so we're going to have to take some shortcuts."

"Some? Keep going."

"She also focuses on the importance of setting," Zara said, her eyes unconsciously glancing around the sparse, businesslike hotel room before stopping on the open bags of weapons, explosives, and ammunition. "It's very important to create the right mental state before the session can begin."

"Right."

Zara made a face as she reached into her jacket pocket. "I also bought a scented candle. Pumpkin spice. It was half price."

Gideon slowly lowered himself against the bed. Groaning, he muttered, "How could this go wrong?"

FORTY-SEVEN

"How does it taste?"

"Like raindrops and sugar plums," Gideon grimaced, almost retching a couple of times as he knocked back about a third of the cup of steeped mushroom juice. "Am I supposed to chew the lumps?"

Zara made a face. "Can't hurt."

She opened her laptop, ensured it was plugged into main power, and brought up a YouTube video titled "TEN HOURS OF CALMING CLASSICAL," which delivered exactly what it promised.

"That sounds AI generated," Gideon pointed out.

"Probably was," she agreed, next opening a Word document and titling it with the date. "Why don't you get comfortable? I don't know how long it takes to kick in."

"Sure thing, doc," Gideon said.

Gideon swilled a glass of water around his mouth to wash away the taste of the mushroom infusion. He smacked his lips with satisfaction. "Much better."

He seemed relaxed, as quick to laugh and joke as he'd been

ever since they met a few days earlier. But Zara sensed that he was putting on an act. She couldn't tell who he was trying to reassure more.

"You need to do something for me," he said after a few minutes, the lightness fading from his face in an instant.

"Sure. Anything."

"Don't stop. When I'm under, I mean. No matter what. We need to know."

Zara swallowed. His expression was...not earnest, exactly.

Decided.

They passed about half an hour chatting about nothing in particular, talking about favorite cuisines—Gideon was certain he liked Mexican food, if little else—and places they'd like to visit once this was all over. When he wasn't paying attention, Zara made a note that some aspects of his memory seemed unaffected—he was well aware of country names, their capitals, the languages spoken in Japan and Austria, even the names of a random politician or celebrity.

It was only specific details about his past that seemed buried. She wondered whether his torturers had been hunting for a specific memory when they drugged him with datura, or whether his brain had simply shut down completely to protect itself.

The longer they talked, the more relaxed Gideon seemed to grow. He closed his eyes and lay back against the headrest, his answers growing slower and more languid with every few minutes that passed. Zara, by contrast, became increasingly alert.

And anxious.

This is crazy, she realized after Gideon had fallen silent for about thirty seconds partway through a conversation about corndogs and the Utah State Fair while deliberating whether it was possible he'd either tasted the former or been to the latter.

She was no doctor. She was certainly not a head doctor. The first aid classes at the Farm had given her a basic grounding in stabilizing physical wounds and common ailments—at least enough information to be useful. But the human brain was the most complex organ in the most complex organism on the planet.

Who am I to go poking around in it?

Zara swallowed hard, looking up to the ceiling as she whispered a prayer to the God she'd neglected in the last few years. Since joining the Agency she'd thought of little else except her mission. She lived for her work. Loved her job and had been—still was—willing to sacrifice everything for it.

"Why the long face?" Gideon said.

She looked down and saw that his eyes had snapped open. He seemed to have forgotten about their conversation about corndogs, which was probably for the best. His pupils were slightly dilated, but not obviously so. Were the mushrooms kicking in? Or was she just overanalyzing things?

Don't stare, she reminded herself, remembering that the two most important features of the Spohn protocol were the same as for any hippie swallowing a patch of LSD: set and setting. Setting was simple: the person consuming the psychedelics had to be as comfortable as possible. They'd done their best—turning down the overhead lights, piling spare pillows and blankets up on the bed, and of course the generic classical music tinkling out of the laptop's tinny speakers.

Set was short for mindset. Psychedelics could induce paranoia or intense fear. To maximize success, the Spohn protocol indicated that it was best to go into a trip with a positive disposition. But just as important was what the subject saw while under the influence.

"You look more freaked out than I feel," he said when she

didn't respond, before pushing an amused puff of air through his nostrils.

The feel of this seemed to delight Gideon. He breathed out hard through his nose several more times before starting to chuckle. This became all-out mirth, leaving him bent double on the bed, heaving in fits of laughter that left him struggling to breathe.

"You don't get it, do you?" he spluttered after at least five or ten seconds of intense—and solo—amusement. "The long face... Like a horse."

Gideon descended back into fits of laughter before his attention was caught by a fly doing lazy loops near the dim bulb of the lights on the ceiling. He stared at it for almost fifteen minutes without saying anything, completely entranced by its movement.

"It's so high up," he finally breathed. "Don't you worry that the air is too thin up there?"

Zara's eyes flickered toward the half-drunk cup of mushroom infusion, wondering if she should have been more cautious with the dosing. She'd done a little research before buying the bag that morning, but all it revealed was that it was impossible to know exactly how much psilocybin was in any single mushroom —or how a given individual would respond to the chemical.

It's too late for second thoughts now...

She spoke softly, almost maternally. "For what?"

"For its wings. Look how little they are..."

By contrast, Gideon's tone was one of wonder. It was as though the housefly was the most miraculous creature he'd ever seen.

Who needs Nat Geo?

"It looks just fine to me," she said. "It has a tiny body. So maybe it only needs little wings."

"Yeah," Gideon said slowly. He seemed comforted by the thought. "Yeah, you're right."

Zara let him savor the wonder of the chemicals flooding through his brain for a few minutes longer. The most mundane of the budget hotel room's details provoked childlike fascination in him. It warmed her heart to see him so happy. But another part of her realized that she was putting off a task that she feared.

"Gideon?"

"Yes?"

"Can you do something?"

"Sure!"

"Lay back against the bed for me and get comfy."

"Okay."

When he was horizontal once again, Zara asked him to close his eyes—mainly to distract him from the fly, which was still holding in the figure of eight pattern near the foot of the bed. He did so without argument—the influence of the psychedelic making him visibly suggestible.

"Now breathe with me. Slowly in one, two. Hold, one, two. Out, one, too."

She kept this up for at least ten minutes, until she too was so relaxed she was in danger of falling asleep. The flood of oxygen in her bloodstream was hypnotic in itself.

For Gideon it had to be a double whammy.

"How do you feel, Gideon?"

"Good," he said, practically stumbling over the word. "Sleepy..."

"Is it okay with you if I ask a few questions?"

The journal article in which Doctor Spohn had laid out her protocol focused on the importance of gaining the patient's consent. Failing to do so risked inflicting more mental and emotional damage.

"Sure…" he mumbled.

"If you get uncomfortable at any time, just tell me, okay? I'm here to help you. I'm here to make sure you're safe."

"Thank you. I feel safe. Warm."

"Good," Zara said, matching his tone. "That's what we want. You know who I am, right?"

"You're Zara," Gideon replied, as if it was the most obvious answer in the world.

"That's right. You wanted me to help you to remember who you were before the château. Is that still okay?

"Yes, please. I want to remember."

Zara switched tabs, her practiced eyes quickly speed-reading through her notes on the protocol that she had already committed to memory. "That's good. I want you to imagine something for me. Picture yourself as a child. Can you do that?"

Gideon nodded. She examined him quickly from a distance. He seemed completely hypnotized.

"Tell me what you see."

"I'm, I'm in a big room. There are beds in a long row on either side. There are lots of children here."

Zara quietly tapped a note. Doctor Spohn's journal article indicated that the patient could be hallucinating as easily as recalling real memories. It didn't really matter.

As long as Gideon's brain hadn't suffered permanent physical damage, it was possible that his memories were simply lodged behind some form of psychological defense mechanism. His brain was protecting him from something: the only way it knew how was to block off access entirely.

Her job was to retrain the brain, to let it know that it was safe to relax. To let down its guard. To let Gideon remember.

"Is it a hospital?"

"No."

Zara frowned, wondering if Gideon was narrating a hallucination rather than a memory. A large room with beds and children. What could that be?

"Are you at summer camp?"

"I don't know what that is."

"Describe what you see," she said.

"I count fifteen, sixteen, seventeen, eighteen beds," Gideon said, moving his head from side to side as his eyes flickered beneath his eyelids. "Each bed has a metal box at the end. Like...a chest. I think I might live here."

"Why do you think that, Gideon?"

"I've been here for a long time. I don't know how I know, I just do."

Boarding school, maybe? Where else did kids live in dormitories for long periods of time?

"I want you to walk to the door and go outside," she said.

Gideon stiffened, and Zara instantly knew that she'd said the wrong thing—though she did not know why.

"What's wrong, Gideon?"

"We can't leave," he hissed, as if trying to avoid being overheard. "They'll beat us, don't you remember?"

Zara stared at the terrified expression on his face and wondered if she should pull the cord now. Was this ethical? Was she doing more damage to Gideon's already broken brain? Her heart raced in her chest.

"Don't stop," she whispered under her breath, remembering what Gideon had told her. "No matter what."

"Okay, let's stay here," she said quickly. "We won't go outside. But who would beat us if we did?"

"The instructors," he said as if it was the most obvious thing in the world.

Instructors? Was he at military school, maybe?

It was possible. But did military schools still inflict physical violence on their students? She decided that in some more unrefined states, that was still likely the case. She tapped another note.

"What are they instructing us?"

"To fight. To be strong. To never give in. And to believe."

"Believe in what?"

"No, in who," he replied.

"Who do we believe in, Gideon?"

"I don't trust him," he said, reverting to the hissing tone he'd used earlier.

"Okay. Let's leave this room and go somewhere else," Zara said hurriedly. It certainly didn't sound like a military school that Gideon was describing. It was more like a...*cult*.

"Yeah. Please."

"Gideon, can you tell me what a Nomad is?" Zara asked next, referring to the list of terms that he'd mentioned to her.

"I'm a Nomad."

"Am I a Nomad?"

"No," he replied, a twinge of amusement on his lips.

"Why not?"

"You're a girl."

"Why can't girls be Nomads?"

"Because it's the law."

"So what do girls do?"

"I—" his forehead knotted into a frown. "I don't know."

Zara quickly typed a note, wishing she'd thought to record the entire session. "Don't you see them?"

"Not since I was, I don't know. Eleven?"

"How old are you now?"

"Fourteen."

Her eyes widened. Was this all just some kind of fantasy—or was it really possible that for three years Gideon hadn't even seen a member of the opposite sex?

"What do you do all day, Gideon?"

"In the morning we have class. I'm great at math. But I only have two more months of school left."

Zara made a note to return to that train of thought in a second.

"What do you do in the afternoons?"

"PT. Weights, running, climbing, boxing, wrestling. And weapons practice, of course."

He said the last activity so casually Zara almost didn't comprehend it. *Of course...*

"What kind of weapons?"

"Everything. I'm an expert marksman. Most of us are. But I'm the best. We train with knives and clubs as well. We'll need it to survive the Trial."

Trial? Zara typed.

"Why do you only have two more months left of school?"

"After that my apprenticeship starts."

"With who?"

"The Chosen."

Zara's head was swimming with questions. Almost every word that Gideon spoke provoked another question. What the hell was the Trial—and who were the Chosen? It all sounded too crazy to be true. And yet... That kid Caleb. Gideon had described how he seemed to worship him.

"Who are they?"

"The elite. They are the warriors of our faith. They protect us all."

"And that's what you want to do?"

Gideon half-shrugged. "It's not what I want. It's my destiny."

"Tell me about the Trial."

Again, Gideon stiffened. In fact, this time his body went almost entirely rigid—as if signaling that this topic was even more psychologically stressful than that of the instructors.

"I'm not sure I want to," he whispered in a boyish tone.

"You can stop if you want. But it's important," Zara said, hating herself for applying the pressure. But she was getting somewhere—and that was almost a high of its own.

"Okay. I can do it."

"Does every boy go through a Trial?"

"No," Gideon said, shaking his head. "Just the apprentices for the Chosen."

"What does it involve?"

"It's a test. They don't tell us exactly what we have to do. There are rumors..."

"Like what?"

"It lasts forty days," Gideon said, seeming confident about that detail. "They give you a knife. Nothing else. You eat what you kill, or you don't eat at all."

"Forty days?" Zara said, surprise audible in her tone. "Like Jesus in the desert?"

Gideon frowned. "Who?"

What the hell? She was certain Gideon knew what the Christian faith was. He'd been a legionnaire, which meant he would have been exposed to French military chaplains, not to mention the thousands, possibly tens of thousands of places of worship across France.

But maybe the fourteen-year-old version of Gideon didn't know about Jesus. Because that was who she was talking to, not the man she'd come to know.

"It doesn't matter. So you have to survive for forty days, is that right?"

"Some of the apprentices say that they strip you naked," he said, his expression uncertain. "Or that you just get a loincloth. But I don't know. I don't want to do it."

"Why not?"

"I'm not worried about doing my time in the desert!"

Gideon said loudly—defensively. "I can survive. I know how to make fire, how to set traps. But I don't want to kill."

"You don't want to hunt animals?"

Gideon's jaw tightened. His eyes flickered wildly beneath his eyelids. He sounded exasperated. "Don't you get it? I don't want to kill another man!"

FORTY-EIGHT

Gideon stared blankly at his hands. The visual hallucinations had mostly faded, and it was only when he blinked that he saw a red shimmering outline around his palms and fingers. But it returned *every* time he blinked.

"Say it," he growled, his voice as flat and dull as his emotional state.

Zara had remained almost completely silent while he sobered up from the psilocybin infusion. He hadn't dared look up at her, terrified that he would see horror in her eyes. But he felt her brooding presence in the corner. Like a traumatized child, he lashed out before he could be hurt again.

"Say what, Gideon?"

"That you're disgusted by me. That you're done."

"Gideon, look at me."

He resisted the command, unwilling to reach out for the offered hand out of fear that it would be withdrawn at the last second. In the space of a few breaths, his emotional state gyrated from hope to fear to despair and back again.

Zara's clothes rustled as she moved, and he closed his eyes

as anguish flooded over him. He couldn't bear watching her walk out that door. She was going to leave him alone. Just like he'd been all these years. Just like he would be for the rest of his life.

"Oh, Gideon," she whispered as she instead climbed onto the bed and sat at his side. "I'm sorry. For *everything*."

"You don't believe that," he replied, turning away from her.

When Zara spoke, her tone was businesslike. "Listen. Right now your brain is flooded with chemicals. You burned out all the serotonin stored in your mind—that's the happiness hormone, and you're all out. What you're feeling is natural. It will fade. And I'll still be here when it does."

She was right. It took hours, but the hollow emptiness in Gideon's chest began to fade and he slowly felt human again. She lay by him the entire time, not reaching out and embracing him, but staying just close enough that he knew she was there.

He kept lying with his eyes closed long after his comedown had faded. Because he remembered now. Remembered who he was and how he had come to be this way.

And now he wanted to forget. But it was too late for that.

"Thank you," he said finally, still unable to meet her gaze.

"It's okay. You'd do it for me."

"I'm not so sure about that."

"Gideon," she said in frustration. "I know you. You're a good person. You risked your own life to save me, so I'm pretty sure you'd give me a fucking hug if I needed one. But you need a little tough love. Stop feeling so damn sorry for yourself. That's not going to fix anything. We have to do that. Together."

Gideon shook his head. He finally pulled himself upright and leaned against the headrest. He chewed his lip and tentatively looked up into her eyes, dreading what came next.

"You deserve to know who I really am," he said. "I'll tell

you everything I remember. After that, it's up to you. I won't blame you if you leave."

"Gideon—"

He held up his hand. "Let me say what I have to."

Her face tightened, but she nodded. "Okay."

"The details are still hazy, but I remember the broad strokes now," he said slowly, closing his eyes and frowning as he tried to corral the story in his mind. "There's more going on than we realized."

"Go on..."

"Did you ever hear the story of the princes in the tower?"

Zara frowned, clearly baffled by where he was going. "Rapunzel?"

Gideon couldn't keep the corners of his lips from turning up with amusement. "Princes, not Princess. I guess some English king died hundreds of years ago, leaving two sons behind. The eldest was next in line to the throne—but he was only twelve years old. Too young to take control."

"Right..."

She was looking at him like he'd gone mad, but Gideon continued anyway. "The prince's uncle—Richard—was named Lord Protector. He was responsible for managing the boy's coronation as king. Instead, he locked both brothers in the Tower of London. They were never seen again."

"So long live King Richard?" Zara said.

"Exactly."

"I don't get what this has to do with you."

"I guess I'm a prince," Gideon said. Once again, he held up a finger to forestall Zara's interruption. "I'm not saying I have royal blood or anything. Not exactly. But I grew up on a commune in Texas. I think it's the largest single ranch in the entire country—at least when you count up all the different parcels of land that have been purchased over the years."

"And you were supposed to inherit it?"

"I wish it was that simple. My father was a complicated man, and that's putting it mildly. I didn't even know he was my dad until I was ten. All of us kids were raised in one big group. I just figured that was normal.

"Throughout my entire childhood, we started every day with prayer. But not to Jesus or God, Buddha, Allah, or even the freaking flying spaghetti monster. To my dad."

Zara blinked stupidly for several seconds, her eyes flickering as she processed what he was telling her. "You grew up..."

"In a cult," he nodded. "But you don't know that until you leave. I just thought it was normal."

"So if your dad was the old king, who's the new one? Senator McKinney?"

Gideon shook his head firmly. "Senator McKinney's just one part of it. A big part, no doubt, but not the whole thing. I'll get to him. I pieced some of this together over the years. It's strange, I remember it—but it feels like somebody else's memories."

"That's natural," Zara said. "I read about it. The memories will take time to bed back in. Your brain is essentially reprocessing each of them as if for the first time."

"I'm not sure I want to remember," Gideon snorted blackly. "It's too messed up."

"You don't have to tell me—"

"Yes, I do. I'm just not sure where to start."

"Why don't you go back to the beginning?"

"I had a lot of siblings. But we were more like...cousins, I guess, because of the way we were raised. Mostly they were born to different women."

Zara wrinkled her nose. "Your dad was a predator."

Gideon nodded. "It took me years to see it. But like I said, we didn't know any different. Dad *was* God. That's what we were told every morning, that's what we whispered in our prayers every night."

"Sorry," Zara said, grimacing. "I interrupted. Go on."

"I had an older brother. Unlike the rest of my siblings, I didn't see him much. He lived with Dad."

"You didn't?"

"No. I lived in the dormitories, like everybody else. We were the only two boys, though. I know that. And I have a sister from the same mother. We were close. Her name is Julia."

He gritted his teeth as a wave of guilt flooded over him.

"Anyway, my brother died when I was young. It was an accident. I don't know the details. It was only then that Dad took an interest in me. He decided I needed to be toughened up, and he placed me with the Chosen."

Zara raised an eyebrow.

"The commune—cult—it's organized on military lines. I don't know exactly how many people live on the ranch, but it's in the thousands, at least. Maybe as many as fifteen or twenty across all the little towns. Maybe even more by now. Everybody does military service, like ROTC, except you start at primary school."

"It sounds more like North Korea."

"More or less," Gideon shrugged. "I heard rumors that it wasn't always that way. At one point people lived freer lives. But my dad was a paranoid man, and it got worse and worse with every year that passed. After I got out, I put some of the details together. Everything started going crazy in the mid-90s, about the time I was born."

"Why?"

Gideon shrugged. "I don't know for sure. But my theory is it has to do with Waco. Dad didn't want to go out like that. He could've gone two ways—but instead of not being a lunatic, he decided to become so strong that nobody would dare take him on."

"A lot like North Korea," Zara muttered.

"After school, everybody was required to do military service. But it's like conscription in Israel or Korea—once you've done a year full time, you return to regular life. Some people were farmers, cleaners, or whatever and just did their three weeks of refresher service each year. Except for the Chosen. They were full-time."

Gideon could tell by the increasingly confused—if not quite doubtful—expression on Zara's face that a part of her found his story difficult to believe. Another part, just as clearly, was balancing this news against the evidence of her own eyes. Back in Marseille. At the airfield.

"How many of them are there, these Chosen?"

"I couldn't say for sure," Gideon admitted. "There were fifty in my cohort of apprentices, and a new cohort every year. But they got larger and larger. I don't know that the earlier cohorts would've been so big. But you have to be talking hundreds, at a minimum."

"This is insane…" Zara whispered. "You're telling me there's an army of religious whackjobs on some ranch in Texas just waiting for—what, exactly?"

"Dad thought the world was going to end," Gideon said, closing his eyes as a sensation of referred embarrassment came over him. "He told everyone that he was there to lead them into the afterlife. I know how cliché that sounds. But he also constantly worried about the federal government—FBI, ATF, whoever—shutting the ranch down. That's what the Chosen were for. To protect us."

"And he thought he could go toe to toe with the Bureau?" Zara asked skeptically.

"The Chosen was formed just to provide security for the

ranch back in, I don't know, the late '70s, maybe? Way before Waco, anyway. Sometime in the '80s, a bunch of Vietnam vets found their way to us. A couple of them were special forces types. They built a professional organization. It was small but well trained. Now I'm not so sure about the small part."

"I know, but still…"

"Remember that we were training from the age of ten years old. I could break a rifle down, clean and reassemble it before I was eight. They made us into child soldiers. I had years of quasi-military experience before I turned sixteen. That was when my dad died."

"I'm sorry. That's so young."

"I'm not," Gideon replied harshly. "He was a sociopath I barely knew. Good riddance."

"Okay. And this is where King Richard fits in?"

Gideon nodded. "I never wanted to take over from Dad. I liked being an apprentice. I got to fire guns and ride helicopters and jump out of planes. Joining the Chosen sounded a hell of a lot more fun than preaching all day."

"So who took over?"

"Gabriel Clark. Or Father Gabriel, as he started to style himself. He was in charge of the paramilitary wing—the Chosen, the reserves, everything. He controlled the guns. Some of the people on the commune didn't agree. But he made his point. Firmly."

"So why didn't he kill you?"

"I think that's where McKinney fits in," Gideon said.

FORTY-NINE

"I guess my dad realized that security came in two forms: the ability to fight back and political influence. At some point, he decided that we needed friends in local government to help smooth over all the land purchases. And then state government. And eventually at the national level, too."

"So he funded political campaigns?" Zara asked doubtfully. "That's no guarantee of success."

"Politics is a dirty business," Gideon said. "But when you can send armed sicarios to threaten your rivals or dispatch a woman to tempt a married politician to bed so that you can blackmail them with the photos..."

"Right," Zara breathed. "I get it."

"We always had missionaries, right from the very start of the commune. People would leave for a month or a year and point lost souls in our direction. You'd be surprised to learn how many broken people just want to find a home."

"But politicians can't disappear to some ranch for most of the year," Zara objected.

"Exactly. The commune's political representatives—ambassadors, Dad called them—were selected partly based on their devotion to Dad. They came back every few weeks but spent most of their time away from the rest of us. And I guess over the years their faith faded."

"Senator McKinney doesn't strike me as the religious type," Zara agreed.

"The ambassadors became a threat to my dad's power base. I've only put this together through whispers and scraps of information, but my theory is that he settled into an uneasy equilibrium with them. The commune provided the finances—and, when necessary, the muscle—that benefited their political careers. In return, they wielded political influence to protect the commune."

"And then your dad died."

"Father Gabriel immediately seized control. But—and this is just my theory—he still needed the support of the commune's ambassadors. Some of them, like Senator McKinney, had grown extremely powerful in the real world by then.

"Killing me would have sent them the wrong signal about the new regime. It was too risky when his new regime wasn't completely secure. And maybe he didn't want to rock the boat with the rest of the commune's inhabitants. At least—at first. After all, I was still an apprentice. Not yet a man. It was still a couple of years until my Trial."

"Trial?"

"I'll explain."

He trailed off, his stomach suddenly gripped by a knot of nerves. He had to come clean with Zara about what he'd done. But what if she rejected him? She was about the only person in the world he thought he could trust. He wasn't sure he could stand her turning her back on him.

But he didn't have a choice. She deserved to know. He

would have to accept the consequences, wherever the chips fell.

"I only saw the senator at the ranch once. At least, that I remember. It was a couple of days before my Trial."

Zara's eyes widened. He couldn't read the emotion contained within those dark orbs. "How old were you?"

"Eighteen. Some of the other nomads hadn't had their birthdays yet, but everybody was roughly the same age."

"Before, you said you were sent out into the desert to survive?"

"It was like a tribal manhood ritual," Gideon confirmed, his expression tightening into a flash of fury at the memory. "No clothes. Just underwear and a knife. There's a huge area of the ranch that's basically open country. Thousands upon thousands of acres. You've got hogs and coyotes roaming around, and they send you out drugged out of your mind."

"Drugged?"

"We were given some kind of paste to swallow. I don't know what's in it exactly. But it makes you delirious. I hallucinated like crazy. I heard it drives some kids mad."

"Datura?"

Gideon nodded. "I think so. At least as one of the components. Once you swallow the paste, you become a nomad. You aren't allowed back into the commune for forty days and forty nights. No matter if you get injured or sick."

"But kids—nomads—must die all the time?"

He shrugged. "It happened. But remember, we weren't ordinary teenagers. Save for the drugs and the length, the Trial wasn't that different from other survival challenges we'd faced before. But accidents happen."

"How do they hide these deaths?"

Gideon laughed. "As far as the state of Texas is concerned, we don't exist."

"We?"

He grimaced and tapped his temple. "Sorry. It's all a bit of a mess up there. I mean the Brotherhood. New Eden."

"You don't have to answer this if you don't feel up to it," Zara said sensitively. "But when you were under, you mentioned not wanting to kill someone. Was that part of the Trial?"

Gideon stared blankly at a spot somewhere past Zara's head. He didn't dare look directly at her for fear of seeing judgment staring back. "Yeah."

"How?"

"You can only join the Chosen by taking another apprentice's knife and returning with their blood on the blade. You don't have to kill them… but accidents happen. And some nomads want to make a name for themselves."

Zara's eyes widened.

Gideon carried on, the words now spilling out from deep within. "The rules were strict. For the first thirty-nine days of the Trial, our only task was to survive. You could return to camp anytime you wanted, but nobody did. It would be too shameful. Most of the kids I knew would rather have killed themselves than fail that way."

"And on the last day?"

"The instructors fired red flares into the sky the night before to warn us that come first light the hunt was on. Every year some apprentices chose to run or hide rather than fight. And for the rest of us, that meant they were prey," he said, stony-faced.

"You didn't hide?"

Gideon shook his head. The motion was jerky. "I had too much pride. I knew who I was by then. Who my father was. The others looked for me to fail. Maybe not openly, but they thought it. I was determined to prove them wrong."

"So what happened?" Zara asked, her voice barely above a whisper. Her tone was hesitant, as if she really didn't want to know the answer.

"I spent the entire day searching for a nomad who had gone to ground. I figured they would be weaker, perhaps injured—and definitely less of a threat than another hunter like me."

He paused, hoping that Zara would say something—anything—but only silence answered him.

"The Trial ended at sunset. I searched for hours, followed trails, but every time I came up empty. The second those red flares were fired into the sky, everybody split. We all knew what was coming. Twice I found bodies—I was too late."

He dragged his palm down the side of his face, pressing firmly so that the friction almost burned his skin. "That pissed me off. I wasn't upset by the sight of a body—I was angry that I didn't get there first. The two dead nomads were weak. Emaciated. They would have been easy pickings."

Zara inhaled sharply. Gideon still didn't dare look at her. But he was certain that she would've looked as disgusted with him as he felt.

"It was starting to get dark. The rules were that you had to return to camp with the knife by sunset for it to count. So I knew that the other nomads would have to head to the same place. And so I set myself up to lie in wait."

He closed his eyes, not just picturing the scene but practically reliving it. His system spiked with adrenaline and cortisol, his breathing grew ragged and droplets of sweat began beading on his temples. He made a fist.

"Adam came out of nowhere. I'd known him my entire life, even before I apprenticed with the Chosen. We played together when we were just three or four years old. We sat next to each other in class."

Gideon fell silent there, a muscle on his temple twitching

as he relived the fight over and over in his mind. He might've stopped completely. But remembering the event had broken a dam within him. He couldn't help it. The story tumbled out.

"I heard him at the last second. He should have crept a couple more steps before he sprinted toward me. I managed to turn and duck underneath his blade. I had mine in my hand already, so I sliced up and caught him on the wrist. But it was only a glancing blow."

He started panting, almost hyperventilating from the stress of reliving a memory that felt as real to him now as it had almost a decade earlier.

"But he was quick. God, he was quick. He was always faster than me, stronger. I guess I kind of looked up to him for a few years. In the moment I saw it in his eyes: he planned to kill me. I didn't think I was going to survive."

"You did," Zara said. He couldn't read her tone.

"Yeah. He cut me across the stomach. Maybe a quarter of an inch deep. It bled like crazy, but I got away without internal damage. I faked like I was hurt worse than I was. Took a couple steps back and slowed my movements. He thought I was bleeding out. I don't blame him. It was everywhere, my clothes were soaked, hands covered in blood. It was hard to keep hold of my knife."

Gideon's eyelids flickered rapidly as his mind re-created the trauma.

"I tripped. Made it look like I tripped, I mean. He came at me with a killing blow, but he was too overconfident. Too slow. I stabbed him deep in the thigh. Must have hit an artery because the second I pulled out my blade, the wound started spurting with blood. The leg gave way underneath him."

He exhaled slowly. Shakily. "I could have let him live. He wasn't a threat to me anymore. I could move and he couldn't. I could have saved his life. Stopped the bleeding. But I didn't."

"What did you do?"

"I froze. I guess my mind kind of shut down. It couldn't take the guilt of what I'd done. I just stood there and watched my best friend bleed out on the ground. He tried to say something at the end, but he didn't have the strength. And then he was gone."

"Did you take his blade?"

Gideon shook his head. "I was in shock. I couldn't think. I don't know how long I stood there, but I couldn't bring myself to go to his body. I didn't want to face my guilt."

"So you never joined the Chosen?" Zara asked.

"I didn't get the chance. I still had time to pull myself together and take his knife before sunset. Maybe I would have done it. But two men appeared out of the darkness. I figured they were Chosen, but when they came closer, I didn't recognize them."

"Who were they?"

"McKinney's people. But I didn't know that then. When they came close, one of them drew a pistol and told me not to move. I couldn't have if I wanted to, but I guess he didn't know that. The other must have stuck me with a sedative because that's the last thing I remember."

FIFTY

"Look at me, Gideon," Zara said.

Gideon sank back against the bed, first cupping his palms against his face, then shrinking away as the touch brought back a flash of memory—his friend's blood spraying out and coating his fingers.

"I'm sorry," he said, his voice husky and raw with emotion. "I didn't know who I was. I swear."

"Gideon," Zara said, reaching out and squeezing his arm. "Listen to me. It's okay."

"It's not okay," he exploded, springing upright and leaping off the bed.

His stomach was knotted, and his hands clenched and unclenched reflexively as he tried—failed—to process the flood of emotions coursing through him as his mind reprocessed three decades of his existence in a matter of minutes.

"I'm a fucking psychopath!" He spat the words derisively, his expression dripping with disdain for his actions. "I should have let him kill me. Instead, I played the Brotherhood's game.

You know what I used as my call sign all those years in the Legion? Hell—even after I left, I stuck to it."

"I don't."

"Nomad," Gideon hissed, once again making a fist and drawing back his elbow as if to punch the wall—if only to feel something that wasn't raw, unrestrained guilt. "Like I was fucking Peter Pan, forever a child. But I wasn't, was I? I killed him. *I became a man.*"

Zara sprung off the bed, landing lightly just a couple of steps in front of him. She stared at him for several long seconds, her gaze burning with fury—so intense he quailed and almost pulled away from her.

She didn't give him a chance.

Instead of storming out of the cheap motel room and leaving him behind—as he expected—she opened up her palm, twisted her torso, and slapped him as hard as she could. The blow rocked him back and left him momentarily stunned—his anger and self-pity and guilt disappearing in the fierce white heat of pain.

Gideon blinked dumbly as his senses returned. His face still stung from the force of the impact—Zara had spared little effort. Though she was almost a foot shorter than him, she packed a hell of a punch.

"Now listen," she said, sparks practically crackling from her vibrating frame. "You were a child. I don't care if you were eighteen. You were groomed, Gideon. You said it yourself—you weren't a normal teenager. You were programmed, like a fucking machine. And so you did the only thing you knew how to do. You killed your friend. And maybe you'll live with that guilt until the end of your life."

She gritted her teeth, leaned forward, and grabbed either side of his face. She spoke in a fierce, low whisper. "But it wasn't your fault."

"I killed him."

"We don't blame cars for hitting pedestrians. We blame their drivers. You weren't in control, not really. It might feel that way to you, but I'm calling bullshit, Gideon."

Zara released her grasp of his head and took a step back. She folded her arms and appeared to take a deep breath to calm herself. "But now you have a choice: You can either stay here and wallow in self-pity or you can decide to do something about it."

"Self-pity?" Gideon snapped, anger momentarily overcoming the remorse that was clouding his judgment and sapping his strength. "I'm a murderer, Zara. I didn't just kill my friend; I stood there and watched him die when I could have saved him. But that's not even the worst of it..."

"Then what is?"

"I left my sister behind," Gideon admitted, fury giving way to exhaustion. He sank down and sat on the end of the bed.

"By the time I woke up in the back of a pickup truck, McKinney's thugs had already driven me across state lines. They took me to a safe house, where he came to me directly. He offered me the world: If I worked with him and his partners, then they would make me the new leader of the commune. All I had to do was follow his instructions. Be his puppet."

"But you didn't," Zara said flatly.

"I ran," Gideon replied, his tone and body limp. "I told them what they wanted to hear. After a few weeks, my guards got careless. I was able to slip away. I spent months living on the streets, stealing cash and struggling to stay warm. Somehow, I learned about the Legion, that they offered a new identity—a fresh start. It sounded too good to be true, but what did I have to lose?

"I made it to the port in Savannah. Nobody cares much about people trying to *leave* the US illegally. The boat got me to Europe. I spent the next five years hiding. Hoping to be forgotten. And I abandoned Julia to that hellhole."

He started to shake. Almost a decade of repressed guilt hit him in an instant. Some deep, recessed part of his mind knew that this wasn't rational. And yet he couldn't stop himself.

Zara eyed him intently. "So what's your decision?"

"What?"

"I asked what I asked."

At first, Gideon didn't understand what she was saying. He was too overpowered by his attack of conscience and, yes, self-pity to think straight. But something about Zara's unflinching stare was clarifying. It forced him to push aside his primitive emotional response.

To think.

Zara had asked him what he planned to do to change the situation. The implication was clear: All those years ago, when he'd fled the commune and McKinney's henchmen, he'd still been a boy. His failure to go back and fight, to sluice away his guilt, it had been understandable then. Not okay, but understandable.

But now he was a man.

Are you?

Gideon closed his eyes. Not to hide from Zara's gaze but so that he could think. So that he could picture Julia's face—intentionally, rather than having it thrust upon him in his dreams. And so that he could remember his friend Adam as a boy, before the chaos and the evil of their time as apprentices.

Neither stared back at him with reproach. They asked nothing of him. He didn't have to go back. He knew he could hide from the Brotherhood for the rest of his life. He had enough money now to find an island somewhere in the Pacific where he could start a bar or a surf shop, work that would fill his days and allow him to drink his nights away.

But something in him physically recoiled at the thought.

His eyes flickered open. He found Zara's and matched her stare. "I guess we better nail these bastards to the wall."

FIFTY-ONE

"God, that's good," Gideon groaned as he bit into his burger. It was loaded with crispy, thick strips of bacon, doused in trans fats, American cheese, salt, and almost every other component of the average cardiac arrest.

And it was perfect.

He washed down a bite of the burger with a swig of Coke so that he could add diabetes to the list of ailments he really didn't give a shit about right now.

Do I have a family history? Who the hell knows?

The burger joint was luckily just over the road from their hotel. It had dingy windows, didn't take credit, and had absolutely no security cameras, so they felt safe in not taking too many precautions to avoid being spotted. If the Brotherhood—or McKinney's connections in the intelligence community—had eyes on this place, then they had no hope of winning anyway.

Zara pulled open her laptop as Gideon finished his burger. She'd wolfed hers down with surprising alacrity—and not a hint of embarrassment—for somebody so small.

"Okay, here's the way I see it," she began—before stopping as Gideon signaled for the server. She arrived quickly and he ordered two beers. She cleared away the table before departing.

"Sorry," Gideon grinned. "Carry on."

She rolled her eyes. "If you'd bothered asking, I prefer IPAs, and Budweiser isn't fit for cleaning out the toilet."

Gideon chuckled. "Lady, you're not at the Agency right now. You might have craft beer tastes, but we sure don't have a craft beer budget. Until we can figure a way of safely withdrawing funds from my Panama account, we have about $20,000 to our name. When that runs out..."

"I didn't say I wouldn't drink it," Zara pointed out as the beers arrived. She looked pointedly at him. "Okay with you if I continue?"

"Be my guest."

"If the Brotherhood are even half as strong as your story suggests, we don't have a chance of taking them head-on."

"Way to keep up morale," Gideon said, tipping his head back and swigging from his mug of beer. He had to admit—at least in his head—that she was right. An IPA would have been much nicer.

"It's simple math. We can't keep getting lucky, not with hundreds of well-trained shooters arrayed against us. It's the old story: We have to be lucky every time."

"And they only have to get lucky once," Gideon nodded.

"Exactly."

Sensing that she wasn't finished, Gideon prompted her. "But you have a plan?"

Zara nodded. "I have a plan. Here's what I think: When Senator McKinney and Mariella Tilley set up the trap that captured you back in France, they still hoped to use you exactly as they did all those years ago when they took you from the commune. You look the part. You're energetic, charismatic... If

I wanted to replace a cult leader, I'm not sure I could think of a better candidate."

"Thanks..." Gideon said hesitantly, but he wasn't sure whether he was supposed to take that as a compliment. "But how can you be certain?"

"I can't. But it stands to reason. If they wanted you dead—perhaps to remove any chance that their previous duplicity would be discovered—then they could have killed you at the start. No point interrogating you. As you proved, that would have been an unnecessary risk."

"Okay," Gideon said. "Makes sense. What about the hit at the château? Because that really didn't feel too friendly. I think they wanted me off the board."

"I think you're probably right. Any hope they had of keeping their operation under the radar died the second you turned Rambo and had your face snapped on security cameras at the hospital in Cannes. From that point onward, they wouldn't be able to deny their involvement to Father Gabriel."

"And he still had reason to want me dead," Gideon said slowly. "Because as long as I'm alive, there's still the tiniest possibility that I might threaten his position."

"Precisely. So McKinney attempted to take you out—probably before Father Gabriel could send a team of the Chosen. When that failed, he got desperate and subcontracted the hit out to local talent in Marseille. Anything to avoid Gabriel getting his hands on you."

"How does this help us?"

Gideon realized that he'd almost finished his beer—and so had Zara—and gestured to the bar for two more.

"By this point, Gabriel must suspect that McKinney is coloring outside the lines. He might not know exactly how he was involved in all this, but if your father thought that the ambassadors posed a threat to his position, then that has to be doubly the case for Gabriel."

"Okay..." Gideon said, feeling the warm rush of alcohol beginning to wash through his veins.

His excuse for drinking was that it helped him think. But really, he just needed to relax. Even if the sensation was fake and would cost him in the morning, that was tomorrow's problem. Right now it felt too good to resist.

"I don't know who killed Mariella Tilley in Cannes. But in a sense, it doesn't really matter. Either it was McKinney because he wanted to tie up a loose end—someone who could connect him to the plot. Or it was Father Gabriel because he no longer trusted her."

"Or she just couldn't take it anymore," Gideon pointed out. "Maybe if it looks like a duck and it quacks like a duck, it's just a suicide."

"That doesn't change anything. McKinney would only need her dead if he was worried about one of Gabriel's people getting to her. And that would only be a concern if she didn't have enough of an insurance policy to keep the Brotherhood at bay."

Gideon frowned. "But McKinney does have enough leverage, is that what you're saying?"

"You got it. You got out of the Brotherhood almost a decade ago. That's a long time for a paranoid, sociopathic cult leader to keep someone around that they didn't trust. The only explanation that makes any sense is that McKinney has a hell of a policy. Enough dirt on a dead man's switch to bring the entire Brotherhood down."

"We saw what was on Mariella Tilley's computer," Gideon mused, taking the baton. "The way I figure it, the Brotherhood's ambassadors aren't just supposed to be politicians or lobbyists. They are more like...an Agency Chief of Station.

They must run networks of lower-level agents of influence and coordinate kompromat operations alongside their day jobs. But Cannes can't be that important of a posting. Not like DC. Not like the chairman of the Senate Intelligence Committee."

Zara's eyes shone with enthusiasm. "Right. Paranoid sociopathic cult leaders are a lot of things—but stupid isn't one of them. McKinney's too big to fail. Or at least, he's too powerful to take on before you're certain of striking a killing blow. Until that point, it's easier to let a cold war fester."

Gideon drummed his fingers on the table. Their drinks had both been reduced to little more than dregs. There wasn't yet enough alcohol in his system to cloud his thoughts, but he felt significantly less stressed than he had a few hours earlier.

He let out a sigh. "I still don't see where this gets us. If he's too big for the Brotherhood to take down, what hope do we have?"

"You're wrong," Zara said flatly. "Our advantage is that we don't have anything to lose. We're already burned. Marked for death, whatever you want to call it. We're dead men—and women—walking."

"That's a cheery thought," Gideon replied. "I'm glad I didn't order you a gin and tonic."

"I'll have you know that I'm a happy drunk," Zara said, reaching for the remnants of her beer and draining the glass in one. "Think of it this way: Why did the Soviets never nuke us during the Cold War? It got pretty toasty at times, but nobody ever pushed the big red button."

"Because both sides had too much to lose."

"We don't," Zara pressed. "Father Gabriel can't risk striking at McKinney in case the senator has a fail-safe system set up to release his files in the event of his death. But we don't have to worry about that. If anything, it works in our favor."

"As long as he really does have this insurance policy you're so sure about."

"Believe me, he does. I knew his reputation before I ever got dragged into this mess. He is a seriously slippery operator. Probably has files on half of Washington."

"Okay. Let's say the files exist, and that we plan to go for them. How?"

"That," Zara said, snapping her laptop lid closed theatrically before signing an imaginary check in midair to let the server know they were done, "is a conversation we need to have over something a hell of a lot stronger than this cat piss."

FIFTY-TWO

They traded up from Budweiser to a 7 percent IPA, and when that was done, Zara ordered a scotch. It was a Wednesday evening, so the bar was relatively quiet. They found an isolated booth where they could talk without being overheard, but they didn't turn back to business until they moved on to liquor.

"As far as I know, the senator has two residences in the DC area. A townhouse in Georgetown and a country house near Middleburg, Virginia," Zara said as she pulled out her laptop once again.

Gideon raised an eyebrow. "You planning on knocking on his front door?"

"It's an option," she mused thoughtfully. "But let's leave it on the back burner for now. To run a play like that and have any hope of walking out alive, we'd need leverage on McKinney, and we don't have any."

She opened two tabs on her Internet browser and pulled up a street view image of the Georgetown townhouse in the first, and a satellite image in the second.

"Private road," she explained. "This is the best we've got."

Gideon used the mouse cursor to spin the street view lens around. He didn't recognize the exact road, but he knew the area. It was home to countless current and former members of Congress, senators, and senior executives in the federal government's vast bureaucracy. Security would be tight. Metropolitan PD probably ran a beefed-up roster of regular patrols in that neighborhood.

And that was before they even made it to the senator's house itself.

"He's going to have a serious security system" he said. "I don't think he has around-the-clock protection, at least not from the government. But Capitol PD, the Secret Service, and most likely the Bureau will have been consulted on the installation. Local cops will be on a hair trigger for any alarm. In that part of town, I'd guess they'd measure their response time in seconds, not minutes."

"You know a lot about DC," Zara said in an inscrutable tone.

He shrugged. "I did a couple of close protection jobs there after leaving the Legion. Easy work."

"And did you ever check in on the senator?"

Gideon flushed red. "I went to the public gallery in the Senate chamber once. Looked at him from afar. And I didn't do shit."

"It doesn't sound like you gave up hope, either," she commented.

Before he could answer, she clicked over to the second tab —the one of the Middleburg home. "You're right about reaction times in DC. It's too risky. This place is a better option."

"For what?" he asked. "We still don't have an actual plan."

Zara leaned against the back of the booth and took a deep swig of her scotch.

"He wants you dead," she said thoughtfully as she set the

glass back down on the table in front of her. "And he wants it done quietly. It's better if he puts a bullet in the back of your head and buries you somewhere where you won't be found."

"You said you were a happy drunk," Gideon pointed out.

"That's what McKinney wants. Which means that's our leverage."

"It's not a lot," he said doubtfully.

"No, it's not. But it's enough to arrange a meeting—somewhere quiet."

"Like his place in Virginia."

"Exactly," Zara grinned. "You're not just a pretty face."

Gideon felt his cheeks flush with blood. He knocked back a third of his remaining scotch to hide his embarrassment, regretting the decision a moment later as the liquor scalded his throat.

Zara didn't seem to notice his discomfort. "He's not stupid. He'll arrange protection. But he'll have to do so *quietly*. He can't risk Father Gabriel getting wind of what he's up to. So we won't be up against an army."

"There's still just two of us," Gideon pointed out, though he felt a rush of excitement in his chest regardless. It was a stupid, hair-thin plan that was shot through with holes. If he was in his right mind he would run as far away from it as his legs would carry him. "We'll need some help—unless we want this to turn into a suicide mission."

Zara theatrically glanced around the quiet, cozy bar. "You have anyone in mind? Because I'm all out of hired help."

He nodded slowly. "Maybe."

She grinned back at him and raised her glass in a mock salute. "Then this might just work."

One glass of scotch became two became three—and after that, Gideon stopped counting. Zara could handle her liquor as well as any legionnaire he'd ever served with. At first, they drank to forget the stress of the past few days. Then they drank because neither wanted the night to end.

It was only closing time that prevented them from continuing into the early hours—perhaps saving them from an even worse hangover than they were already signed up for.

Zara pulled herself out of the booth, stumbling slightly as she stood back up.

"You're drunk," Gideon said as he levered himself upright.

Maybe there really was some kind of cosmic justice because as he got to his feet, a sudden rush of blood to his head made him unsteady. He swayed and had to reach out and grab the back of the seat to stop himself from falling.

Snorting with laughter, Zara held out her hand for him to grasp onto for support.

"Yes," she said, tears in her eyes as she finally regained the ability to speak, "but I'm a happy drunk."

"Touché."

Gideon didn't even notice that they were still holding hands until they were halfway back to the hotel. His cheeks reddened more than they already were from the effects of the alcohol. He was about to drop Zara's hand before he abruptly caught himself.

Will she think that's weird?

He couldn't just let go, could he? Not now. Zara might think he was being rude—or worse, it might just draw attention to what they were doing.

"Gideon?"

When he didn't respond, Zara repeated the question. "Gideon?"

"Huh?"

"If you keep squeezing my fingers that tight, they might fall off," she said, mirth gleaming in her eyes.

"Shit," he said, quickly letting go. "Sorry."

"Don't be. It was nice—at least, until you tightened the screws."

Nice?

Had he heard her right? Gideon cursed himself for drinking so much. His brain was definitely working slower than it was supposed to. But right now he wasn't sure whether he could blame the alcohol alone.

Zara turned to face him. Her eyes were glossy, her cheeks as red as his felt. There was a slight chill in the springtime air this far north, but it did little to quench what Gideon belatedly, stupidly realized was his growing attraction for her.

He cleared his throat. "It's late..."

"Yeah," Zara said dryly. "It's late."

He glanced toward the hotel in the distance. It seemed impossibly far away. "We've—we've got a long day ahead of ourselves tomorrow. I guess we should get to bed."

"I guess we should," Zara said, this time taking a step closer to him. "So—are you going to take me with you?"

It wasn't just the words; it was the way she said them that broke through Gideon's last line of defense. There was some distant part of his brain that warned him that following this path might make everything a whole lot more difficult.

But that was tomorrow's problem.

Gideon reached out and took Zara's hand from her side. "I'll be more careful," he said with a smile as he pulled her toward him.

The kiss wasn't fierce or passionate or any of the usual adjectives used to describe such things. But neither was it empty. It was a moment of connection for two people who were adrift in the world except for each other.

And it lingered.

"Well," Zara whispered as they finally broke apart. "What was that you were saying about taking me to bed?"

FIFTY-THREE

"I thought you left me," Zara said sleepily, her lithe frame sadly still covered by the messy bedsheets. "Stole away in the middle of the night so you didn't have to wake up by my side."

"What a chore that is," Gideon laughed, happily finding that there was no awkwardness between them as he balanced the cardboard take-out drink holder in his left hand and the brown paper McDonald's bag in his right. He nudged the hotel door closed with his right knee. "Not gourmet, I'm afraid."

Zara let the sheets fall away from her body as she sat upright in bed, gratefully accepting one of the two paper coffee cups.

"I guessed your order," Gideon said, tossing the cup holder in the trash can and finally taking a well-earned swig of his own beverage. He put the food bag on the hotel room's small but functional work desk, then set his cup down alongside it. "But I pretty much got one of everything on the breakfast menu."

"Sausage McMuffin?" Zara asked hopefully.

He rummaged inside the bag. "You're not allergic to eggs, are you?"

"Even better," she replied as he tossed the paper-wrapped breakfast item through the air toward her. "I'm going to have to go on a serious health kick once this is all over."

"I like your optimism."

"Nobody ever rode their luck by expecting they were going to die," she shrugged. She took a big bite of the McMuffin. "I really shouldn't enjoy these as much as I do. You know why I joined the Agency?"

"Was it to defend democracy? Or just because you *really* like planning coups?"

"A little from column A, a little from column B, but mostly I just wanted to extend the hegemony of McDonald's franchises across the globe. You ever hear the fact that no two countries with a McDonald's have ever gone to war?"

"Yeah."

"It's bullshit. But it sounds good."

They fell silent as Gideon worked his way through a bacon and cheese biscuit, an Egg McMuffin, and a sausage burrito for good measure.

"You really weren't kidding, were you?" Zara observed. He couldn't read the expression on her face as he leaned against the wall on the other side of the room devouring his way through the entire menu.

"There's more if you want?" he replied, picking up the bag —which was still disconcertingly full—and offering it to her.

"I'm only doing this because you made me," she said.

They were on the road by 9 a.m. and off the road by 10 to empty their bladders. Zara worked on her laptop in the passenger seat to find them a suitable safe house. Both agreed it would probably be unwise to prepare for the kind of operation they had in mind in a hotel room. It only took one maid missing the do-not-disturb hanger for a SWAT team to bust down the door and spoil both their days.

"I found a place," Zara finally announced as road signs for the DC area grew more and more frequent. "It's a half-hour drive from Middleburg. Close enough to allow us to conduct recon as often as we like, far enough that we shouldn't have any problem staying hidden."

"You'll need to direct me," Gideon said, gesturing at the ancient 4 x 4's dashboard. "This thing doesn't exactly come with all the mod cons."

"Another man who doesn't appreciate real beauty," she grumbled from the passenger seat.

Gideon glanced sideways. "You sure about that?"

Zara quickly looked away. They hadn't exactly talked about what had happened between them the previous night. At least not since leaving the hotel room. Gideon wondered whether they'd closed the door on that chapter when they left Boston. Maybe last night was nothing more than two lonely people finding a moment's peace.

Whatever it was, thinking about it was distracting—and distractions could get them both killed. He had to park those thoughts until this was all over.

"We need a plan," he said, mostly to break a slightly awkward silence that was beginning to develop.

"Take the next exit," Zara said, pointing at an overhead road sign they were swiftly approaching. "Last night you said you might have a lead on some assistance."

"Maybe," Gideon prevaricated, no longer so certain without the alcohol clouding his judgment. "Leclerc offered me his help."

"Leclerc?" Zara said, screwing up her face in surprise. "He'll be handcuffed to a French hospital bed right now."

"It's possible," Gideon said thoughtfully. "But I don't think so. He's a survivor. And he has powerful friends in the French establishment. Maybe he'll be in the doghouse for a while. But two French agents are dead, and the Directorate-General for Internal Security doesn't fuck around. They'll be perfectly happy to lie down with us dogs if it helps them get revenge, and they won't think twice about picking up fleas by doing it."

"You think the French state is going to help us take down McKinney?" Zara said doubtfully. He thought he felt her gaze flick toward him, presumably to check whether he'd suffered a head injury she hadn't noticed.

"No. I think they're going to look the other way."

"And why would Leclerc lift a finger to help us? We can't pay."

"I have some money," Gideon mused. His newly recovered memories still felt strange to him, as though he was reading a foreign newspaper. Everything was the same—but different. "But I don't think he'll take it. He's a man of the Legion."

"What does that have to do with anything?"

"The château—," Gideon said, intentionally using the shorthand to describe the institution where he had recovered, "it's sort of a spiritual home for the Foreign Legion. It was built during France's war in Indochina—Vietnam. Legionnaires were dying there before the US ever decided to get involved. Generations of veterans have recuperated there, tending the fields alongside serving soldiers every harvest season. Every legionnaire has sweated alongside our veterans."

"Having respect for the past is one thing," Zara said, still doubtful. "Being willing to risk your life for it is another entirely."

Gideon shrugged. "We'll see."

"How do you intend to get a message to him?"

"There was a private forum we used to use. I don't even know if he's alive, or in any fit state to answer even if he is. But it's worth a shot."

"That solves one part of the equation," Zara said, drumming her fingernails against the lid of her laptop. "Possibly. But we also need to get a message to the senator without it being intercepted by the Brotherhood's agents."

"I was thinking about this," Gideon said. "I know why we want to meet him. And I know why he would want to be in the same room with us. But what story are we telling him to make it happen? He's going to suspect that we are playing him."

"I'll make a spy of you yet," Zara grinned. "Breaks your brain a little bit, doesn't it?"

"A lot bit."

"It's a good point," she said, before directing him to take the next right. They were off the highway now, and green fields spotted with white and brown horses stretched out in every direction.

"But I don't think it really matters. Whatever we say, he's going to expect us to double-cross him. And he's going to prepare to do the exact same thing to us. That's just the way it works. I say we get a message to him asking for money. A lot of money—$5 million or maybe ten. Enough that it'll hurt him to pay it. And in return, we promise to disappear. He'll suspect it's a trap, but he doesn't have any other choice."

"And how do we get a message to him?"

"I've been thinking about this. His fixer, Ronan Haynes, was my point of contact with the senator at the start. I guess later on McKinney couldn't resist quarterbacking the operation from his own armchair. But he must have trusted Ronan implicitly for him to be looped in on the Marseille operation."

"So what, we send him an email?"

Zara smiled with such malevolence that Gideon made a note to remember never to get on her bad side. "I have a better idea."

FIFTY-FOUR

They set up in the single-story home north of Purcellville that Zara had found for rent on a local message board. It had two bedrooms, fast Wi-Fi, and a kitchen that came stocked with a chilled bottle of white wine courtesy of the owner—who had retired to Florida and would thankfully not be poking her nose into their business.

It was also situated on about ten acres of land and was three-quarters of a mile from its nearest neighbors. The land was fenced and gated, so it was unlikely they would receive any uninvited guests.

It was perfect.

They'd stopped on the way to purchase supplies—mostly food and drink, but also fresh clothes and toiletries. They had both wrung about as much use out of the clothes they'd been wearing since Turin as they could.

Neither of them had chosen bedrooms yet. It was as though that topic was parked.

"Let's hope neither of us sleepwalks," Zara said. She was sitting on her laptop at the breakfast bar and had looked up from her research to find that Gideon was in the process of concealing weapons in a number of unlikely spaces around the home.

Gideon grinned as he closed an otherwise empty cupboard door, leaving a loaded pistol inside it. "Just as long as you don't go looking for a midnight snack, we should be fine."

"Okay, I've gotten about as far as I'm going to get," Zara said with a tight, frustrated shake of her head. "Using commercial databases for this is like trying to read under the covers at night without a flashlight."

"Show me what you've got," Gideon said, unconsciously adopting a soothing tone. He performed a quick scan around the room to check that his hiding places were suitably concealed, then walked over to stand at Zara's side.

She had a notepad by her laptop that she'd filled with countless pages of a tight, ugly scrawl. "Don't bother trying to read that," she said. "I barely can."

Zara clicked over to her Internet browser and brought up a preloaded tab. It contained a street-view image of a typical American house. A line of text at the bottom of the page indicated that it was located near the town of Vienna, Virginia.

Gideon frowned. "What's this?"

"This is the home of Ronan Haynes, McKinney's fixer. At least," she scrunched up her nose, "I think it is. According to the county's property records, it was purchased twenty-three years ago for a little over $400,000."

He let out a low whistle. "I guess that's why they tell you to buy houses. They really aren't making any more of them."

"Not round there," Zara agreed.

The house in question was a two-story affair with three-sided bay windows and a gabled roof, out of which rose a traditional brick chimney. The resolution on the street view shot wasn't perfect, but even so, it was obvious that the house was in good repair. The sidings were pale and edged with blue trim that matched the front door.

"Looks like McKinney's the sharing type."

"Whoever said that crime doesn't pay was a fat liar," Zara agreed. "But it makes sense. Mafia dons always like to keep their underbosses happy. It's not a good investment in the long term to piss off men with guns and years of dirt on you."

"I guess not."

"Haynes keeps a low profile," Zara said, flicking to the next tab. "I've only found a couple of photographs of him—usually in the background of press shots of the senator."

Gideon leaned forward to examine the first of the images. He puffed out his cheeks. Zara was right, the photo told him little. The man was in his mid-fifties, at a guess, with a trim figure and only a thin crown of gray hair remaining around his temples. He resembled a middle manager in some bland federal bureaucracy—the US Fish and Wildlife Service, maybe—the kind of individual you might walk past on a street and forget the moment he disappeared from your eyeline.

"Have you ever seen him before?" she asked.

Gideon shook his head. "Never laid eyes on him."

At least, I don't think I have.

Zara flicked through a few more similar shots, but Gideon lost interest. They didn't reveal any additional information. Maybe he was five foot ten—perfectly average in both height and build. The photos told him nothing about his skill with weapons or in hand-to-hand combat.

"Okay, so who is he?"

"Like I said, low profile. If I had access to my Agency credentials, I'd be able to tell you more. But here are the basics: Haynes was born in Des Moines, Iowa, in 1969. He has a military background—deployed to Kuwait during the First Gulf

War—but I couldn't tell you whether he saw combat or not. A couple of years after the war, he dropped off the radar.

"I found an article in the online archives of the *Des Moines Register* indicating that he was listed as a missing person in 1997. After that, nothing."

"Maybe he went to Texas," Gideon mused, rubbing his chin thoughtfully. "He fits the profile of a recruit. Lost, looking for guidance..."

"That's what I'm thinking. Anyway, there's nothing until 2005. He was stopped by Metropolitan PD with a firearm in his vehicle—no permit."

"Did he do time?"

Zara shook her head. "Charges were dropped. The records I have access to don't say why."

"I think I have a good idea," Gideon snorted.

"Yeah..." Zara said softly. "I can tell you one thing though—from my personal experience of him. I only ever spoke to him on the phone. But he's one scary dude. His voice is just...cold. Empty. I got the sense that he would snap my neck without ever thinking about it again. He probably wouldn't even feel anything while he did it."

Gideon felt his right fist clench at the thought. "Go back to the street view tab."

Zara clicked over, and he zoomed in on the front of the house. He couldn't see any evidence of a home security system, but the front door was mostly blurred out by the tech platform's privacy system. A camera could have been positioned behind the hidden patch. It didn't have to be high-end. Even a simple Ring doorbell would provide excellent coverage and motion detection.

"We need to scope it out in person."

Gideon reached for the laptop as Zara climbed to her feet to stretch. He closed his eyes for a few seconds as he remembered the precise string of randomized letters and numbers that made up the web address for the private forum Leclerc's contractors used to bid for work, then typed them into the browser bar. A password dialogue opened up, and though he had no idea what the password was, his fingers filled in the blanks.

"OK," he muttered. "I'm in."

"What are you going to say?"

Gideon's eyes widened as he saw a message thread titled with his name. "No need. Leclerc's alive. And he wants to know what I—we—need."

"You're sure it's him?"

He turned the laptop screen so Zara could see it. Before a dense paragraph of text was a cellphone selfie of Leclerc in a hospital gown. He had a broad smile on his face. "Pretty sure. And he says some old friends want to help."

"COMFY?" Zara asked from the front seat of the 4 x 4 several hours later. The afternoon had been eaten up by preparing their opening offer to Sheldon McKinney—a recorded testimony of everything Zara had done, seen and heard. The video wouldn't be enough to clear her name or give justice to the families of the dead French agents.

But if released online it might just be enough to bring McKinney down.

The news that Leclerc was onside—and that John Stamp and Victor Glenn, the two legionnaires who'd been held captive at the Cannes villa with Gideon all those months ago—had given their pursuit of McKinney a new lease on life. Help was on the way. Right now it was their job to lay the groundwork for any future operation.

And one was coming, there was no doubt about that.

In the meantime they'd folded down the rear seats to give Gideon a level shooting position. He was presently lying underneath the blanket that concealed his frame. It would take a very observant set of eyes getting extremely close to notice either his own gaze—or the barrel of the rifle underneath the fabric. Zara had verified that fact herself.

"I need to take up yoga," Gideon said with a pained grunt.

"ETA five minutes," Zara replied, glancing to her left at the stack of flyers she'd liberated from a Chinese takeout restaurant local to Haynes's place to use as cover.

She'd also purchased about ninety bucks' worth of food to heat up later that evening. The bag was also concealed underneath the blanket, and it filled the old SUV with the pungent aroma of well-spiced Szechuan dishes. It was a neat addition to her cover that was mostly for her own enjoyment. If Haynes got close enough to the car to detect the scent, then it was probably game over.

Her own disguise was relatively simple. She was wearing a baseball cap and let her hair fall messily to hide most of her face. A little judicious use of eye makeup and foundation that significantly lightened her complexion completed the picture.

It was late evening when they arrived in Vienna. Zara felt her stomach contract as they got closer and closer to Holly Bush Lane—where Haynes's house was located. The neighborhood was beautiful, the homes well separated and hidden from each other by well-maintained foliage and mature tree growth.

"Comms check when you get out," Gideon reminded her.

"I hadn't forgotten," she said acidly.

"Don't take it personally. Every operation is a freshly shaken snow globe. If you wing it you're bound to trip up. All we can do to put the odds in our favor is make sure that we've considered every variable."

"That's a long-winded way of saying that everybody has a plan until they get punched in the mouth," she observed back at him.

But as her fingers whitened around the steering wheel, she realized that he was right—and she was allowing her anxiety to get the better of her.

Zara set her jaw tight, then sighed to release the tension. "Comms check when I get out. If no connection, then we scrub the mission. I only post flyers on the houses on Haynes's side of the street. I stay in your sight line at all times."

"If I tell you to drop, you drop," Gideon said, his voice perfectly even. "If I tell you to run, you run. And if I have to shoot, you get back to the car as fast as you can. Are we good?"

"We're good," Zara confirmed softly as she took the last turn onto Haynes's road. The yards were as perfectly manicured as the rest of the neighborhood. She maintained an even ten miles an hour, noting the signs on the lampposts indicating that kids played in the area, though she could see none out right now.

Probably inside glued to their phones.

Zara bit her lip and forced herself to concentrate. She ran through the mission parameters in her mind once again. The blue-trimmed two-story house that she recognized from the Google Street View image as Haynes's slowly came into view, and she stepped off the gas and feathered the brake until the car came to a stop on the far side of the street and almost directly opposite his house. But not exactly opposite—she was parked far enough away to ensure that Gideon had a clear field of fire.

"If he's home, you post the flyer through the mailbox, and then you get out," Gideon reminded her as she fiddled with the camera app on his cell phone. She set it to record, then slipped it into a front pocket—lens facing out. He paused. "Good luck."

She didn't respond. Part of her wanted to back out. They could replan the reconnaissance and make Gideon run point instead. It had sounded sensible back at the safe house to do it this way—he was the better shot and could cover her effectively from the back seat. She wasn't nearly as confident with her long gun marksmanship.

She swallowed, grabbed the stack of flyers, and opened the door. As she climbed out of the vehicle, her pistol bit into her lower back. It was well concealed by the bulky clothing she'd chosen, which also made it impossible to gauge her weight to closer than ten or fifteen pounds.

"Can you hear me?" she asked, pretending to scratch the back of her head but actually fiddling with the earpiece they'd liberated from the Brotherhood's SUV back in Maine.

"Loud and clear," Gideon confirmed. "Don't forget to lock the car. I'll pull it open from inside if I need to get out."

Zara clicked her tongue twice in confirmation—something she'd worked out she could do without moving her lips. She inserted the key into the lock and twisted it. The mechanism clicked into place and felt somehow symbolic.

She was committed now.

Her breath grew shaky as she walked to the other side of the street. She found herself aiming directly for the front steps up to Haynes's covered porch and consciously directed herself away—thankful for Gideon's insistence on drilling the plan into her mind.

"Road's clear," Gideon said.

She found herself irrationally grateful for the sound of his voice in her ears.

Two clicks.

Zara dropped a flyer through the last two mailboxes on Haynes's side of the street before retracing her path and climbing up to his front porch. It was painted a deep maritime blue that contrasted with the house's pale sidings exceptionally well. There was a printed sign that said: "No soliciting. No flyering." She found herself wondering whether he'd hired a designer.

Eyes on the fucking prize.

As she reached the top step, Zara's gaze darted left and right. The blinds were half-drawn on the bay windows, but enough was visible to know that the latter were original features. It was likely they would find similarly fragile windows at the back of the house. She saw no magnetic window sensors that would indicate a home security system, no stickers on the window by the front door with the badge of a local security company, no doorbell camera.

"Don't react. Car approaching. SUV, black." Gideon reported tersely.

Zara felt herself freezing and forced herself to keep moving. She grabbed a flyer and opened the front of the mailbox before stuffing it inside. She used the time to glance through the windows on either side of the front door. She saw a coatrack with a few dark jackets hanging off of it. No wiring that might be connected to a security system. No cameras.

Doesn't mean they aren't there...

"It's slowing. Might be a neighbor."

She turned back to the street as slowly as possible to maximize her visual time on target. Even so, a second later she was facing the road. She watched as a black SUV braked smoothly and came to a halt directly in front of Haynes's residence.

"Keep walking," Gideon instructed. "Nice and smooth."

Zara did so, though she felt her muscles growing stiff and imagined that her gait must be jerky. Haynes would know it was her—he had to know. She heard a car door open then slam shut. And then two words that chilled her to the core.

"It's him."

FIFTY-FIVE

"Can't you fucking read?"

At first, Zara tried to ignore Haynes's mocking tone. It was definitely him. He was wearing a dark suit that hung off his frame as though he'd recently lost weight. He didn't look particularly physically impressive, but there was an obvious underlying strength. He moved like a manual laborer, not a desk jockey.

"Hi," she said lamely from the bottom step as he strode toward her.

She turned the stack of flyers sideways-on so that he would be able to see what they were. Adrenaline surged through her system, tightening her chest and making it difficult to think straight.

Don't say too much. He's heard your voice before.

Zara tilted her chin down so that the peak of the baseball cap covered more of her face and angled herself away from Haynes. He was carrying a backpack in his right hand—probably grabbed from the passenger seat—and now dropped it onto the ground.

"Stay calm," Gideon said, his tone ice cold in contrast to the stress that was rampaging through Zara's mind. "I've got him covered. Just keep walking."

"Don't walk away from me!" Haynes snarled. He'd gone from 0 to 100 in a matter of seconds. He reached out and grabbed Zara's left wrist and raised it—and the stack of flyers—high above her shoulder. "I asked you a question."

"I'm coming out," Gideon said instantly. "I don't have a clear shot."

"No!" Zara said insistently, hoping that her hair was still covering the earpiece in her right ear. The downside of using the Brotherhood's comms tech was that Haynes would probably recognize it if he saw it. "Don't!"

"Don't what?" Haynes asked, his face creasing into a frown.

"Don't make me call the cops," Zara said, turning her face away from his gaze as she tried to pull her hand free. "I'm just doing my job."

Haynes released her wrist grudgingly. "You're lucky I didn't call the police on you. Didn't you see the sign?"

"What sign?"

He pointed up the steps. "It says it right there. *No flyering.*"

"Is that the whole neighborhood?" Zara asked, rubbing her wrist. "I didn't see it on any of the other houses."

Haynes sneered at her. "I don't give a shit what my neighbors do. Just stay away from my house."

And then, as Zara backed away from him, his gaze narrowed. His chin crept forward an inch as if he was confirming a suspicion. "I know you."

Zara turned to run, but before she'd even made it two paces Haynes's pistol was up and aimed. "Don't fucking move," he hissed.

Shit, Zara thought, her mind otherwise bereft of direction. She'd never imagined that the barrel of a pistol could look that wide. There was something more ominous about it than all the danger she faced until now.

Perhaps it was the fact that Haynes's hand didn't even tremble.

"Zara, reach into your pocket for the car keys," Gideon said calmly through her earpiece. "Take them out and when he asks, tell him he's not going to shoot you in the middle of his own street."

Her chest rose and fell rapidly. For a moment it was difficult for Zara to even process Gideon's words. She blinked several times before her senses began to reassert themselves.

"You're not going to shoot me here," she said, hating the way her voice shook as she reached into her pocket as instructed.

"Stop that," Haynes snapped, frowning at what she was doing.

Zara's fingers closed around the keys.

"Good," Gideon said immediately. "Now walk to the car."

Hesitantly Zara took a step.

"Don't move!" Haynes ordered in a low hiss. Strangely that increased Zara's confidence. He was still trying to avoid attracting attention. Despite the fact that nobody was obviously looking out of their windows, that could change if she started to scream.

Or if somebody started shooting.

"Tell him to look at me," Gideon said. The evenness in his voice helped calm her nerves.

"Can you see that car?" Zara said, jerking her thumb behind herself.

"What are you talking about?"

Her own voice was completely calm now. "Look at the backseats."

For a moment Haynes didn't respond. Finally his gaze

shifted, a twitchiness to the movement indicating he planned only to glance for a second. But his eyes widened.

"You can see me, can't you?" Gideon called out—this time speaking from across the street and not over the radio.

Haynes didn't answer.

"I advise you not to touch that trigger. I can't be held liable for my actions if you do."

Zara heard movement on the other side of the street—the scuffling sound of somebody climbing out of the car—before rapid footsteps behind her announced Gideon's arrival. He stepped past her and fanned out to the right, raising his rifle so that Haynes was in his sights.

"What do you want?" Haynes said, keeping his pistol aimed at her despite Gideon's arrival.

"To end this," Zara said.

"You think it matters if you kill me?" Haynes snorted. "They won't stop hunting you. Either of you. I'm just a pawn. A bit part player."

"We know," Gideon said dryly. "If we wanted you dead, we'd have shot you from the car."

"Then what are you doing here?" Haynes asked, still not taking his attention away from Zara, despite the fact that Gideon was holding a weapon on him.

"The problem with being an internationally wanted criminal is that you can't just call up your senator's office and ask for a meeting," Zara said.

Haynes looked surprised for the first time. "Why the hell would he meet you?"

"Because we don't want any part of this power play he has going on," Gideon said evenly. "I never wanted to be anybody. I still don't. I want to be left alone."

"What does the boss have to do with that?"

"All we want is to disappear and leave this mess behind us,"

Zara answered. "We know we can't fight the Brotherhood. We don't want to try."

"Then what are you doing here?"

"We need money. Lots of money," Zara said. "Enough to buy the best passports and pay all the right bribes. I know McKinney's reputation. He can arrange everything we need. Ten million ought to do it."

Haynes snorted. "Why would he do that?"

Zara reached into the back pocket on her jeans for the USB drive she'd prepared earlier and tossed it toward him. "Tell him to watch this."

FIFTY-SIX

"You've checked it for viruses?" McKinney said, glancing sideways at the USB drive in Haynes's hand.

He nodded. "It's clean."

"What do they want?"

"It's easier if you watch."

Haynes plugged the drive into the computer on McKinney's desk. The PC was high-end, and it only took a second before the contents flashed up on the screen. As Haynes had seen on his own laptop the previous night, it contained only two files: one video, the other audio. He double-clicked on the former.

Zara's frozen face appeared on the computer monitor. Her mouth was half open, the pause icon hovering over it like a cloud. He tapped the space bar and the video began to play.

"My name is Zara Walker," she said. "I am an employee of the Central Intelligence Agency. My immediate supervisor is the station chief at the embassy in Paris, France. For security reasons I will not name him, however, I have provided a number of journalists with his name."

"What is this?" McKinney growled.

Haynes didn't answer.

"Approximately two days ago, I was ordered by my supervisor to assist a senior Washington politician." Zara paused, and her face twinged with something that—if McKinney hadn't known better—he might have believed was real anguish. "To my shame, I did so."

On screen, Zara chewed her lip. "I'm ashamed because I knew what I was doing was wrong. I was trying to save my career, and in doing so I betrayed my country."

McKinney reached out and paused the video. His face was thunderous. "I don't want to watch any more of this," he said in a brutal tone of voice. "What does she want?"

Haynes had long ago mastered an impassive demeanor. He wore it now.

"She's threatening to release this video—she calls it her testament—to the press, congressional authorities, the FBI, and social media. She confesses to everything—her initial orders, watching the two French agents die in Marseille, and she names both of us."

"She has no proof," McKinney snapped back.

Haynes pointed at the folder open on the senator's screen. "She recorded her phone calls. With both of us. We can claim the recordings are fakes, but it'll just attract more attention to the story."

"Dammit," McKinney said, flexing and releasing his fist. His face had turned an alarming shade of puce.

"Our people at the Bureau can play defense on any investigation. And we can apply pressure on the media and Congress. For a while."

"Say what you want to say, Ronan."

"If this gets too loud, all bets are off. They can upload that video to social media faster than we can take it down. We can try, but that'll only make the cover-up look more suspicious. You can bet that hundreds, then thousands of people will share their own copies. It'll be like fighting a wildfire with a fire extinguisher."

McKinney exhaled. Already the outward evidence of his rage was fading. There was a reason the Brotherhood had sent him to the nation's capital—he was the consummate Washington dealmaker. And Ronan knew better than anyone that everybody had a price.

"What does she want?"

Haynes shrugged. "Money, mostly. Ten million and the promise that you'll let them disappear. And they want to look you in the eye and hear you say it."

McKinney looked dumbfounded. "Say that again?"

"That's what the video says. They want to meet you here, in Middleburg, in twenty-four hours. And they want the money in cash. No transfers."

"Why would they do that?" McKinney mused. "Why risk it?"

"It's possible they're overconfident. They might think that you wouldn't risk moving against them so long as they can release these clips. Or perhaps they think we'll be able to trace a wire transfer. They're probably right."

"Or it's a trap," McKinney mused.

"It's possible," Haynes agreed. He watched his boss expectantly. When the senator remained silent, he asked, "What do you want me to do?"

"Arrange for a few reliable men. Do it quietly. We can't afford New Eden finding out about this."

"You want to take them out when they get here? What about the video?"

"They'll give it up," McKinney said, his nostrils flaring. "Or you will make life very unpleasant for them."

A knock sounded at the door to the senator's library office. McKinney's wife didn't bother waiting for approval before pulling it open and stepping inside.

"What do you want, Julia?"

Haynes discreetly unplugged the USB drive as the young woman walked over. She was clothed demurely in a blue floral dress that fell past her knees. He intentionally looked away from her, knowing that despite the senator's antipathy for the woman who had been foisted upon him, he was still a jealous man.

"I packed my things," she said, her voice strangely girlish, as they all were. The affectation was drilled into them. It had creeped Haynes out in the beginning. But you got used to it. "When are we driving back into the city?"

"We're not," McKinney said, seeming to make a decision as he spoke the words.

"Why not?" Julia replied, her lips forming into a pout. "You know I don't like this place. It's too cold."

McKinney rose slowly. "Because I said so."

"But why?"

Even though Haynes suspected it was coming, the speed of the older man still startled him. The senator reached out with an open palm and slapped his wife hard on her cheek. The blow rocked her back and sent her tumbling to the floor. For a few seconds, she didn't even cry with pain.

"Pick her up," McKinney said, gesturing toward his wife, who lay in a fetal position on the floor. His lip was curled with disgust.

Julia started crying as Haynes slipped his hands underneath her arms and hoisted her to her feet. She didn't make a sound, but the tears slid silently down her cheeks. Her face was already red and beginning to swell.

McKinney was entirely unimpressed by his wife's evident

shock. He looked her up and down, lingering on her belly before finally meeting her gaze. To Julia's credit, she matched it, despite the fact that her ears must have been ringing from the force of the blow.

"Don't question me again, girl," he said coldly.

Julia said nothing. Sensing that she was capable of supporting her weight once again, Haynes released his grasp and stepped back. He wanted to leave the room but knew that McKinney enjoyed these displays of power. He liked others to watch.

"What is your purpose?"

"I'm—I'm your partner. Your servant," Julia said, her voice shaky. "I just want to help you, sir. That's all I've ever wanted."

McKinney's eyes flashed with a black rage. He stepped forward and grabbed his wife by the roots of her hair. "No. Your purpose is to give me a son. And I have no son, do I, Julia?"

She shook her head, the tugging of her hair causing her eyes to water more.

"You'll be in my bed tonight," McKinney said, relinquishing his grip and pushing her away with an air of disdain. "And clean up your face. You look disgusting."

Haynes was careful not to react as Julia fled the office, her steps uneven. She pulled the door closed behind her, but it failed to latch.

McKinney turned away, as if he'd already forgotten the intensity of the emotion he'd experienced just moments before. "Arrange for those men. This ends tomorrow night."

FIFTY-SEVEN

"We've got company," Gideon said, crouching down to peer out the window that looked out onto the driveway to the front of their rented bungalow. A slate-gray sedan was rumbling along the uneven half-paved road. He flexed his grip around the pistol in his right hand. The weight of the weapon was as comforting as it always was.

But he longed not to have to feel that way. There was nothing natural about living life like this.

"It'll be them," Zara said, barely looking up from her computer screen. "They're right on time. What car are they driving?"

"Toyota Corolla."

"Just like they texted from the airport," she said, reaching out and closing the lid of her laptop. "Relax."

"We're being chased by a homicidal globe-spanning cult, remember," Gideon grumbled, leaning away from the window.

"Oh," Zara said, looking around with mock surprise. "I thought this was a surprise vacation."

A minute later they heard the thunk of two car doors slamming, then the click of a trunk opening, and a third slam as it shut. Gideon held up his palm as Zara rose to greet their guests.

"Stay there," he said in a low voice.

She was right that these new arrivals were following the protocol that he'd communicated to Leclerc via the private web forum. But the last few days had made him paranoid enough to at least doubt the truth of his own senses. He wouldn't be certain that their communications hadn't been intercepted until he laid eyes on Stamp and Glenn himself. It'd been three months since he helped them escape from the villa in Cannes but his recollection of their descriptions had been reinforced by the photos in Leclerc's personnel files.

The wooden floorboards creaked underneath him as he walked slowly to the door. He heard footsteps on the other side of the panels, boots scraping against gravel, then a hollow thud as the first foot stepped onto the porch.

Gideon twisted the door handle and pulled it open in one swift movement. He kept his pistol down at his side, but his arm was poised to raise up and fire it in a fraction of a second.

"There's close enough," he called out.

The two men stopped. They were both wearing dark blue jeans; one was in an olive-green field jacket, the other in a tan Carhartt. The one in the Carhartt stopped midstride and dropped a black duffel bag at his side.

"Come now, Ryker," he said cocking his head with surprise. "That ain't no way to treat an old friend."

Gideon exhaled slowly. It was John Stamp. And judging from the broad smile on the man's face, it was extremely unlikely that this was a trap.

"Put the gun away, Gideon," Zara said, pushing past him and swatting his pistol-wielding hand. "If they wanted to hurt us, they already would have."

"And just for the record, ma'am, we do not," Victor Glenn

said. He didn't seem as friendly as his partner, but there was an easiness about him.

"Good. Gideon, come grab his bag," she said, ushering Stamp inside.

Gideon blinked slowly, sensing mild amusement dancing in Glenn's eyes. He wasn't exactly sure how he planted himself in this situation, following orders from a woman he'd barely met.

And somehow not minding it...

"You like her," Glenn said quietly as he walked up onto the porch.

"Thanks for coming," Gideon answered without addressing his statement. "You didn't have to."

"Yeah, we did," Glenn said seriously. "You saved both our lives."

"I put you both in danger," Gideon said, grimacing as a wave of guilt washed over him. Neither of the two men who had flown to him at the drop of a hat would have been hurt in the first place if it wasn't for him.

"Bullshit" was the reply. "You didn't know. Somebody else made that choice. And I really don't like people fucking with my life."

Gideon reached out and embraced Glenn. They didn't know each other too well. They'd served in the Legion at roughly the same time but never in the same regiment. But he'd answered the call. Fulfilled the warrior's code of arms.

He was here.

"Come on inside," he said, taking Glenn's bag off him. "It's a little cramped, but we'll find you somewhere to sleep."

Stamp was already introducing himself to the crate of beers that Gideon had stocked the fridge with. He pulled out four, popping the caps with a bottle opener on the back of his wallet.

"Never go anywhere without it," he grinned.

"Least after he stopped opening them with his teeth,"

Glenn snorted. "Couldn't afford the dental cover once he came back home."

"Don't believe a word that comes out of his mouth, ma'am," Stamp said, gallantly offering the first beer to Zara. "I take good care of my pearly whites."

"It's Zara," she said, clinking bottles first with him, then Glenn. "Thanks for coming."

"I needed a vacation anyway," he replied, rolling his shoulder and plastering a feigned grimace on his face. "I'm not exactly fully recovered."

"What exactly happened?" Gideon asked, his face tightening. "It's still hazy."

"I'm not surprised," Glenn said after sighing with satisfaction, his bottle already a third drained.

"Long journey," he said by way of explanation, though none of them cared. He gestured at Stamp then back at himself. "Those motherfuckers had both of us in cages. Didn't bother giving us food or water for going on two days. Guess they figured they were going to dispose of us when it was all over anyway, so why bother?"

The question was rhetorical, but he looked around anyway before fixing his gaze on Gideon. "They flipped the script on us not long after we arrived at the villa. That bitch kept up the facade that everything was normal until she was sure we didn't have a support team or something. They came for us at night, when only I was on shift. You guys were sleeping."

"We both woke up to a gun in the face," Stamp chimed in. "Gideon reacted faster than I did. Knocked the gun aside, damn near broke the guy's wrist. But there were three of them for every one of us, and they were prepared. Ain't nothing you can do to fight numbers like that. They beat the daylights out of us."

"Anyway, it didn't take long to figure out that they didn't

give a shit about me and John," Glenn said, a wry grin on his face. He pointed at Gideon. "Only this special snowflake over here. You'd have thought he was our Lord and Savior come back down to earth by the way they were going on."

"They let us be, mostly," Stamp said, his humor fading. "Only brought us out when they wanted to teach Gideon here a lesson. They had him strapped down to a chair and were shooting him up with all kinds of shit. I thought he was going to lose his damn mind. When he started speaking in tongues, that's when I wondered if he really was sent to save us."

"And he did," Glenn agreed. "Still don't know how. We were both too weak by then to move. They'd whaled on us a couple times. Nearly broke my arm. I was spitting up blood for almost three weeks after we escaped. After Gideon here set us free."

"He was off his damn face," Stamp said, gritting his teeth forcefully. "If I hadn't seen it with my own eyes I wouldn't have believed it, you know? I could barely lift my head up off the floor. They shot him up with another vial of that drug. He seemed to pass out. After about ten minutes, one of them came over to check his vitals. Gideon snapped his neck."

"He cut himself free with the guy's knife," Glenn said, carrying on the tale. "Killed the other guy in the basement before he could even cry out with surprise. Then carried us both up out of that hellhole with his bare hands."

Stamp gazed intently into Zara's eyes. "If it wasn't for this man right here, I wouldn't be standing here. I owe him my life. And I don't give a shit how this started. I'm here to end it."

Glenn started a slow, theatrical clap. "That's our hero right there," he said, and Gideon was unsure whether he was referring to him or Stamp.

His friend rolled his eyes. "All right. What's the plan?"

"It's kind of free-form," Gideon admitted.

"Ain't it always."

Zara cleared the table in front of her and spread out a map of the Middleburg area. Senator McKinney's house was marked with a small black cross.

"You both need to know who we're going after," she said.

"Doesn't matter," Stamp said instantly. "We're with you all the way."

"You might not say that when she's done," Gideon said dryly.

"This is Sheldon McKinney's country house," Zara said, tapping the cross.

"You mean *the* Sheldon McKinney," Glenn said slowly. "The Chairman of the Senate Intelligence Committee Sheldon McKinney?"

"The one and only," Zara confirmed coolly. "He's behind what happened to all of you in France. He caused the deaths of two French intelligence agents in Marseille three days ago. He wants us dead, and he won't give up until he gets his way."

"Or we stop him first," Gideon said.

"What are the rules of engagement?" Stamp asked. His posture was tense, his mouth a thin line.

"Whatever it takes. McKinney's a member of a cult called the Brotherhood. It has thousands of members and tentacles deep into Washington and most of the three-letter agencies. He's probably not a true believer; it's worse than that. He's using his position to enrich himself. To secure his own power."

"Okay, then," Stamp said with a sharp nod. "Just checking we were all aligned."

"That didn't scare you off?"

"Not one bit."

"Good. We believe that McKinney has an insurance policy that's stopping the Brotherhood from taking him out. That's what we're after."

"Trouble in paradise?" Glenn asked.

"Something like that."

"Ain't that always the way."

Zara reached for her laptop and spun it around. She ran her finger across the trackpad and the screen flashed into life. She double-clicked an icon and two video feeds appeared on screen.

"We did a recce first thing this morning and installed these cameras. This one," she said, tapping the feed on the left side of the screen, which displayed a large wooden driveway gate, "covers the entrance to McKinney's property. The road to the house is about half a mile in length. The other is a distance shot of the building itself."

"His security system's good," Gideon said, taking up the baton. "Cameras on the exterior fence, sometimes a pair of local cops parked just up from the gate."

"So what do you plan to do?"

Gideon shrugged casually. "Drive right in."

FIFTY-EIGHT

"The cops drive through the gate and do a circle of the interior perimeter every three hours," Zara said, glancing at her watch. "Should be any moment now."

"We'll arrive right after they do their check," Gideon explained. "From what we've seen, they just wave visitors through. They probably note down license plates, maybe even run them through the system. But we'll show up clean."

"And then what?" Glenn asked skeptically. "You two just stroll right into the lion's den?"

"Something like that," Gideon confirmed. "But it'll just be me."

Zara shot him a fierce look.

He held up his hands. "We've been through this. Having you on the outside gives us options. He can't move on me if he's worried about you uploading those tapes to the net."

"If he's as ruthless as you guys think, he might roll the dice anyway," Glenn said. "Gideon's the one he really wants. *Needs*. Maybe he figures he can ride out the storm. He's got enough dirt on people in this town to be sure he'll never be prosecuted for what he's done. He might have to retire in disgrace, but so do half the politicians in this town. And as long as he has Gideon and this insurance policy, then the Brotherhood can't take him out, either."

"That's where you guys come in," Gideon said. "We'll be in constant contact. If I go dark for any reason, you come get me. That's the first part of the plan, anyway."

"It's risky," Stamp mused out loud, drumming his fingertips against the map lying on the table as he alternated his attention between it and the video feeds on screen.

"That's why we're paying you the big bucks," Gideon said.

"Do you have photos of the exterior of McKinney's place?" Stamp asked, before adding, "I wasn't aware you were paying us a damn thing."

"About that," Gideon said as Zara pulled up photos they'd taken on a quick reconnaissance trip to Middleburg using a long-distance lens. They weren't brilliant quality, but it would've been too risky to linger long enough to frame the shots perfectly. "The deal we set up is that McKinney pays us off, and we disappear for the rest of our lives. If the cash is real, then we split it four ways."

"How much's a life worth?" Glenn asked.

"Five million," Zara said, gesturing first at herself, then at Gideon. "For each of us."

He let out a low whistle. "Not bad."

"What's the second part?" Stamp said. "You said that this was the first part of the plan. So what's the second?"

"We're not doing this for the money," Gideon said, folding his arms. "I don't want to look over my shoulder the rest of my life."

"Neither do I," Zara agreed.

"I'm going to snatch the senator," Gideon explained. "If he hands over his insurance policy, then I'll let him go. Kidnapping someone of his stature would set all of law enforcement on our tail."

"And if he doesn't?"

Zara answered that. "Then we kill him. If he doesn't hand over the insurance policy, then the only way to guarantee its release is to trip his dead man's switch."

"Literally," Glenn grumbled. "Shit. You really ain't here to play."

"If you want to back out, then now's the time," Gideon said. "I wouldn't blame you. I'm asking too much."

Stamp leaned forward and examined the photos on Zara's screen in greater detail. He kept drumming his fingers on the table, his eyes squinted as if deep in thought.

Finally he stood up and announced, "This plan of yours, it isn't going to work. It's half a mile from the fence to the house. Even if we can climb it without being detected, it'll be five minutes in full battle rattle before we get inside the house. It'll take too long."

"And calling it a plan is a bit grandiose, even for you," Glenn added. "We're in, by the way. To the bitter end."

Gideon spread his hands wide and said, "If you have a better idea, I'm all ears."

Stamp exchanged a look with Glenn. They appeared to be communicating almost telepathically. After a couple of seconds they came to a decision. Gideon and Zara waited expectantly to hear what it was.

"What's that thing the kids are saying these days?" Stamp asked rhetorically.

"Enlighten me..." Gideon said, raising his eyebrows as he waited for the punchline.

The two ex-legionnaires grinned as Stamp intoned, "All cops are bastards."

Gideon frowned, not yet understanding where the two men were going with this.

Zara got there first. "I see two problems with your plan."

"Fugitives in glass houses shouldn't throw stones," Stamp said. "But go on..."

"First," she said, counting off her points on her index finger as the corners of her mouth turned up with amusement, "you'll need to make a donation to the benevolent fund. It won't do their careers any good to be tied up in the trunk of their own squad car."

"I can do that," he agreed. "And second?"

Her smile grew. "You'll need a driver."

FIFTY-NINE

"Radio check," Stamp said over the encrypted earpieces Gideon and Zara had liberated from the Brotherhood SUV back in Maine.

"Walker, copy," Zara said.

"Glenn, loud and clear. I have visual on the cop car. Looks like they are about to do their rounds."

Gideon paused before giving his answer. He hesitated for a moment, then said, "Nomad, good copy."

Over the course of the afternoon, it had become clear that Leclerc had arranged for the two legionnaires to bring a few goodies with them. How exactly the Frenchman had managed to source a pair of Swedish AT4 shoulder-fired antitank weapons on such short notice wasn't exactly clear, but nobody asked too many questions.

In addition to the AT4s was a veritable bounty of explosives, detonators, grenades, and small-arms ammunition, along with personal protective equipment and night vision aids. Combined with the plunder from the Brotherhood SUV that Gideon and Zara still had in the back of the Wrangler, they had enough hardware to topple the government of a small Caribbean nation.

Of course, if they had to use any of it, then things would have gone horribly wrong.

Gideon was currently sitting in the driver's seat of the car the two legionnaires had brought with them. His ass felt uncomfortably warm, and his palms were drenched with sweat. It had nothing *directly* to do with the fact that he was about to drive into a situation that was very likely to be a trap.

No. It turned out that Stamp was something of a connoisseur when it came to explosives, particularly the jerry-rigged improvised kind. He'd packed every hidden compartment in the car with plastique and attached a radio-controlled detonator.

I'm sitting on a fucking bomb.

He exhaled slowly. He was waiting in a lay-by about a mile down the road from McKinney's Middleburg mansion. They'd done one last careful sweep of the vicinity and detected no sign that the senator had brought in reinforcements for the night's clandestine meeting.

The two cameras they'd planted on the roads leading toward his house hadn't detected any unusual activity—only the senator's car entering and exiting, along with a couple of vehicles that appeared to belong to domestic help.

"Cops look nice and relaxed. Big guy in the passenger seat's working his way through a family-size bag of Reese's Pieces," Glenn reported.

That was a good sign, wasn't it? If the cops had been switched with experienced shooters, Ronan Haynes would probably have picked men in the prime of their lives. From Glenn's description, these guys weren't that.

"Sixty seconds."

Gideon's right knee bounced restlessly against the steering

wheel. He tried to still it with his hand, but it was hopeless. His mind was filled with all the ways this could go wrong. The cops might notice movement in the darkness and call for help before Glenn and Stamp were able to silence them.

There could be a hidden camera somewhere—maybe even an infrared sensor they had missed. If the house's defenders got a warning they were about to be infiltrated, then this would likely go sideways. Fast.

"Okay, looks like they're checking in with dispatch," Glenn said, rendering all speculation moot. "It's go time."

STAMP FLASHED his partner a hand signal and received an accompanying nod. They were hidden in the foliage on either side of the road. The cop car was hidden from the senator's front gate by a thick section of trees. Men like McKinney didn't like to think about the people who risked everything to keep them safe.

It gave them a window. A short one. They had to jump the cops and secure them in a matter of seconds so that the delay in the usual rounds didn't attract curiosity or suspicion from inside the house.

"We'll make it up to you," he whispered, seeing the larger cop's face lit up by the screen of his cell phone. The guy was in his mid-fifties. He didn't deserve what was about to happen.

But it was the only way.

Three clicks over the radio.

Two.

Go.

Stamp sprinted out of the trees, his rifle bouncing against his chest where it was clipped to his vest. He had a pistol in his right hand. He only needed to cover about five yards, and he was as fit as he'd ever been, despite the rigors of his experience in France.

He made it to the passenger door before the big cop even looked up. He snatched at the door handle, holding his breath as he did so. If the vehicle was locked, then this was going to get a whole lot louder.

It wasn't.

The door swung open easily, and Stamp reached inside and grabbed the cop by his neck, instantly checking to see whether the man was wearing his seat belt. He was not.

His eyes flashed with shock and fear. "What the hell—?"

The second he knew that his prey was free, Stamp reversed his momentum, pulling the man out of the vehicle and throwing him to the ground. As the cop hit the ground, a whoosh of air released from his lungs, almost certainly winding him.

As adrenaline flooded his veins, Stamp blocked out the noise of a similar scuffle on the other side of the car. The air was filled with grunts, slight exhalations of breath, and the scrabbling of hands and the rustling of cloth.

Stamp pressed the muzzle of his pistol against the big cop's temple, and the man instantly stilled his feeble struggles. He was turning red, sucking in breaths that never seemed to fill his lungs. Dammit, he was purple now.

What the fuck?

"What's wrong with you?" he hissed.

"Asthma," the cop managed to get out, his eyes practically rolling back in his skull. "Need...inhaler."

"Christ," Stamp hissed. This could be a ruse, but he didn't think so. The cop appeared to be choking now. This was costing them time they didn't have. If this man had been his enemy, he would've left him to die.

But he wasn't. He was probably a good man with a wife

and kids at home. He wasn't here out of choice. He didn't know what kind of man McKinney was or the evils he was responsible for. And he damn sure didn't deserve to die because of that.

Stamp knelt at his side and hurriedly patted him down. He found the inhaler in the cop's right pocket, pulled off the cap and shoved it between his lips, depressing the metal cylinder half a dozen times before pausing and pumping another couple of doses through the man's lips in time with his breath—which he saw to his relief was now easing.

"What's the holdup?" Glenn called out in a low voice.

"Working on it," Stamp replied, his own tone clipped.

Another sixty seconds passed before he judged that the officer had recovered enough to be restrained. He stripped the man's jacket from his shoulders, as Glenn had done with his target, and shrugged it on. They tied the two men to a tree far from the road, gagged them, and left them there.

Zara edged out of the forest. "Ready?"

Stamp nodded. "Shit, that didn't go as easily as planned."

"But it's done."

They found two broad-brimmed campaign-style hats on the back seat. Zara took one and climbed into the back, then passed the other forward to Glenn who had taken the passenger seat and was in the process of unclipping his rifle from the sling around his vest. He placed it onto his head, then zipped up the uniform jacket.

She checked her watch. "Time to go."

Stamp exhaled sharply as he fired up the cruiser's engine. This was the unknown speed bump that could scotch their plan. If the cops had a password to get through the gate, then their plan was over before it had a chance to get started.

He accelerated gently as he pulled out onto the road, before spinning the wheel to the left and braking in front of the gate. The cruiser drew to a halt, and Glenn prepared to climb out. Stamp held out a hand to hold his friend up.

"Wait a sec," he muttered, depressing the lever to the side of the steering wheel and flashing the cruiser's front lights twice.

It's worth a shot.

He held his breath as he waited for a response. Several seconds ticked by and nothing happened. Just as he was about to release Glenn to walk up to the intercom, a buzz rang out in the gloom, and a green LED light blinked into life on the speaker panel.

The gates swung silently open.

"THEY'RE IN," Zara announced quietly over the radio net about fifteen minutes later. Gideon breathed a sigh of relief.

"Any sign of trouble?"

"None. I dropped them off behind the thick copse of trees. Was in the front seat and moving again within about ten seconds. Don't think we were detected."

"Good job," Gideon radioed. "Stay safe. I'm going in."

SIXTY

Gideon traced their path a couple of minutes later. He resisted the urge to glance toward the police cruiser as he drove past. According to the plan, Zara would be inside, monitoring the house's front entrance.

He didn't like it. She was exposed out here. But as she, Glenn, and Stamp had forcefully emphasized, it wasn't like they had any other choice. And he'd seen the way she operated in the field. She was good.

I'm just a control freak.

It was a truth that made entering McKinney's house unarmed particularly difficult to bear. They'd all agreed that it was pointless to try to smuggle in a weapon. Ronan Haynes was too experienced not to pat him down.

The only play that remained open to them was for Gideon to acquire a gun from somewhere inside the house. However, he wasn't exactly going in without a trick under his sleeve. The twenty kilos of plastic explosive packed into the vehicle was enough to cause a hell of an explosion. He would be the only person in there who knew not only that it existed in the first place but also the precise moment it would detonate.

The distraction would rattle his brains. But at this point he figured he must have some kind of immunity to further brain damage.

He stopped in front of the gate, climbed out of the vehicle, and walked up to the intercom panel. It was a steel plate with a numeric keypad at the bottom and two small circles at the top. He puzzled over what they were in the gloom as he tapped the call button.

His answer came quickly. The circle on the left lit up and spilled out a pool of electric light at an angle that drilled directly into his eyes. He winced from the discomfort, covered his eyes, and whispered a prayer for his now-departed night vision. The illumination was enough for him to realize that the other circle was a small camera lens.

"Smile," he muttered.

"Lift up your jacket," a voice crackled through the speaker. It was probably Haynes, but the quality was too poor to be sure. "And turn three-sixty degrees."

Gideon did as he was instructed, going further by pulling up his pants legs to show that he didn't have a spare piece strapped to either ankle.

"Okay. Drive up to the house. When you get here, pop the trunk."

The light on the security panel clicked off, and Gideon climbed back into the car as the gates swung open. His palms were now completely dry. His breathing was easy. In fact, he felt as relaxed as he could remember.

He was in the endgame now.

Spotlights angled up the trunks of the apple trees planted in neat rows down the full length of the driveway. It was still early spring, so the branches were only just beginning to bud.

The skeletal structure above swayed in the gentle breeze, causing fingers of shadow to stretch out across the road surface.

The asphalt driveway gave way to a gravel drive directly in front of the big red-brick house. It was two stories with a tile roof and had to be a couple of hundred years old. Thick vines of ivy had crept up almost to the guttering, finding purchase in every tiny crevice. The decorative tapestry seemed to be consuming the old house, squeezing the life out of it.

Two men were standing just out of the doorway when he arrived. He only recognized one—Haynes. The other man was most likely a hired shooter. He was roughly six feet tall, with a lean, muscular CrossFit-style build. He was carrying an AR-pattern rifle, which he aimed at Gideon's vehicle.

Gideon ignored Haynes's gestured instructions to stop until he pulled in the car to just a few feet from the open doorway to the house. If they were forced to detonate the explosives, it was possible that very little of the facade of the brick building would survive.

"Hands where I can see them," the shooter instructed as Gideon opened the car door.

He nodded, leaning his wrists on the steering wheel and splaying his fingers. The last thing he needed was for a B-grade mercenary to splatter his brains across the dashboard tonight.

"I'm going to reach down and pop the trunk," he said in a calm voice. "That okay?"

"Slowly."

Gideon waited a beat before complying to give the guy the added assurance that he wasn't going to do anything stupid. He could feel Haynes's attention scouring his face as he did so. He didn't bother repaying the favor. After a couple of seconds, he reached for the button on the center console and opened the trunk.

"Now climb out of the vehicle."

Again, Gideon complied slowly. The shooter kept his rifle trained on him, sidestepping to allow Haynes to pat him down without crossing his field of fire. Gideon felt rough hands tousling every inch of his body.

"You won't find anything," he said, keeping his hands raised and open. "I'm just here to talk."

"Where's the girl?" Haynes asked curtly when he stepped back, apparently satisfied that Gideon had come unarmed.

"Who?"

"Walker," came the answer, laced with withering disdain.

"Oh," Gideon said theatrically. "I didn't realize you were talking about a seasoned CIA case officer."

"A fuck-up."

"Let's agree to disagree," he said coolly. "Anyway, she's a long way from here. I walk out of here with the money, and we disappear. But if anything should happen to me..."

Haynes drew his weapon and gestured for the muscle to check the car. He held out his free hand, palm facing up, and said, "Keys."

"I'd rather keep hold of them myself."

"I don't give a shit what you'd rather."

"Fine." Gideon shrugged. He reached languidly into his pocket and pulled out the key fob. He deliberately paid little attention to the man ransacking the car, even as his blood pressure ticked inexorably higher with every passing second.

"Here," he said, tossing the keys toward Haynes, just a little beyond the fixer's reach, forcing him to grope for them in an awkward, ungainly lunge.

Gideon allowed himself a sly grin as Haynes pocketed the keys. McKinney's hatchet man couldn't lash out at the slight while maintaining his dignity, but he clearly wanted to.

"Well?" he said, scowling at the shooter. "Any weapons?"

"Looks like it's clean," came the reply that Gideon was

hoping for. He kept his expression relaxed, knowing better than to look relieved.

"Inside," Haynes said, pointing through the open doorway.

"How will I know where I'm going?"

"Just walk," the man growled. Gideon watched out of the corner of his eye as he reached into his pocket and placed the Corolla's keys on a silver tray on a thin antique stand by the door.

The house was appointed in an English country style, with flagstone flooring and rich wallpaper—a luxurious maroon with needlepoint gold stripes. A fire was lit in the entrance hallway, though only a handful of embers glowed in the hearth.

"Nice place," Gideon observed as he walked into the house. "Didn't know a senator's salary stretched this far."

To his dismay, Haynes didn't take the bait. He kept walking in a straight line down the long hallway. To the left was a kitchen, the door ajar only a couple of inches. The work surfaces were of thick beams of oak or another similar hardwood. They had been polished until they almost shone.

"Take a right," Haynes instructed.

As he turned, Gideon caught a glimpse of the two men trailing him. He made a note of the fact that they were walking about six feet behind him, way too far for him to close the distance before they pumped him full of lead.

He'd known that Haynes was a canny operator. This was confirmation that the hired help wasn't too bad, either. But they'd expected that.

If Haynes and McKinney were operating under ideal circumstances, then there was no way this meeting would have gone down like this. Haynes would have hidden a dozen or more gunmen in the house and grounds and probably had dog and handler teams ready to search him as he entered.

But everybody in this picture was operating with one hand tied behind their back. The risk of the Brotherhood learning what was going on was too high for anybody to properly arm themselves.

And so he'd been able to drive a car bomb right up to McKinney's front door.

Of course, making use of that "advantage" was a dicey prospect. There was a reason that most kids learned that holding their breath until they passed out wasn't a useful negotiation strategy in adult life. Deliberately blowing yourself up had to be even less likely to work.

But you played the cards you were dealt.

A staircase appeared in front of Gideon. He paused in front of it.

"Why did you stop?" Haynes snapped.

"You told me to follow your instructions," Gideon said, raising his voice a little bit for the benefit of his earpiece. It was designed to transmit when it detected a voice. "If you want me to go upstairs, you just have to ask."

"Climb the damn stairs."

Gideon heard a slight intake of breath behind him and wondered whether the hired shooter had found his deliberate intransigence amusing. It was possible. But a compatible personality wasn't likely to help him if it came to a shootout. He'd spent time around mercenaries. Glenn and Stamp were the good kind.

But there weren't many of them.

The stairs creaked as they climbed, and for the first time, Gideon felt a flicker of anxiety in his chest. It seemed darker upstairs somehow, though he wasn't sure whether it was just a figment of his imagination.

"Is the senator joining us, or do I have to make do with your company all night?" he said. "Not that it isn't riveting."

It sounded like Haynes opened his mouth to respond. But he was cut off before he had the chance.

"It's good to see you, Gideon," a deeper, rougher voice rang out as he reached the top step. "It's been a long time."

JULIA CREPT toward the door of her bedroom. Even on the occasions her husband deigned to be intimate with her, like the previous night, he never allowed her to sleep in his bed. Out here in the country they didn't even sleep on the same floor.

She twisted the door handle and pulled it open a couple of inches, holding her breath as she did so. Several armed men had appeared on the property earlier that day. She recognized none of them—but she was certain they weren't Brotherhood people, and they definitely weren't from the government.

Ronan Haynes had ordered her to her bedroom two hours earlier. He'd told her that Sheldon wanted her to remain there until further notice. She'd known something was up then.

It was why she'd contacted her handler.

She heard voices further down the hallway and saw a man with a gun walking away from her toward the stairwell. She held her breath until he disappeared out of sight, then tip-toed down the hallway until she could hear the voices more clearly. It only took a few seconds of listening to confirm what she already suspected.

He's here.

SIXTY-ONE

"That's not my name," Gideon said, feeling his diaphragm clench and his heart rate begin to rise at the sight of McKinney. Looking at photos of the man was one thing. Proximity was quite another. It summoned an ancient fear from somewhere deep inside him.

From before he was a man.

"What would you like me to call you?" McKinney asked, his voice supremely confident. He was wearing suit pants, black oxford shoes, and a dark gray cashmere quarter-zip sweater. The clothing looked expensive and well cut, but it couldn't disguise the man's spreading frame. "Nomad?"

Behind the senator was another armed man. Gideon didn't recognize him but guessed he was another hired gun. The man's gaze tracked his every step, and his weapon was held ready to fire. Gideon wondered whether Haynes had managed to acquire more security personnel on such short notice.

"I see you don't want to play. Pity," McKinney said, turning to the guard behind him and saying, "Get my wife."

I guess not, Gideon thought.

McKinney had only sent the man off once Haynes and the other shooter arrived. The man sidled past his employer and passed the new arrivals on his way toward the stairs.

What has his wife got to do with anything?

Gideon pushed that thought out of his mind. It would be answered soon enough. If it was important, he'd find out then. No sense worrying about it now. But the vignette revealed one thing: They were probably only facing three armed men. That was better odds than they had any right to expect. One-on-one, he'd wager the skills and grit of any three legionnaires against anyone else the mercenary world could offer.

He glanced around and saw that McKinney was standing in a large, wide hallway. At the far end was a wide set of double wood doors that wouldn't have looked out of place in a European church. Just to the left of the doorway, another narrower corridor led deeper into the house.

The area he was standing in was a luxuriant display of wasted square footage. In any other home, it would have been several bedrooms. Here it was just a place to display bland modern art and expensive floor lighting.

"Moving toward the house," Stamp whispered in his earpiece. "Thirty feet out."

Gideon schooled his features and studied those of his guests. Haynes had maneuvered himself to take the place of the departed mercenary, leaving the other shooter behind him. That meant he could see both McKinney's and Haynes's expressions. Neither seemed to have any idea that armed men were on the property.

At least, men who weren't on their payroll.

"I'm here to do business," Gideon said, ignoring McKinney's jibes about his name. He refused to give the senator the satisfaction of a reaction. "I understand you are a reasonable man. In your position I guess you kind of have to be."

"And what position is that?"

"You're balanced on a ledge between two shark-infested pools. In one you have the Brotherhood, and in the other the government. If you tumble into either, you'll be ripped apart. So you make choices. Bend when you have to—so that you don't end up having to break."

"And that's all you're asking for, is it?" McKinney said, a twitch of irritation crossing his face at the moment Gideon mentioned the Brotherhood. A poorly concealed glance at the shooter behind Gideon revealed that the man didn't know anything about the cult whose tentacles had led him here. "In my book ten million would cause a lot of men to break."

"But not you. It's the cost of doing business," Gideon said, continuing to buy time to analyze the situation. He was temporarily facing only two opponents. Was now the best time to strike? If he waited, the risk was that the other merc would return with McKinney's wife and the odds would be further stacked against him.

"We're behind cover," Stamp reported. "Fifteen feet to the southern wall of the house. There's something weird out here."

Gideon stiffened, but the transmission didn't continue. He had no way of asking for more information. Weird could cover a lot of bases.

Dammit, Stamp.

"Join me in my office," McKinney said, seeming to reach a decision. He gestured toward the double doors at the end of the hallway.

"You, stay here," Haynes growled.

For a moment, Gideon held still, thinking the fixer was pointing at him. It took a moment to realize that he was instructing the mercenary behind him. He slowly eased himself forward, his brain instantly revving into higher gear.

This was it. He wasn't going to get a better moment to take

his chance than the next couple of minutes. Assuming a squad of special forces operators wasn't waiting in McKinney's office, the senator was going to be guarded only by Haynes.

The fixer was a canny, tough fighter, there was no doubt about it. It was in the way he moved. But he also looked to be in his fifties. As any observer of professional sport could tell you, reflexes begin to fade before a player's thirtieth birthday. It's only downhill from there.

And so it was for men of violence. You never lost your tactical brain or your skill with a weapon.

But the speed with which you could deploy those skills was another matter. It would happen to Gideon himself one day.

But not yet.

All that flashed through Gideon's mind in a matter of seconds as McKinney turned and strode toward his office door. It took several seconds down the long hallway before he reached it, stepping forward and reaching out with both hands to push the heavy doors aside.

Haynes walked backward, keeping his pistol trained steadily on Gideon. He clearly sensed the calculus in the former legionnaire's mind.

The question was: Was there anything he could do about it?

Gideon began to follow. He checked in with every joint and limb to ensure that he was in peak physical condition, or as close to it as could be expected after the events of the past few days. The bullet wound remained and his legs ached, but they wouldn't fail.

He picked up the pace, closing the distance on Haynes while remaining surreptitious about it.

"So you got the money?" Gideon called out, keeping his voice calm.

McKinney stepped through the office door. Gideon realized that it was actually a library that stretched almost forty feet lengthwise and twenty in width. It contained a couple of comfortable leather sofas and a desk with a computer monitor on it. The walls were lined with books, many of which appeared to be leather-bound legal or historical texts.

At the far end of the room, underneath the windowsill, were several objects that looked distinctly out of place. Five large black duffel bags stacked in a stubby pyramid.

Could just be newspaper, Gideon thought as he reached the office's threshold. Haynes backed away from him, stepping deeper into the office and always keeping six feet of separation from him. Too far to lash out and grab his weapon. He would have to somehow engineer an opportunity.

"I have certain means," McKinney said in a voice that seemed designed to carry no further than the doorway Gideon was about to step through. "But I need assurances."

"What kind of—?"

Gideon fell silent as the lights in the library office—in fact, throughout the entire house and grounds—went dark. The sudden change startled him. And contrary to his theory, Haynes reacted faster.

"What the fuck is this?" the fixer snapped. "Hands behind your head."

Blinking rapidly as he tried to process what the hell was going on, Gideon complied. It seemed the easiest way to buy himself time to think. Were Stamp and Glenn responsible for this somehow?

He loosely interlaced his fingers, his subconscious mind keeping them relaxed and slightly parted so that he would be able to spring into action the second he was required to.

"Luke, get in here," Haynes called, gesturing for the shooter in the hallway to join them in the office.

"What's going on, Ronan?" McKinney asked. There was a quaver of fear in his voice.

Gideon rejected the possibility that this was a ruse. The two men would have to be Oscar-winning actors to pull it off, and they were not. But neither did he see how—or why—his two accomplices could have killed the power. It wasn't part of their plan.

A storm? There was nothing on the weather forecast.

A short in the local substation? Possible—but the timing was hinky.

To say the least.

"Cover him," Haynes said in a cold voice as the merc named Luke arrived behind Gideon.

The second his gun was on Gideon, Haynes turned toward the computer on the desk. He leaned forward in front of it, set his pistol down, and shook the mouse.

"Power's out," he muttered before quickly crouching to the side of the computer.

"I hadn't noticed," McKinney fired back acidly.

Haynes fiddled with a box on the floor. In the gloom, Gideon was unable to make out what he was looking at. An instant later, Haynes connected a wire, and the computer began whirring back to life, throwing enough illumination from a cluster of LCD lights to identify a backup battery.

Gideon slowly, subtly reached into his ear with his right thumb, making as though he was scratching an itch. In reality, he attempted to discreetly adjust his earpiece before tapping it twice with his thumbnail to send out a bat signal.

"What are you doing?" Luke asked suspiciously.

CRACK.

This time Gideon reacted instantly. He didn't know the cause, but his brain identified the sound as a shotgun blast. Before a flash of light and the echo of an explosion—much larger than any shotgun shell he'd ever seen—rattled the library's windows, he spun toward Luke.

The mercenary's attention had been attracted by the disturbance outside. Gideon made him pay for it. He knocked the rifle to one side with his left forearm, then reached out and snatched it from the man's grasp with all the strength of his right arm. He turned and had his back to a wall of books, with the rifle trained on McKinney before Luke even knew the gun was gone.

"Stamp, report," he snapped, no longer needing to disguise the existence of the earpiece. "What the hell's happening out there?"

No reply. A creeping sensation of doubt ran up his spine.

"Glenn?"

Still nothing.

The pieces began to fall into place. The power was out. Communications were down. Neither McKinney nor Haynes had any more of an idea of what was going on than he did. There was only one real explanation: A third party had entered the arena. There was only one that made sense.

The Brotherhood.

SIXTY-TWO

"Drop the fucking weapon!" Haynes yelled, his own pistol somehow already back in his hand and aimed directly at Gideon's head.

"Don't think I'll be doing that," Gideon said as calmly as he could manage. He angled his head so that the majority of his attention was on Haynes, leaving McKinney in his peripheral vision so the senator didn't get the idea to make an escape attempt.

"You came to take me out," McKinney said, his face somewhat pale, but his voice still strong.

Gideon grimaced. "I did," he admitted. "But I didn't knock out the power. And I sure as shit didn't take out my own comms. You got any bright ideas who might have the balls to make a move on your home? Because I'm guessing if it was the government, your little birds would have warned you."

McKinney's face grew even paler. A slight tremor shook his right hand as he spoke. "Who's to say that this isn't a trap?"

"It might be," Gideon allowed, keeping his gaze trained on

Haynes. The other mercenary was somewhere to his left, but he wouldn't act without instructions.

I hope.

"But you're going to have to take a leap with me and trust that I'm not playing 4D chess, okay?" Gideon continued, gesturing out the window with his elbow. "If that was who I think it was, what are we looking at?"

A chatter of gunfire exploded outside, barely muffled by the colonial mansion's thick brick walls. It was impossible to be certain, but Gideon thought the weapons responsible sounded close to the house.

Stamp and Glenn?

The development appeared to make up Haynes's mind. He lowered his weapon, briefly closing his eyes as a look of dismay crossed his face. "It's a DAG team."

"A what?" Gideon asked, screwing up his face as he racked his brain for any memory of the term. Nothing jumped out.

"After your time," Haynes said, hustling toward the window at the far end of the room. He stopped and inched toward it, his back to the walls. "Short for Direct Action Group. Modeled on Delta's ODA's. Twelve-man teams recruited out of the best of Chosen. Well-trained. And complete fanatics. They're true believers."

Gideon slowly lowered his weapon. He tried radioing his accomplices again but still got nothing. If he was to believe what Haynes was telling him—and he had no reason not to—then instead of just Haynes and a couple of shooters, he was facing an entire Brotherhood hit squad.

And even if he got through them, McKinney's hired help were still the sting in the tail.

"Shit," he whispered. Operations never went to plan. But they didn't usually have all the teeth knocked out of them before even landing a single punch.

"What are you doing?" McKinney half-yelled, gesturing at Haynes. "He could kill me right now."

"We have to work together," Haynes said, apparently grasping the conclusion that Gideon had reached long before his boss did. "DAG teams usually operate alongside a screening squad of Chosen fighters. We could be facing thirty guys with guns. Maybe even more."

"I need ammo," Gideon said quickly, before gesturing at Luke. "And he needs another gun. Tell me you're Second Amendment types."

Haynes still had his back to the wall by the window, and now his cheek was pressed up against it as he attempted to peer out into the darkness without getting shot. There was a little moonlight, but not much beneath the clouds that swept across the sky.

"I can't see shit," Haynes swore.

The comment fired off a neuron in Gideon's brain.

"Close the curtains," he said, jogging down the hallway past the mercenary who was standing half-dazed by a wall of books. "All of them. Drones."

The one-word explanation was enough. All of them had seen the flash of light in the sky a few seconds earlier. And Gideon had personal—and very recent—experience with the Brotherhood's use of the aerial machines.

He swept curtains closed along the hallway until the space was consumed by darkness. When he returned to the office, now only lit by the glow of the computer, Haynes was standing somewhat frozen, pushing his hands through his hair.

Gideon quickly grasped that he was a follower, not a leader. He was capable of executing a plan and probably had a far better tactical mind than his boss, but without orders he was useless. Maybe that was how he'd been dragged into the Brotherhood in the first place. Perhaps susceptibility to such a cult required a certain personality type.

"Guns," he repeated.

Haynes nodded quickly, his expression lightening.

"Luke, with me." He ran out of the room, the mercenary trailing quickly behind.

A muffled explosion rang out somewhere below. Gideon's brain quickly categorized it as a breaching charge. That could mean it was the two legionnaires.

Or the Brotherhood.

The magazine in his rifle contained just twenty rounds. If he was forced to commence battle before Haynes returned—if Haynes returned—then it wasn't going to be a long fight.

He stood in the enormous, dark room with only his thoughts and McKinney's breathing for company. He turned to the older man and eyed him up and down.

"I should kill you right now," he said. "I'll never get a better chance."

"Do it then," McKinney replied, chin to his chest, shoulders slumped. "It's over. I can't survive this."

Footsteps downstairs. Men's boots. A low shout.

Gideon spun back to cover the staircase. "Is that the only way up?"

"My career's over," McKinney groaned.

"Career?" Gideon said, momentarily stunned that the senator could even think of his lifetime of deceit and corruption in those terms. "It doesn't matter. Just answer the fucking question."

"It's the only way up," Haynes confirmed, his tone strained from exertion. Gideon glanced to his right to see the fixer coming out of the hallway festooned with ammunition boxes and canvas bags. Luke appeared a moment later, similarly equipped.

The two men dumped the hardware on one of the sofas in the library. Haynes sent Luke back for more, before grabbing a rifle of his own, pushing in a magazine, and chambering a round.

"I need ammo," Gideon called out, still keeping his rifle trained on the staircase.

"Coming up," a voice called. "Don't shoot, okay? We're friendly."

Haynes sprinted over, his finger on the rifle's trigger.

Gideon reached out and pushed the muzzle down to the floor. He shook his head, his body relaxing with relief. "They're with me."

Feet scraped against creeping stairs as dark silhouettes rounded the break in the staircase. Gideon's night vision had mostly returned by now. He squinted at the shapes. The faces came into view hazily.

He didn't recognize either of them.

Wait, that wasn't true. He'd seen the first before: the mercenary McKinney had dispatched to get his wife. Which, by process of elimination, meant that the woman to the man's side, wearing a tight pantsuit and her hair tied up in a bun, had to be the senator's other half.

And half was the right word, that was for sure. There was no way she was more than a day over half the man's age.

"Found them lurking downstairs," Glenn said. He was heavily loaded, an antitank rifle slung over one shoulder, his rifle over the other. He carried a pistol in his right hand aimed a few inches down and to the left of the mercenary's back. Close enough that he could fix the target before the man could so much as fart wrong. "Figured they might as well join the party."

Gideon said nothing. He was staring at the senator's wife, his gaze locked onto her pale, bloodless skin. She looked terrified, but that wasn't what was attracting his attention. Nor was her obvious beauty. She was in excellent shape and well attired despite the hour.

But he recognized her.

"We took down a drone just before it blotted us out," Stamp explained, seemingly oblivious to Gideon's distraction as he neared the top of the staircase. "Got a little scratched up by shrapnel, but nothing that won't go down well with the ladies."

"Got eyes on at least half a dozen shooters," Glenn said more earnestly. "Pinned them down for long enough to make a run for it to the house. Guess we weren't the only people to hear about the money."

"Julia..." Gideon whispered.

That was it. She was nearly a decade older than when he'd last seen her. She was only a girl back then. To the version of him that was eternally trapped in his dreams, she was fourteen, just a few years younger than him.

But now she wasn't.

Her face wrinkled with confusion. For a time no recognition flickered in her eyes. But finally the wrinkles on her forehead relaxed.

"Gideon?"

He felt a hand grasp his left shoulder roughly. He fell back, too stunned to react to the unexpected physical touch. He saw McKinney's stubbled face leering at him in the darkness.

"We don't have time for a family reunion," the old man thundered. "If you don't get your shit together, we all die."

The floor swayed underneath Gideon's feet like the deck of a ship. A distant part of his self-conscious was pleased that the senator had come around to the working together part of the plan. But that portion was currently overwhelmed by the unreality of what he was seeing.

"You know her?" Stamp asked, jogging toward a large

wardrobe that stood on the right-hand side of the hallway. He deposited his rifle and ammo against the wall before saying, "You should have said you had someone on the inside. We could have just knocked. Vic—give me a hand with this."

Gideon wrestled himself back into the moment, tearing his peripheral vision away from Julia's face. He hated the fact that Senator McKinney was right. He really didn't have time to process this emotional tsunami right now.

He stumbled toward the couch in the library and filled his pockets with as much ammunition for his rifle as he could find. Resting against the back of the couch was another similar long gun, except this one came equipped with an infrared scope. Figuring it would come in handy in this environment, he exchanged his own weapon for it.

Fragments of memories flew past him as he cracked open a box of grenades. Sharing his lunch with Julia when she was on report. Teaching her how to make a fire from charred cloth and straw. Her helping him with his math homework, despite being barely over half his age.

There was an almighty crash from behind him, and he spun to see that the two legionnaires had toppled the wardrobe in front of one of the curtained windows. He quickly realized they had created a makeshift firing position—the window itself was raised above head height.

Gideon passed Julia as he jogged back over to the window but didn't dare meet her gaze. He wasn't prepared to come to terms with what this meant. Not yet.

He gestured to the legionnaires with his rifle. "I got this. Check the cache on the couch. And get the others organized."

He hopped up onto the wardrobe, feeling the damaged wood shift and creak underneath his weight, then disappeared behind the curtains. He reached down and powered up the infrared scope, then removed the lens cap. It took a few seconds before a grayscale display appeared behind the reticle.

"Christ," Stamp whistled with approval. "What were you preparing for—the end of the world as we know it?"

"Today was always coming," Haynes growled in response, his voice muffled by the upholstery.

"Wish I'd picked a different day to visit."

Gideon brought the rifle up, slowly opening the window with his other hand. He pushed it out inch by inch so the movement didn't attract unwanted attention, then rested the weapon on the ledge. He swung it gently left and right across the country home's grounds.

Glowing dots lit up like fireflies in the night sky, volcanic against the dark, cool gray of the lawn.

"Five, six, seven…" he counted out loud. "We've definitely got company."

Not that that was in any doubt.

"They'll be inside in sixty seconds," he called out in a low voice, angling his head behind him before returning his cheek to the side of the rifle. He breathed deeply in and out, steadying his heart rate—or trying to. It felt like a herd of Broncos was bucking inside his chest.

He watched as pairs of men leapfrogged each other toward the house, each sprinting about fifteen yards before taking a knee behind a garden feature or a tree and signaling for the other to follow.

"You," he whispered, picking out the closest of them, who had only just gone to ground. He had a few seconds.

Gideon took careful aim. It had been a while since he'd practiced a shot like this. Everything was harder in the dark. But there was little wind, and the range was within sixty yards.

He sighted on the man's chest. A headshot would've been neater, but he would only have the element of surprise once.

Better not to miss. At this range and with this caliber of bullet, even if the guy was wearing armor plate, the bullet would still do real damage.

Exhale.

Pause.

Fire.

SIXTY-THREE

Gideon's first target dropped like a stone. He shifted his aim to the Brotherhood fighter's partner without waiting for a damage assessment. All that mattered now was speed. He wouldn't have long.

He didn't.

Just as he squeezed the trigger of his rifle a second time, on this occasion firing two shots in quick succession toward the center mass of the second shooter, a crackle of gunfire erupted in his peripheral vision. It wasn't just visible through the scope; the muzzle flashes were like camera flashes popping off in the dark.

The first few dozen rounds went wide. But they also impacted within seconds of him firing at his second target. Even as he threw himself away from the window, chunks of masonry cut into his cheeks—thrown by the weight of the incoming gunfire.

Before long, the ceiling on the far side of the hallway was peppered with black bullet holes. Plaster dust rained down like snow.

"Glenn—AT4. Now."

The ex-legionnaire stared back at him in the gloom with a look of shock on his face. "It's suicide."

Gideon didn't wait. He set the rifle on top of the toppled wardrobe and grabbed one of the two AT4 antitank rounds by the canister's carrying handle. He snatched at the safety pin and tossed it aside. The weapon was now armed, but it would not fire accidentally due to the remaining safety catch.

"Clear the area!" he yelled over the rattle of incoming gunfire, only vaguely aware that the other two legionnaires were already moving as one, pushing the others back into the library to clear the hallway, which would shortly be filled with the compressive back blast from the recoilless rifle.

The suppressive fire from the lawn below began to fade, though the gaps between incoming rounds—most of which impacted the walls around the window itself rather than punching through the open window into the ceiling—measured in single-digit seconds. It wasn't much of a margin of safety.

"Only one I'm getting," Gideon muttered to steady his nerves.

"Clear!" a voice yelled from behind him, muffled by the now-closed wooden library doors.

Gideon didn't acknowledge the warning. He hopped up onto the wardrobe, braced himself firmly in a low squat to absorb the force of the round, and crouched just below the lip of the window.

Time seemed to slow. He experienced each incoming round, each beat of his heart as discrete events, as if captured in amber.

The suppressive fire all but faded away. There was a risk that it was a trap. But he didn't have time to wait them out. The more of the enemy that made it into the house, the worse things would very shortly be. He slid the safety catch into the fire position. His finger grazed the trigger.

He breathed out.

Another rattle of shots popped through the window, sending brick dust up and coating his hair as he rose and steadied the antitank weapon's canister on the window ledge. He looked out into the darkness speckled by the occasional muzzle flash. He aimed for a spot about forty yards away and directly ahead. He had no idea if anyone was down there.

And he fired.

The room filled with a flash that he barely noticed as a clap of sound buffeted his hearing. The force of the ignition shook his entire body, but force of habit compelled him to toss the now-empty weapon cylinder out the window and jump away from danger.

He hit the floor at the moment of impact. Another explosion rumbled through the old house. Somewhere glassware clinked, and the bookshelves in the library groaned.

"Everyone into firing positions," Gideon yelled, his voice muffled. He shook his head to clear his hearing and found that the world was moving slower than it was supposed to.

A friendly hand clapped him on the shoulder. Somehow Stamp had made it over to him, seemingly unaffected by the quicksand that gripped Gideon's boots.

"Good job, you lunatic," he whispered. Except his lips were contorted, his mouth opened wide in a yell.

"Can't hear," Gideon answered, tapping his ears. The ringing and dullness would fade. The permanent damage would not.

No time to worry about that now.

There was nothing more they could do to stop the Brotherhood's direct action group from making it into the house. Occasional suppressive fire targeted the windows along the lawn-view wall, but they invariably hit too high to do any damage.

But that wasn't the point.

"I hear 'em," Glenn called out, his voice sounding more normal than Stamp's had just a few moments earlier. "Won't be long."

Gideon picked up the rifle that he'd set down on the wardrobe and crouched at the legionnaire's side behind the heavy wooden piece of furniture as if it would do anything to shield him from a wave of lead. He saw Haynes take a knee, shielding half of his body behind the hallway wall just to the left of the library door. The two mercenaries were lying prone, weapons aimed at the staircase.

He couldn't see Julia. Or McKinney.

"Don't fucking shoot me, all right?" Stamp yelled, before jogging toward the banisters overlooking the stairwell.

Muffled shouts downstairs were coupled with the occasional grenade or flash-bang detonation and the incessant rattle of gunfire. It seemed that the assaulting party—however many of them remained—were being pretty liberal with their use of firepower as they cleared the lower floor of the building.

"They're just wasting their ammo," he called out to steady everybody's nerves.

He didn't say that it was unlikely they would run dry.

The tension built with every passing second. Soon it was so thick that he could practically chew it. Sweat trickled down his temple. Heavy, strained breathing echoed in a chorus all around him.

"Who has a grenade?" he called.

"Yeah," Stamp answered, letting his rifle fall against his chest rig and reaching into the pockets on both sides of his pants.

"Ditto," Glenn confirmed, along with similar answers from both Haynes and the two mercenaries.

"Good. You know what to do."

Silence returned.

And then it was time.

A single burst of gunfire rang out at the bottom of the staircase. Gideon instinctively peered toward the source of the sound. Even as his pupils widened in the darkness, he realized the gravity of his situation.

"Cover your eyes!" he yelled exactly in time with a heavy thump on the stairwell below. He nestled his upper face between the crook of his elbow and grimaced at the exact instant the flash-bang grenade detonated.

And a second, and a third.

Head ringing, hearing once again kaput, Gideon reached blindly into his pockets. The flash had penetrated his eyelids, but only with sufficient intensity to damage his night vision, not stun him completely.

His fingers closed around the now-warm metal of a grenade's casing and clamped against the spoon. He inserted the index finger of his free hand into the loop of the pin, then yanked it free. "Now!"

He saw half a dozen arms pull back all around him. The catapults levered forward at slightly different times. The result was the same. Six distinct grenades flew through the air, their dark green casings almost invisible in the gloom.

Three.

Two.

The heavy metal objects thumped downward right as boot steps traveled in the opposite direction.

Gideon didn't need to count out the last second. The grenades detonated almost simultaneously, filling the stairwell, then the hallway with clouds of dust and smoke that briefly glowed with flame before the explosions collapsed in on themselves.

He leapt over the wardrobe as Stamp brought up his rifle once again and began firing blindly into the chaos below him. He joined the legionnaire at his side and followed suit, firing the entire magazine into the base of the stairwell.

As the blast noise faded, screams of injured, mangled men filled the air. Gideon had heard them before. They had haunted his dreams for a time. Now he exulted in them. These men were here to kill him. To kill his friends.

To kill my sister.

And he would not, could not allow them to succeed.

"They'll come again," he thought when the worst of the screaming had faded—presumably as the injured were dragged away from the danger zone or had merely succumbed to their injuries. "We have to be ready."

SIXTY-FOUR

Every ten seconds or so, the wall overlooking the lawn shook from the impact of grenades fired from rifle-mounted underslung launchers. The larger detonations were punctuated with eruptions of suppressive fire designed to keep the defenders' heads down. At the bottom of the stairwell, an enemy shooter was firing single rounds every three seconds or so, like clockwork.

A very slow clock, anyway.

"We need to punch out of here," Stamp growled. "No sense in sticking around until they kill us off, one by one."

Gideon nodded. They'd completed a check of their weapons and ammunition. Plenty of small-arms ammo remained, but they were running low on grenades—only five among all of them. The second antitank round was a trump card—but difficult to fire inside a building in the middle of a gunfight due to the backblast effect.

According to Haynes, there was another cache of munitions on the first floor, behind a false wall in the walk-in refrigerator. But that was a long way away, and the incessant rattle of gunfire chewing chunks of brick and mortar out of the wall just to their side was a reminder that the enemy's reinforcements were arriving.

They had none.

"Keep watch," he said to the two legionnaires. "I'll be back."

He jogged away from the stairwell in a low crouch, not rising up to his full height until he was near the doors to the office. Haynes and his two hired shooters were squatting on their haunches around the couch in the center of the room, loading magazines from a crate of fresh rounds.

"Catch," Haynes said, tossing several magazines toward Gideon, who caught them easily and dumped the one full mag he'd expended so far.

"Thanks."

"We have to make a break for it," Haynes said, gesturing to the far end of the room with a jerk of his head. "I took a peek out of that window just now. Saw at least half a dozen fresh bodies sprinting toward the house before they got a bead on me."

Gideon noted the information, but his attention was stolen by the sight of Julia. She was sitting on the room's other couch, her hands folded over her knees. No—folded over a pistol that rested on her knees. Senator McKinney sat by her side—in fact, separating her from the others. He was perspiring heavily.

"Share the extra ammo around," he said. "Be ready to move in sixty seconds."

He wasn't sure how he'd become the group's de facto leader, and yet that was indisputably the case. An hour earlier, Haynes would have happily put a bullet in the back of his head. Now they were in this together.

Until the moment they weren't.

If we survive that long...

Gideon decided there was no point worrying about Haynes's men double-crossing him right now. To even get to that point, they had to survive. And right now their odds weren't exactly looking good.

He exhaled, his gaze still on Julia. He decided he needed to go over to her. To say something. What exactly that was, he didn't know. She clearly remembered him. And yet she was sitting by her husband's side.

Deciding that in a few minutes they might all be dead, Gideon figured he might as well go over. He was about halfway to the couch when two things happened at once. First, Julia looked at him, and her face softened from a mask of fear. Another emotion lurked in her eyes that he couldn't make out. But he was certain there was still some affection there.

Second, John Stamp let out a long, low whistle. As Gideon snapped back around, he saw the legionnaire's face was dark and grim. "We're out of time, ladies. They're back."

Gideon figured the initial DAG team had to be down to no more than fifty percent strength by now—two casualties from his sniper shots and an unknown but sizable number from the hail of grenades they'd thrown. He didn't know what exactly was about to happen. But he was sure the enemy wouldn't repeat the same tactic twice.

So neither could they.

"Glenn, give me a hand," he said, sprinting toward the wardrobe before planting both his palms on the vertical side. He braced his legs and began to push.

"Huh? Oh. I get it."

The two men drove the wardrobe forward as Stamp watched tensely just ahead. They didn't stop pushing until the wooden cabinet formed a kind of barricade at the top of the staircase.

"Back," Stamp cautioned.

"Haynes," Gideon yelled. "Set up firing points to defend the office. We'll hold the stairs as long as possible. I'll signal when we have to fall back. Just don't catch us in the crossfire."

A disconcerting silence filled the hallway after Haynes acknowledged and ordered his men to change their positions. Gideon and Glenn crouched behind the wardrobe, leaving Stamp exposed but with a better firing position standing over the banisters that looked down over the stairwell. Glenn had switched to his shotgun—a pump-action military variant that was perfect for clearing tight spaces like the descending staircase in front of them.

Gideon glanced around and took in the state of the once-pristine hallway for the first time. It smelled of smoke and blood, and the walls were cracked from the impact of bullet holes and the force of the many detonations that had rocked the house.

"Here we go," Stamp yelled.

Instead of flash-bangs, this time the Brotherhood tossed smoke grenades. *Lots* of smoke grenades. Gideon heard half a dozen distinct thunks as smoke canisters hit the lower steps, then a low hiss as the incendiaries began to deploy a thick blanket of confusion.

Gideon glanced through his thermal scope but gave up almost instantly. The smoke particles were still too warm, obscuring the thermal signature of any attackers just as effectively as his eyes had been foiled.

He cocked his head and listened instead. The stairs were old and creaky. No matter how stealthy the Brotherhood fighters were, they still had to lumber up them armed with heavy weapons—and just as blind as the house's defenders. The disguise was a double-edged sword.

He reached for a grenade but held steady before pulling

the pin, still listening. The smoke also deadened sound. Something was happening down there, he was sure of it. But what...

No, he'd heard that before.

"Down!"

He yelled the warning barely a second before an FPV drone burst out of the cloud of smoke, followed shortly by a second. Both drones carried small black objects underneath their frames. Almost certainly explosives.

Glenn spun at Gideon's side, eyes tracking upward. The drones had no running lights and were almost invisible in the gloom. The other legionnaire squeezed his trigger, and the shotgun rang out, spewing a cloud of shot toward the ceiling. One of the drones sparked out and clattered harmlessly to the floor—miraculously without detonating the grenade slung to it.

The fans powering the other drone ramped up to high pitch. Glenn racked another shell into his weapon and fired again but missed. Gideon was torn between the fight that was doubtless approaching up the staircase and the possible death of friends—and family—behind him.

He pulled the pin of his grenade and tossed it down the stairs. Stamp fired blindly into the smoke; both men knew an attack was coming. The sound of the drone's engine seemed to be fading, but he realized it was only flying away from him.

Toward the office.

Toward Julia.

As that realization struck him, Gideon spun. He turned just in time to see the second FPV drone detonate about three feet inside the office's doors. One of Haynes's shooters—at least one—died almost instantly.

And then the assault began once again. Two silhouettes charged out of the smoke only to throw themselves against the unexpected barrier posed by the wardrobe. Glenn, Stamp, and

Gideon fired as one, butchering the two attackers before they were able to get a shot off. Their bodies fell backward.

"Take that, motherfucker," somebody yelled. It didn't matter who. The emotion was catching.

But more followed.

A grenade detonated behind Gideon, probably thrown over his head by someone in the smoke below. The shrapnel missed him, but the force of yet another explosion buffeted his exhausted body.

He squeezed the trigger. The gun bucked against his shoulder. He dumped his expended magazine. He squeezed the trigger. The gun bucked—

An enormous man loomed out of the smoke just as all three legionnaires were in the process of reloading. It was a lucky break. He hurdled over the wardrobe, apparently learning from his dead comrades' mistakes, and jumped off, throwing himself two-footed directly into Gideon's chest.

He didn't have time to react or spin out of the way, let alone fire his weapon. Only suffer the explosion of pain that burst behind his eyelids and sent him slipping toward unconsciousness.

Out of the corner of his fading peripheral vision, Gideon saw Stamp turn, rack a round, and squeeze his trigger. The berserker's body jerked, but he didn't fall until at least half a dozen rounds had cut through him. And he didn't fall without firing one of his own. It hit Glenn in the upper thigh.

"I'm hit!"

Gideon's lungs wheezed in his desperate attempt to acquire oxygen. He sounded like a dying cancer patient as he turned onto his side and attempted to roll onto his front. There was no way he could push himself upright yet—

"Gideon, we need to fall back," Stamp yelled over the chaos as he tossed his last remaining grenade over the banisters. He emptied most of a magazine down the staircase, catching yet another zombie-like figure emerging from the billowing smoke.

"No doubt," he coughed in response, pushing himself back to his feet with a supreme effort of will. "You take Glenn. I'll cover."

A fresh burst of adrenaline salved Gideon's immediate pain, and he took advantage of it to feed a fresh magazine—his last—into his weapon. He hopped up onto the wardrobe and fired several clipped bursts down the stairwell.

Glenn yelled and swore with pain as his friend dragged him back toward the office. Matching screams of pain echoed from downstairs. It was impossible to say how many lives the carnage had swallowed, but Gideon could see at least half a dozen bodies scattered in just the visible part of the hallway and staircase. A couple were still moving, but barely, feebly.

It seemed that for now—again—they had halted the Brotherhood's assault.

But did we kill enough of them?

That was the only question that mattered. Even brainwashed fanatics had some desire for personal survival. During the campaigns against ISIS that he'd been part of in Mali, it had been well known in the Legion that some "suicide" bombers actually had their vests detonated remotely, since the poor bastards wearing them didn't always want to go through with it.

If they'd killed enough of the leaders—perhaps like the big berserker—then maybe this would be over. The survivors would retreat to lick their wounds.

He had to make sure of it.

Gideon sprinted down the stairs. Some part of his mind screamed at him that he only had eleven rounds remaining in his weapon, so he grabbed a rifle from a fallen corpse and slung it over his left shoulder.

The smoke the Brotherhood fighters had deployed was

almost completely gone now. He rounded the bend in the staircase, hurdling over bodies. There was so much blood, so much pain and needless waste that he almost wanted to vomit.

All this for one man.

Finally he found himself on the first floor. An injured fighter was slumped against the wall just to his left. He went for his weapon—but slowly.

Pathetically.

Gideon automatically shifted his aim toward the fallen shooter as his peripheral vision interrogated the remainder of the space. It was chewed up and scarred and blackened by the half dozen or more grenades they'd tossed down here. A couple of bodies were just chunks of seared flesh. Military hardware lay abandoned everywhere.

As far as he could see, there were no more Brotherhood shooters left to fight.

"Don't do it," he warned the man who had finally, laboriously closed his fingers around the grip of his pistol. "I don't give a shit about you. I'll let you—"

As the man brought the pistol up with surprising speed, Gideon was forced to react. He squeezed the trigger of his rifle. It bucked against his shoulder, and in an instant the fighter's skull was split in two.

"—live," he whispered.

Gideon let himself breathe for a few seconds. Let the ringing in his ears fade, and the revulsion at what he'd been forced to do—well, that would hang around for a while.

And then he slowly, methodically cleared the ground floor of the house. A couple of Brotherhood fighters were so badly injured they barely reacted as he passed them. He kicked their weapons aside more out of habit than need.

Finally he reached a shattered window on the exterior of the house. He brought his rifle up and stared out through the infrared scope. He counted five glowing silhouettes making their way from the house. Some limping, others sprinting, one barely even moving.

Part of him knew he should show no mercy. They wouldn't for him.

But his soul was tired. And this fight was over.

Not quite.

SIXTY-FIVE

Gideon ran back upstairs, discarding the rifle he'd carried this far in favor of the one he'd taken from the Brotherhood corpse on the stairs. He also looted a couple of fresh magazines and flicked off the weapon's safety.

Just in case.

He was inured to the death and destruction by the time he hopped back over the wardrobe and landed in the hallway. He followed the trail of blood that Glenn had left as Stamp dragged him toward the office.

Too much blood.

Senator McKinney and Julia—his wife—were still huddled at the far end of the office when he arrived. Haynes's two mercenaries were both definitely dead. One had bled out from a gut wound; the other must have taken a round through the chest at some point in the fighting. Stamp and the fixer were crouched over Glenn's body, both their postures tense.

"We're good downstairs," Gideon said as he slowed in front of them, paying as much attention to their body language as he was to Glenn's condition. "For now. What's the deal here?"

"Vic needs a hospital," Stamp said, his shoulders slightly hunched with exhaustion as he rose to his feet. He was holding his pistol. "I got a tourniquet on, but the bullet nicked an artery. He needs a surgeon."

"Shit," Gideon swore. He glanced hopefully toward the senator, as if the man's clout could somehow open the doors of a major trauma center and get Glenn admitted as a patient—and all without attracting the attention of law enforcement.

"He's going to wake up with a handcuff on his wrist," Stamp growled.

"But at least he'll wake up."

"Either way, we need to get him to a hospital fast. The tourniquet's stopped the bleeding, but he'll lose the leg if he doesn't go under the knife within the hour."

"I know," Gideon replied. "Dammit."

He tapped his earpiece. "Zara, you out there? Say something."

Nothing.

He exhaled. Thought for a second, then took a step back and raised his rifle, leveling it directly at Haynes's chest. The fixer's eyes widened, but otherwise, he didn't react. Stamp immediately swept into action, aiming his own pistol in McKinney's direction.

"Is the money in those bags real?" Gideon said in a low, deadly voice.

Haynes nodded. "I zipped them up myself."

"Then you have a choice to make. I'll let you leave with one of them, no questions asked. But you drop that weapon and walk out of here, and you don't look back."

"What's the alternative?"

"I drop you right now."

"And the senator?"

"Whatever choice you make, he's no longer your business."

Haynes chewed his lip. Finally, he nodded. "It's a fair trade, I guess."

"You piece of shit, Ronan," McKinney swore. "You traitorous fuck."

The fixer unslung his rifle—slowly—and dumped it unceremoniously on the floor. His pistol followed shortly after. He walked quickly toward the back of the room—two muzzles on him the entire way—and picked up one of the black duffel bags as Senator McKinney berated him the entire time.

Gideon tuned the man out.

No. He tried. As Haynes passed him, he traded places to let Stamp cover the fixer and walked over to McKinney. He paused for a second to think over what he was about to do, then gave a slight nod of satisfaction.

He drove the stock of his rifle into the man's stomach.

"That's better," he said. He glanced sideways at Julia, whose expression was guarded. She was still clutching the pistol, and he debated whether he should take it off her. He couldn't remember whether women at New Eden were given weapons training.

He would do it after, he decided. The situation right now was still too volatile. And she'd managed to make it through not just one but two chaotic assaults without shooting herself. She'd survive just fine now.

More than anything, he wanted to simply sit with her, to hug her and console her and ask how she'd been all these years. But they were in a smoking war zone, with the possibility that Brotherhood assets might still try to attack them—and if not, then law enforcement would be close on their tail.

And right now he had a job to do.

He let his rifle fall against the sling around his shoulder and grabbed McKinney by the chest. He pushed him back against the wall, holding him in place with his left hand pressed against the man's chest as he frisked him professionally with his right.

He was clean.

"You're a real man, huh?"

"Says you," McKinney coughed.

A thump of an explosion outside—a reasonable distance away—caught Gideon's attention. He couldn't see a flash, but by the sound of it, it had come from somewhere near the gate.

"Nomad, how copy?" Zara's voice crackled through his earpiece. "Gideon? John? *Anyone?*"

The last word was delivered with such trepidation that Gideon's heart almost broke for her.

He stepped back from McKinney, keeping his eyes on the man the entire time, then tapped the side of his earpiece. "We're here. Vic's hurt bad, but the rest of us are okay."

"What about the package?"

Gideon met McKinney's smoldering gaze. "Working on it."

"I just took out a portable jamming system," Zara reported. "But there's a screening force at the bottom of the drive with heavy weapons. What do you want me to do?"

"You still have access to a ride?"

"Yep. I drove away from the house when I saw their convoy approaching. Something just smelled off. I guess they decided it was better if the cops were out of earshot before they started their attack."

Gideon exhaled slightly. It was a lucky break. It might just give them a way out of here. "Stay put. We have to get Vic to a doctor. Give me sixty seconds and I'll get back to you with a plan."

"Copy."

Gideon began to fold his arms, but then changed his mind and raised his rifle once again. McKinney's lips were shiny with saliva, and a line of drool glistened halfway down his chin.

The clock was ticking.

"John," he said without turning.

"Yeah?"

"Can you get Vic to the front drive without help?"

"Sure."

"Take Julia and find a vehicle. I have an idea for the Corolla."

"I'm staying here," his sister said forcefully.

Don't have time for this.

"Fine. Go."

As Stamp grunted with the effort of hauling his friend up into a fireman's carry, and Glenn moaned insensibly with pain, McKinney stared challengingly back at him. "What? You want to hurt me, Richter?"

"My name is Ryker," he fired back.

"It wasn't."

"Well, it damn well is now. And no, I don't want to hurt you." He glanced down contemptuously at the duffel bags by the window. "I don't want your money, either."

"Then what?"

"I want your insurance policy."

"My—*what?*" McKinney answered. He screwed his face up with confusion, but it was forced. Feigned.

Gideon twitched his aim just a couple of inches to the right and squeezed the trigger without ceremony. The rifle kicked, and the plaster behind McKinney's left elbow shattered. A chunk of masonry behind it cut through his still-pristine cashmere sweater, which was now stained with fresh blood.

"What the fuck is wrong with you?" McKinney said, some of his earlier bravado fading. He looked at Gideon with true fear in his eyes.

"Next one goes through your knee." Gideon shrugged.

"What makes you think I have an insurance policy?"

"The fact I haven't had a lobotomy," Gideon answered with a tired sigh. "And the fact you're still alive. Three—"

"Wait!" McKinney snapped, holding up his bare palms in entreaty. The stain of blood around his elbow was growing. His face was pale.

"Two," Gideon intoned.

"He'll fucking kill me," McKinney said, his voice coming out in a whine.

"I'll fucking kill you," Gideon said coldly. "I get the insurance policy either way. Right?"

He stared directly into McKinney's eyes. When the man didn't try to refute his assertion, he knew he was correct. "Don't make me count to one."

"Okay," McKinney whispered, his shoulders slumping. "I have a copy here."

"I'm coming up the drive now, Gideon," Zara said through his earpiece.

Time's running out.

Gideon waited, but McKinney didn't move. Finally he gestured with his rifle to give the senator permission. McKinney, now seeming older and smaller, shuffled toward his computer but didn't stop there. He pulled a book off the shelf behind it. It was leather bound and gold embossed, though the leaf was dull and faded. He handed it to Gideon.

"What is this?"

"Open it."

He did so and found a small hard drive in a pocket where the pages should have been. An insert had been cut out of the paper, just large enough to nestle the small black drive.

"By the wall," Gideon snapped, pointing to a spot about six feet away from the computer.

As McKinney shuffled toward it, he pulled the hard drive out of the book and tossed the latter object to the floor. He examined the drive and found that a USB cable—just a couple of inches—was tucked into an indent at the top. He pulled it out and plugged it into the senator's home computer.

It didn't take long for the drive to mount. When he double-clicked it, a dialogue box popped up asking for a password.

"Don't make me ask," he growled.

"No deal," McKinney mumbled. "Get me out of here and I'll tell you. But you can't leave me to Gabriel's dogs. They'll kill me."

Gideon snapped his rifle up and aimed it directly at the senator's chest. "Don't try me. Give me the fucking password."

McKinney shook his head. His expression was beaten but on this matter at least there was a resolve in his gaze. "Only if you get me out of here."

Gideon glanced around and saw Glenn's blood all over the floor. He didn't have time for negotiation. "What guarantee do I have that you will tell me then?"

"If I don't, kill me," McKinney shrugged. "You'll get your answers one way or another."

"Shit," Gideon snapped, briefly casting his eyes up to the ceiling which was now pockmarked with bullet holes and shrapnel scars. He made a snap decision. Glenn's life was more important. "Fine. But fuck with me again and I won't hesitate to pull the trigger."

He resisted the urge to yank the cable out of the port and grimaced as he slogged through the process of manually ejecting the drive.

"Time to go," he said, pocketing it as he ran toward the stack of duffel bags by the window, keeping his peripheral vision on McKinney's defeated form the entire time. He grunted as he hefted one over his shoulder. It had to weigh a hundred pounds.

"Julia, come on," he repeated, turning toward her when he realized she hadn't moved.

"I can't," she answered in a voice that was barely more than a whisper. She was trembling. "Gideon, you have to go."

"What—?"

She moved faster than he could have imagined, raising the pistol she'd carried this entire time through the air and leveling it at his head. Her face was torn, disfigured. Tears began streaming down her cheeks, and her formerly impeccable, carefully styled hair was messy and free.

"Now, Gideon," she said, seeming to concentrate when she used his new, unfamiliar name. "Your friend doesn't have long."

"Shoot him!" McKinney yelled from across the room, his face too enlivened and twisted. The cause of that emotion was much clearer to Gideon. He was enraged.

Julia turned toward the senator, her body lithe and coiled. She moved like a predator, Gideon thought, still too stunned to react to this turn of events. As he watched from a detached, analytical place in his mind, she squeezed the trigger before her torso had even come to a halt.

The bullet hit home an inch from McKinney's skull, tearing a spray of paper from the book wall. "Shut your mouth," she said, trembling with anger—more than anger. Hatred, maybe. "This isn't about you."

McKinney blinked wildly, seemingly barely able to process his wife's betrayal.

"Come with me," Gideon said, holding out his hand. He didn't bother turning his weapon on her. What was he going to do, shoot his own sister? She didn't seem to want to hurt him.

"I can't," she said, tears freely coursing down her face now. "You don't understand. I love him."

"Who—McKinney?"

"Not him. Father Gabriel saved me, Gideon. After you left, I was lost. I owe him everything."

"Julia, you're—," Gideon said, before stumbling to a halt. What was he going to say, that she was brainwashed? He didn't know a lot about deprogramming, but it sure as hell wasn't that easy.

"Go," she whispered, a strange light gleaming in her eyes. She was trembling again. "I don't want to have to hurt you, Gideon. I don't want you to make me hurt you. But I will."

The entire time, her grip on the pistol in her hand remained steady. Gideon saw that she really would shoot him, even though it might break her to do so.

He didn't have a choice. Glenn's life wouldn't wait for him to change Julia's mind. He didn't have time.

"What are you going to do?" he whispered, a great, aching pain in his chest.

"Gideon, what's the holdup?" Stamp radioed, sounding harried. "I found wheels. Vic's strapped in. We need to go!"

He kept his eyes fixed on Julia's tear-stained face.

His sister gritted her teeth and gestured at McKinney with the pistol. "I'm going home. And I'm taking him with me."

SIXTY-SIX

Gideon sprinted through the smoldering shell of McKinney's once-fine mansion, hurdling bodies and debris despite the great weight of the duffel on his back. Blood splattered the walls, and fragmentation shards had punctured holes in thousands upon thousands of dollars' worth of art and sculptures. Smoke still hung heavy in the confined hallways and reception rooms.

He retraced his footsteps through the house, grabbing the keys for the Corolla from the tray in the entrance lobby before bursting out of the main exit. In the distance, from the edge of the mansion's grounds, the occasional scattered bursts of gunfire and muzzle flashes continued. No doubt the Chosen screening force was chasing shadows. Occasionally, a round zipped by overhead and buried itself in the masonry halfway up the house.

"Come on!" Stamp yelled from the front driveway. He'd found a black SUV somewhere and was standing on the ledge inside the driver's door laying down covering fire. The ejected shell casings tinkled on the vehicle's roof before rolling off and falling to the ground in a waterfall of brass.

As Gideon approached, Stamp slithered back to the ground. "Where's your sister?"

"Long story. She's staying put."

"Must be a hell of a Thanksgiving dinner," Stamp said, shaking his head as he rammed a fresh magazine home. "Get in the passenger seat. I already opened up the sunroof."

Gideon instantly grasped his plan. Stamp knew he couldn't drive and shoot at the same time, but if they wanted any chance of busting through the screening force at the entrance gate, someone needed to lay down suppressive fire. And that someone was going to be him: a makeshift top-gunner without a stabilized heavy machine gun.

"I have a better idea," he said, taking a second to reach into his pants pocket for the hard drive. He made to toss it to Stamp, then thought better of risking everything they'd come here for. Despite hating the loss of the precious seconds, he walked it over to the ex-legionnaire and placed it in the man's open palm. "Give this to Zara if I don't make it, okay?"

"What the hell are you talking about?" Stamp said, his fingers closing around the drive. "We don't have time for this. Glenn's bleeding out, for fuck's sake."

Gideon held his old comrade's gaze for a single long second. "I know. I'm going to clear us a route out. Don't move until it's done."

"How will I know?"

Gideon grinned mercilessly, then tossed the duffel bag at Stamp's feet. "You'll figure it out."

With that, he turned and sprinted for the Corolla. The trunk was still popped, but he didn't bother taking the time to close it. He wasn't too worried about the car's aerodynamics. Not right now.

"Zara," he radioed. "You still there?"

"Yep," she replied, her voice barely above a whisper. "I'm

right behind the main screening party. I'll keep their heads pinned down soon as you give the word."

"Don't worry about that," he grunted as he started the car's engine and instantly fed it a full pedal's worth of gas. The tires screeched and burned against the gravel driveway, kicking out shards of stone and a plume of dust. "I need you to do something for me."

"You got it."

"Two seconds after I give the mark, punch the detonator and get your head down. Can you do that?"

"Sure," she replied, pausing for just a heartbeat of hesitation before adding, "What are you doing?"

Gideon wrestled the underpowered sedan's steering wheel around, feeling the car's chassis groan under the unusual demand he was putting on it. He took his foot off the gas as the car's nose swung back around to face down the private road to the entrance gate just so he didn't overshoot the turn.

And then he gunned it.

The needle on the speedometer hit twenty, thirty, forty, then fifty miles an hour in a matter of seconds. The slight incline down the hill helped, as did the fact that the accelerator pedal was flat against the floor.

Gideon's chest rose and fell steadily. Suddenly he felt completely and utterly calm. It was as if he'd been born for this exact moment.

"Gideon?" Zara called out, her voice pitching up with concern. "Are you in that car?"

"I won't be," he assured her, his voice steady.

"You can't be serious. This will never work."

"It will," he said. "Just count to two and then hit the button. And Zara?"

"Yeah?"

"It was nice to meet you."

The speedometer hit eighty miles an hour. The nose of the sedan was angled straight down toward the gate now. It was only eighty yards away. Close enough that even through the darkness he could see the faint outlines of men. Men with guns.

And then muzzle flashes.

He couldn't hear the gunshots over the noise of the car's engine and the wind buffeting its chassis. But he felt the first impact as a bullet punched through the passenger side of the windshield and sent cracks spidering through the entire sheet of glass.

Fifty yards.

Gideon reached for the door latch and pulled it open, maintaining enough pressure on the handle that it remained mostly closed. The needle hit ninety miles per hour.

He had a matter of seconds now. Less than that.

"Zara, MARK!"

The instant the words left his mouth, Gideon flung the driver's side door open and kicked out with all the strength in his exhausted legs. The car was moving so fast, the lip of the door collided with his ankle and started him spinning through the air.

One.

Gideon hit the ground with a concussive impact. Somewhere between being flung from the car and making landfall, he lost his grip on the rifle. It banged against him once and then spun off into the darkness as he kept sliding across grass that was slick with condensation. The force of the landing punched the oxygen from his lungs.

Two.

Twenty kilograms of plastic explosive went up in a flash that lit up the sky and even lifted the blackness of unconsciousness that was beginning to swallow Gideon's vision. The searing brilliance of the explosion traveled faster than the sound and the heat and the blast wave.

But they followed, buffeting Gideon's already bruised and battered body into submission. Pieces of metal and plastic fell from the sky all around him. The engine block landed thirty feet away and chewed a crater out of the earth.

"Gideon?" A distant voice buzzed in his earpiece. He was sure she sounded familiar; he just couldn't place her. "Gideon! Can you hear me?"

The last thing Gideon saw before he slipped under and the flash of the explosion faded into nothingness was a smoking hole where the car gate had been and little more than burning scraps of flesh and cloth around it.

"John," he mumbled, or maybe just thought. "Drive!"

EPILOGUE

The high from his near-death escape had so far lasted three days. Long enough that Gideon was beginning to feel that the damage done to his brain might just have righted itself. As his head hit the pillow every night—usually in a different city, ideally in a different state—he feared that the depersonalization that had dogged him for weeks would return.

But every morning, he felt like himself.

He rolled over in bed, this time in a dingy motel on the outskirts of Parkersburg. The cool kiss of the air conditioning replaced the warmth radiated by Zara's body and caused him to shiver as the fuzzy red lines on the alarm clock's display wobbled before steadying. It was 4:57 a.m.

This morning, Gideon felt like shit. The culprit wasn't the bottle of bourbon that sat on the table opposite the bed because it was still unopened.

Today was Jean-Luc's funeral. And he wasn't going to be there.

Gideon reached out and canceled the alarm two minutes before it would have sounded. As usual, his body had awakened him right on time. He rolled over and extended his hand toward Zara's back. Before his fingers met the fabric of her tank top, she stirred slightly and groaned.

"I'm awake," she whispered. "Couldn't sleep."

"Coffee?"

"Please."

He rose and padded silently across the stained and frayed carpet toward the coffee machine, wincing as he twisted his torso and listened to the answering pops from his neck and spine. Jumping from a car doing ninety miles an hour onto uneven ground wasn't exactly chiropractor-approved. But he wasn't doing too bad, all things considered.

Gideon fed the first pod into the espresso machine and waited for the noise of grinding gears to stop and the hiss and sizzle of brewing coffee to begin. He popped the machine open and began the process of making his own cup before walking the first over to Zara.

"Thanks," she said, smiling through bleary eyes as she accepted the offering of caffeine. They drank in silence together, both occupied by their own thoughts, and then they showered and dressed. It wasn't yet light outside.

Gideon's phone buzzed twenty minutes later, right when he expected it to. He didn't recognize the number, but he answered the video call anyway. A familiar face—bruised, scratched, and still exhausted from the events at McKinney's mansion several days earlier—popped up on screen.

"John," he said in greeting. "Thanks for doing this."

"Anytime, anyplace," Stamp replied. The smile on his lips didn't quite match his eyes, but he seemed genuinely pleased to see Zara and Gideon. "Although next time you can stump up for first class. I can't fly coach. Especially not after last week. And no more excuses about how the cash needs washing."

He winked, then flipped the camera around and showed

them the scene in front of him—the dusty cemetery in Puyloubier that housed the Legion's memorial and many of its dead. Gideon knew it well, though it had never looked like this. Several dozen narrow white folding chairs had been set up on the gravel facing the memorial wall. The hundreds of names inscribed on the marble slabs were too indistinct to make out individually, but Gideon felt a chill run down his spine even so.

His own name could have been written on that wall. He'd faced death on numerous occasions while in the Legion, but he always survived. But if he'd died, his life would have been preserved for posterity, surrounded by the assumed names of all those other men who'd given their lives for France.

The cemetery filled over the course of the next half hour. The camera briefly focused on a man in a wheelchair being pushed into the cemetery for several seconds until the view was blocked out by other mourners.

Stamp tucked his phone into the breast pocket of his jacket as the service commenced to avoid attracting undue attention, so the audio was muted but audible. Halfway through, Gideon twisted the cap off the bourbon bottle and filled the now-washed coffee cups with a hefty home pour of liquor. He offered one to Zara, who accepted it even though it was still dark out, then tried to let the heat of the liquor sear away his grief.

"Jean-Luc was the best of us," Colonel Fournier finished, bowing his head. "And he will rest here under the sun for eternity, close to those he loved the most. Please, bow your heads with me as we pay our final respects."

Gideon tightened his jaw and closed his eyes as a row of active-duty legionnaires in dress uniform—black combat boots, blue sashes around their waists, and the customary white "kepi" peak—filed to the front. They carried polished ceremonial rifles, which they raised to the sky.

He flinched at the first report of gunfire.

Zara reached out and placed a comforting hand on his shoulder. She kept it there until the gun salute was finished and much longer still as Gideon shook with all the grief he'd repressed during the previous week at the death of the man who had nursed him back from the brink of his own mortality.

Hot tears flowed down his cheeks, first in a continuous stream that seared the skin, then one by one before they left only dry streaks of salt. An emptiness replaced the white heat that had pushed him forward ever since the attack on the Institution.

Stamp said nothing as the memorial service ended and the majority of the mourners filed out the tree-lined path to the gate. Silence descended once again among the vineyards at the foothills of the Montagne Sainte-Victoire before he finally broke it.

"Gideon," he said. "There's somebody here who wants to speak to you."

The camera feed shook and broke up several times as the audio transmitted the sound of Stamp's footsteps crunching on gravel across the cemetery. Gideon frowned as he waited for a hint about whom Stamp was referring to. He caught the flash of a gray tire and a man's thigh as Stamp's phone was passed over.

"My friend," Leclerc said as the video feed stabilized once more. "It is good to see your face."

"And yours," Gideon replied, smiling at the sight of the old gunrunner, mercenary broker, and sometimes French intelligence asset who it seemed was the man in the wheelchair. "I'm glad you made it."

"Thanks to your friend here." Leclerc smiled. "Or so I understand. I owe you my thanks for saving my life. I will be indebted to you as long as I live."

Zara flushed. "It's all good," she replied. "You repaid me by arranging for Glenn's treatment. He's going to make a full recovery. I had no idea veterinarians were so skilled with humans as well as pets."

"I'll pretend you didn't say that," Leclerc smiled mischievously. "A favor from me can be a very valuable treasure. And besides, Glenn's one of my most valuable boys. It just wouldn't be good business to let him die over a misunderstanding."

The genial smile on his face gave lie to the idea that he thought of his people as expendable. But Gideon didn't need confirmation of that. He remembered.

"Jacques, can I ask you something?" Zara ventured hesitantly.

"Of course."

"The two DGSI agents. What's happening with their families?"

Leclerc's head briefly dipped. "They are being taken care of."

"Is...is there a way I can contribute? Those two men are dead because of me. I know I can't make up for what I've done. But I'll spend the rest of my life trying."

"Non," Leclerc said, shaking his head firmly. "It is not the case. Those gangsters were set in motion long before you arrived on the scene. DGSI recovered their cell phones. I have seen this evidence myself."

Zara tensed, almost as if growing defensive. "I lit the spark."

Leclerc shrugged. At least, Gideon thought he did as the camera view briefly jerked toward the sky.

"Maybe. But you did not pour the fuel. Those boys would have come for me to get to Gideon. And the result would have been the same."

Zara closed her eyes and shook silently. It was time for

Gideon to repay the favor. He squeezed her forearm tight and held her until she sighed with release. "Be that as it may. I still wish to contribute to whatever fund is set up to help their families. Guilt doesn't wash clean that easy."

Leclerc bowed his head slowly. "I will make arrangements."

After a suitable pause, Gideon steered the conversation back to safer ground. "How are you doing anyway, Jacques? I'm surprised you're already up and—*uh*—wheeling about."

The Frenchman snorted. "I was a complication nobody wanted to deal with. I simply told the authorities everything they wanted to know."

"And they believed you?"

The wily broker laughed. "I have no doubt they are watching me right now. I suspect they want to know more about you, Gideon. Where you came from, and how my government might use you to its advantage. But that is a conversation for another day. For now I will be—how do you say—squeaky clean?"

Gideon laughed—a real laugh that helped wash away some of the heaviness of the previous hour. Hell, the whole week. "I bet you will, buddy. I bet you will."

"You will come see me sometime?"

"If you provide the documents." Gideon shrugged. "Then it's a date."

"What now?" Zara said after Gideon thanked Stamp for making the journey to France and ended the call.

Gideon wrinkled his nose. It was finally light outside, and the added illumination only revealed more of the dusty motel room's flaws. "We find somewhere to hole up that doesn't risk us needing tetanus shots. And we figure out what's on that damn hard drive."

"And your sister?" Zara asked softly.

"She has doubts," Gideon said after a short pause. He'd thought of little other than Julia for days. "I saw it in her eyes. She wouldn't have let me escape if there wasn't a part of her that knew everything she's been fed is a lie. The Julia I know is still in there somewhere."

Zara squeezed his hand. "Then let's get her out."

AUTHOR'S NOTE

Hey,

Thanks for finishing *Code of Arms*. I hope you liked what you read, because I've been writing furiously and you don't have long to wait for *Test of Faith*, the second book in the *Gideon Ryker* series.

    I got the idea for this series after doing a little background reading on Jeffrey Epstein. You know, the convicted pedophile who committed suicide in a New York prison while the guards who was supposed to be watching him were conveniently asleep. Oh, and the video footage conveniently disappeared. That guy.

    I always found it very interesting that Epstein got a sweetheart non-prosecution deal from a prosecutor who ended up getting elected to the U.S. Senate in 2017 despite mountains of credible evidence that he was in fact a serial sex abuser.

    I also found it interesting that nobody ever questioned where all his money came from. He was supposedly a financial manager for the very rich – but only one of his clients was ever known to the public. There are theories that some of it came from a Ponzi scheme, or that he was an asset for a foreign intelligence service, but I doubt we'll ever know for sure.

Of course what we do know is that during a raid on his Palm Beach mansion in 2005, police found hidden cameras in private areas. Other witnesses described an extensive security system in his Manhattan townhouse that used pinhole cameras in bedrooms and restrooms and a setup that monitored every single room in the house twenty-four hours a day.

We also know that he trafficked and abused young women and instructed them to have sexual relations with his guests.

It doesn't seem like too much of a jump to suggest that he was creating blackmail material—what the Russians call kompromat. You can imagine that kind of leverage being useful in at least two ways: first, parting wealthy people from some of their money; and second cultivating political connections to protect from legal consequences.

I took this general idea and applied it to another longtime topic of interest for me—how a Waco-like cult could protect themselves from the government. And so the Brotherhood was born.

It's been great fun writing a new action series with zero expectations. There was something freeing about creating Gideon—a character who starts out knowing as little about himself as I did!

As well as *Test of Faith*, before the end of the year you can also expect another *Blake Larsen* crime novel and the next installment in the *Jason Trapp* series—*Eyes Only*. Depending on how productive I am over the summer there may also be a couple more *Gideon Ryker* books before the year is out. They are easy writing!

Before I sign off, I recently took a look at my royalty statements and realized to my surprise that almost a million readers have now picked up one of my books, which is as hard to believe as it is a great honor.

My thanks to every single one of you for allowing me to do this as a career—and of course to my lovely wife, who now handles the entire business side and is the person you can thank for cracking the whip on my procrastination. Thanks to her 2024 will be my most productive year since I started in 2019.

There's plenty more coming. Thanks for reading.

Jack.

NEXT IN THE SERIES

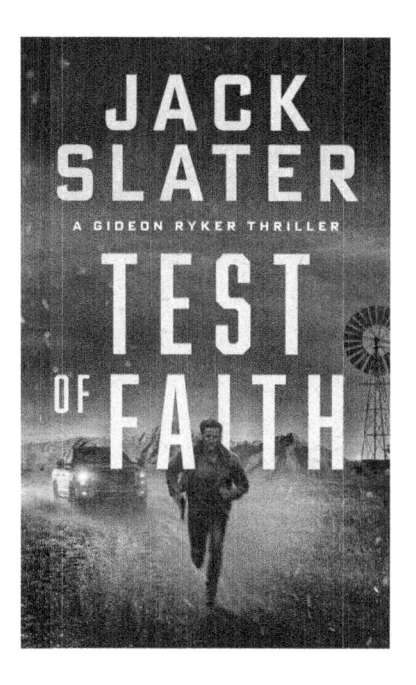

The Nomad returns this summer in **Test of Faith**, the exhilarating second Gideon Ryker thriller. Pre-order now on Amazon!

A month ago, Gideon Ryker's sister betrayed him to the cult known as the Brotherhood. He nearly lost his life. A whole lot of Chosen thugs died trying to capture him. And then Julia let him go...

Four weeks on, all Gideon wants is to lay down his arms. But he's no fool. The second he stops running, the Brotherhood will catch up to him—and destroy everything he holds dear. And in ex-CIA officer Zara Walker, he's found someone worth fighting for.

The problem is: they know that too.

Gideon wants peace. And he's prepared to kill for it.

Pre-order *Test of Faith* (*Gideon Ryker Book 2*) by heading to Amazon.

Release date: July 2024.

FOR ALL THE LATEST NEWS

I hope you enjoyed *Code of Arms*. If you did, and don't fancy sifting through thousands of books on Amazon and leaving your next great read to chance, then sign up to my mailing list and be the first to hear when I release a new book.

 Visit - www.jack-slater.com/updates

You can also visit Amazon to leave a review on *Code of Arms*, for which as ever I would be most grateful.

Thanks so much for reading!

Jack.

THE JACK SLATER STORE

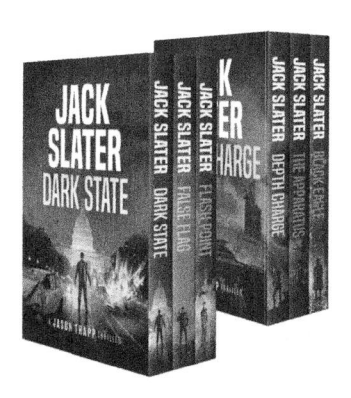

Head to the brand new Jack Slater store for exclusive online only paperback bundles! Use the code **WELCOME10** for 10% off your first order.

CODE OF ARMS AUDIOBOOK

Head to Audible to listen to the Code of Arms audiobook!

Printed in Great Britain
by Amazon